Ruth Prawer Jhabvala was born in Germany of a Polish father and German mother and came to England in 1939 at the age of twelve. She graduated from Queen Mary College, London University, and married the Indian architect C.S.H. Jhabvala.

As well as her numerous novels and short stories, Ruth Prawer Jhabvala wrote scripts for film and television. She worked mostly in collaboration with James Ivory and Ismail Merchant. The screenplays for *A Room with a View* and *Howard's End* won Academy Awards for Best Adapted Screenplay. She won the Booker Prize for *Heat and Dust* in 1975, the Neil Gunn International Fellowship in 1978, the MacArthur Foundation Fellowship in 1984 and was made a CBE in the 1998 New Year's Honours List.

Ruth Prawer Jhabvala died in 2013.

LEFTOVER SHARDS AT QUTB
C. S. H. Jhabvala

Ruth Prawer Jhabvala

AT THE END OF
THE CENTURY

Little, Brown

LITTLE, BROWN

First published in Great Britain in 2017 by Little, Brown

1 3 5 7 9 10 8 6 4 2

A CIP catalogue record for this book
is available from the British Library.

ISBN 978-1-4087-0952-8

Typeset in Sabon by M Rules
Printed and bound in Great Britain by
Clays Ltd, St Ives plc

Papers used by Little, Brown are from well-managed forests
and other responsible sources.

MIX
Paper from
responsible sources
FSC® C104740

Little, Brown
An imprint of
Little, Brown Book Group
Carmelite House
50 Victoria Embankment
London EC4Y 0DZ

An Hachette UK Company
www.hachette.co.uk

www.littlebrown.co.uk

Contents

Introduction

Alipur Road, Old Delhi, 1955

Alipur Road was a wide avenue lined with enormous banyan trees, and my mother and I would go for walks along it – to Maiden's Hotel, which had a small library, or further on to the Quidsia Gardens. And, across the road, I'd see a young woman pushing along a perambulator with a baby seated in it and a little girl dancing alongside it. She was a married woman, clearly, and I a student at the University of Delhi, but glancing across the road at her, I felt an instinctive relation to her. Why?

She was revealed to be a young woman of European descent – German and Polish – who was married to an Indian architect, Cyrus Jhabvala, and lived in rooms in a sprawling bungalow just off Alipur Road. When her mother, a German Jewish woman from London, visited her, Ruth searched for someone she could talk to. I think it might have been Dr Charles Fabri, the Hungarian Indologist who lived in the neighbourhood, who suggested she might meet my German mother, who had also come to India on marrying an Indian, thirty years ago in the 1920s.

A coffee party – a *kaffeeklatsch* – was arranged so the two could indulge in their shared language in this foreign setting.

I can't imagine how or why, but Ruth decided to follow their meeting, after her mother had returned to England, with many others, on a different level – that of daughters. With extraordinary kindness and generosity she would have me over to their house, one filled with books, the books she had brought with her from England where she had been a student at the University of London when she had met Jhab. Perhaps it touched her that I was so excited about being among her books, talking to her about books. After that, whenever I came away with an armful of books on loan, with her talk still in my ears, I felt elated, a visitor to another world, the writer's world I had only imagined and which now proved real. I would go home to scribble at my desk with a new, unaccustomed sense of the validity of such an occupation. I had met someone who, like myself, regarded writing as a very private, almost secret practice, a product of the interior space of shadows and silence. (This was very, very long before the age of readings, literary conferences and book festivals at which writers now meet and talk almost incessantly.)

One day she placed in my hands a copy of *To Whom She Will*, her first novel that had been published in faraway England, an unimaginable distance from Alipur Road, Old Delhi. Holding it, I felt I had touched something barely con-sidered possible – that the scribbling one did in one's hidden corner of the world could be printed, published and read in the world beyond. Could our drab, dusty, everyday lives yield material that surely belonged only to the genius of a Chekhov, a Jane Austen, a Woolf or a Brontë? Taking home the copy Ruth inscribed for me and reading it, I made the discovery that Ruth had found, in this ordinary, commonplace world I so belittled, the source for her art, the material for her writ-ing, using its language, its sounds and smells and sights with a veracity, a freshness and immediacy that no other writer I had read had. The message like an electric current: yes, this is our world, our experience, it can be our writing too.

Many years, much experience later, we once had an unexpected encounter in the airport at Frankfurt. She was on her way from New York to India and I was on my way from India to New York. Alarmed at my lack of proper clothing, she insisted on giving me her duffel coat that she would not need in India but I would in New York. So we made our separate ways, across the hemispheres, safely.

In the years that followed, we shared so much or, looked at differently, so little: our lives were small, restricted. The Jhabvalas moved to the beautiful house designed by Jhab on Flagstaff Road, and there were now three daughters – and two enormous German shepherd dogs. I too married and had children and would take them over for tea, which they would greatly look forward to because Ruth always had her cook, Abdul, bake a cake for them and Jhab would come back from his office to entertain them with his repertoire of magic tricks.

In the summers we met in the 'hill-station' of Kasauli where the Jhabvalas booked rooms at the Alasia Hotel every year while I stayed in a rented cottage nearby. Our children would run wild in the pine woods on the hillsides while Ruth and I went for our more sedate walks and occasionally met with Khushwant Singh, the Sikh historian and novelist who also had a home there.

In all these orderly, regulated, uneventful years, Ruth wrote prolifically: novels and short stories that seemed to draw upon a bottomless well of material. She always had such an air of existing in a separate world, in isolation and perfect stillness – so where did all this come from? Where, how, did she come to know the men and women who peopled her books?

We need to listen to her: in her 1979 Neil Gunn Fellowship lecture she said that as a Jewish refugee from Europe, the loss of her inheritance made her 'a cuckoo forever insinuating myself into others' nests', 'a chameleon hiding myself in false or borrowed colours'. Also that 'You take over other people's backgrounds and characters. Keats called it "negative capability".'

It was a contrast to what E.M. Forster and Paul Scott had done in their writing about India as outsiders and visitors, if fascinated observers. Caryl Phillips has remarked that 'she was postcolonial before the term had been invented'. Ruth's own explanation was typically understated and wry: 'Once a refugee, always a refugee', which is why John Updike called her 'an initiated outsider'.

Once when she had V.S. Naipaul to tea and passed him a plate of cakes, he pointed at it with a trembling finger and cried, 'There's a fly on it!' 'Oh,' she said, 'just take off your glasses. I always do.' But not when she was writing, when her vision was laser-sharp; nothing was glossed or obscured.

This would explain stories such as 'The Widow', whose central character longs for a life other than that of marriage to an old man, mean and vindictive, and after his death lusts after her tenant's young son, pathetically pursuing him with promises of the fine clothes his mother can't buy him and even the motor scooter he yearns for, only to be spurned and having return to her watching and waiting circle of relatives, a cast of sly and avaricious dependants. The voice, the point of view, is so perfectly captured, one would not add or alter a single word for greater effect. 'Expiation', a story so wrenching it is almost unbearable, is about the owner of a cloth shop in a small town and the unconditional love he has for his younger brother, a wastrel who falls in with a criminal and commits a murder for which both are hanged, then brings himself, in a supreme act of love and forgiveness, to perform the necessary last rites for both of them.

Both are word-perfect; one might be hearing the protagonists themselves speaking. And Ruth's characters were not likely to be speaking English, they would be speaking Hindi or Urdu or Hindustani. So there was a translation going on – yet there was no hint of the strain and uneasiness of crude, satirical and parodied translation of an Indian language into English that we encounter today. Hers was a total absorption. Ruth, like a great actress, becomes her characters and presents them to us from the inside out, not the outside in. She does not criticize them or satirize them – as so many Indian readers accused her of doing – she becomes those she portrays.

It was her fate to be presented to Western readers as a Jane Austen, but although she does share her wit, precision and asperity of style, she was not ever Jane Austen at a ball, watching the flirt, the sharp-eyed mother or the tittering gossip – she entered into and inhabited her characters, herself withdrawing.

I think none of us in India knew what an immense drain this was upon her energy, her resources. Not until we read her extraordinary essay 'Myself in India', in which she wrote of the split, the fracture between her Western sensibility and her Eastern experience which is made plain in the first line: 'I have lived in India for most of my adult life. My husband is Indian and so are my children. I am not, and less so every year.' She went on to reveal the exhaustion relating to the constant to and fro of her love and loathing for her adopted land. 'I think of myself as strapped to a wheel that goes round and round and sometimes I'm up and sometimes I'm down.'

This was when the subject of her work changed to the Europeans who came to India, the hippies of the 1960s and 1970s, unlike herself in search of the exotic – whether spiritual or sexual, they hardly knew themselves, often confusing the two and finding it in the figure of the charismatic and unscrupulous guru.

In 'An Experience of India' the heroine, a woman married to an English correspondent posted to Delhi, becomes infatuated with a young Indian musician, practically kidnaps him and drags him, miserably, home to her husband and their very Western apartment. He flees from her and returns to his family, and she becomes very ill. Her husband contrives a transfer to Geneva so she may recover there, but when it comes to it she refuses with unexpected ferocity to go, choosing instead the life of a destitute pilgrim, still in search for what she had set out to discover.

Over and over again the stories are about the spirit longing for a physical manifestation of the ideal although, in the devastating story 'Desecration', a marriage to a fine, honourable man is abandoned for an affair with a coarse, brutal man as if degradation was what was wanted even if it destroys.

Ruth herself became ill, her family worried about her. In those days if she ever saw I was myself going through some anguish over the life I was living and the writing I was struggling to do, she would not question or probe but instead rally me – and perhaps herself – by quoting Thomas Mann: 'He is mistaken who believes he may pluck a single leaf from the laurel tree of art without paying for it with his life', or ask, laughingly, 'What would you rather be – the happy pig or the unhappy philosopher?' making light of it – but not taking it lightly herself.

It must have been at this time that James Ivory and Ismail

Merchant entered her life when they came to India in search of material for a film. They found it in an early novel of hers, *The Householder*, which she adapted for the screen for them. She said, 'Films made a nice change for me. I met people I wouldn't have done otherwise: actors, financiers, con men,' and she moved to New York, buying herself an apartment, a tiny eyrie in a building on the Upper East Side where Ismail and Jim lived.

In the summers she joined them in James Ivory's country house in the upper Hudson river valley that became a gathering place for their far-flung families and friends. Ismail bought Ruth a camper's travelling desk to set up under the trees by the lake so she could work there. Claverack was the scene for some great occasions, like the fiftieth anniversary of Ruth and Jhab's wedding, attended by all their daughters and grandchildren, at which they were presented with a replica of Henry James's 'golden bowl' and Ruth surprised everyone by standing up and delivering a speech, flawlessly. She spoke so little, but when she did it was always carefully considered and precisely worded as if she were writing, pen on paper.

I saw less of her in these years, although I moved to America myself, not to the film world but the academic one of New England, but kept in touch through her writing. Apart from the film scripts she wrote for Merchant Ivory Productions, and the adaptations of novels by E.M. Forster and Henry James for which she won Academy Awards, she now wrote only short stories that she said she loved 'for their potential of compressing and containing whatever I have learnt about writing and about everything else'.

She found a new, rich vein in the lives of the Jewish European refugees, the people she might have known in the past, who had come to America and could be observed in the grand hotels and restaurants of New York and Los Angeles.

One can discern in these stories her continued fascination with the false guru who in America takes the form of the temperamental artist, the supposed genius, attracting women who submit to their stormy tempers and selfish demands. Very often the solution to these tangled, tortuous relationships presents itself in the form of the ménage, as in the story by that name: a temperamental pianist is attracted to two sisters; each of them puts up with his dark moods and unruly life and do everything to help his genius flourish. When they age and tire, the daughter of one steps in to replace them. In 'Pagans', one of two sisters, married to a powerful studio head in Hollywood, stays on after his death, acquiring a devoted young admirer, Shoki. Her sister arrives to persuade her to return to New York, but falls for Shoki herself and when her husband, a prosperous banker, comes to take her back, he fails and the threesome in Hollywood is happy and complete without him. The ménage in these stories is brought about through understanding and acceptance that is not easily come by but welcomed when it is.

For such a quiet, still person it is extraordinary what strong passions each story, novel and film contains. She never shied away from them and continued to address their immense potential for both joy and destruction with a clarity of vision, unobscured by any wisp of illusion. Clear, cool, dry and infused by wit and insight, her style was the mirror of her person, the poise and elegance of her being.

Anita Desai
May 2017

A Loss of Faith

Ram Kumar could not remember his father, who had been a printer and had died of a sudden fever, leaving his wife and five small children to be supported by his brother, a postal inspector. The impression that Ram Kumar's mother gave of her husband was, on the one hand, that of a man all tenderness and generosity and, on the other, of one very much like his brother the postal inspector – that is to say, a man who was often drunk on raw liquor, was careless of his family and beat his wife. In her moments of depression – which were frequent, for her life among her sisters-in-law and mother-in-law was not easy – she favoured the first impression: 'Ah,' she would say, 'if my children's father were still alive, it would be different for me'; and then she would suggest how her husband in his lifetime had cared for her, brought special foods for her when she was pregnant, given her and the children warm things to wear in the winter, and on festival days had taken them to see fairs and processions. But when things were not going too badly for her, she gave a different picture. Then she spoke with a kind of bitter satisfaction of the way all men were the same, all given to drink, selfishness and wife-beating; and she compressed her lips and nodded her head up and down, suggesting that, if called upon, she

1

could tell many a tale from her own experience of married life to illustrate this truth.

Her eldest child – not Ram Kumar, who was the third – was fortunately a boy, and all her hope was in him. Vijay was a strong, healthy, daring boy, and she could hardly wait for him to grow up and earn money and take her and her other children away to live with him. But when he finally did grow up, he turned out to be too fond of strolling through the bazaars, going to the cinema and having fun with his friends to give much of his attention to the jobs that were found for him; so that within two years he had run through fourteen such jobs – all of the nature of office messenger or contractor's errand boy – and it became clear even to his mother that he would not hurriedly earn a lot of money. After these two years, he disappeared and was not heard of for another two; at the end of which time he came back and said he had been to Calcutta, where he had earned a lot of money and had been about to send for them when a thief had come in the night and stolen it all from under his bed. He was now in no hurry to look for another job, but stayed around in his uncle's home during the day and went out towards evening to enjoy life with his numerous acquaintances.

At first he went out quite often with his uncle and the two came back late in the night, very drunk and very friendly. But the friendship did not last long, and soon the uncle came to be tired of feeding a large, strong, healthy nephew who made no attempts to find another job. Quarrels between them became more and more frequent: watched by women cowering against the wall and clutching their hair, the two of them flung bitter words against one another; until one day the nephew ended another such quarrel by smashing his fist in his uncle's face and, stepping over the prostrate body, disappeared out of the house. When he next reappeared, he was wearing a beautiful suit of smuggled silk and a big ring on his little finger and was working in some rather shady capacity for a big business magnate. But though he now really seemed to be earning a lot of money, he made no attempts to take away his mother and his younger brother and sisters. Nor did he come to see them very often or, when he did, speak much of his affairs; so that it was only by devious routes that they finally discovered him to be spending much of his time and most of his money on a very beautiful young Muslim lady, who employed her abilities at singing and dancing to entertain at certain kinds of parties. His mother took this news as she had taken all her other afflictions: with tears, with resignation, with pleas to God to lighten her lot.

Meanwhile Ram Kumar too was growing up, and his mother tried to turn her hopes to him. But, unlike his brother, he was not very promising. Where Vijay was broad and strong and good-looking, Ram Kumar was small and weak, with a pinched face to go with his pinched body. And he was always afraid. At the little charity school he attended he was afraid both of the master and of the other boys. He worked feverishly so that the master should have nothing with which to reproach him, and he hunched himself up to an even smaller size in the hope that the boys would not notice him. He was so successful that nobody, neither master nor boys, ever did notice him, and he remained unknown, unbefriended and – which was what he had aimed for – unmolested.

At home he tried the same tactics, though less successfully. The whole family lived together in one room and one veranda. There were Ram Kumar, his mother and his two sisters – his elder sister had been married to a policeman in Saharanpur, and Vijay, of course, was no longer living with them – the postal inspector uncle with his wife and children, as well as one widowed aunt and a grandmother.

Their room was in a row of six quarters built on one side of a courtyard which had on its other side the workshop of a dry-cleaner and the office with cyclostyle of an Urdu weekly of limited circulation. On summer nights all the families slept outside in the courtyard, but summer days were hot and long and the room small, and even Ram Kumar could not always escape notice. He suffered especially from his thin, hard, old grandmother and the widowed aunt, who looked just as old as the grandmother. They were often angry with him and beat him and abused him while he cowered in a corner and wept into his hands.

There was no one who could protect him against them. His mother could not even put in a good word for him because, if she had done so, they would have begun to beat and abuse her too. As it was they did this often enough. They pinched her and pulled her hair and poked her with sharp cooking-irons. 'Evil eye', they called her, 'killer of your husband, bringer of death'. She had to accept everything, for it was true she was a widow and guilty of the sin of outliving her husband. Ram Kumar had to watch the beatings meted out to his mother as she had to watch his; but it did not bring him any closer to her. On the contrary, he even resented her because she was weak and could not protect him. So when she tried to comfort him after his beatings, petting and stroking and whispering to him, he sat there passive and unmoved with his face closed and the tear-marks on his cheeks; and when she whispered into his ear, 'When you are grown up and are earning a lot of money, you will take me away to live with you', he did not reply and even tightened his lips, for though he had, in his wilder moments, hopes of

4

going away himself, he never entertained the idea of taking her with him.

He liked to sit on the opposite side of their courtyard, in the poky little office of the old man who wrote, cyclostyled and distributed the Urdu weekly. The old man sat on the floor with a tiny desk in front of him and lingered lovingly with a quill pen over the flowering Urdu script in which he wrote his paper. Ram Kumar was not interested in what he was writing, but he liked the peace and order of the little room – the smell of black ink and the gentle sucking noise the old man made between his teeth as he wrote. Very few visitors ever came to disturb him; but it was through one such visitor, a relative of the old man's, that Ram Kumar got a job. It happened that the relative sat talking to the old man about this and that – a sick sister, a journey to Lucknow – and mentioned in passing that a boy was wanted to help in the shop in which he was employed. The old man jerked his head back to where Ram Kumar sat quietly behind the cyclostyle and said, 'Take him.' Ram Kumar was startled: he was not used to the old man taking any notice of him. But that 'Take him' came at a right time. He had left school, his uncle was trying to find him a job, his grandmother and aunt abused him for being idle. So he went gratefully to the shop.

He loved it from the first. It was a draper and outfitter's shop, but not an ordinary shop, not one of the little booths in the city bazaars which was the only kind of shop he and his like ever visited. This was in the fashionable shopping centre of New Delhi, where the rich went, and it was a big shop with a door to go in by and two glass windows in which were displayed samples of all the beautiful things sold inside. There were two counters inside, and behind the counters stood the assistants, serving the customers. Ram Kumar watched them with eager eyes, he darted forward to be of assistance to them in taking the goods from the shelves, his lips moved with theirs as they offered the customers all there was at their disposal. It did not take him long to know more about stock and prices than any other employee in the shop; for though he was only the general boy, hired to go out on errands, wrap parcels and tidy up counters, he had soon learned so much that the others began to rely on him, and it was he who was asked, 'Ram Kumar, has the new voile come in yet?' 'Ram Kumar, is there a baby vest, size 2?' 'Ram Kumar, how much for Hind Mill sheets, single-bed size?'

After about a year, they began to allow him to change the goods in the windows. He spent sweet hours displaying newly arrived stock, not with taste but with love; reverently he laid out or hung up materials, blankets, ladies' underwear and children's clothing. Inside the shop, on the edge of one of the counters, stood a pale wax doll, two feet high and rather peeling, with a mouse-tooth smile, one hand with a finger missing outstretched, its feet painted with white socks and black anklestrap shoes. Once a week, Ram Kumar changed its clothes, making it display now a pink satin frock with lace trimmings, now a boy's sailor suit or a hand-embroidered skirt with cap to match. He loved the doll and loved dressing it, but there was no element of play in the way he handled it; this was work for him, something important and deadly earnest.

He did not spend much time at home any more. He left early in the morning, carrying the little parcel of food which his mother had cooked for him at dawn, and he returned late in the night, so tired that he could only eat his supper and roll up in his corner to sleep. He slept well, and was not easily disturbed. Only sometimes, when the noise in the room rose to a pitch, he woke up and opened startled eyes to scenes which, though he had seen them all his life, were still scenes of horror to him. His uncle might be reeling round the room, drunk, bedraggled, desperate, shouting: 'Let me be! Let me live!' tearing his hair and then knocking his head against the wall and whimpering in anguish. Hands clutched at him, his wife, his sister, his mother; shrill tearful voices implored him to lie down and sleep, till suddenly he broke loose and roared like a madman: 'They are eating me up!' in a voice of pain and despair. The women reeled back and it was always at that point that he began to beat his wife. He struck out at her wildly, staggering and falling like a wounded animal, sometimes hitting and sometimes missing, while she screamed on one long high-pitched note and dodged him fairly successfully. 'I will kill her!' he shouted, hitting out with both arms and tears streaming down his face. 'Kill them all!' he sobbed. Ram Kumar, woken up from his sleep, clutched his tattered blanket to his chest and stared with horrified eyes at the drunken man and the screaming women, the little flame in the kerosene lamp flickering and dying for want of oil, and the grandmother on her knees praying with uplifted hands to God to save them all.

But in the shop it was different. Here there were comfortably well-to-do customers, courteous assistants, and the proprietor who sat all day at a table in a corner of the shop. Ram Kumar had a great respect for the proprietor. He admired the way he sat poring over business letters and accounts while remaining alert to everything that went on in the shop, every now and again rapping out an order or rising himself to help satisfy a difficult customer. He was a morose man, with a clean blue shave and rimless spectacles, who never talked much and suffered from a bad stomach. If he had any personal feelings, he never showed them in the shop: an inefficient assistant was got rid of, however piteously he might plead poverty and promise reform; salaries were docked with ruthless impartiality for a damage to stock and unpunctuality. But he showed the same impartiality in recognizing merit. Ram Kumar found himself step by step promoted, first to assistant salesman, then to salesman, then to deputy head salesman and finally, after seven years, when he was twenty-two years old, to head salesman and staff manager.

He was earning good money now. His status in the family increased and, with his, his mother's. Nobody beat her now, nobody called her 'evil eye'; she was no longer the widow of her husband but the mother of her son and, as such, worthy of respect. She held her head high, bought a new sari and gave sharp answers. But she was not yet satisfied. She still wanted, as she had wanted ever since her widowhood, to be taken away by her son and set up in a home of her own. Every night she urged this on him, in cajoling whispers; every night he made no reply but turned over in his corner and went to sleep. He wanted a different domestic life, but he was always too tired, after his day at the shop, to formulate thoughts of getting it. But one day she told him she had heard of a place they could have at low rent, and after that he began to think about it. And with his mother nagging him and pleading constantly, it was easier to give way than to hold out. So they moved, he and his mother and his two younger sisters, to a ground-floor room in a tenement, and he became head of a family.

Here he had his first taste of domestic bliss. It was good to come home, late in the evening, to the quiet room which the women kept scrupulously clean, and to eat the food they had prepared for him with such love and care. They treated him, their sole support, with high respect and he, in return, took his responsibility towards them very seriously. His senior position in the shop had already given him an air of authority, a certain dignity of bearing, which he could now afford to take home with him. He had also borrowed his employer's somewhat sour expression of face, and his principles were strict. Not that he was very sure of any principles; but he knew how life should not be and deduced from that how perhaps it should. He was sure it should not be as he had known it in his uncle's house – disorderly, dirty and violent; and in opposition he set up an ideal of quiet and orderliness, of meekness and domestic piety. To this he wished his women to adhere. He liked to think of them quietly following their household duties, taking in some sewing work and keeping themselves modestly to themselves.

This last was perhaps the most important: for the tenement was full of people who led the sort of lives he wanted to get away from. On the top floor was a Muslim insurance clerk whose two wives were for ever quarrelling and abusing one another, and underneath them a crippled astrologer, who augmented his income by selling love potions and whose dissatisfied clients frequently reported him to the police. Next to Ram Kumar on the ground floor lived a traveller in rugs and carpets, whose wife and daughter, left often alone, did not conduct themselves with the decorum Ram Kumar could have wished for in his neighbours. They stood out in the street and laughed and joked, the mother as well as her daughter, showing off their big breasts and healthy cheeks. It was this family that Ram Kumar feared most, for they made overtures of friendliness and the girl was the same age as his sisters. He found it necessary to instruct his mother to avoid all contact with them, which she agreed to do, denouncing them with some fervour for loose morals and shameless conduct.

In appearance Ram Kumar remained as he had been as a child – small, weak and wholly unremarkable. Yet he was getting the habit of authority: at home there was no one but he who counted; in the shop he was next only to the proprietor. He became exacting, tight with money and slightly bad-tempered. His mother forbade everything to his sisters in his name – 'Your brother will be angry' – and every evening, just before his homecoming, she as well as the two girls began to fidget about the room, tidying everything up more than was necessary. And Ram Kumar looked round, pursed his lips and thrust out his thin stomach, and felt himself master of the house.

Except when his brother was there. Vijay came to see them sometimes, and his presence had what Ram Kumar felt to be a deplorable effect on the household. For Vijay, with his silk suit, his big ring, his oiled and scented hair, at once upset that prim orderliness which Ram Kumar had imposed. The mother and sisters became flushed and excited, they hovered around Vijay, listened to his stories, tittered and fussed and were restrained only by the presence of Ram Kumar, at whom they threw frequent guilty glances. Vijay himself hardly noticed his brother. As far as he was concerned, Ram Kumar's status had not changed from the time he had been the puny and insignificant younger brother who kept out of everyone's way. Sometimes, in the face of his contempt, Ram Kumar felt like asserting himself: after all, it was he who was now the head of the family and kept the mother and sisters, not Vijay, who did nothing for them. Yet most of the time he was glad not to be noticed by Vijay; for he was still afraid of him.

There was to him something alien and terrible about his

elder brother. He was not sure quite what work he did for the big business magnate who kept him in his retinue, but he sensed that it was something rather shady of which no one ever spoke. And that to him characterized Vijay's life altogether – it was something of which one could not speak and should not even think about. Where did he live, and with whom? A shudder passed through Ram Kumar when he thought of this. He could never forget the young Muslim lady they had been told about, who sang and danced. The tunes Vijay hummed he had perhaps first heard from her, this liquor of which he smelled he had drunk with her, the ring he wore had been given by her, when he smiled like that and smoothed his hair he was thinking of her. And all this he brought with him into their room, it was behind his eyes and voice as he joked with the mother and sisters, and Ram Kumar could do nothing and say nothing and wait only for him to be gone again.

Sometimes Vijay did not go so quickly. It seemed there were periods when he was out of work or had temporarily quarrelled with his employers or simply did not feel like working, and then he hung around his brother's home, unwashed and dishevelled, sleeping with abandon, going out at nights to drink with his friends. Ram Kumar suspected that during these periods his mother supplied him with funds out of her housekeeping money, but he dared not ask and pretended not to notice. He pretended also not to notice the suppressed excitement which shone in the faces of the mother and her daughters, as if they were having a much better time than they wished him to know. But he did not wish to know and was even afraid of knowing. He went to the shop and lost himself in work. There was comfort in dressing the doll in a different outfit and hovering tender fingers over a newly arrived stock of silk underwear.

Once, on coming home, he found the wife and daughter of the traveller in rugs and carpets in the room. They all seemed to be on the friendliest terms together. Ram Kumar's mother and his sisters looked shocked when he came in, but Vijay and the visitors went on talking and laughing undisturbed. Their laughter was loud and improper, and the girl flung back her head from a strong, healthy throat and let Vijay look down into her bosom. Ram Kumar retired into a corner and ate his food, while his mother whispered to him, 'What could we do? They came to visit.' He did not answer. When she lied, his mother's face bore a prim, innocent expression. He hated her and hated his sisters and hated the home he had made. The traveller's daughter looked at him over her shoulder; she looked sly and laughing, and her little gold earring shook against her plump cheek. He knew she was laughing at him and he felt ashamed for not being like Vijay. Yet he was angry too, because it was he who supported the family and paid the rent of the room in which they sat enjoying themselves, not Vijay.

After that, he often thought about the neighbours. He thought about the plump, shameless girl and felt indignant. He also felt it was time for him to marry off his sisters. His mother had been telling him so for some time: 'Find someone for my girls,' she told him in the urgent whisper she always used when she wanted something; 'it is time they were off your hands.' Then she looked coy, gazing at him with her head on one side and too sweet a smile on her lips: 'And after that is finished, we can start thinking of you.' She tried to stroke his face but he turned it away. He was not ready to think of his own marriage yet.

But he set earnestly and methodically about doing something for his sisters. He studied the matrimonial advertisement columns in the newspapers, inserted an advertisement of his own and, after some correspondence, settled things to everyone's satisfaction. For their dowries he had to borrow from a moneylender at the usual rate of interest, but he knew that with his salary he would have little difficulty in repaying this by monthly instalments. He was pleased with himself, so was his mother. Her hints about his own marriage became more frequent, and he was more ready to listen to her.

He often saw the wife of the traveller in carpets nowadays, and her daughter. They always seemed to be outside their room when he passed in the mornings and in the evenings. The mother was very obsequious to him; she smiled humbly and inquired after his health, while the daughter hovered behind her, her head covered by her sari with a becoming, if uncharacteristic, air of modesty. Ram Kumar never looked at her, but when he passed her, he could not help thinking of the way she had glanced at him over her shoulder that night when he had seen her in his room, and her earring shaking against her round, glowing cheek.

His mother began frequently mentioning these neighbours to him; at first hesitantly, but when she saw that he was inclined to listen, more fully and boldly. He had been, she said, mistaken about them. They were decent, respectable people, and the girl a jewel of a girl – modest and skilled in household duties; and moreover, the father, travelling around in a hired horse-drawn carriage with his rugs and carpets rolled up at the back, earned good money, he would be able to give a fine dowry with his only daughter. Ram Kumar listened and felt flattered. It was he who was being persuaded to take this plump pretty girl, he who was wanted for her husband, not someone else, not Vijay. Every night his mother talked to him, every morning and night he saw the girl and her mother waiting for him outside their door. His face remained sour and perhaps he even exaggerated his frown of ill humour, to hide the strange feelings that were growing inside him. These surprised him, for he had not known that one could have such feelings.

He did not have them for long after he married her. She soon stopped smiling for him, and his mother soon stopped finding any virtue in her. Every day the two women quarrelled, and the girl's mother would rush in and take her daughter's part. When Ram Kumar came home, his mother at once began complaining to him against his wife, who, tossing her head and keeping a menacing silence, glowered at him as if she dared him to say anything to her. And he never did dare; instead he got angry with his mother, and told her not to worry him with her women's quarrels.

He was afraid of his wife in the same way as he was afraid of Vijay. He knew that his high position in the shop and the important frown he wore on his face did not impress her. When he came to her with his passion, she pushed him away as one would push away a troublesome little animal; and even when she let him come to her, she remained aloof and impatient, so that afterwards he was ashamed and turned from her with an embarrassed look on his face. He could refuse her nothing, not because he loved her any more but because of this fear he had of her. When she wanted money, he had to give it, though it was always painful for him to part with money. Sometimes he dared to protest – 'I have given money for the household' – but it was never any use; in the end he had to fumble in his pocket, feeling unhappy and defeated, while she stood there with one hand on her hip and the other insolently outstretched; and his mother, whom he had always kept very short, looked on with hungry, angry eyes.

When Vijay came, Ram Kumar's wife was quite different. Then all her contempt and nonchalance dropped from her; she smiled again as she had smiled before she was married, dimples appeared in her fat cheeks and her sari was allowed to slip from her bosom. And Vijay looked at her with a knowing air, which made her laugh more and put up a hand to caress her hair and turn herself casually to show off her hips. Ram Kumar was in the shop all day and it was easy for him there not to think about them. When he was at home, he frowned in his usual way and pretended to notice nothing. He did not talk to anyone, and only his mother tried to talk to him.

It was difficult to know how his mother felt about the situation. At times she looked at Vijay with pride and gentle, wistful, motherly sighs; and at others at Ram Kumar with what was perhaps pity. She tried to talk to Ram Kumar sometimes; and strangely enough, always about his father, the long-dead printer. 'What a man,' she would say; and she sighed and smiled and wiped at a tear. She may have been talking about him in his gentle family-man respect; yet it seemed more likely – from her tone of womanly respect and the way she looked, pityingly and comparingly, at Ram Kumar – that she was referring to him in his role of swaggering drunkard and lusty wife-beater. What Ram Kumar still liked best in the shop, after all these years, was serving the customers. He stood waiting behind the counter, with just the right mixture of dignity and obsequiousness, his hands folded in repose at chest-level and inclining his body in a brisk, neat bow. He brought out the requisite goods almost before his customer had finished asking for them, and spread them with respectful triumph on the counter. He did not have to say, 'This is the best you can buy anywhere': his quiet, pride, his attitude of caressing reverence towards his goods, made that clear enough. But at the least sign of hesitation on the part of the customer, he was ready to push aside the first item and startle with something even more suitable. He reached up, reached down, swooped here and darted there to bring out more stock, snapped his fingers in the air for one of the assistants to whom he delivered terse and almost silent commands, and all this so unobtrusively, and as it were with his left hand, that his customer never for one moment felt released from his ardent attention. Sometimes, in the most respectful manner possible, he put forward a question-mark of discreet suggestion and if this met with a favourable response, began gently to guide his customer's desires. His patience and solicitude never slackened, and he remained all-absorbed till the last moment when he handed back change and cash-memo and bowed his customer off the premises with the same self-immolating grace, his hands folded, his eyes lowered, with which he had welcomed him. He felt himself alive and significant with the customers. Here he was the salesman, perfect in his role, whom no one could ignore or despise or challenge in authority.

His wife had children whom he could not care for as much as he might have done if he had been sure that they were his. Yet he provided for them, clothed them and sent them to school. He provided for everybody. His uncle, the postal inspector, died, and while his widow and smaller children went into the care of a grown-up son, the grandmother and aunt, tough old roots who lived for ever, were sent to Ram Kumar. Vijay was now often not working. He lay around in Ram Kumar's home and quarrelled with Ram Kumar's wife. He had become bloated and morose. Though he still went on his drinking bouts at night, he could not carry his liquor so well and often, when he came home, he could be heard to retch and moan right up till morning. He was mostly in a depressed mood nowadays. He sat against the wall, with his knees drawn up and his head lowered, wiping his hands in his tousle of dank hair, and grew philosophical. 'All the good things in life,' he would say, 'are like shaky teeth in the mouth, which will drop out and leave us.' Gold ring, silk suit, Muslim lady – all had gone. He was a tired, ageing man and mostly out of work. It seemed the business magnate had withdrawn his protection, and Vijay now only got work here and there from old associates. Whatever he earned, he spent, and then he wheedled Ram Kumar's wife, who abused him but finally got him what he wanted from her husband. Money began to be very short in the house. Ram Kumar found he often had to turn to moneylenders, and the debts mounted and so did the interest on them. Sometimes he could not keep up with the monthly repayments and then the moneylenders came to the house and had to be cajoled.

His relations with the proprietor of the shop had never changed, in all the years he had worked there. The proprietor sat, sour and impersonal, behind his table, doing his accounts and keeping an eye on what was going on in the shop; Ram Kumar as head assistant was his right-hand man but by no means his confidant. They had no private relationship at all. Ram Kumar had shyly revealed his marriage and, later, the birth of his wife's first son, but both these items of news had been received too non-committally for him ever to venture to impart any other. He respected his employer's complete lack of interest in the lives of his employees. He understood there was a barrier as between a king and his subjects, or a guru and his disciples, and that was right to maintain that barrier. Yet he felt closer to the proprietor than to anyone else in the world. They shared one overriding passion – their passion for the shop – and this to Ram Kumar seemed like a deep source of orderliness and virtue, of Goodness and Truth.

And yet, as he got older and things at home became more hopeless, he began to want something further from the proprietor. He felt sometimes, as they were checking stock together or counting the day's takings, that there were other things he wished to talk about besides the business in hand. He was not sure quite what those other things might be, and yet he felt an urge to start talking from the heart; to say, perhaps, 'Sir, my wife has always been unfaithful to me', or 'Sir, I have my mother, my grandmother, my aunt, my brother to support'. And, still more, he wanted to ask questions. There was a new *why* in his life that he wanted to put to someone. He could not understand how things had come to this pass: he had always worked so hard; had wanted to keep everything decent and orderly and different from what it had been in his uncle's house. Yet, in spite of his efforts, the same disorder there had been in his uncle's house, the same sense of too much and too violent a humanity, had come to swallow his own life. He felt as if everything were closing in on him – the Muslim wives fighting upstairs, the crippled astrologer and, in his own room, the monstrous shapes of his mother, his wife, his grandmother, the shrill voices, the quarrels, dirt and poverty and moneylenders who had to be cajoled. He remembered how his uncle had clutched at his head and screamed: 'They are eating me up!' and that was how he was feeling himself, devoured and eaten.

He did not know any way in which to tell this to the proprietor, so that there was nothing for him to do but push back his rising heart and continue checking stock. And afterwards, when the shop closed at night, he wandered round by himself, his lips moving slightly as he talked in imagination to the proprietor, explaining himself fully and without reservation.

Often, when he got home, his wife at once began to ask him for money; and when he had to refuse her, for it frequently happened nowadays that he really had nothing, she was angry and shouted at him, while his mother listened with tightdrawn lips.

Once he tried to defend himself, he waved trembling hands in the air and cried, 'But what can I do?'

That drove her to such fury that she began to look round for something to strike him with; and she would undoubtedly have found something, if Vijay had not at this point intervened.

He turned to Ram Kumar and said, 'Why don't you ask for more money in your shop?'

But that suggestion shocked Ram Kumar; he had got to the top of the salary scale, and the salary scale was to him like a law of God or Nature, incontrovertible.

Vijay laughed at him and his wife shouted, 'What is it to him if we all starve!'

Vijay mocked, 'He belongs to his shop, not to us'; but after a time he stopped mocking, and his face assumed the bitter expression which nowadays was the most characteristic of him. He said, 'Yes; all your life you have slaved for the shop, and where are you now?'

Ram Kumar's wife said, 'The fool, his own family is nothing to him—'

'Keep quiet,' Vijay said, without even turning round to her; she looked sullen, but said nothing further. 'Look at both of us,' said Vijay to his brother. 'You have worked all your life and I—' here he stopped and laughed, with an echo of his old free laughter in which there was also some surprise and admiration at all the things he had done in *his* life. 'And now we are both here,' he said.

19

Ram Kumar listened to him, which was not something he had often done before; but now, for the first time, he felt almost a kind of response to what his brother was saying.

After that, he listened more frequently when Vijay sat on the floor in his bitter moods, running his hands through his hair and muttering against the world. 'The world sucks the juice out of us and then spits us out like an empty shrivelled skin,' said Vijay. And Ram Kumar pretended to be minding his own business, as usual, but inwardly he nodded. It was so, he knew now; he had always worked and hoped hard, but had got nothing. His attitude towards the shop and the proprietor changed, and he began to doubt whether they really represented all goodness and virtue, as he had so unquestioningly believed all these years. He still worked as hard as ever and received customers with the same grace and ceremony; but now he went about these things stiffly and hollowly and without joy, like a man who has lost his faith.

One day Vijay, when returning from one of his drinking bouts, was knocked down by a motorcycle-rickshaw. He was brought to a hospital where it took him three days to die. They covered him with a red cloth and carried him on a plank down to the Jumna. The pall bearers were Ram Kumar and several cousins and brothers-in-law. Behind them walked other male relatives and friends. Everyone chanted: 'God, God, you are Truth!' Ram Kumar chanted too, but he did not believe it; he did not believe there was any God or any Truth or anything at all.

Since Vijay had no sons, it was Ram Kumar who had to feed the fire of his brother's pyre. He ladled in clarified butter and heard its sizzle and saw the flames shoot up; and it was not long before it was all finished and they could go home again. At home the women were mourning. They wailed and screamed and knocked themselves against the floor and walls to hurt themselves. Ram Kumar's wife clutched at her own throat as if she wished to strangle herself and screamed to her dead and burned brother-in-law: 'Stand up just once more!' The mother hit her fist against her forehead and chanted about the feelings she had when she was carrying Vijay, and about his childhood and beautiful manhood. The grandmother, who was very old and not sure who was dead, stamped her feeble feet and wrung her hands to Heaven. Even very distant relatives, who had hardly known Vijay, showed extravagant grief. It was what was done at every death – what must have been done, though Ram Kumar could not remember it, at his own father's death, what had been done at his uncle the postal inspector's, and what no doubt would be done at his own death, by these women who went on for ever.

There was no spark in him to kindle him into a rebel. And yet, as he smiled and bowed to customers, he asked himself sometimes, why am I doing this; and he looked at the proprietor – sitting at his table, blue-shaved, with rimless spectacles, growing every year richer and more sour – and strange feelings rose in his heart. Meanwhile at home money became tighter and tighter. His mother developed some disease, which made her feet and hands swell up. She had to be taken to doctors, and the doctors had to be paid money, which Ram Kumar did not know how to come by. Once she said to him, 'If I could die, son, things would be easier for you'; she could no longer walk and sat all day on a piece of matting, looking down in astonishment at her purple, swollen hands that lay in her lap like dead animals. At last Ram Kumar asked for a rise in salary. The salary scale had, like everything else, ceased to be sacred to him, so it was no longer impossible for him to ask; but he expected to be refused, which he was.

His one act of rebellion was quite unpremeditated and came as a surprise even to himself. He was dressing the doll, changing its attire from a silk blouse and velvet shorts to a blue dressing-gown with braidings, when he dropped it. He never quite knew whether he had done it on purpose. He remembered thinking, just before the fatal accident, that the doll's mouse-tooth grin was rather stupid; he also remembered the surge of pleasure when it went hurtling, with some violence, down from the counter. Everyone in the shop gasped and came crowding round; the proprietor rose from his table. They all stood and looked at the broken fragments and from them at Ram Kumar, who kept his eyes lowered and said nothing. He would not apologize, would not say he did not know how it could have happened. He was almost enjoying this little unexpected moment, though he would no doubt have enjoyed it more if he had not known that the cost of a new doll would be taken, month by month, out of his salary.

The Widow

Durga lived downstairs in the house she owned. There was a small central courtyard and many little rooms opening from it. All her husband's relatives, and her own, wanted to come and live with her; they saw that it would be very comfortable, and anyway, why pay rent elsewhere when there was that whole house? But she resisted them all. She wouldn't even allow them to live in the upstairs part, but let it out to strangers and took rent and was a landlady. She had learned a lot since she had become a widow and a property owner. No one, not even her elder relatives, could talk her into anything.

Her husband would have been pleased to see her like that. He hated relatives anyway, on principle; and he hated weak women who let themselves be managed and talked into things. That was what he had always taught her: stand on your own, have a mind, be strong. And he had left her everything so that she could be. When he had drafted his will, he had cackled with delight, thinking of all his relatives and how angry they would be. His one anxiety had been that she would not be able to stand up to them and that she would give everything over into their hands; so that his last energies had been poured into training her, teaching her, making her strong.

She had grown fond of him in those last years – so much so that, if it hadn't been for the money and independent position with which he left her, she would have been sad at losing him. That was a great change from what she had felt at the beginning of her marriage when, God forgive her, she had prayed every day for him to die. As she had pointed out in her prayers, he was old and she was young; it was not right. She had hated everyone in those days – not only her husband, but her family too, who had married her to him. She would not speak to anyone. All day she sat in a little room, unbathed, unkempt, like a woman in mourning. The servant left food for her on a tray and tried to coax her to eat, but she wouldn't – not till she was very hungry indeed and then she ate grudgingly, cursing each mouthful for keeping her alive.

But the old man was kind to her. He was a strange old man. He did not seem to expect anything of her at all, except only that she should be there in his house. Sometimes he brought saris and bangles for her, and though at first she pretended she did not want them, afterwards she was pleased and tried them on and admired herself. She often wondered why he should be so kind to her. He wasn't to anyone else. In fact, he was known as a mean, spiteful old man, who had made his money (in grain) unscrupulously, pressed his creditors hard and maliciously refused to support his needy relatives. But with her he was always gentle and even generous, and after a while they got on very well together.

So when he was dead, she almost missed him, and it was only when she reminded herself of other things about him – his old-man smell, and his dried legs, when she had massaged them, with the useless rag of manhood flopping against the thigh – that she realized it was better he was gone. She was, after all, still young and healthy and hearty, and now with the money and property he had left her, she could lead the life she was entitled to. She kept two servants, got up when she wanted and went to sleep when she wanted; she ate everything she liked and as much as she liked; when she felt like going out, she hired a tonga – and not just any tonga, but always a spruce one with shining red leather seats and a well-groomed horse wearing jingling bells, so that people looked round at her as she was driven smartly through the streets.

It was a good life, and she grew plump and smooth with it. Nor did she lack for company; her own family and her husband's were always hovering around her and, now that she had them in the proper frame of mind, she quite enjoyed entertaining them. It had taken her some time to get them into that proper frame of mind. For in the beginning, when her husband had just died, they had taken it for granted that she was to be treated as the widow – that is, the cursed one who had committed the sin of outliving her husband and was consequently to be numbered among the outcasts. They had wanted – yes, indeed they had – to strip her of her silken coloured clothes and of her golden ornaments. The more orthodox among them had even wanted to shave her head, to reduce her diet to stale bread and lentils and deprive her from ever again tasting the sweet things of life: to condemn her, in fact, to that perpetual mourning, perpetual expiation, which was the proper lot of widows. That was how they saw it and how their forefathers had always seen it; but not how she saw it at all.

There had been a struggle, of course, but not one of which the outcome was long in doubt. And now it was accepted that she should be mistress of what was hers and rule her household and wear her fine clothes and eat her fine foods: and out of her abundance she would toss crumbs to them, let them sit in her house and talk with them when she felt like talking, listen to their importunities for money and sometimes even perhaps – not out of pity or affection, but just as the whim took her – do them little favours and be praised and thanked for it. She was queen, and they knew it.

But even a queen's life does not bring perfect satisfaction always, and there were days and even weeks at a time when she felt she had not been dealt with as she had a right to expect. She could never say exactly what had been left out, but only that something *had* been left out and that somehow, somewhere, she had been short-changed. And when this realization came over her, then she fell into a black mood and ate and slept more than ever – not for pleasure, but compulsively, sunk in sloth and greed because soft beds and foods were all that life had given to her. At such times she turned her relatives away from her house, and those who nevertheless wheedled their way in had to sit respectfully silent round her bed while she heaved and groaned like a sick woman.

There was one old aunt, known by everyone as Bhuaji, who always managed to wheedle her way in, whatever Durga's mood. She was a tough, shrewd old woman, small and frail in appearance and with a cast in one eye which made it seem as if she was constantly peeping round the next corner to see what advantage lay there. When Durga's black mood was on her, it was Bhuaji who presided at the bedside, saw to it that the others kept suitably mournful faces and, at every groan of Durga's, fell into loud exclamations of pity at her sufferings. When Durga finally got tired of all these faces gathered round her and, turning her back on them, told them to go away and never come back to be a torture and a burden on her, then it was again Bhuaji who saw to it that they left in haste and good order and suitably on compassionate tiptoe; and after locking the door behind them all, she would come back to sit with Durga and encourage her not only to groan but to weep as well and begin to unburden herself.

Only what was there of which she could unburden herself, much as, under Bhuaji's sympathetic encouragement, she longed to do so? She brought out broken sentences, broken complaints and accusations, but there was nothing she could quite lay her finger on. Bhuaji, always eager and ready to comfort with the right words, tried to lay it on for her, pointing out how cruelly fate had dealt with her in depriving her of what was every woman's right – namely, a husband and children. But no, no, Durga would cry, that was not it, that was not what she wanted: and she looked scornful, thinking of those women who did have husbands and children, her sisters and her cousins, thin, shabby, overworked and overburdened, was there anything to envy in their lot? On the contrary, it was they who should and did envy Durga – she could read it in their eyes when they looked at her, who was so smooth and well-fed and had everything that they could never even dream of.

Then gradually, Bhuaji began to talk to her of God. Durga knew about God, of course. One had to worship Him in the temple and also perform certain rites such as bathing in the river when there was an eclipse and give food to the holy men and observe fast days. One did all these things so that no harm would befall, and everybody did them and had always done them: that was God. But Bhuaji talked differently. She talked about Him as if He were a person whom one could get to know, like someone who would come and visit in the house and sit and talk and drink tea. She spoke of Him mostly as Krishna, sometimes as the baby Krishna and sometimes as the lover Krishna. She had many stories to tell about Krishna, all the old stories which Durga knew well, for she had heard them since she was a child; but Bhuaji told them as if they were new and had happened only yesterday and in the neighbourhood. And Durga sat up on her bed and laughed: 'No, really, he did that?' 'Yes, yes, really – he stole the butter and licked it with his fingers and he teased the young girls and pulled their hair and kissed them – oh, he was such a naughty boy!' And Durga rocked herself to and fro with her hands clasped before her face, laughing in delight – 'How naughty!' she cried. 'What a bad bad boy, bless his heart!'

But when they came to the lover Krishna, then she sat quite still and looked very attentive, with her mouth a little open and her eyes fixed on Bhuaji's face. She didn't say much, just listened; only sometimes she would ask in a low voice, 'He was very handsome?' 'Oh very,' said Bhuaji, and she described him all over again – lotus eyes and brows like strung bows and a throat like a conch. Durga couldn't form much of a picture from that, but never mind, she made her own, formed it secretly in her mind as she sat there listening to Bhuaji, and grew more and more thoughtful, more and more silent.

Bhuaji went on to tell her about Krishna's devotees and the rich rewards granted to those whose hearts were open to receive him. As Durga avidly listened, she narrated the life of Maya Devi, who had retired from the world and built herself a little hut on the banks of the Ganges: there to pass her days with the baby Krishna, whom she had made her child and to whom she talked all day as to a real child, and played with him and cooked for him, bathed his image and dressed it and put it to sleep at night and woke it up with a kiss in the morning. And then there was Pushpa Devi, for whom so many advantageous offers had come but who rejected them all because she said she was wedded already, to Krishna, and he alone was her lord and her lover; she lived with him in spirit, and sometimes in the nights her family could hear her screams of joy as she lay with him in their marital rite and gave him her soul.

Durga bought two little brass images of Krishna – one of him playing the flute, the other as a baby crawling on all fours. She gave them special prominence on her little prayer table and paid her devotions to him many times a day, always waiting for him to come alive for her and be all that Bhuaji promised he would be. Sometimes – when she was alone at night or lay on her bed in the hot, silent afternoons, her thoughts dwelling on Krishna – she felt strange new stirrings within her which were almost like illness, with a tugging in the bowels and a melting in the thighs. And she trembled and wondered whether this was Krishna descending on her, as Bhuaji promised he would, showing her his passion, creeping into her – ah! great God that he was – like a child or a lover, into her womb and into her breasts.

She became dreamy and withdrawn, so that her relatives, quick to note this change, felt freer to come and go as they pleased and sit around in her house and drink tea with a lot of milk and sugar in it. Bhuaji, indeed, was there almost all the time. She had even brought a bundle of clothes and often stayed all day and all night, only scurrying off to have a quick look at her own household, with her own old husband in it, and coming back within the hour. Durga suspected that, on these home excursions of hers, Bhuaji went well provided with little stocks of rice and lentils and whatever other provisions she could filch from the kitchen store. But Durga hardly cared and was, at any rate, in no frame of mind to make a scene. And when they asked for money, Bhuaji or the other relatives, as often as not she gave – quite absent-mindedly, taking out her keys to unlock the steel almira in which she kept her cash-box, while they eagerly, greedily, watched her.

At such moments she often thought of her husband and of what he would say if he could see her being so yielding with these relatives. She could almost imagine him getting angry – hear his shrill old man's voice and see him shaking his fist so that the sleeve of his kurta flapped and showed his plucked, dried arm trembling inside. But she did not care for his anger; it was her life, her money, she sullenly answered him, and she could let herself be exploited if she wished. Why should he, a dead old man, dictate his wishes to her, who was alive and healthy and a devotee of Krishna's? She found herself thinking of her husband with dislike. It was as if she bore him some grudge, though she did not know what for.

The relatives sat in the house and got bolder and bolder, until they were giving their own orders to the servants and complaining about the quality of the tea.

It was about this time that the tenants who had rented the place upstairs gave notice – an event which brought great excitement into the lives of the relatives, who spent many happy hours apportioning the vacant flat out among them-selves (Bhuaji, of course, was going to move her old husband into one room, and she left the others to fight for the remain-ing space). But here suddenly Durga showed herself quite firm again: tenants meant rent, and she had no intentions, not even to spite her husband, of sacrificing a regular monthly income. So only a few days after the old tenants moved out, and the relatives were still hotly disputing among themselves as to how the place was to be apportioned, a new family of tenants moved in, consisting of one Mr Puri (a municipal tax inspector) with his wife, two daughters and a son. Their

belongings were carried upstairs to loud, remonstrative cries
from the relatives; to which Durga turned a deaf ear – even
to the plaints of Bhuaji, who had already brought her old
husband and her household chattels along and now had to
take them back again.

Durga had been worshipping her two images for so long now,
but nothing of what Bhuaji had promised seemed to be happening to them. And less and less was happening to her. She
tried so hard, lying on her bed and thinking of Krishna and
straining to reproduce that wave of love she had experienced;
but it did not return or, if it did, came only as a weak echo of
what it had been. She was unsatisfied and felt that much had
been promised and little given. Once, after she had prayed
for a long time before the two images, she turned away and
suddenly kicked at the leg of a chair and hurt her toe. And
sometimes, in the middle of doing something – sorting the
laundry or folding a sari – she would suddenly throw it aside
with an impatient gesture and walk away frowning.

She spent a lot of time sitting on a string cot in her courtyard, not doing anything nor thinking anything in particular,
just sitting there, feeling heavy and too fat and wondering
what there was in life that one should go on living it. When
her relatives came to visit her, she as often as not told them to
go away, even Bhuaji; she did not feel like talking or listening
to any of them. But now there was a new person to stake a
claim to her attention. The courtyard was overlooked by a
veranda which ran the length of the flat upstairs. On this
veranda Mrs Puri, her new tenant, would frequently appear,
leaning her arms on the balustrade and shouting down in
friendly conversation. Durga did not encourage her and
answered as drily as politeness permitted; but Mrs Puri was

a friendly woman and persisted, appearing twice and three times a day to comment to Durga on the state of the weather. After a while she even began to exercise the prerogative of a neighbour and to ask for little loans – one day she had run out of lentils, a second out of flour, a third out of sugar. In return, when she cooked a special dish or made pickle, she would send some down for Durga, thus establishing a neighbourly traffic which Durga had not wished for but was too lethargic to discourage.

Then one day Mrs Puri sent some ginger pickle down with her son. He appeared hesitantly in the courtyard, holding his glass jar carefully between two hands. Durga was lying drowsily on her cot; her eyes were shut and perhaps she was even half-asleep. The boy stood and looked down at her, not knowing what to do, lightly coughing to draw her attention. Her eyes opened and stared up at him. He was perhaps seventeen years old, a boy with large black eyes and broad shoulders and cheeks already dark with growth. Durga lay and stared up at him, seeing nothing but his young face looming above her. He looked back at her, uncertain, tried to smile, and blushed. Then at last she sat up and adjusted the sari which had slipped down from her breasts. His eyes modestly lowered, he held the jar of pickle out to her as if in appeal.

'Your mother sent?'

He nodded briefly and, placing the jar on the floor by her cot, turned to go rather quickly. Just as he was about to disappear through the door leading out from the courtyard she called him back, and he stopped and stood facing her, waiting. It was some time before she spoke, and then all she could think to say was, 'Please thank your mother.' He disappeared before she could call him back again.

Durga had become rather slovenly in her habits lately, but that evening she dressed herself up in one of her better saris and went to call on Mrs Puri upstairs. A visit from the landlady was considered of some importance, so Mrs Puri, who had been soaking raw mangoes, left this work, wiped her hands on the end of her sari and settled Durga in the sitting-room. The sitting-room was not very grand, it had only a cane table in it and some cane stools and a few cheap bazaar pictures on the whitewashed walls. Durga sat in the only chair in the room, a velvet armchair which had the velvet rubbed bare in many places and smelled of old damp clothes.

Mrs Puri's two daughters sat on the floor, stitching a quilt together out of many old pieces. They were plain girls with heavy features and bad complexions. Mr Puri evidently was out – and his wife soon dwelt on that subject: every night, she said, he was sitting at some friend's house, goodness knows what they did, sitting like that, what could they have so much to talk about? And wasting money in smoking cigarettes and chewing betel, while she sat at home with her daughters, poor girls, and wasn't it high time good husbands were found for them? But what did Mr Puri care – he had thought only for his own enjoyment, his family was nothing to him. And Govind the same . . .

'Govind?'

'My son. He too – only cinema for him and laughing with friends.'

She had much to complain about and evidently did not often have someone whom she could complain to; so she made the most of Durga. The two plain daughters listened placidly, stitching their quilt; only when their mother referred to the urgent necessity of finding husbands for them – as she did at frequent intervals and as a sort of capping couplet to each particular complaint – did they begin to wriggle and exchange sly glances and titter behind their hands.

It took Durga some time before she could disengage herself; and when she finally did, Mrs Puri accompanied her to the stairs, carrying her burden of complaint right over into her farewell and even pursuing Durga with it as she picked her way down the steep, narrow stone stairs. And just as she had reached the bottom of them, Govind appeared to walk up them, and his mother shouted down to him, 'Is this a time to come home for your meal?'

Durga passed him in the very tight space between the doorway and the first step. She was so close to him that she could feel his warmth and hear his breath. Mrs Puri shouted down the stairs: 'Running here and there all day like a loafer!' Durga could see his eyes gleaming in the dark and he could see hers; for a moment they looked at each other. Durga said in a low voice, 'Your mother is angry with you,' and then he was halfway up the stairs.

Later, slowly unwinding herself from her sari and staring at herself in the mirror as she did so, she thought about her husband. And again, and stronger than ever, she had that feeling of dislike against him, that grudge against the useless dead old man. It was eighteen or nineteen years now since they had married her to him: and if he had been capable, wouldn't she have had a son like Govind now, a strong, healthy, handsome boy with big shoulders and his beard just growing? She smiled at the thought, full of tenderness, and forgetting her husband, thought instead how it would be if Govind were her son. She would not treat him like his mother did – would never reproach him, shout at him down the stairs – but, on the contrary, encourage him in all his pleasures so that, first thing when he came home, he would call to her – 'Mama!' – and they would sit together affectionately, more like brother and sister, or even two friends, than like mother and son, while he told her everything that had happened to him during the day.

She stepped closer to the mirror – her sari lying carelessly where it had fallen round her feet – and looked at herself, drawing her hand over her skin. Yes, she was still soft and smooth and who could see the tiny little lines, no more than shadows, that lay round her eyes and the corners of her mouth? And how fine her eyes still were, how large and black and how they shone. And her hair too – she unwound it from its pins and it dropped down slowly, heavy and black and sleek with oil, and not one grey hair in it.

As she stood there, looking at herself in nothing but her short blouse and her waist-petticoat, with her hair down, suddenly another image appeared behind her in the mirror: an old woman, grey and shabby and squinting and with an ingratiating smile on her face. 'I am not disturbing?' Bhuaji said.

Durga bent down to pick up her sari. She began to fold it, but Bhuaji took it from her and did it far more deftly, the tip of her tongue eagerly protruding from her mouth.

'Why did you come?' Durga said, watching her. Bhuaji made no reply, but went on folding the sari, and when she had finished, she smoothed it ostentatiously from both sides. Durga lay down on the bed. As a matter of fact, she found she was quite glad that Bhuaji had come to see her.

She asked, 'How long is it since they married me?'

'Let me see,' Bhuaji said. She squatted by the side of the bed and began to massage Durga's legs. 'Is it fifteen years, sixteen . . .'

'No, eighteen.'

Bhuaji nodded in agreement, her lips mumbling as she

worked something out in her head, her hands still skilfully massaging.

'Eighteen years,' Durga said reflectively, 'I could have been—'

'Yes, a grandmother by now,' said Bhuaji, smiling widely with all her empty gums.

Durga suddenly pushed those soothing, massaging hands away and sat upright. 'Leave me alone! Why do you come here, who called you?'

Instead of sitting in her courtyard, Durga was now often to be found pacing up and down by the door which led to the staircase. When Govind came down, she always had a word for him. At first he was shy with her and left her as quickly as possible; sometimes he waited for her to go away before he came down or went up. But she was patient with him. She understood and even sympathized with his shyness: he was young, awkward perhaps like a child, and didn't know how much good she meant him. But she persevered; she would ask him questions like: 'You go often to the cinema?' or 'What are you studying?' to prove to him how interested she was in him, interested like a mother or a favourite aunt, and ready to talk on any topic with him.

And slowly he responded. Instead of dashing away, he began to stand still at the bottom of the steps and to answer her questions; at first in monosyllables but soon, when his interest was stirred, at greater length; and finally at such great length that it seemed pointless to go on standing there in that dark cramped space when he could go into her house and sit there with her and drink almond sherbet. He kept on talking and told her everything: who were his friends, who his favourite film stars, his ambition to go abroad, to become an aircraft engineer. She listened and watched him while he spoke; she watched and watched him, her eyes fixed on his face. She became very familiar with his face, yet always it was new to her. When he smiled, two little creases appeared in his cheeks. His teeth were large and white, his hair sprang from a point on his forehead. Everything about him was young and fresh and strong – even his smell, which was that of a young animal full of sap and sperm.

She loved to do little things for him. At first only to ply him with almond sherbet and sweetmeats, of which he could take great quantities; later to give him money – beginning with small amounts, a rupee here and there, but then going on to five- and even ten-rupee notes. He wanted money badly and his parents gave him so little. It was wrong to keep a boy short of money when he needed a lot: for treating his friends, for his surreptitious cigarettes, for tee-shirts and jeans such as he saw other boys wearing.

It became so that he got into the habit of asking her for whatever he wanted. How could she refuse? On the contrary, she was glad and proud to give – if only to see the look of happiness on his face, his eyes shining at the thought of what he was going to buy, his smile which brought little creases into his cheeks. At such moments she was warm and sick with mother's love, she longed to cradle his head and stroke his hair. He was her son, her child.

That was exactly what his mother told her: 'He is your son also, your child.' Mrs Puri was glad to see Durga take such an interest in the boy. She taught him to say thank you for everything that Durga gave him and to call her auntie. She made pickle very often and sent it down in jars. She also came down herself and talked to Durga for hours on end about her family problems. So much was needed, and where was it all to come from? Mr Puri's salary was small – 175 rupees a month plus dearness allowance – and he spent a lot on betel and cigarettes and other pleasures. And what was to become of her poor children? Such good children they were, as anyone who took an interest in them was bound to find out. They needed a helping hand in life, that was all. Her boy, and her two girls who ought to have been married a year ago. She sent the girls down quite often, but Durga always sent them quickly back up again.

Towards the beginning of each month, when the rent was due, Govind came down every day with pickle and after a while Mrs Puri would follow him. Dabbing with her sari in the corner of her eye, she would give an exact account of her monthly expenditure, what were her debts and what she had in hand, so that Durga could see for herself how impossible it was to impose any demand for rent on such an overburdened budget. And though Durga at first tried to ignore these plaints, this became more and more difficult, and in the end she always had to say that she would not mind waiting a few days longer. After which Mrs Puri dried her eyes and the subject of rent was not mentioned again between them till the first week of the following month, when the whole procedure was repeated. In this way several months' rent accumulated – a fact which, had it been brought to their notice, would have surprised Durga's previous tenants who had not found her by any means so lenient a landlady.

The relatives were much alarmed at this growing friendship with the Puris, which seemed to them both ominous and unnatural. What need had Durga to befriend strangers when there were all her own relatives, to whom she was bound in blood and duty? They became very indignant with her, but had to keep a check on their tongues; for Durga was short-tempered with them these days and, if they touched on subjects or showed moods not to her liking, was quicker than ever to show them the door. But something obviously had to be said and it was Bhuaji who took it upon herself to say it.

She began by praising Govind. A good boy, she said, that she could see at a glance, respectful and well mannered, just the sort of boy whom one ought to encourage and help on in life. She had nothing at all against Govind. But his mother now, and his sisters – Bhuaji, looking sideways at Durga, sadly shook her head. Alas, she knew women like that only too well, she had come across too many of them to be taken in by their soft speech. Greedy and shameless, that was what they were, self-seeking and unscrupulous, with their one aim to fasten upon and wring whatever advantage they could out of noble-hearted people like Durga. It was they, said Bhuaji, coming closer and whispering behind her hand as if afraid Mrs Puri would hear from upstairs, who incited the boy to come down and ask for money and new clothes – just as a feeler and to see how far they could go. Let Durga wait and in a short time she would see: saris they would ask for, not ten-rupee notes but hundred-rupee ones, household furniture, a radio, a costly carpet; and they would not rest till they had possessed themselves not only of the upstairs part of the house but of the downstairs part as well . . .

Just then Govind passed the door and Durga called out to him. When he came, she asked him, 'Where are you going?' and then she stroked the shirt he was wearing, saying, 'I think it is time you had another new bush-shirt.'

'A silk one,' he said, which made Durga smile and reply in a soft, promising voice, 'We will see,' while poor Bhuaji stood by and could say nothing, only squint and painfully smile.

One day Bhuaji went upstairs. She said to Mrs Puri: 'Don't let your boy go downstairs so much. She is a healthy woman, and young in her thoughts.' Mrs Puri chose to take offence: she said her boy was a good boy, and Durga was like another mother to him. Bhuaji squinted and laid her finger by the side of her nose, as one who could tell more if she but chose. This made Mrs Puri very angry and she began to shout about how much evil thought there was in the world today so that even pure actions were misinterpreted and made impure. Her two daughters, though they did not know what it was all about, also looked indignant. Mrs Puri said she was proud of her son's friendship with Durga. It showed he was better than all those other boys who thought of nothing but their own pleasures and never cared to listen to the wisdom they could learn from their elders. And she looked from her veranda down into the courtyard, where Govind sat with Durga and was trying to persuade her to buy him a motor scooter. Bhuaji also looked down, and she bit her lip so that no angry word could escape her.

Durga loved to have Govind sitting with her like that. She had no intention of buying him a motor scooter, which would take more money than she cared to disburse, but she loved to hear him talk about it. His eyes gleamed and his hair tumbled into his face as he told her about the beautiful motor scooter possessed by his friend Ram, which had many shiny fittings and a seat at the back on which he gave rides to his friends. He leaned forward and came closer in his eagerness to impart his passion to her. He was completely carried away – 'It does forty miles per hour, as good as any motor car!' – and looked splendid, full of strength and energy. Durga laid her hand on his knee and he didn't notice. 'I have something for you inside,' she said in a low, hoarse voice.

He followed her into the room and stood behind her while she fumbled with her keys at her steel almira. Her hand was shaking rather, so that she could not turn the key easily. When she did, she took something from under a pile of clothes and held it out to him. 'For you,' she said. It was a penknife. He was disappointed, he lowered his eyes and said, 'It is nice,' in a sullen, indifferent voice. But then at once he looked up again and he wetted his lips with his tongue and said, 'Only 1,200 rupees, just slightly used, it is a chance in a million' – looking past her into the almira where he knew there was a little safe in which she kept her cash. But already she was locking it and fastening the key back to the string at her waist. He suddenly reached out and held her hand with the key in it – '1,200 rupees,' he said in a whisper as low and hoarse as hers had been before. And when she felt him so close to her, so eager, so young, so passionate, and his hand actually holding hers, she shivered all over her body and her heart leaped up in her and next thing she was sobbing. 'If you knew,' she cried, 'how empty my life has been, how lonely!' and the tears flowed down her face. He let go her hand and stepped backwards, and then backwards again as she followed him; till he was brought up short by her bed which he could feel pressing against the back of his knees, as he stood, pinned, between it and her.

She was talking fast, about how alone she was and there was no one to care for. Yet she was young still, she told him – she invited him to look, look down into her face, wasn't it a young face still, and full and plump? And the rest of her too, all full and plump, and when she was dressed nicely in one of her best saris with a low-cut blouse, then who would know that she wasn't a young girl or at least a young woman in the very prime of her life? And she was good too, generous and good and ready to do everything, give everything for those she loved. Only who was there whom she could love with all the fervour of which her heart was capable? In her excitement she pushed against him so that he fell backwards and sat down abruptly on her bed. At once she was sitting next to him, very close, her hand on his – if he knew, she said, what store of love there was in her, ready and bursting and brimming in her! Then it was his turn to cry; he said, 'I want a motor scooter, that's all,' in a hurt grieved voice, trembling with tears like a child's.

That was the last time he came down to see her. Afterwards he would hardly talk to her at all – even when she lay in wait for him by the stairs, he would brush hurriedly past her, silent and with averted face. Once she called after him, 'Come in, we will talk about the motor scooter!' but all she got by way of reply was, 'It is sold already,' tossed over his shoulder as he ran upstairs. She was in despair and wept often and bitterly; there was a pain right in her heart, such as she had never experienced before. She longed to die and yet at the same time she felt herself most burningly alive. She visited Mrs Puri several times and stayed for some hours; during which Mrs Puri, as usual, talked a lot, and in the usual strain, and kept pointing out how her children were Durga's too, while the two daughters simpered. Evidently she knew nothing of what had happened, and assumed that everything was as it had been.

But, so Durga soon learned, Mrs Puri knew very well that everything was not as it had been. Not only did she know, but it was she herself who had brought about the change. It was she who, out of evil and spite, had stopped Govind from coming downstairs and had forbidden him ever to speak to Durga again. All this Durga learned from Bhuaji, one hot afternoon as she lay tossing on her bed, alternately talking, weeping and falling into silent fits of despair. She had no more secrets from Bhuaji. She needed someone before whom she could unburden herself, and who more fit for that purpose than the ever available, ever sympathetic Bhuaji? So she lay on her bed and cried: 'A son, that is all I want, a son!' And Bhuaji was soothing and understood perfectly. Of course Durga wanted a son; it was only natural, for had not God set maternal feelings to flow sweetly in every woman's breast? And now, said Bhuaji angrily, to have that God-given flow stopped in its course by the machinations of a mean-hearted, jealous, selfish woman – and so it all came out. It was a revelation to Durga. Her tears ceased and she sat up on her bed. She imagined Govind suffering under the restraint laid upon him and yearning for Durga and all her kindness as bitterly as she yearned for him. There was sorrow upstairs and sorrow downstairs. She sat very upright on the bed. After a while she turned her face towards Bhuaji, and her lips were tight and her eyes flashed. She said, 'We will see whose son he is.'

She waited for him by the stairs. He came late that night, but still she went on waiting. She was patient and almost calm. She could hear sounds from upstairs – a clatter of buckets, water running, Mrs Puri scolding her daughters. At the sound of that voice, hatred swelled in Durga so that she was tempted to leave her post and run upstairs to confront her enemy. But she checked herself and remained standing downstairs, calm and resolute and waiting. She would not be angry. This was not the time for anger.

She heard him before she saw him. He was humming a little tune to himself. Probably he had been to see a film with friends and now he was singing a lyric from it. He sounded gay and light-hearted. She peeped out from the dark doorway and saw him clearly just under the lamp-post outside the house. He was wearing an orange tee-shirt which she had given him and which clung closely to him so that all his broad chest and his nipples were outlined; his black jeans too fitted tight as a glove over his plump young buttocks. She edged herself as close as she could against the wall. When he entered the doorway, she whispered his name. He stopped singing at once. She talked fast, in a low urgent voice: 'Come with me – what do your parents ever do for you?'

He shuffled his feet and looked down at them in the dark.

'With me you will have everything – a motor scooter—'

'It is sold.'

'A new one, a brand-new one! And also you can study to be an aircraft engineer, anything you wish—'

'Is that you, son?' Mrs Puri called from upstairs.

Durga held fast to his arm: 'Don't answer,' she whispered.

'Govind! Is that boy come home at last?' And the two plain sisters echoed: 'Govind!'

'I can do so much for you,' Durga whispered. 'And what can they do?'

'Coming, Ma!' he called.

'Everything I have is for you—'

'You and your father both the same! All night we have to wait for you to come and eat your food!'

Durga said, 'I have no one, no one.' She was stroking his arm which was smooth and muscular and matted with long silky hair.

Mrs Puri appeared at the top of the stairs: 'Just let me catch that boy, I will twist his ears for him!'

'You hear her, how she speaks to you?' whispered Durga with a flicker of triumph. But Govind wrenched his arm free and bounded up the stairs towards his mother.

*

It did not take Bhuaji long after that to persuade Durga to get rid of her tenants. There were all those months of rent unpaid, and besides, who wanted such evil-natured people in the house? Bhuaji's son-in-law had connections with the police, and it was soon arranged: a constable stood downstairs while the Puris' belongings – the velvet armchair, an earthenware water pot, two weeping daughters carrying bedding – slowly descended. Durga did not see them. She was sitting inside before the little prayer table on which stood her two Krishnas. She was unbathed and in an old crumpled sari and with her hair undone. Her relatives sat outside in the courtyard with their belongings scattered around them, ready to move in upstairs. Bhuaji's old husband sat on his little bundle and had a nap in the sun.

'Only pray,' Bhuaji whispered into Durga's ear. 'With prayer He will surely come to you.' Durga's eyes were shut; perhaps she was asleep. 'As a son and as a lover,' Bhuaji whispered. The relatives talked gaily among themselves outside; they were in a good, almost a festive mood.

It seemed Durga was not asleep after all, for suddenly she got up and unlocked her steel almira. She took out everything – her silk saris, her jewellery, her cashbox. From time to time she smiled to herself. She was thinking of her husband and of his anger, his impotent anger, at thus seeing everything given away at last. The more she thought of him, the more vigorously she emptied her almira. Her arms worked with a will, flinging everything away in abandon, her hair fell into her face, perspiration trickled down her neck in runnels. Her treasure lay scattered in heaps and mounds all over the floor and Bhuaji squinted at it in avid surmise.

Durga said, 'Take it away. It is for you and for them—' and she jerked her head towards the courtyard where the relatives

45

twittered like birds. Bhuaji was already squatting on the floor, sorting everything, stroking it with her hands in love and wonder. As she did so, she murmured approvingly to Durga: 'That is the way – to give up everything. Only if we give up everything will He come to us.' And she went on murmuring, while stroking the fine silks and running hard gold necklaces through her fingers: 'As a son and as a lover,' she murmured, over and over again, but absently.

The relatives were glad that Durga had at last come round and accepted her lot as a widow. They were glad for her sake. There was no other way for widows but to lead humble, bare lives; it was for their own good. For if they were allowed to feed themselves on the pleasures of the world, then they fed their own passions too, and that which should have died in them with the deaths of their husbands would fester and boil and overflow into sinful channels. Oh yes, said the relatives, wise and knowing, nodding their heads, our ancestors knew what they were doing when they laid down these rigid rules for widows; and though nowadays perhaps, in these modern times, one could be a little more lenient – for instance, no one insisted that Durga should shave her head – still, on the whole, the closer one followed the old traditions, the safer and the better it was.

A Spiritual Call

The river, broad, swift, swollen, was at this season too dangerous to cross in a boat. One had to walk across the bridge, which was holy and thronged with pilgrims chanting salutations as they crossed. On the other side of the bridge began a cluster of tiny temples, all of them made spruce with silver tinsel, peacock fans, gilt ornaments and pink paint. The gods inside them were also painted pink – pink cheeks and rosebud lips – and the plump priests who looked after them were immaculately bathed and their skulls were newly shaven and naked except for their one tuft of hair. Worshippers were constantly passing in and out to leave their offerings and obeisances, while the rest-houses, which alternated with the temples, were equally well populated, though they offered no amenities beyond a dark, bare room of whitewashed brick. But here anyone was welcome to spread their bedding on the floor and put the children to sleep and light the cooking fires and stir in their cooking vessels, and all the time be very merry and make friends with strangers: for coming like this, here to this holy place in quest of grace, lightened the heart and made it loving to all the world.

Beyond the temples and rest-houses came a wood with a path through it; on either side of the path were trees and shrubs and sadhus doing penance. Some of the sadhus were stark naked, some wore animal skins, all had long, matted hair and beards and were immobile, so that it was easy to believe they had been sitting there for centuries, as rooted and moss-grown as the trees and as impervious as they to snakes and any wild animals there might be prowling around. Besides the sadhus, there were beggars and these were not in the least still or immobile but very lively indeed, especially if someone happened to pass by when they would set up voluble claims to alms, holding up their palms and pointing out any sores or other disfigurements that might have laid them victim.

Over everything towered the mountains, receding far up into the blue sky into unknown heights of holiness, steppe upon steppe of them and dissolved from sight at last among mysterious white veils which may have been mist or snow or, who knew, the emanation of a promised Presence.

It was all, in short, too good to be true; a dream, though better than anything, Daphne felt, she could have dreamed of. The coolie, naked except for a loincloth, walked in front of her and carried her baggage on his head; he was her guide and protector who cleared a path for her through the crowd of pilgrims, warded off the beggars and knew exactly where she wanted to go. It was quite a long walk, but Daphne was too entranced to mind; nor did she for one moment doubt that she was being led along the right way. And sure enough, her messenger, like some angel sent direct, brought her at last into the presence she had desired, for many weeks now, and when she was there and saw him again, so great was her relief and her happiness that she burst into tears.

'Welcome!' he said to her, and did ever eyes and smile swell the word with such meaning? And then he said to her tears, 'Now what is this? What nonsense?'

'I'm silly,' she said, wiping away at her eyes but unable to check a further gush of tears.

'Yes, very silly,' he said, and turned to the others around him: 'Isn't she? A silly goose?' and all smiled at her, with him, all of them tender, friendly, saying welcome.

One or two of them she recognized; the cheerful, bearded, athletic young men in orange robes who were his permanent disciples and who had been with him in London. She did not know any of the others. They included quite a number of non-Indians, and these she guessed to be people like herself who had followed him out here to undergo an intensive course of spiritual regeneration. In addition there were many casual visitors constantly passing in and out of the room, devotees come to have a sight of him who sat for a while and then got up and went away while others took their place. Daphne was used to seeing him thus in the midst of crowds. It had been the same in London, where he had been constantly surrounded – by women mostly, rich women in smart hats who bustled round him and besieged him with requests uttered in shrill voices; and he so patient, unruffled, eating ice cream in someone's drawing-room and smiling on them all equally.

Nevertheless, it had seemed to Daphne that his smile had in some way been special for her. There was no reason why she should think so, yet she had been convinced of it. When he looked at her, when he spoke to her (though he said nothing that he did not say to others), she felt chosen. She was not by nature a fanciful girl; on the contrary, she had always been known as straightforward and sensible, good at sickbeds, had done history at Oxford, wore tasteful, unobtrusive, English clothes. Yet after she had met Swamiji, she knew without a word being spoken that he meant her to follow him back to India. It was not an easy path. She was fond of travelling in a way and always spent her summer vacation in France or Italy, and twice she had gone to Greece: but she had never contemplated anything much farther than that. She was quite happy in London – had her few friends, her quite interesting job with a secretarial agency – and though perhaps, if opportunity had knocked that way, she would not have minded a year or two doing some sort of interesting job in America or on the continent, it was not, one would have said, in her nature to go off on a spiritual quest to India.

Everyone was indeed amazed; she herself was, but she knew it was inevitable. No one tried to stand in her way, although of course her mother – a wonderfully energetic lady of middle years prominent on several welfare committees – pointed out quite a few of the drawbacks to her enterprise. But there was nothing she could say that Daphne had not already said to herself: so that the mother, who was tolerant in the best English way and believed in people being allowed to make their own mistakes, had not spoken any further but instead confined herself to bringing forward several aged relatives who had served in India as administrators during the Raj and were thus suited to give Daphne advice on at least such basic questions as to what clothes to take and what diseases to guard against.

Everyone, whatever their private thoughts, had been too tactful outright to warn Daphne of disaster. But if they had done, how triumphantly she could, after some weeks' stay, have contradicted them! She was supremely happy in the ashram. It was not a very grand place – Swamiji had rented it for a few months for himself and his followers, and it consisted merely of three rows of rooms grouped around a courtyard. The courtyard was triangular in shape, and the apex was formed by Swamiji's room, which was of course much bigger than all the others and led to a veranda with a view out over the river. The other rooms were all small and ugly, inadequately lit by skylights set so high up on the walls that no one could ever get at them to clean them; the only pieces of furniture were cheap string-cots, some of which had the string rotting away. The meals were horrible – unclean, badly cooked, and irregular – and the cooks kept running away and had to be replaced at short notice. There were many flies, which were especially noticeable at meal-times when they settled in droves on the food and on the lips of people eating it. Daphne rose, with ease, above all this; and she lived only in the beautiful moments engendered by the love they all bore to Swamiji, by the hours of meditation to which he exhorted them, the harmonious rhythm of their selfless days, and the surrounding atmosphere of this place holy for centuries and where God was presumed to be always near.

The door to Swamiji's room was kept open day and night, and people came and went. He was always the same: cheerful and serene. He sat on the floor, on a mattress covered with a cream-coloured silk cloth, and the robe he wore loosely wrapped round himself was of the same silk, and both of them were immaculate. His beard and shoulder-length hair shone in well-oiled waves, and at his feet there lay a heap of flowers among which his fingers often toyed, picking up petals and smelling them and then rubbing them to and fro. He was not a handsome man – he was short and not well built, his features were blunt, his eyes rather small – yet there was an aura of beauty about him which may have been partly due to the flowers and the spotless, creamy, costly silk, but mostly of course to the radiance of his personality.

He was often laughing. The world seemed a gay place to him, and his enthusiasm for it infected those around him so that they also often laughed. They were very jolly together. They had many private jokes and teased each other about their little weaknesses (one person's inability to get out of bed in the mornings, another's exploits as a fly-swatter, Swamiji's fondness for sweets). Often they sat together and just gossiped, like any group of friends, Swamiji himself taking a lively lead; any more serious talk they had was interspersed among the gossip, casually almost, and in the same tone. They were always relaxed about their quest, never over-intense: taking their cue from Swamiji himself, they spoke of things spiritual in the most matter-of-fact way – and why not: weren't they matter-of-fact? the most matter-of-fact things of all? – and hid their basic seriousness under a light, almost flippant manner.

Daphne felt completely at ease with everyone. In England, she had been rather a shy girl, had tended to be awkward with strangers and, at parties or any other such gathering, had always had difficulty in joining in. But not here. It was as if an extra layer of skin, which hitherto had kept her apart from others, had dropped from off her heart, and she felt close and affectionate towards everyone. They were a varied assortment of people, of many different nationalities: a thin boy from Sweden called Klas, two dumpy little Scottish school-teachers, from Germany a large blonde beauty in her thirties called Helga. Helga was the one Daphne shared a room with. Those dark, poky little rooms made proximity very close, and though under different circumstances Daphne might have had difficulty in adjusting to Helga, here she found it easy to be friendly with her.

Helga was, in any case, too unreserved a person herself to allow reserve to anyone else; especially not to anyone she was sharing a room with. She was loud and explicit about everything she did, expressing the most fleeting of her thoughts in words and allowing no action, however trivial, to pass without comment. Every morning on waking she would report on the quality of the sleep she had enjoyed, and thence carry on a continuous stream of commentary as she went about her tasks ('I think I need a new toothbrush.' 'These flies – I shall go mad!') In the morning it was – not a rule, the ashram had no rules, but it was an understanding that everyone should do a stretch of meditation. Somehow Helga quite often missed it, either because she got up too late, or took too long to dress, or something prevented her; and then, as soon as she went into Swamiji's room, she would make a loud confession of her omission. 'Swamiji, I have been a naughty girl again today!' she would announce in her Wagnerian voice. Swamiji smiled, enjoying her misdemeanour as much as she did, and teased her, so that she would throw her hands before her face and squeal in delight, 'Swamiji, you are not to, please, please, you are not to be horrid to me!'

Swamiji had a very simple and beautiful message to the world. It was only this: meditate; look into yourself and so, by looking, cleanse yourself; harmony and happiness will inevitably follow. This philosophy, simple as its end product appeared to be, he had forged after many, many solitary years of thought and penance in some icy Himalayan retreat. Now he had come down into the world of men to deliver his message, planning to return to his mountain solitude as soon as his task here was achieved. It might, however, take longer than he had reckoned on, for men were stubborn and tended to be blind to Truth. But he would wait, patiently, and toil till his work was done. Certainly, it was evident that the world urgently needed his message, especially the Western world where both inner and outer harmony were in a state of complete disruption. Hence his frequent travels abroad, to England and other countries, and next he was planning a big trip to America, to California, where a group of would-be disciples eagerly awaited him. His method was to go to these places, make contacts, give lectures and informal talks, and then return with a number of disciples whom he had selected for more intensive training. He had, of course, his little nucleus of permanent disciples – those silent, bearded young men in orange robes who accompanied him everywhere and looked after his simple needs – but the people he brought with him from abroad, such as Daphne and Helga and the others, were expected to stay with him for only a limited time. During that time he trained them in methods of meditation and generally untangled their tangled souls, so that they could return home, made healthy and whole, and disseminate his teaching among their respective countrymen. In this way, the Word would spread to all corners of the earth, and to accelerate the process, he was also writing a book, called *Vital Principle of Living*, to be published in the first place in English and then to be translated into all the languages of the world.

Daphne was fortunate enough to be chosen as his secretary in this undertaking. Hitherto, she had observed, his method of writing had been very strange, not to say wonderful: he would sit there on his silken couch, surrounded by people, talk with them, laugh with them, and at the same time he would be covering, effortlessly and in a large flowing hand, sheets of paper with his writing. When he chose her as his secretary, he presented these sheets to her and told her to rewrite them in any way she wanted. 'My English is very poor, I know,' he said, which made Helga exclaim, 'Swamiji! Your English! Poor? Oh, if I could only speak one tiniest bit as well, how conceited I would become!' And it was true, he did speak well: very fluently in his soft voice and with a lilting Indian accent; it was a pleasure to hear him. Daphne sometimes wondered where he could have learned to speak so well. Surely not in his mountain cave? She did not know, no one knew, where he had been or what he had done before that.

Strangely enough, when she got down to looking through his papers, she found that he had not been unduly modest. He did not write English well. When he spoke, he was clear and precise, but when he wrote, his sentences were turgid, often naive, grammatically incorrect. And his spelling was decidedly shaky. In spite of herself, Daphne's Oxford-trained mind rose at once, as she read, in judgement; and her feelings, in the face of this judgement, were ones of embarrassment, even shame for Swamiji. Yet a moment later, as she raised her burning cheeks from his incriminating manuscript, she realized that it was not for him she need be ashamed but for herself. How narrow was her mind, how tight and snug it sat in the straitjacket her education had provided for it! Her sole, pitiful criterion was conventional form, whereas what she was coming into contact with here was something so infinitely above conventional form that it could never be contained in it. And that was precisely why he had chosen her: so that she could express him (whose glory it was to be inexpressible) in words accessible to minds that lived in the same narrow confines as her own. Her limitation, she realized in all humility, had been her only recommendation.

She worked hard, and he was pleased with her and made her work harder. All day she sat by his side and took down the words which he dictated to her in between talking to his disciples and to his other numerous visitors; at night she would sit by the dim bulb in the little room she shared with Helga to write up these notes and put them into shape. Helga would be fast asleep, but if she opened her eyes for a moment, she would grumble about the light disturbing her. 'Just one minute,' Daphne would plead, but by that time Helga had tossed her big body to its other side and, if she was still grumbling, it was only in her sleep. Very often Daphne herself did not get to sleep before three or four in the morning, and then she would be too tired to get up early enough for her meditation.

She could not take this failure as lightly as Helga took her own. When Helga boasted to Swamiji, 'Today I've been naughty again', Daphne would hang her head and keep silent, unable to confess. Once, though, Helga told on her – not in malice, but rather in an excess of good humour. Having just owned up to her own fault and been playfully scolded for it by Swamiji, she was brimming with fun and her eyes danced as she looked round for further amusement; they came to rest on Daphne, and suddenly she shot out her finger to point: 'There's another one just as bad!' and when she saw Daphne blush and turn away, rallied her gaily, 'No pretending, I saw you lie snug in bed, old lazybones!'

Daphne felt awkward and embarrassed and wondered what Swamiji would say: whatever it was, she dreaded it, for unlike Helga she took no pride in her shortcomings, nor did she have a taste for being teased. And, of course, Swamiji knew it. Without even glancing at Daphne, he went on talking to Helga: 'If you manage to do your morning meditation three days running,' he told her, 'I shall give you a good conduct prize.' 'Swamiji! A prize! Oh, lucky lucky girl I am!'

But the next time they were alone together – not really alone, of course, only comparatively so: there were just a few visitors and they sat at a respectful distance and were content with looking at and being near him – as Daphne sat cross-legged on the floor, taking dictation from him, her notebook perched on her knee, he interrupted his fluent flow of wisdom to say to her in a lower voice: 'You know that private meditation is the – how shall I say? – the foundation, the cornerstone of our whole system?'

After a short pause, she brought out, 'It was only that I was—' she had been about to say 'tired', but checked herself in time: feeling how ridiculous it would be for her to bring forward her tiredness, the fact that she had sat up working till the early hours of the morning, to him who was busy from earliest morning till latest night, talking to people and helping them and writing his book and a hundred and one things, without ever showing any sign of fatigue but always fresh and bright as a bridegroom. So she checked herself and said, 'I was lazy, that's all,' and waited, pencil poised, hoping for a resumed dictation.

'Look at me,' he said instead.

She was too surprised to do so at first, so he repeated it in a soft voice of command, and she turned her head, blushing scarlet, and lifted her eyes – and found herself looking into his. Her heart beat up high and she was full of sensations. She would have liked to look away again, but he compelled her not to.

'What's the matter?' he said softly. He took a petal from the pile of flowers lying at his feet and held it up to his nose. 'Why are you like that?' he asked. She remained silent, looking into his face. Now he was crushing the petal between his fingers, and the smell of it, pungent, oversweet, rose into the air. 'You must relax. You must trust and love. Give,' he said and he smiled at her and his eyes brimmed with love. 'Give yourself. Be generous.' He held her for a moment longer, and then allowed her at last to look away from him; and at once he continued his dictation which she endeavoured to take down, though her hands were trembling.

After that she was no longer sure of herself. She was an honest girl and had no desire to cheat herself, any more than she would have desired to cheat anyone else. She felt now that she was here under false pretences, and that her state of elation was due not, as she had thought, to a mystic communion with some great force outside herself, but rather to her proximity to Swamiji, for whom her feelings were very much more personal than she had hitherto allowed herself to suspect. Yet even after she admitted this, the elation persisted. There was no getting away from the fact that she was happy to be there, to be near him, working with him, constantly with him: that in itself was satisfaction so entire that it filled and rounded and illumined her days. She felt herself to be like a fruit hanging on a bough, ripening in his sunshine and rich with juices from within. And so it was, not only with her, but with everyone else there too. All had come seeking something outside of themselves and their daily preoccupations, and all had found it in or through him. Daphne noticed how their faces lit up the moment they came into his presence – she noticed it with Klas, a very fair, rather unattractive boy with thin lips and thin hair and pink-rimmed eyes; and the two Scottish schoolteachers, dumpy, dowdy little women who, before meeting Swamiji, had long since given up any expectations they might ever have had – all of them bloomed under his smile, his caressing gaze, his constant good humour. 'Life,' he once dictated to Daphne, 'is a fountain of joy from which the lips must learn to drink with relish as is also taught by our sages from the olden times.' (She rewrote this later.) He was the fountain of joy from which they all drank with relish.

She was working too hard, and though she would never

have admitted it, he was quick to notice. One day, though she sat there ready with notebook and pencil, he said, 'Off with you for a walk.' Her protests were in vain. Not only did he insist, but he even instructed her for how long she was to walk and in what direction. 'And when you come back,' he said, 'I want to see roses in your cheeks.' So dutifully she walked and where he had told her to: this was away from the populated areas, from the throng of pilgrims and sadhus, out into a little wilderness where there was nothing except rocky ledges and shrubs and, here and there, small piles of faded bricks where once some building scheme had been begun and soon abandoned. But she did not look around her much; she was only concerned with reckoning the time he had told her to walk, and then getting back quickly to the ashram, to this room, to sit beside him and take down his dictation. As soon as she came in, he looked at her, critically: 'Hm, not enough roses yet, I think,' he commented, and ordered her to take an hour-long walk in that same direction every day.

On the third day she met him on the way. He had evidently just had his bath, for his hair hung in wet ringlets and his robe was slung round him hastily, leaving one shoulder bare. He always had his bath in the river, briskly pouring water over himself out of a brass vessel, while two of his disciples stood by on the steps with his towel. They were coming behind him now as he – nimbler, sprightlier than they – clambered round ledges and stones and prickly bushes. He waved enthusiastically to Daphne and called to her: 'You see, I also am enjoying fresh air and exercise!'

She waited for him to catch up with her. He was radiant: he smiled, his eyes shone, drops of water glistened on his hair and beard. 'Beautiful,' he said, and his eyes swept over the landscape, over the rocky plateau on which they stood – the holy town huddled on one side, the sky, immense and blue, melting at one edge into the mountains and at another into the river. 'Beautiful, beautiful,' he repeated and shook his head and she looked with him, and it was, everything was, the whole earth, shining and beautiful.

'Did you know we are building an ashram?' he asked her.

'Where?'

'Just here.'

He gave a short sweep of the hand, and she looked around her, puzzled. It did not seem possible for anything to grow in this spot except thistles and shrubs: and as if to prove the point, just a little way off was an abandoned site around which were scattered a few sad, forgotten bricks.

'A tip-top, up-to-date ashram,' he was saying, 'with air-conditioned meditation cells and a central dining-hall. Of course it will be costly, but in America I shall collect a good deal of funds. There are many rich American ladies who are interested in our movement.' He tilted his head upward and softly swept back his hair with his hand, first one side and then the other, in a peculiarly vain and womanly movement.

She was embarrassed and did not wish to see him like that, so she looked away into the distance and saw the two young men who had accompanied him running off towards the ashram; they looked like two young colts, skipping and gambolling and playfully tripping each other up. Their joyful young voices, receding into the distance, were the only sounds, otherwise it was silent all around, so that one could quite clearly hear the clap of birds' wings as they flew up from the earth into the balmy, sparkling upper air.

'I have many warm invitations from America,' Swamiji said. 'From California especially. Do you know it? No? There is a Mrs Fisher, Mrs Gay Fisher, her husband was in shoe business. She often writes to me. She has a very spacious home which she will kindly put at our disposal, and also many connections and a large acquaintance among other ladies interested in our movement. She is very anxious for my visit. Why do you make such a face?'

Daphne gave a quick, false laugh and said, 'What face?'

'Like you are making. Look at me – why do you always look away as if you are ashamed?' He put his hand under her chin and turned her face towards himself. 'Daphne,' he said, tenderly; and then, 'It is a pretty name.'

Suddenly, in her embarrassment, she was telling him the story of Daphne: all about Apollo and the laurel tree, and he seemed interested, nodding to her story, and now he was making her walk along with him, the two of them all alone and he leaning lightly on her arm. He was slightly shorter than she was.

'So,' he said, when she had finished, 'Daphne was afraid of love ... I think you are rightly named, what do you say? Because I think – yes, I think this Daphne also is afraid of love.'

He pinched her arm, mischievously, but seeing her battle with stormy feelings, he tactfully changed the subject. Again his eyes shone, again he waved his hand around: 'Such a lovely spot for our ashram, isn't it? Here our foreign friends – from America, like yourself from UK, Switzerland, Germany, all the countries of the world – here their troubled minds will find peace and slowly they will travel along the path of inner harmony. How beautiful it will be! How inspiring! A new world! Only one thing troubles me, Daphne, and on this question now I want advice from your cool and rational mind.'

Daphne made a modest disclaiming gesture. She felt not in

the least cool or rational, on the contrary, she knew herself to have become a creature tossed by passion and wild thoughts.

But, 'No modesty, please,' he said to her disclaimer. 'Who knows that mind of yours better, you or I? Hm? Exactly. So don't be cheeky.' At which she had to smile: on top of everything else, how nice he was, how terribly, terribly nice. 'Now can I ask my question? You see, what is troubling me is, should we have a communal kitchen or should there be a little cooking place attached to each meditation cell? One moment: there are pros and cons to be considered. Listen.'

He took her arm, familiar and friendly, and they walked. Daphne listened, but there were many other thoughts rushing in and out of her head. She was very conscious of his hand holding her arm, and she kept that arm quite still. Above all, she was happy and wanted this to go on for ever, he and she walking alone in that deserted place, over shrubs and bricks, the river glistening on one side and the mountains on the other, and above them the sky where the birds with slow, out-stretched wings were the only patterns on that unmarred blue.

Not only did it not go on for ever, but it had to stop quite soon. Running from the direction of the ashram, stumbling, waving, calling, came a lone, familiar figure: 'Yu-hu!' shouted Helga. 'Wait for me!'

She was out of breath when she caught up with them. Strands of blonde hair had straggled into her face, perspiration trickled down her neck into the collar of her pale cerise blouse with mother-of-pearl buttons: her blue eyes glittered like ice as they looked searchingly from Swamiji to Daphne and back. She looked large and menacing.

'Why are you walking like two lovebirds?'

'Because that is what we are,' Swamiji said. One arm was still hooked into Daphne's and now he hooked the other into

Helga's. 'We are talking about kitchens. Let's hear what you have to advise us.'

'Who cares for me?' said Helga, pouting. 'I'm just silly old Helga.'

'Stop thinking about yourself and listen to the problem we are faced with.'

Now there were three of them walking, and Daphne was no longer quite so happy. She didn't mind Helga's presence, but she knew that Helga minded hers. Helga's resentment wafted right across Swamiji, and once or twice she looked over his head (which she could do quite easily) to throw an angry blue glance at Daphne. Daphne looked back at her to ask, what have I done? Swamiji walked between them, talking and smiling and holding an arm of each.

That night there was an unpleasant scene. As usual, Daphne was sitting writing up her notes while Helga lay in bed and from time to time called out, 'Turn off the light' before turning round and going back to sleep again. Only tonight she didn't go back to sleep. Instead she suddenly sat bolt upright and said, 'The light is disturbing me.'

'I won't be a minute,' Daphne said, desperately writing, for she simply had to finish, otherwise tomorrow's avalanche of notes would be on top of her – Swamiji was so quick, so abundant in his dictation – and she would never be able to catch up.

'Turn it off!' Helga suddenly shouted, and Daphne left off writing and turned round to look at her. From the high thatched roof of their little room, directly over Helga's bed, dangled a long cord with a bulb at the end: it illumined Helga sitting up in bed in her lemon-yellow nylon nightie which left her large marble shoulders bare; above them loomed her head covered in curlers which made her look awesome like

Medusa, while her face, flecked with pats of cream, also bore a very furious and frightening expression.

'Always making up to Swamiji,' she was saying in a loud, contemptuous way. 'All night you have to sit here and disturb me so tomorrow he will say, "You have done so much work, good girl, wonderful girl, Daphne". Pah. It is disgusting to see you flirting with him all the time.'

'I don't know what you're talking about,' Daphne said in a trembly voice.

'Don't know what you're talking about,' Helga repeated, making a horrible mimicking face and attempting to reproduce Daphne's accent but drowning it completely in her German one. 'I hate hypocrites. Of course everyone knows you English are all hypocrites, it is a well-known fact all over the world.'

'You're being terribly unfair, Helga.'

'Turn off the light! Other people want to sleep, even if you are busy being Miss Goody-goody!'

'In a minute,' Daphne said, sounding calm and continuing with her task.

Helga screamed with rage: 'Turn it off! Turn it off!' She bounced up and down on her bed with her fists balled. Daphne took no notice whatsoever but went on writing. Helga tossed herself face down into her pillow and pounded it and sobbed and raged from out of there. When Daphne had finished writing, she turned off the light and, undressing in the dark, lay down in her lumpy bed next to Helga, who by that time was asleep, still face downwards and her fists clenched and dirty tear-marks down her cheeks.

Next morning Helga was up and dressed early but contrary to her usual custom, she was very quiet and tiptoed around so as not to disturb her room-mate. When Daphne finally woke

up, Helga greeted her cheerfully and asked whether she had
had a good sleep, and then she told her how she had watched
poor Klas stepping into a pat of fresh cow dung on his way to
meditation. Helga thought this was very funny, she laughed
loudly at it and encouraged Daphne to laugh too by giving her
shoulder a hearty push. Then she went off to get breakfast
for the two of them, and, after they had had it, and stepped
outside the room to cross over to Swamiji's, she suddenly
put her arm round Daphne and whispered into her ear: 'You
won't tell him anything? No? Daphnelein?' And to seal their
friendship, their conspiracy, she planted a big, wet kiss on
Daphne's cheek, and said, 'There. Now it is all well again.'

Swamiji was receiving daily letters from America, and he
was very merry nowadays and there was a sense of bustle
and departure about him. The current meditation course,
for which Daphne and Helga and all of them had enrolled,
was coming to an end, and soon they would be expected
to go home again so that they might radiate their newly
acquired spiritual health from there. But when they talked
among themselves, none of them seemed in any hurry to
go back. The two Scottish schoolteachers were planning a
tour of India to see the Taj Mahal and the Ajanta caves and
other such places of interest, while Klas wanted to go up to
Almora, to investigate a spiritual brotherhood he had heard
of there. Swamiji encouraged them – 'It is such fun to travel,'
he said, and obviously he was gleefully looking forward to
his own travels, receiving and answering all those airmail
letters and studying airline folders, and one of the young men
who attended on him had already been sent to Delhi to make
preliminary arrangements.

Daphne had no plans. She didn't even think of going home;
it was inconceivable to her that she could go or be anywhere

where he was not. The Scottish schoolteachers urged her to join them on their tour, and she half-heartedly agreed, knowing though that she would not go. Helga questioned her continuously as to what she intended to do, and when she said she didn't know, came forward with suggestions of her own. These always included both of them; Helga had somehow taken it for granted that their destinies were now inseparable. She would sit on the side of Daphne's bed and say in a sweet, soft voice, 'Shall we go to Khajurao? To Cochin? Would you like to visit Ceylon?' and at the same time she would be coaxing and stroking Daphne's pillow as if she were thereby coaxing and stroking Daphne herself.

All the time Daphne was waiting for him to speak. In London she had been so sure of what he meant her to do, without his ever having to say anything; now she had to wait for him to declare himself. Did he want her to accompany him to America; did he want her to stay behind in India; was she to go home? London, though it held her mother, her father, her job, her friends, all her memories, was dim and remote to her; she could not imagine herself returning there. But if that was what he intended her to do, then she would; propelled not by any will of her own, but by his. And this was somehow a great happiness to her: that she, who had always been so self-reliant in her judgements and actions, should now have succeeded in surrendering not only her trained, English mind but everything else as well – her will, herself, all she was – only to him.

His dictation still continued every day; evidently this was going to be a massive work, for though she had already written out hundreds of foolscap pages, the end was not yet in sight. Beyond this daily dictation, he had nothing special to say to her; she still went on her evening walk, but he did not again come to meet her. In any case, this walk of hers was now never taken alone but always in the company of Helga, whose arm firmly linked hers. Helga saw to it that they did everything together these days: ate, slept, sat with Swamiji, even meditated. She did not trust her alone for a moment, so even if Swamiji had wanted to say anything private to Daphne, Helga would always be there to listen to it.

Daphne wasn't sure whether it was deep night or very early in the morning when one of the bearded young men came to call her. Helga, innocently asleep, was breathing in and out. Daphne followed the messenger across the courtyard. Everything was sleeping in a sort of grey half-light, and the sky too was grey with some dulled, faint stars in it. Across the river a small, wakeful band of devotees was chanting and praying, they were quite a long way off and yet the sound was very clear in the surrounding silence. There was no light in Swamiji's room, nor was he in it; her guide led her through the room and out of an opposite door which led to the adjoining veranda, overlooking the river. Here Swamiji sat on a mat, eating a meal by the light of a kerosene lamp. 'Ah, Daphne,' he said, beckoning her to sit opposite him on the mat. 'There you are at last.'

The bearded youth had withdrawn. Now there were only the two of them. It was so strange. The kerosene lamp stood just next to Swamiji and threw its light over him and over his tray of food. He ate with pleasure and with great speed, his hand darting in and out of the various little bowls of rice, vegetables, lentils, and curds. He also ate very neatly, so that only the very tips of the fingers of his right hand were stained by the food and nothing dropped into his beard. It struck Daphne that this was the first time that she had seen him eat a full meal: during the course of his busy day, he seemed content to nibble at nuts and at his favourite sweetmeats, and now and again drink a tumbler of milk brought to him by one of his young men.

'Can I talk to you?' he asked her. 'You won't turn into a laurel tree?'

He pushed aside his tray and dabbled his hand in a finger-bowl and then wiped it on a towel. 'I think it would be nice,' he said, 'if you come with me to America.'

She said, 'I'd like to come.'

'Good.'

He folded the towel neatly and then pressed it flat with his hand. For a time neither of them said anything. The chanting came from across the river; the kerosene lamp cast huge shadows.

'We shall have to finish our book,' he said. 'In America we shall have plenty of leisure and comfort for this purpose ... Mrs Gay Fisher has made all the arrangements.'

He bent down to adjust the flame of the lamp and now the light fell directly on his face. At that moment Daphne saw very clearly that he was not a good-looking man, nor was there anything noble in his features: on the contrary, they were short, blunt and common, and his expression, as he smiled to himself in anticipation of America, had something disagreeable in it. But the next moment he had straightened up again, and now his face opposite her was full of shadows and so wise, calm and beautiful that she had to look away for a moment, for sheer rapture.

'We shall be staying in her home,' he said. 'It is a very large mansion with swimming pool and all amenities – wait, I will show you.' Out of the folds of his gown he drew an envelope, which he had evidently kept ready for her and out of which he extracted some colour photographs.

'This is her mansion. It is in Greek style. See how gracious these tall pillars, so majestic. It was built in 1940 by the late Mr Fisher.' He raised the lamp and brought it near the photograph to enable her to see better. 'And this,' he said, handing her another photograph, 'is Mrs Gay Fisher herself.'

He looked up and saw that light had dawned, so he lowered the wick of the lamp and extinguished the flame. Thus it was by the frail light of earliest dawn that Daphne had her first sight of Mrs Gay Fisher.

'She writes with great impatience,' he said. 'She wants us to come at once, straight away, woof like that, on a magic carpet if possible.' He smiled, tolerant, amused: 'She is of a warm, impulsive nature.'

The picture showed a woman in her fifties in a pastel two-piece and thick ankles above dainty shoes. She wore a three-rope pearl necklace and was smiling prettily, her head a little to one side, her hands demurely clasped before her. Her hair was red.

'The climate in California is said to be very beneficial,' Swamiji said. 'And wonderful fruits are available. Not to speak of ice cream,' he twinkled, referring to his well-known weakness. 'Please try and look a little bit happy, Daphne, or I shall think that you don't want to come with me at all.'

'I want to,' she said. 'I do.'

He collected his photographs from her and put them carefully back into the envelope. There was still chanting on the other side of the river. The river looked a misty silver now and so did the sky and the air and the mountains as slowly, minute by minute, day emerged from out of its veils. The first bird woke up and gave a chirp of pleasure and surprise that everything was still there.

'Go along now,' he said. 'Go and meditate.' He put out

his hand and placed it for a moment on her head. She felt small, weak and entirely dependent on him. 'Go, go,' he said, pretending impatience, but when she went, he called: 'Wait!' She stopped and turned back. 'Wake up that sleepy Helga,' he said. 'I want to talk to her.' Then he added: 'She's coming with us too.' 'To America?' she said, and in such a way that he looked at her and asked, 'What's wrong?' She shook her head. 'Then be quick,' he said.

A few days later he sent her a present of a sari. It was of plain mill cloth, white with a thin red border. She put it away but when, later, he saw her in her usual skirt and blouse, he asked her where it was. She understood then that from now on that was what he wanted her to wear, as a distinguishing mark, a uniform almost, the way his bearded young attendants always wore orange robes. She put it on just before her evening walk; it took her a long time to get it on, and when she had, she felt awkward and uncomfortable. She knew she did not look right, her bosom was too flat, her hips too narrow, nor had she learned how to walk in it, and she kept stumbling. But she knew she would have to get used to it, so she persevered; it seemed a very little obstacle to overcome.

Instead of going on her usual route, she turned today in the opposite direction and walked towards the town. First she had to pass all the other ashrams, then she had to go through the little wood where the sadhus did penance and the beggars stretched pitiful arms towards her and showed her their sores. In these surroundings, it did not seem to matter greatly, not even to herself, what she wore and how she wore it; and when she had crossed the wood, and had got to the temples and bazaars, it still did not matter, for although there were crowds of people, none of them had any time to care for Daphne. The temple bells rang and people bought garlands and incense and sweetmeats to give to their favourite gods. Daphne crossed the holy bridge and, as she did so, folded her hands in homage to the holy river. Once or twice she tripped over her sari, but she didn't mind, she just hitched it up a bit higher. When she came to the end of the bridge, she turned and walked back over it, again folding her hands and even saying, 'Jai Ganga-ji', only silently to herself and not out loud like everyone else. Then she saw Helga coming towards her, also dressed in a white sari with a red border; Helga waved to her over the heads of people and when they came together, she turned and walked back with Daphne, her arm affectionately round her shoulder. Helga was wearing her sari all wrong, it was too short for her and her feet coming out at the end were enormous. She looked ridiculous, but no one cared; Daphne didn't either. She was glad to be with Helga, and she thought probably she would be glad to be with Mrs Gay Fisher as well. She was completely happy to be going to California, and anywhere else he might want her to accompany him.

Miss Sahib

The entrance to the house in which Miss Tuhy lived was up a flight of stairs between a vegetable shop and a cigarette and cold-drink one. The stairs were always dirty, and so was the space around the doorway, with rotted bits of vegetable and empty cigarette packets trampled into the mud. Long practice had taught Miss Tuhy to step around this refuse, smilingly and without rancour, and as she did so she always nodded friendly greetings to the vegetable seller and the cold-drink man, both of whom usually failed to notice her. Everyone in the neighbourhood had got used to her, for she had lived there, in that same house, for many years.

It was not the sort of place in which one would have expected to find an Englishwoman like Miss Tuhy, but the fact was, she was too poor to live anywhere else. She had nothing but her savings, and these, in spite of her very frugal way of life, could not last for ever; and of course there was always the vexed question of how long she would live. Once, in an uncharacteristically realistic moment, she had calculated that she could afford to go on for another five years, which would bring her up to sixty-five. That seemed fair enough to her, and she did not think she had the right to ask for more. However, most of the time these questions did not arise for she tended to be too engrossed in the present to allow fears of the future to disturb her peace of mind.

She was, by profession and by passionate inclination, a teacher, but she had not taught for many years. She had first come to India thirty years ago to take up a teaching post at a school for girls from the first families, and she had taught there and at various other places for as long as she had been allowed. She did it with enthusiasm, for she loved the country and her students. When Independence came and all the other English teachers went home, it never for a moment occurred to her to join them, and she went on teaching as if nothing had changed. And indeed, as far as she was concerned, nothing did change for a number of years, and it was only at the end of that time that it was discovered she was not sufficiently well qualified to go on teaching in an Indian high school. She bowed her head to this decision, for she knew she wasn't; not compared with all those clever Indian girls who held MA degrees in politics, philosophy, psychology and economics. As a matter of fact, even though they turned out to be her usurpers, she was proud of these girls; for wasn't it she and those like her who had educated them and made them what they now were – sharp, emancipated, centuries ahead of their mothers and grandmothers? So it was not difficult for her to cede to them with a good grace, to enjoy her farewell party, cry a bit at the speeches and receive with pride and a glow in her heart the silver model of the Taj Mahal which was presented to her as a token of appreciation. After that, she sailed for England – not because she in the least wanted to, but because it was what everyone seemed to expect of her.

She did not stay long. True, no one here said she was not well qualified enough to teach and she had no difficulty in getting a job; but she was not happy. It was not the same. She liked young people always, and so she liked the young people she was teaching here; but she could not love them the way she had loved her Indian pupils. She missed their playfulness, their affection, their sweetness – by comparison the English children struck her as being cool and distant. And not only the children but everyone she met, or only saw in streets and shops: they seemed a colder people somehow, politer perhaps and more considerate than the Indians among whom she had spent so many years, but without (so she put it to herself) *real love*. Even physically the English looked cold to her, with their damp white skins and pale blue eyes, and she longed again to be surrounded by those glowing coloured skins; and those eyes! the dark, large, liquid Indian eyes! and hair that sprang with such abundance from their heads. And besides the people, it was everything else as well. Everything was too dim, too cold. There was no sun, the grass was not green, the flowers not bright enough, and the rain that continually drizzled from a wash-rag sky was a poor substitute for the silver rivers that had come rushing in torrents out of immense, dark blue monsoon clouds.

So she and her savings returned, improvidently, to India. Everyone still remembered her and was glad to see her again but, once the first warm greetings were over, they were all too busy to have much time to spare for her. She didn't mind, she was just happy to be back; and in any case she had to live rather a long way from her friends because, now that she had no job, she had to be where rents were cheaper. She found the room in the house between the vegetable seller and the cold-drink shop and lived there contentedly all the week round, only venturing forth on Sundays to visit her former colleagues and pupils. As time went on, these Sunday visits became fewer and further between, for everyone always seemed to be rather busy; anyway, there was less to say now, and also she found it was not always easy to spare the bus fare to and fro. But it didn't matter, she was even happier staying at home because all her life was there now, and the interest and affection she had formerly bestowed on her colleagues and pupils, she now had as strongly for the other people living in the house, and even for the vegetable seller and the cold-drink man though her contact with them never went further than smiles and nods.

The house was old, dirty and inward-looking. In the centre was a courtyard which could be overlooked like a stage from the galleries running all the way round the upper storeys. The house belonged to an old woman who lived on the ground floor with her enormous family of children and grandchildren; the upper floors had been subdivided and let out to various tenants. The stairs and galleries were always crowded, not only with the tenants themselves but with their servants. Everyone in the house except Miss Tuhy kept a servant, a hill boy, who cleaned and washed and cooked and was frequently beaten and frequently dismissed. There seemed to be an unending supply of these boys; they could be had very cheaply, and slept curled up on the stairs or on a threshold, and ate what was left in the pot.

Miss Tuhy was a shy person who loved other people but found it difficult to make contact with them. On the second floor lived an Anglo-Indian nurse with her grown-up son, and she often sought Miss Tuhy out, to talk in English with her, to ask questions about England, to discuss her problems and those of her son (a rather insipid young man who worked in an airlines office). She felt that she and Miss Tuhy should present a united front against the other neighbours, who were all Hindus and whom she regarded with contempt. But Miss Tuhy did not feel that way. She liked and was interested in everyone, and it seemed a privilege to her to be near them and to be aware of what seemed to her their fascinating, their passionate lives.

Down in the courtyard the old landlady ruled her family with a rod of iron. She kept a tight hold of everything and doled out little sums of pocket money to her forty-year-old sons. She could often be heard abusing them and their wives, and sometimes she beat them. There was only one person to whom she showed any indulgence – who, in fact, could get away with anything – and that was Sharmila, one of her granddaughters. When Miss Tuhy first came to live in the house, Sharmila was a high-spirited, slapdash girl of twelve, with big black eyes and a rapidly developing figure. Although she had reached the age at which her sisters and cousins were already beginning to observe that reticence which, as grown women, would keep them away from the eyes of strangers, Sharmila still behaved with all the freedom of the smaller children, running round the courtyard and up and down the stairs and in and out of the homes of her grandmother's tenants. She was the first in the house to establish contact with Miss Tuhy, simply by bursting into the room where the English lady lived and looking round and touching things and lifting them up to examine them – 'What's that?' – all Miss Tuhy's treasures: her mother-of-pearl pen-holder, the photograph of her little niece as a bridesmaid, the silver Taj Mahal. Decorating the mantelpiece was a bowl of realistically shaped fruits made of plaster-of-paris, and before leaving Sharmila lifted a brightly coloured banana out of the bowl and held it up and said, 'Can I have it?' After that she came every day, and every day, just before leaving, helped herself to one more fruit until they were all finished and then she took the bowl.

Sharmila was lazy at school all the year round, but she

always panicked before her class promotion exams and came running for help to Miss Tuhy. These were Miss Tuhy's happiest times, for not only was she once again engaged in the happy pursuit of teaching, but she also had Sharmila sitting there with her all day long, bent ardently over her books and biting the tip of her tongue in her eagerness to learn. Miss Tuhy would have dearly loved to teach her the whole year round, and to teach her everything she knew, and with that end in view she had drawn up an ambitious programme for Sharmila to follow; but although sometimes the girl consented to submit to this programme, it was evident that once the terror of exams was past her interest sharply declined, so that sometimes, when Miss Tuhy looked up from a passionate reading of the romantic poets, she found her pupil fiddling with the strands of hair which always managed to escape from her sober pigtail and her mouth wide open in a yawn she saw no reason to disguise. And indeed Miss Tuhy had finally to admit that Sharmila was right; for what use would all this learning ever be to her when her one purpose in life, her sole duty, was to be married and give satisfaction to the husband who would be chosen for her and to the inlaws in whose house she would be sent to live?

She was just sixteen when she was married. Her grandmother, who usually hated spending money, excelled herself that time and it was a grand and memorable occasion. A big wedding marquee was set up in the courtyard and crammed tight with wedding guests shimmering in their best clothes; all the tenants were invited too, including Miss Tuhy in her good dress (white dots on a chocolate-brown background) and coral necklace. Like everyone else, she was excitedly awaiting the arrival of the bridegroom and his party. She wondered what sort of a boy they had chosen for her Sharmila. She

wanted a tall, bold boy for her, a soldier and a hero; and she
had heightened, almost mythological visions of the young
couple – decked out in jewels and gorgeous clothes – gaily
disporting themselves in a garden full of brightly coloured
flowers. But when at last the band accompanying the bridegroom's party was heard, and everyone shouted, 'They have
come!' and rushed to the entrance to get the first glimpse,
then the figure that descended from the horse amid the jubi-
lation of the trumpets was not, in spite of his garlands and his
golden coat, a romantic one. Not only was Sharmila's bridegroom stocky and ill at ease, but he was also no longer very
young. Miss Tuhy, who had fought her way to the front with
the best of them, turned away in bitter disappointment. There
were tears in her eyes. She knew it would not turn out well.

Sharmila came every day to visit her old home. At first she
came in order to boast, to show off the saris and shawls and
jewellery presented to her on her marriage, and to tell about
her strange new life and the house she lived in and all her new
family. She was brimming over with excitement and talked
non-stop and danced round the courtyard. Some time later
she came with different stories, about what her mother-in-
law had said to her and what she had answered back, about
her sisters-in-law and all the other women, how they tried to
get the better of her but how she soon showed them a trick
or two: she tucked in her chin and talked in a loud voice and
was full of energy and indignation. Sometimes she stayed
for several days and did not return till her husband came to
coax her back. After a year the first baby arrived, and a year
later the second, and after a few more years a third. Sharmila
became fat and matronly, and her voice was louder and more
raucous. She still came constantly, now with two of the children trailing behind her and a third riding on her hip, and

79

she stayed longer than before, often refusing to go back even when her husband came to plead with her. And in the end she seemed to be there all the time, she and her children, so that, although nothing much was said on the subject, it was generally assumed that she had left her husband and her in-laws' house and had come back to live with her grandmother.

She was a little heavy now to go running up and down the stairs the way she used to: but she still came up to Miss Tuhy's room, and the English lady's heart still beat in the same way when she heard her step on the stair, though it was a different step now, heavier, slower and accompanied by children's tiny shuffle and patter. 'Miss Sahib!' Sharmila would call from the landing, and Miss Tuhy would fling her door wide open and stand there beaming. Now it was the children who moved from object to object, touching everything and asking to know what it was, while Sharmila, panting a little from her climb up the stairs, flung herself on the narrow bed and allowed Miss Tuhy to tuck a pillow behind her back. When the children had examined all the treasures, they began to play their own games, they crawled all over the floor and made a lot of noise. Their mother lay on the bed and sometimes she laughed and sometimes she sighed and talked about everything that came into her head. They always stayed for several hours, and when they left at last, Miss Tuhy, gorged with bliss, shut the door and carefully cleaned out her little room which the children had so delightfully disordered.

When she didn't feel like going upstairs, Sharmila stood in the middle of the courtyard and shouted, 'Miss Sahib!' in her loud voice. Miss Tuhy hurried downstairs, smoothing her dress and adjusting her glasses. She sat with Sharmila in the courtyard and helped her to shell peas. The old grandmother watched them from her bed inside the room: that terrible old woman was bedridden now and quite unable to move, a huge helpless shipwreck wrapped in shawls and blankets. Her speech was blurred and could be understood only by Sharmila, who had become her interpreter and chief functionary. It was Sharmila, not one of the older women of the household, who carried the keys and distributed the stores and knew where the money was kept. While she sat with Miss Tuhy in the courtyard, every now and again the grandmother would make calling noises and then Sharmila would get up and go in to see what she wanted. Inside the room it was dark and smelled of sickness and old age, and Sharmila was glad to come out in the open again.

'Poor old Granny,' she said to Miss Tuhy, who nodded and also looked sad for Granny because she was old and bedridden: as for herself, she did not feel old at all but a young girl, sitting here like this shelling peas and chatting with Sharmila. The children played and sang, the sun shone, along the galleries upstairs the tenants went to and fro hanging out their washing; there was the sound of voices calling and of water running, traffic passed up and down on the road outside, a nearby flour mill chucked and chucked. 'Poor old Granny,' Sharmila said again. 'When she was young, she was like a queen – tall, beautiful, everyone did what she wanted. If they didn't she stamped her foot, and screamed and waved her arms in the air – like this,' Sharmila demonstrated, flailing her plump arms with bangles up to the elbow and laughing. But then she grew serious and put her face closer to Miss Tuhy's and said in a low, excited voice: 'They say she had a lover, a jeweller from Dariba. He came at nights when everyone was asleep and she opened the door for him.' Miss Tuhy blushed and her heart beat faster; though she tried to check them, a thousand impressions rippled over her mind.

'They say she was a lot like me,' said Sharmila, smiling a little and her eyes hazy with thought. She had beautiful eyes, very large and dark with heavy brows above them; her lips were full and her cheeks plump and healthy. When she was thoughtful or serious, she had a habit of tucking in her chin so that several chins were formed, and this too somehow was attractive, especially as these chins seemed to merge and swell into her very large, tight bust.

But her smile became a frown, and she said, 'Yes, and now look at her, how she is. Three times a day I have to change the sheets under her. This is the way it all ends. Hai,' and she heaved a sigh and a brooding look came on her face. The children, who had been chasing each other round the courtyard, suddenly began to quarrel in loud voices; at that Sharmila sprang up in a rage and caught hold of the biggest child and began to beat him with her fists, but hardly had he uttered the first cry when she stopped and instead lifted him in her arms and held him close, close to her bosom, her eyes shut in rapturous possessiveness as if he were all that she had.

It was one of the other tenants who told Miss Tuhy that Sharmila was having an affair with the son of the Anglo-Indian nurse from upstairs. The tenant told it with a lot of smiles, comments and gestures, but Miss Tuhy pretended not to understand, she only smiled back at the informer in her gentle way and said 'Good morning', in English and shut the door of her room. She was very much excited. She thought about the young man whom she had seen often and sometimes talked to: a rather colourless young man, with brown hair and Anglo-Indian features, who always dressed in English clothes and played cricket on Sunday mornings. It seemed impossible to connect him in any way with Sharmila; and how his mother would have hated any such connection!

The nurse, fully opening her heart to Miss Tuhy, never tired of expressing her contempt for the other tenants in the house who could not speak English and also did not know how to live decently. She and her son lived very decently, they had chairs and a table in their room and linoleum on the floor and a picture of the Queen of England on the wall. They ate with knife and fork. 'Those others, Miss Tuhy, I wouldn't like you to see,' she said with pinched lips (she was a thin woman with matchstick legs and always wore brown shoes and stockings). 'The dirt. Squalor. You would feel sick, Miss Tuhy. And the worst are those downstairs, the—' and she added a bad word in Hindi (she never said any bad words in English, perhaps she didn't know any). She hated Sharmila and the grandmother and that whole family. But she was often away on night duty, and then who knew – as the other tenant had hinted – what went on?

Miss Tuhy never slept too well at nights. She often got up and walked round her room and wished it were time to light the fire and make her cup of tea. Those night hours seemed very long, and sometimes, tired of her room, she would go out on the stairs and along the galleries overlooking the courtyard. How silent it was now with everyone asleep! The galleries and the courtyard, so crowded during the day, were empty except where here and there a servant boy lay sleeping huddled in a corner. There was no traffic on the road outside and the flour mill was silent. Only the sky seemed alive, with the moon sliding slowly in and out of patches of mist. Miss Tuhy thought about the grandmother and the jeweller for whom she had opened the door when it was like this, silent and empty at nights. She remembered conversations she had heard years ago among her English fellow-teachers. They had always had a lot to say about sensuality in the East. They whispered to each other how some of the older boys were seen in the town entering certain disreputable alleys, while boys who came from princely or landowner families were taught everything there was to know by women on their father's estates. And as for the girls – well, they whispered, one had only to look at them, how quickly they ripened: could one ever imagine an English girl so developed at thirteen? It was, they said, the climate; and of course the food they ate, all those curries and spices that heated the blood. Miss Tuhy wondered: if she had been born in India, had grown up under this sun and had eaten the food, would she have been different? Instead of her thin, inadequate, English body, would she have grown up like the grandmother who had opened the door to the jeweller, or like Sharmila with flashing black eyes and a big bust?

Nothing stirred, not a sound from anywhere, as if all those lively people in the house were dead. Miss Tuhy stared and stared down at Sharmila's door and the courtyard washed in moonlight, and wondered was there a secret, was something going on that should not be? She crept along the gallery and up the stairs towards the nurse's door. Here too everything was locked and silent, and if there was a secret, it was being kept. She put her ear to the door and stayed there, listening. She did not feel in the least bad or guilty doing this, for what she wanted was nothing for herself but only to have proof that Sharmila was happy.

She did not seem happy. She was getting very bad-tempered and was for ever fighting with her family or with the other tenants. It was a not uncommon sight to have her standing in the middle of the courtyard, arms akimbo, keys at her waist, shouting insults in her loud, somewhat raucous voice. She no longer came to visit Miss Tuhy in her room, and once, when the English lady came to be with her downstairs, she shouted at her that she had enough with one old woman on her hands and did not have time for any more. But that night she came upstairs and brought a little dish of carrot halwa which Miss Tuhy tried to refuse, turning her face away and saying primly that thank you, she was not hungry. 'Are you angry with me, Missie Sahib?' coaxed Sharmila with a smile in her voice, and she dug her forefinger into the halwa and then brought it to Miss Tuhy's lips, saying 'One little lick, just one, for Sharmila', till Miss Tuhy put out her tongue and shyly slid it along Sharmila's finger. She blushed as she did so, and anger and hurt melted out of her heart.

'There!' cried Sharmila, and then she flung herself as usual on the bed. She began to talk, to unburden herself completely. Tears poured down her cheeks as she spoke of her unhappy life and all the troubles brought down upon her by the grand-mother who did not give her enough money and treated her like a slave, the other family members who were jealous of her, the servants who stole from her, the shopkeepers who cheated her – 'If it weren't for my children,' she cried, 'why should I go on? I'd make an end of it and get some peace at last.'

'Sh,' said Miss Tuhy, shocked and afraid.

'Why not? What have I got to live for?'

'*You?*' said Miss Tuhy with an incredulous laugh, and looked at that large, full-bloomed figure sprawled there on the narrow bed and rumpling the bedcover from which the embroidery (girls carrying baskets of apples and pansies on their arms) had almost completely faded.

Sharmila said, 'Did I ever tell you about that woman, two doors away from the coal merchant's house? She was a widow and they treated her like a dog, so one night she took a scarf and hung herself from a hook on the stairs. We all went to have a look at her. Her feet were swinging in the air as if there was a wind blowing. I was only four but I still remember.'

There was an eerie little pause which Miss Tuhy broke as briskly as she could: 'What's the matter with you? A young woman like you with all your life before you – I wonder you're not ashamed.'

'I want to get away from here! I'm so sick of this *house*!'

'Yes, Miss Tuhy,' said the Anglo-Indian nurse a few days later, when the English lady had come to pay her a visit and they both sat drinking tea under the tinted portrait of the Queen, 'I'm just sick and tired of living here, that I can tell you. If I could get out tomorrow, I would. But it's not so easy to find a place, not these days with the rents.' She sighed and poured the two of them strong tea out of an earthenware pot. She drank in as refined a way as Miss Tuhy, without making any noise at all. 'My boy's wanting to go to England, and why not? No future for us here, not with these people.'

Miss Tuhy gave a hitch to her wire-framed glasses and smiled ingratiatingly: 'No young lady for him yet?' she asked, and her voice quavered like an inefficient spy's.

'Oh, he goes with the odd girl or two. Nothing serious. There's time yet. We're not like those others – hurry-curry, muddle-puddle, marry them off at sixteen, and they never even see each other's face! No wonder there's trouble afterwards.' She put her bony brown hand on Miss Tuhy's knee and brought her face close: 'Like that one downstairs, the she-devil. It's so disgusting. I don't even like to tell you.' But her tongue was already wiping round her pale lips in anticipation of the telling.

Miss Tuhy got up abruptly. She dared not listen, and for some unknown reason tears had sprung into her eyes. She went out quickly but the nurse followed her. It was dark on the stairs and Miss Tuhy's tears could not be seen. The nurse clung to her arm: 'With servants,' she whispered into Miss Tuhy's ear. 'She gets them in at night when everyone's asleep. Mary Mother,' said the nurse and crossed herself. Instantly a quotation rose to Miss Tuhy's lips: 'Her sins are forgiven, for she loved much. But to whom little is forgiven, the same loveth little.' The nurse was silent for a moment and then she said, '*She*'s not Christian,' with contempt. Miss Tuhy freed her arm and hurried to her own room. She sat in her chair with her hands folded in her lap and her legs trembling. A procession of servants filed through her mind: undersized hill boys with naked feet and torn shirts, sickly but tough, bent on survival. She heard their voices as they called to each other in their weird hill accents and laughed with each other, showing pointed teeth. Every few years one of them in the neighbourhood went berserk and murdered his master and ran away with the jewellery and cash, only to be caught the next day on a wild spree at cinemas and country liquor shops. Strange wild boys, wolf boys: Miss Tuhy had always liked them and felt sorry for them. But now she felt most sorry for Sharmila, and prayed for it not to be true.

It could not be true. Sharmila had such an innocent nature. She was a child. She loved sweet things to eat, and when the bangle seller came, she was the first to run to meet him. She was also very fond of going to the cinema, and when she came home she told Miss Tuhy the story. She acted out all the important scenes, especially the love scenes – 'Just as their lips were about to meet, quick as a flash, with her veil flying in the wind, she ran to the next tree and called to him – Arjun! – and he followed her and he put his arms round the tree and this time she did not run away – no, they stood looking at each other, eating each other up with their eyes, and then the music – oh, Missie, Missie, Missie!' she would end and stretch her arms into the air and laugh with longing.

Once, on her little daily shopping trip to the bazaar, Miss Tuhy caught sight of Sharmila in the distance. And seeing her like that, unexpectedly, she saw her as a stranger might, and realized for the first time that the Sharmila she knew no longer existed. Her image of Sharmila was twofold, one superimposed on the other yet also simultaneous, the two images merged in her mind: there was the hoyden school-girl, traces of whom still existed in her smile and in certain glances of her eyes, and then there was Sharmila in bloom, the young wife dancing round the courtyard and boasting about her wedding presents. But the woman she now saw in the bazaar was fat and slovenly; the end of her veil, draped carelessly over her breasts, trailed a little in the dust, and the heel of her slipper was trodden over to one side so that she seemed to be dragging her foot when she walked. She was quarrelling with one of the shopkeepers, she was gesticulating and using coarse language; the other shopkeepers leaned out of their stalls to listen, and from the way they grinned and commented to each other, it was obvious that Sharmila was a well-known figure and the scene she was enacting was one she had often played before. Miss Tuhy, in pain, turned and walked away in the opposite direction, even though it meant a longer way home. For the first time she failed to greet the vegetable seller and the cold-drink man as she passed between their two shops on her way into the house, and when she had to step round the refuse trodden into the mud, she felt a movement of distaste and thought irritably to herself why it was that no one ever took the trouble to clean the place. The stairs of the house too were dirty, and there was a bad smell of sewage. She reached her room with a sigh of relief, but it seemed as if the bad smell came seeping in from under the closed door. Then she heard again Sharmila's anguished voice crying, 'I want to get away! I'm so sick of this *house*!' and she too felt the same anguish to get away from the house and from the streets and crowded bazaars around it.

That night she said to Sharmila, in a bright voice, 'Why don't we all go away somewhere for a lovely holiday?'

Sharmila, who had never had occasion to leave the city she was born in, thought it was a joke and laughed. But Miss Tuhy was very much in earnest. She remembered all the holidays she had gone on years ago when she was still teaching. She had always gone to the Simla hills and stayed in an English boarding house, and she had taken long walks every day and breathed in the mountain air and collected pine cones. She told Sharmila all about this, and Sharmila too began to get excited and said, 'Let's go,' and asked many more questions.

'Sausages and bacon for breakfast every morning,' Miss Tuhy reminisced, and Sharmila, who had never eaten either, clapped her hands with pleasure and gave an affectionate squeeze to her youngest child playing in her lap: 'You'll like that, Munni, na? Shaushage? Hmmm!'

'They'll get wonderful red cheeks up there,' said Miss Tuhy, 'real English apple cheeks,' and she smiled at the sallow city child dressed in dirty velvet. 'And there'll be pony rides and wild flowers to pick and lovely cool water from the mountain streams.'

'Let's go!' cried Sharmila with another hug to her child.

'We'll go by train,' said Miss Tuhy. 'And then a bus'll take us up the mountains.'

Sharmila suddenly stopped smiling: 'Yes, and the money? Where's that to come from? You think *she*'d ever give?' and she tossed her head towards the room where her grandmother lay, immobile and groaning but still a power to be reckoned with.

Miss Tuhy waved her aside: 'This'll be *my* treat,' she said.

And why not? The money was there, and what pleasure it would be to spend it on a holiday with Sharmila and the children! She brutally stifled all thoughts of caution, of the future. Money was there to be spent, to take pleasure with, not to eke out a miserable day-by-day existence which, in any case, might end – who knew? – tomorrow or the day after. And then what use would it ever be to her? Her glasses slipped and lay crooked on her nose, her face was flushed: she looked drunk with excitement. 'You'll get such a surprise,' she said. 'When we're sitting in the bus, and it's going up up up, higher and higher, and you'll see the mountains before you, more beautiful than anything you've ever dreamed of.'

Unfortunately Sharmila and the children were all very sick in the bus that carried them up the mountains, and so could not enjoy the scenery. Sharmila, in between retching with abandon, wept loudly that she was dying and cursed the fate that had brought her here instead of leaving her quietly at home where she belonged and was happy. However, once the bus had stopped and they had reached their destination, they began to enjoy themselves. They were amused by the English boarding house, and at mealtimes were lost in wonder not only at the food, the like of which they had never eaten, but also at the tablecloths and the cutlery. Their first walk was undertaken with great enthusiasm, and they collected everything they found on the way – pine cones and flowers and leaves and stones and empty cigarette packets. As Miss Tuhy had promised, they rode on ponies: even Sharmila, gasping and giggling and letting out loud cries of fright, was hoisted on to the back of a pony but had to be helped down again, dissolving in fits of laughter, because she was too heavy. Miss Tuhy revelled in their enjoyment; and for herself she was happy too to be here again among familiar smells of pine and wood fires and cold air. She loved the pale mists that rose from the mountainside and the rain that rained down so softly. She wished they could stay for ever. But after the third day Sharmila and the children began to get bored and kept asking when they were going home. They no longer cared to go for walks or ride on ponies. When it rained, all four of them sat mournfully by the window, and sighed and moaned and kept asking, what shall we do now? and Sharmila wondered how human beings could bear to live in a place like this; speaking for herself, it was just the same as being dead. Miss Tuhy had to listen not only to their complaints but also to those of the management, for Sharmila and the children were behaving badly – especially in the dining-room where, after the third day, they began demanding pickles and chapattis, and the children spat out the unfamiliar food on the tablecloth while Sharmila abused the hotel servants in bazaar language.

So they went home again earlier than they had intended. They had been away less than ten days, but their excitement on seeing the old places again was that of long-time voyagers. They had hired a tonga at the station and, as they neared home, they began to point out familiar landmarks to each other; by the time they had got to their own neighbourhood bazaar, the children were bobbing up and down so much that they were in danger of falling off the carriage, and Sharmila shouted cordial greetings to the shopkeepers with whom she would be fighting again tomorrow. And at home all the relatives and friends crowded into the courtyard to receive them, and there was much kissing and embracing and even a happy tear or two, and the tenants and servants thronged the galleries upstairs to watch the scene and call down their welcome to the travellers. It was a great homecoming.

Only Miss Tuhy was not happy. She did not want to be back. She longed now for the green mountains and the clean, cool air; she also missed the boarding house with its English landlady and very clean stairs and bathrooms. It was intensely hot in the city and dust storms were blowing. The sky was covered with an ugly yellow heat haze, and all day hot, restless winds blew dust about. Loudspeaker vans were driven through the streets to advise people to be vaccinated against the current outbreak of smallpox. Miss Tuhy hardly left her room. She felt ill and weak, and contrary to her usual custom, she often lay down on her bed, even during the day. She kept her doors and windows shut, but nevertheless the dust seeped in, and so did the smells and the noise of the house. She no longer went on her daily shopping and preferred not to eat. Sharmila brought food up for her, but Miss Tuhy did not want it, it was too spicy for her and too greasy. 'Just a little taste,' Sharmila begged and brought a morsel to her lips. Miss Tuhy pushed her hand away and cried out, 'Go away! I can't stand the smell!' She meant not only the smell of the food, but also that of Sharmila's heavy, perspiring body.

It was in these days of terrible heat that the grandmother at last managed to die. Miss Tuhy dragged herself up from her bed in order to attend the funeral on the bank of the river. It was during the hottest part of the day, and the sun spread such a pall of white heat that, seen through it, the flames of the pyre looked colourless and quite harmless as they first licked and then rose higher and enveloped the body of the grandmother. The priest chanted and the eldest son poured clarified butter to feed the fire. All the relatives shrieked and wailed and beat their thighs in the traditional manner. Sharmila shrieked the loudest – she tore open her breast and, beating it with her fists, demanded to be allowed to die, and then she tried to fling herself on the pyre and had to be held back by four people. Vultures swayed overhead in the dust-laden sky. The river had dried up and the sand burned underfoot. Everything was white, desolate, empty, for miles and miles and miles around, on earth and, apart from the vultures, in the sky. Sharmila suddenly flung herself on Miss Tuhy and held her in a stifling embrace. She wept that now only she, Miss Tuhy, was left to her, and promised to look after her and tend and care for her as she had done for her dear, dead granny. Miss Tuhy gasped for air and tried to free herself, but Sharmila only clung to her the tighter and her tears fell on and smeared Miss Tuhy's cheeks.

Miss Tuhy's mother had died almost forty years ago, but Miss Tuhy could still vividly recall her funeral. It had drizzled, and rich smells of damp earth had mixed with the more delicate smell of tuberoses and yew. The clergyman's words brought ease and comfort, and weeping was restrained; birds sang cheerfully from out of the wet trees. That's the way to die, thought Miss Tuhy, and bitterness welled up into her hitherto gentle heart. The trouble was, she no longer had the fare home to England, not even on the cheapest route.

A Course of English Studies

Nalini came from a very refined family. They were all great readers, and Nalini grew up on the classics. They were particularly fond of the English romantics, and of the great Russians. Sometimes they joked and said they were themselves like Chekhov characters. They were well off and lived gracious lives in a big house in Delhi, but they were always longing for the great capitals of Europe – London, Paris, Rome – where culture flourished and people were advanced and sophisticated.

Mummy and Daddy had travelled extensively in Europe in easier times (their honeymoon had been in Rome), and the boys had, one by one, been abroad for higher studies. At last it was Nalini's turn. She had finished her course in English literature at Delhi's exclusive Queen Alexandra College and now she was going to the fountainhead of it all, to England itself. She tried for several universities, and finally got admission in a brand-new one in a Midland town. They were all happy about this, especially after someone told them that the new universities were better than the old ones because of the more modern, go-ahead spirit that prevailed in them.

'Dearest Mummy, I'm sorry my last letters haven't been very cheerful but please don't get upset! Of course I love it here – who wouldn't! – and it was only because I was missing you darlings all so much that I sounded a bit miserable. Now that I know her better I can see Mrs Crompton is a very nice lady, she is from a much better class than the usual type of landlady and I'm really lucky to be in her house. I have a reading list as long as my arm from classes! It's a stiff course but terribly exciting and I can hardly wait to get started on it all. The lecturers are very nice and the professor is a darling! Social and cultural activities have begun to be very hectic, there are so many societies to choose from it is difficult to know where to start. There are two music societies, one for classical music and the other for pop. You won't have to guess very hard which is the one I joined ... '

Yes, there was the classical music society, and more, a poetry society, and the town had symphony concerts and a very good repertory company playing in a brand-new theatre financed by the Arts Council. It was a good place, full of cultural amenities and intelligent people, and the university was, as Nalini and her family had been told, modern and go-ahead, with a dynamic youngish Vice-Chancellor in charge. Nalini's letters home – she wrote three or four times a week – were full of everything that went on, and her mother lived it all with her. Sometimes, sitting in her drawing-room in Delhi on the yellow silk sofa, the mother, reading these letters, had tears in her eyes – tears of joy at the fullness and rapture of life and her own daughter a young girl at the very centre of it.

But Nalini was not as happy as she should have been. She did everything that she had always dreamed of doing, like going for walks in the English countryside and having long discussions over cups of coffee, but all the same something that she had expected, some flavour that had entered into her dreams, was not there. It was nothing to do with the weather.

She had expected it to be bleak and raining, and she had spirits high enough to soar above that. She had also learned to adjust to her landlady, Mrs Crompton, who had 'moods' – as indeed it was her right to have for she had been the injured party in a divorce suit – and to be sympathetic when Mrs Crompton did not feel up to cooking a hot meal. Of course, she missed Mummy and Daddy and the boys and the house and everything and everyone at home – *dreadfully!* – but it was the price she had been, and still was, willing to pay for the privilege of being in England. Besides, there was always the satisfaction of writing to them and as often hearing from them, and not only from them but from all the others too, her cousins and her college friends, with all of whom she was in constant correspondence. Every time the postman came, it was always with at least one letter for Nalini, so that Mrs Crompton – who wasn't really expecting anything but nevertheless felt disappointed to have nothing – sometimes became quite snappish.

Nalini was not lonely in England. She got to know the people at college quite quickly, and even had her own group of special friends. These were all girls: they were friendly with the men students, and of course saw a lot of them during classes and the many extracurricular activities, but special friendships were usually with members of one's own sex. So it was with a number or just a single girl friend that Nalini roamed over the college grounds, or sat in the canteen, or went to a concert, or out for a walk; and very pleasant and companionable it always was. Yet something was missing. She never wrote home about anything being missing, so they all thought she was having as grand a time as her letters suggested. But she wasn't. Really, in spite of everything, all England at her disposal, she was disappointed.

One day she was out walking with her friend Maeve. They had left the town behind them and were walking down the lanes of an adjoining village. Sometimes these lanes were narrow and hemmed in by blackberry bushes that were still wet with water drops from recent rains; sometimes they opened up to disclose pale yellow fields, and pale green ones, and little hills, and brindled cows, and a pebbled church. The air was clear and moist. It was the English countryside of which the English poets – Shakespeare himself – had sung, and of which Mummy had so often spoken and tried to describe to Nalini. Maeve was talking about Anglo-Saxon vowel changes and the impossibility of remembering them; she was worried about this because there was a test coming up and she didn't know how she was ever going to get through it. Nalini also did not expect to get through, but quite other thoughts occupied her mind. Although she was fond of Maeve – who was a tall strong girl and looked like a big robin with her ruddy cheeks and brown coat and brown knitted stockings – Nalini could not help wishing that she was not there. She wanted to be alone, in order to give vent to the melancholy thoughts with which she felt oppressed. If she had been alone, perhaps she would have run through the fields, with the wind whipping her face; or she might have leaned her head against a tree, in which a thrush was singing, and sighed, and allowed the tears to flow down her cheeks.

The men students at the university were all very nice boys: eager and gentle and rather well mannered in spite of the long hair and beards and rough shirts that so many of them affected. One could imagine a charming brother-and-sister relationship with them, and indeed that seemed to be what they themselves favoured when they went as far as establishing anything more personal with any of the girls. It would not have done for Nalini. She had enough brothers at home, and what she had (even if she didn't at the time know it) come to England for, what she expected from the place, what everything she had read had promised her, was love and a lover.

A girl in such a mood is rarely disappointed. One of the lecturers was Dr Norman Greaves. He took the classes on Chaucer and his Age as well as on the Augustans, and although neither of these periods had ever been among Nalini's favourites, she began to attend the lectures on them with greater enthusiasm than any of the others. This was because Dr Greaves had become her favourite teacher. At first she had liked the professor best – he was handsome, elegant, and often went up to London to take part in television programmes – but, after she had written her first essay for Dr Greaves, she realized that it was he who was by far the finer person.

He had called her to his office and, tapping her essay with the back of his hand, said, 'This won't do, you know.'

Nalini was used to such reactions from the lecturers after they had read her first essays. She could not, like the other English students, order her thoughts categorically, point by point, with discussion and lively development, but had to dash everything down, not thoughts but emotions, and moreover she could only do so in her own words, in the same way in which she wrote her letters home. But all the lecturers said that it wouldn't do, and when they said that, Nalini hung her head and didn't know what to answer. The others had just sighed and handed her essay back to her, but Dr Greaves, after sighing, said, 'What are we going to do about you?' He was really worried.

'I'll work harder, sir,' Nalini promised.

'Yes, well, that's nice of you,' said Dr Greaves, but he still looked worried and as if he thought her working harder wouldn't do all that much good. Nalini looked back at him, also worried; she bit her lip and her eyes were large. She feared he was going to say she wasn't good enough for the course.

'"In *Troilus and Criseyde*",' read Dr Greaves, '"Chaucer shows how well he knows the feelings in a woman's heart". That's all right, but couldn't you be a bit more specific? What passages in particular did you have in mind?'

Nalini continued to stare at him; she was still biting her lip.

'Or didn't you have any in mind?'

'I don't know,' she said miserably; and added – not, as far as she was concerned, at all inconsequentially – 'I think I'm a very emotional sort of person.'

He had given her essay back to her without any further comment; but there had been something in his manner as he did so which made her feel that a bad essay, though unfortunate, was not the end of the world. The others had not made her feel that way. Dr Greaves soared above them all. He was not handsome like the professor, but she found much charm in him. He was rather short – which suited Nalini who was small herself – and thin, and exceptionally pale; his hair was pale too, and very straight and fine, of an indeterminate colour which may have been blond shading into grey. He was no longer young – in his thirties, at the end of his thirties indeed, perhaps even touching forty.

Nalini's life took on colour and excitement. She woke up early every morning and lay in bed wondering joyfully how many times she would see him that day. Tuesdays, Thursdays and Fridays she was secure because those were days when he lectured; the other two days she was dependent on glimpses in corridors. These had the charm of sudden surprises, and there was always a sort of exquisite suspense as to what the next moment or the next corner turned might not reveal. But of course the best were lecture days. Then she could sit and look at him and watch and adore an hour at a time. He walked up and down the dais as he talked, and his pale hands fidgeted ceaselessly with the edges of his gown. His head was slightly to one side with the effort of concentration to get his thoughts across: he strove to be honest and clear on every point. His gown was old and full of chalk, and he always wore the same shabby tweed jacket and flannel trousers and striped college tie. He was not, unlike the professor and several others of the lecturers, a successful academic.

Weekends would have been empty and boring if she had not got into the habit of walking near his house. He lived on the outskirts of town in a Victorian house with a derelict garden. There had been several rows of these old houses, but most of them had been pulled down and replaced by new semi-detached villas which were sold on easy instalments to newly-weds. Dr Greaves was not newly wed; he had many children who ran all round the house and down the quiet lanes and out into the fields. These children were never very clean and their clothes were obviously handed down from one to the other. The babies of the young couples in the villas wore pink and blue nylon and were decorated with frills. All the young couples had shiny little cars, but Dr Greaves only had a bicycle.

One Saturday Nalini met him coming out of his house wheeling this bicycle. He was surprised to see her and wondered what she was doing there; and although she did not quite have the courage to tell him that she had been lingering around for him, neither did she stoop to tell him a lie. They walked together, he wheeling his bicycle. He called 'Mervyn!'

to a little boy who came dashing round a corner and was, to judge by his unkempt appearance, a son of his, but the boy took no notice and Dr Greaves walked on patiently and as if he did not expect to have any notice taken.

It was a sunny day. Dr Greaves was going into town on a shopping tour and Nalini accompanied him. They went into a supermarket and Dr Greaves took a little wire basket and piled it up with a supply of washing soap and vinegar and sliced loaf and many other things which he read out from a list his wife had prepared for him. Nalini helped him find and take down everything from the shelves; sometimes she brought the wrong thing – a packet of dog biscuits instead of baby rusks – and that made them laugh quite a bit. Altogether it was fun; they were both slow and inexpert and got into other people's way and were grumbled at. Dr Greaves was always very apologetic to the people who grumbled, but Nalini began to giggle. She giggled again at the cash desk where he dropped some money and they had to scrabble for it, while everybody waited and the cashier clicked her tongue. Dr Greaves went very pink and kept saying, to the cashier and to the people whom he kept waiting, 'I'm most awfully sorry, do forgive me, I am so sorry.' Finally they got out of the shop and he stood smiling at her, blinking his eyes against the sun which was still shining, and thanked her for her help. Then he rode away, rather slowly because of the heavy load of shopping he had to carry from the handlebars.

The next Saturday it was raining, but nevertheless Nalini stood and waited for him outside his house. At first he did not seem to be very pleased to see her, and it was only when they had walked away from the house for some distance, that he made her sit on the crossbar of his bicycle. They rode like that together through the rain. It was like a dream, she in his arms and feeling his breath on her face, and everything around them, the trees and the sky and the tops of the houses, melting away into mist and soft rain. They went to the same shop and bought almost the same things, but this time, when they came out and she already saw the smile of farewell forming on his lips, she quickly said, 'Can't we have coffee somewhere?' They went to a shop which served home-made rock cakes and had copper urns for decoration. It was full of housewives having their coffee break, so the only table available was one by the coat rack, which was rather uncomfortable because of all the dripping coats and umbrellas. Nalini didn't mind, but Dr Greaves sat hunched together and looking miserable. His thin hair was all wet and stuck to his head and sometimes a drop came dripping down his face. Nalini looked at him: 'Cold?' she asked, with tender concern.

'How can you bear it here,' he said. 'In this dreadful climate.' There was an edge to his voice, and his hand fidgeted irritably with the china ashtray.

'Oh, I don't mind,' said Nalini. 'I've had so much sun all my life, it makes a change really.' She smiled at him, and indeed as she did so, she radiated such warmth, such a sun all of her own, that he, who had looked up briefly, had at once to look down again as if it were too strong for him.

'And besides,' she added after a short silence, 'it's not what the weather is like outside that matters, but what you feel here, inside you.' Her hand was pressed between her charming little breasts. Her eyes sought his.

'I hope,' he said foolishly clearing his throat, 'that you're happy in your work.'

'Of course I am.'

'Good. I thought your last essay showed some improvement, actually. Of course there's still a long way to go.'

'I'll work hard, I promise!' she cried. 'Only you see, I'm such a funny thing, oh dear, I simply can't learn anything, I'm stupid, my mind is like a stone – till I find someone who can *inspire* me. Now thank goodness,' and she dropped her eyes and fidgeted with the other side of the ashtray, and then she raised her eyes again and she smiled, 'I've found such a person.' She continued to smile.

'You mean me,' he said brusquely.

This put her off. She ceased to smile. She had expected more delicacy.

'My dear girl, I'm really not a fit person to inspire anyone. I'm just a hack, a workhorse. Don't expect anything from me. Oh my God, please,' he said and held his head between his hands as if in pain, 'don't look at me with those *eyes*.'

'Are they so awfully ugly?'

'Leave me alone,' he begged. 'Let me be. I'm all right. I haven't complained, have I? I'm happy.'

'No, you're not.' She sagely shook her head. 'I've read it in your face long ago. Why are these lines here,' and she put out her finger and traced them, those lines of suffering running along the side of his mouth which she had studied over many lectures.

'Because I'm getting old. I'll be forty in May. *Forty*, mind you.'

'Sometimes you look like a little boy. A little boy lost and I want to comfort him.'

'Please let me go home now. I've got to buy fish and chips for Saturday lunch. They'll all be waiting.'

'If you promise to meet me tomorrow. Promise? Norman?' She lightly touched his hand, and the look with which she met his was a teasing, victorious one as if she were challenging him to say no, if he could.

At home her landlady, Mrs Crompton, was feeling unwell. She hadn't cooked anything and lay in bed in the dark, suffering. Nalini turned on the lights and the fires and went down in the kitchen and made scrambled eggs on toast. Then she carried a tray up to Mrs Crompton's bedroom and sat on the side of Mrs Crompton's bed and said, 'Oh you poor thing you,' and stroked the red satin eiderdown. Mrs Crompton sat up in bed in her bedjacket and ate the scrambled eggs. She was a woman in early middle age and had a rather heavy, English face, with a strong nose and thin lips and a lowish forehead: it looked even heavier than usual because of the lines of disappointment and grief that seemed to pull it downwards. From time to time, as she ate, she sighed. Her bedroom was very attractively furnished, with ruffled curtains and bedcovers and a white rug, but it was sad on account of the empty twin bed which had been Mr Crompton's and now just stood there parallel with Mrs Crompton's, heavily eloquent under the bedcover which would never again be removed.

Nalini felt sorry for her and tried to cheer her up. She held one of Mrs Crompton's large, cold hands in between her own small, brown, very warm ones and fondled it, and told her everything amusing that she could think of, like how she forgot her sari out on the washing line and it got soaking wet again in the rain, all six yards of it. Mrs Crompton did not get cheered up much, her face remained long and gloomy, and at one point a tear could be seen slowly coursing its way along the side of her nose. Nalini watched its progress and suddenly, overcome with pity for the other's pain, she brought her face close to Mrs Crompton's and kissed that dry, large-pored skin (how strange it felt! Nalini at once thought of Mummy's skin, velvet-smooth and smelling of almond oil) and as she did so, she murmured, 'Don't be sad,' she kept her face down on the pillow with Mrs Crompton's and hidden against it, which was just as well, for although she really was so full of sympathy, none of this showed on her face which was blooming with joy.

'Dearest Mummy, Sorry sorry sorry! Yes you're right I've been awful about letters lately but if you knew how much work they pile on us! I've been working like a slave but it's fun. My favourites now are the Augustans. Yes darling, I know you're surprised and at first sight they do look cold like we've always said but they are very passionate underneath. I go out quite often into the country, it is so peaceful and beautiful. Sometimes it is windy and cold but it's funny, you know I always feel hot, everyone is surprised at it.'

Norman usually wore a polo-neck sweater under his sports jacket, but Nalini never more than an embroidered shawl thrown lightly over her silk sari. Whenever they met, they went out into the country. They had found a place for themselves. It was a bus ride away from town, and when they got off the bus, they had to walk for about half a mile through some fields and finally through a lane which wound down into a small valley. Here there were four cottages, hidden away among trees and quite separate from each other. At the rear their gardens ran out into a little wood. The owners of the fourth and last cottage – a devoted old couple whom Norman had known and sometimes visited – had both died the year before and their cottage was for sale. At the bottom of its garden, just where the wood began, there was a little hut built, plank by loving plank, by the old dead owners themselves as a playroom for visiting grandchildren. Now it served as a secret, hidden shelter for Norman and Nalini. No one ever came there – at most a cat or a squirrel scratching among the fallen leaves; and the loudest sounds were those of woodpeckers and, very occasionally, an aeroplane flying peacefully overhead.

Nalini, who was really in these matters quite a practical girl, always brought all necessary things with her: light rugs and air cushions, packets of biscuits and sausage rolls. If it was cold and wet, they carpeted the hut with the rugs and stayed inside; on fine days, they sat in the wood with their backs leaning against the trunk of a tree and watched the squirrels.

Nalini loved picnics. She told Norman about the marvellous picnics they had at home, how the servants got the hampers ready and packed them in the back of the car, and then they drove off to some lovely spot – it might be a deserted palace, or an amphitheatre, or a summer tank, always some romantic ruin overgrown with creepers and flowers – and there rugs were spread for them and they lay on them and looked at the sky and talked of this and that, recited poetry and played jokes on each other; when the hampers were unpacked, they contained roast chickens, grapes and chocolate cake.

'Yes,' said Nalini, 'it was lovely but this,' she said and ate a dry Marie biscuit, 'this is a million billion times better.'

She meant it. He lay beside her on the rug they had spread; it was a fine day, so they were under a tree. Dead leaves crunched under the rug every time they moved; there weren't many left up on the branches, and some of them were bright red and hung in precarious isolation on their stalks.

Norman too sighed with contentment. 'Tell me more,' he said. He never tired of hearing about her family life in their house in Delhi or, in the summer, up in Simla.

'But you've heard it all hundreds of times! Tell me about you now. You never tell me anything.'

'Oh me,' said Norman. 'My life's tended to be rather dowdy up till now.'

'And now?'

He groaned with excess of feeling and gathered her into

his arms. He kissed her shoulder, her neck, one temple; he murmured from out of her hair, 'You smell of honey.'

'Do you think of me when I'm not there?'

'Constantly.'

'When you're lecturing?'

'Yes.'

'When you're with your wife?'

He released her and lay down again, and shut his eyes. She bent close over him; her coil of hair had come half-undone and she made it brush against his cheek. 'Tell me how you think of me,' she said.

'As a vision and a glory,' he said without opening his eyes. She drank in his face: how fine it looked, the skin thin and pale as paper with a multitude of delicate lines traced along the forehead, and the two deeply engraved lines that ran from his nose to his lips. It was a face, she felt, designed to register only the highest emotions known to mankind.

'What sort of a vision?' she asked. And when he didn't answer, she begged him, 'I want to hear it from you, tell me in beautiful words.'

He smiled at that and sat up and kissed her again; he said 'There aren't any words beautiful enough.'

'Oh, yes, yes! Think of Chaucer and Pope! Do you ever write poetry, Norman? You don't have to tell me – I know you do. You're a poet really, aren't you? At heart you are.'

'I haven't written anything in years.'

'But now you'll start again, I know it.'

He smiled and said, 'It's too late to start anything again.'

But she would never let him talk like that. If he referred to his forty years, his family, the moderateness of his fortunes, she would brush him aside and say that from now on everything would be different. She did not say how it would be different, nor did she think about it much; but she saw grand vistas opening before them both. Certainly it was inconceivable that, after the grand feelings that had caught them up, anything could ever be the same for either of them again. For the time being, however, she was content to let things go on as they were. She would be here for another two years, finishing her course; and although of course it would have been marvellous if they could have lived together in the same house, since that could not be, she would carry on with Mrs Crompton and he with his family. When the two years were up, they would see. Meanwhile, they had their hut and one another's hearts – what else mattered? She was perfectly happy and wanted, for the moment, nothing more.

It was he who was restless and worried. She noticed during lectures that his hands played even more nervously with the edges of his gown than before; his face looked drawn, and quite often nowadays he seemed to have cut himself shaving so that the pallor of his cheeks was enhanced by a little blob of dried blood. Once in her anxiety she even approached him after lectures and, under cover of asking some academic question, whispered, 'Is something wrong? Are you ill?' A frightened expression came into his eyes.

Afterwards, when they were alone together in their own place, he begged her never again to talk to him like that in class. She laughed: 'What's it matter? No one noticed.'

'I don't care if they noticed or not. I don't want it. It simply frightens me to death.'

'You're so timid,' she teased him, 'like a little mouse.'

'That's true. I always have been. All my life I've been terrified of being found out.'

At that she tossed her head. She certainly had no such fears and did not ever expect to have them.

Then he said, 'I rather think I *have* been found out,' and added, 'It's Estelle.'

'Have you told her?'

'When you've been married to someone as long as that, they don't need to be told anything.'

After a short pause, she said, 'I'm glad. Now everything is in the open.'

She knew certain steps would have to be taken, but was not sure what they were. It was no use consulting with Norman, he was in no state to plan anything; and besides, she wanted to spare him all the anxiety she could. In previous dilemmas of her life, she had always had Mummy by her side, and how they would discuss and talk and weigh the pros and cons, sitting up in Mummy's large, cool bedroom with the air conditioner on. Now Mummy was not there, and even if she had been, this was a matter on which she would not be able to give advice. Poor Mummy, Nalini thought affectionately, how restricted her life had always been, how set in its pattern of being married and having children and growing older, and tasting life only through books and dreams.

Her English friends at college were also not fit to be let into an affair of such magnitude. Nalini was fond of them, of Maeve and the rest, but she could no longer take them quite seriously. This was because they were not serious people. Their concerns were of a superficial order, and even when they had connections with the men students, these too remained on a superficial level; never, at any point, did their lives seem to touch those depths of human involvement where Nalini now had her being. Once she had a long heart-to-heart talk with Maeve. Actually, it was Maeve who did most of the talking. They were in her room, which was very cosy, with a studio couch and an orange-shaded lamp and an open fire in the grate. They sat on the floor by the fire and drank coffee out of pottery mugs. Maeve talked of the future, how she hoped to get a research studentship and write a thesis on the political pamphlets of the early eighteenth century; for this she would have to go to London and spend a lot of time in the British Museum Reading Room. She spoke about all this very slowly and seriously, sitting on the floor with her long legs in brown knitted stockings stretched out in front of her and her head leaned back to rest against a chair; she blew smoke from her cigarette with a thoughtful air. Nalini had her legs tucked under her, which came easily to her, and her sari billowed around her in pale blue silk; sometimes she put up her hand to arrange something – her hair, a fold of her sari – and then the gold bangles jingled on her arms. There was something almost frivolous in her presence in that room with all the books and the desk full of notes and Maeve's favourite Henry Moore study on the wall. Yet it wasn't Nalini who was frivolous, it was large, solid Maeve. How could anyone, thought Nalini, endeavouring to listen with a sympathetic expression to what her friend was saying, talk with so serious an air of so unserious a future – indeed, how could a future spent in the British Museum Reading Room be considered as a future at all? She pitied Maeve, who looked healthy and human enough with her bright red cheeks and her long brown hair, but who did not appear to have as much as an inkling of what riches, what potentialities, lay waiting within a woman's span of life.

Mrs Crompton seemed to know more about it. She carried, at any rate, a sense of loss, the obverse side of which postulated a sense of possibilities: she knew a woman's sorrow and so must have, Nalini inferred, some notion of a woman's joy. Mrs Crompton was not an easy person to get along with. She was hard and autocratic, and ran her household with an iron discipline. Every single little thing had its place, every action of the day its time: no kettle to be put on between ten in the morning and five in the afternoon, no radio to be switched on before noon. She did not encourage telephone calls. Nalini, who at home was used to a luxuriantly relaxed way of life, did not, after the initial shock, find it too difficult to fall in with Mrs Crompton's rigid regime and always did her best to humour her. As a result, Mrs Crompton trusted her, even perhaps liked her as far as she was capable of liking (which was not, on the whole, very far – she was not by nature an affectionate person). They spent quite a lot of their evenings together, which suited both of them for, strangely enough, Nalini discovered that she was beginning to prefer Mrs Crompton's company to that of the girls at college.

Indeed, in the evenings Mrs Crompton became a somewhat different person. When the day was done and its duties fulfilled, when the curtains were drawn and chairs arranged closer to the fire, at this cosy domestic hour her normally stern daytime manner began if not to crumble then at any rate to soften. Memories surged up in her, memories of Mr Crompton – though not so much of their life together as of their final parting. This seemed to have been the event in her life which stirred her deeper than anything that had ever gone before or come after. It had played, and was still playing, all her chords and made her reverberate with feelings of tremendous strength. Nalini admired these feelings: it was living, it was passion, it was the way a woman should be. She never tired of listening to Mrs Crompton's story, she was the unfailing attendant and sympathizer of the tears that were wrung from this strong person. Nalini heard not only about Mr Crompton but also, a lot, about the other woman who had taken him away. There was one incident especially that Mrs

Crompton often rehearsed and that Nalini listened to with special interest. It was when the other woman had come to visit Mrs Crompton (quite unexpectedly, one morning while she was hoovering in the back bedroom) and had asked her to give Mr Crompton up. Mrs Crompton had been at a disadvantage because she was only in her housedress and a turban tied round her head, while the other woman had had her hair newly done and was in a smart red suit with matching bag and shoes; nevertheless Mrs Crompton had managed to carry off the occasion with such dignity – without showing anger, without even once raising her voice, doing nothing more in fact than in a firm voice enunciating right principles – that it was the other woman who had wept and, before leaving, had had to go to the bathroom to repair her make-up.

Nalini was careful to wear her plainest sari when she went to call on Estelle Greaves. She had no desire to show Norman's wife up to an even greater disadvantage than she guessed she already would be. She had not, however, expected to find quite so unattractive a person. She was shocked, and afterwards kept asking Norman: 'But how did you ever get married to her?'

Norman didn't answer. There were dark patches of shadow under his eyes, and he kept running his hand through his hair.

'She can't ever have been pretty. It's not possible, how can she? Of course, probably she wasn't so fat before but even so – *and* she's older than you.'

'She's the same age.'

'She looks years older.'

'For God's sake,' Norman said suddenly, 'shut up.'

Nalini was surprised, but she saw it was best to humour him. And it was such a beautiful day, they ought really to be doing nothing but enjoying it. There was a winter stillness in the air, and a hint of ice in its sharp crystal clearness against which the touches of autumn that still lingered in fields, trees and hedges looked flushed and exotic. 'Let's walk a bit,' she said, tucking her hand under his arm.

He disengaged himself from her: 'Why did you do it?' he said in a puzzled, tortured way. 'Whatever possessed you?'

'I wanted to clear the air,' she said grandly; and added, even more grandly, 'I can't live with a lie.'

He gave a shout of exasperation; then he asked, 'Is that the sort of language you used with her?'

'Oh, with her.' Nalini shrugged and pouted. 'She's just impossible to talk to. Whenever you try and start on anything serious with her, she jumps up and says the shepherd's pie is burning. Oh Norman, Norman, how do you stand it? How can you live with her and in such an atmosphere? Your house is so – I don't know, uncared for. Everything needs cleaning and repairing. I can't bear to think of you in such a place, you with your love for literature and everything that's lovely—'

He winced and walked away from her. He did not walk through the wood but along the edge of it, in the direction of the next house. This was a way they usually avoided, for they wanted to steer clear of the old people living around. But today he seemed too distraught to care.

'Why are you annoyed with me?' she asked, following him. 'I did right, Norman.'

'No,' he said; he stopped still and looked at her, earnestly, in pain: 'You did very, very wrong.'

She touched his pale cheek, pleadingly. Her hand was frail and so was her wrist round which she wore three gold bangles. Suddenly he seized her hand and kissed its palm many times over. They went back to their hut where they bolted the door, and at once he was making love to her with the same desperate feverishness with which he had kissed her hand.

She was well pleased, but he more guilty and downcast than before. As he fastened his clothes, he said, 'You know, I really mustn't see you any more.'

She laughed: 'Silly billy,' she said, tenderly, gaily, in her soft Indian accent.

But from this time on, he often declared that it was time they parted. He blamed himself for coming to meet her at all and said that, if he had any resolution in him, he would not show up again. She was not disturbed by these threats – which she knew perfectly well he could never carry out – but sometimes they irritated her.

She told him, 'It's your wife who's putting you up to this.' He looked at her for a moment as if she were mad. 'She hates me,' Nalini said.

'She hasn't said so. But of course you can't expect—'

'Well I hate her too,' Nalini said. 'She is stupid.'

'No one could call Estelle stupid.'

'I've met her, so you can't tell me. She has nothing to say and she doesn't even understand what's said to her. It's impossible to talk to her intelligently.'

'What did you expect her to talk to you intelligently *about*?'

'About you. Us. Everything.'

He was silent, so she assumed she had won her point. She began to do her hair. She took out all her pins and gave them to him to hold. But it turned out that he had more to say.

'It was so wrong of you to come to our house like that. And what did you want? Some great seething scene of passion and renunciation, such as Indians like to indulge in?'

'Don't dare say anything bad against my country!'

'I'm not, for God's sake, saying anything bad against your country!'

'Yes, you are. And it's your wife who has taught you. I could see at one glance that she was anti-Indian.'

'Please don't let's talk about my wife any more.'

'Yes, we will talk about her. I'll talk about her as much as I like. What do you think, I'm some fallen woman that I'm not allowed to speak your wife's name? Give me my pins.' She plucked them from out of his hand and stabbed them angrily into her coil of hair. 'And I'll tell you something more. From now on everything is going to change. I'm tired of this hole-and-corner business. You must get a divorce.'

'A splendid idea. You're not forgetting that I have four children?'

'You can have ten for all I care. You must leave that woman! It is she or I. Choose.'

Norman got up and let himself out of the hut. At the door he turned and said in a quiet voice, 'You know I'm no good at these grand scenes.'

He walked away through the garden up on to the path which would lead him to the bus stop. He had a small, lithe figure and walked with his head erect, showing some dignity; he did not look back nor lose that dignity even when she shouted after him: 'You're afraid! You're a coward! You want to have your cake and eat it!'

They made it up after a day or two. But their separate ideas remained, his that they must part, hers that he must get a divorce. They began to quarrel quite frequently. She enjoyed these fights, both for themselves and for the lovely sensations involved in making them up afterwards. He found them exasperating, and called her a harridan and a fishwife: a preposterous appellation, for what could be further from

116

the image of a harridan and a fishwife than this delicate little creature in silk and gold, with the soft voice and the soft, tender ways. Once he asked her: 'All right – supposing I get a divorce, what next? What do you suggest? Do we stay here, do I go on teaching at the university and support two families on my princely salary? You tell me.'

'Oh no,' she said at once, 'I'll take you with me to India.'

This idea amused him immensely. He saw himself taken away as a white slave boy, cozened and coddled and taught to play the flute. He asked her to describe how they would live in India, and she said that she would dress him up in a silk pyjama and she would oil his hair and curl it round her finger and twice a day, morning and evening, she would bathe him in milk. It became one of their pastimes to play at being in India, a game in which he would loll on the rug spread on the floor of their hut and she would hold his head in her lap and comb him and pet him and massage his cheeks: this was fun, but it did not, Nalini reflected, get them any further.

'Dearest Mummy, How I long for one of our cosy chats up in the bedroom. I have so much to tell you. Darling Mummy, I have found someone with whom I want to share my life and I know you too will love him. He is exactly the sort of person we have always dreamed of, so sensitive and intelligent like an English poet.' But she never sent that letter. Mummy was so far away, it might be difficult for her to understand. Besides, she could not really do anything yet to solve their practical problems. One of these was particularly pressing just now. Winter had come on, and it was beginning to get too cold to use their hut. Icy blasts penetrated through the wooden boards, and Norman's teeth never stopped chattering. But where else could they go? Norman said nowhere, it just meant that they must not see each other any more, that the cycle of seasons was dictating what moral right had already insisted on long ago. Nalini had learned to ignore such defeatist talk.

It was around this time that she first confided in Mrs Crompton. This came about quite naturally, one evening when they were both sitting by the fire, Mrs Crompton with her large hands in her lap, Nalini crocheting a little rose bed-jacket for herself. Sometimes Nalini lowered her work and stared before her with tragic eyes. It was silent in the room, with a low hum from the electric fire. Nalini sighed, and Mrs Crompton sighed, and then Nalini sighed again. Words were waiting to be spoken, and before long they were. Nalini told her everything: about Norman, and Estelle, and the children, and the hut, and the cold weather. Also how Norman was going to get a divorce and go away with her to India. Mrs Crompton listened without comment but with, it seemed, sympathy. Later, when they had already said goodnight and Nalini had gone up to her room and changed into her brushed nylon nightie, Mrs Crompton came in to tell her that it would be all right if she brought Norman to the house. Nalini gave a big whoop and flung her arms round Mrs Crompton's neck, just as she used to do to Mummy when Mummy had done something lovely and nice, crying in a voice chock-full of gratitude, 'Oh you darling, you darling you!'

Norman hated coming to the house. He kept saying he was sure Mrs Crompton was listening outside the door. Once Nalini abruptly opened the door of her room, to convince him that no one was there, but he only shook his head and said that she was listening through the ceiling from downstairs. Certainly, they were both of them – even Nalini – very much aware of Mrs Crompton's presence in the house. Sometimes they heard her moving about and that put them out, and sometimes they didn't hear any sound from her at all and that put them out even more. When it was time for Norman to leave and they came down the stairs, she was invariably there, waiting for them in the hall. 'Do have a cup of tea before you go,' she would say, but he always made some excuse and left hurriedly. Then she would be disappointed, even a little surly, and Nalini would have to work hard to soothe her.

Nalini had made her room so attractive with lots of photographs of the family and embroidered cushions and an Indian wall-hanging, but Norman was always uncomfortable, all the time he was there. Sometimes even he would make an excuse not to come, he would send a note to say he had a lecture to deliver at an evening class, or that he was suffering from toothache and had to visit the dentist. Then Mrs Crompton and Nalini would both be disappointed and turn off the lights and the fires and go to bed early.

She boldly went up to him after classes and said, 'You haven't been for a *week*.' He raised his eyes – which were a very pale, almost translucent blue, and remarkably clear among the dark shadows left around them by anxiety and sleepless nights – and he looked with them not at her but directly over her head. But he came that evening. He said, 'I told you you mustn't ever do that.'

'I had to – you didn't come so long.'

He sighed and passed his hand over his eyes and down his face.

'You're tired,' she said. 'My poor darling, you've been working too hard.' With swift, graceful movements, which set her bangles jingling, she settled pillows on her bed and smoothed the counterpane invitingly. But he didn't lie down. He hadn't even taken his coat off.

'Please let me go, Nalini,' he said in a quiet, grave voice.

'Go where, my own darling?'

'I want us not to see each other any more.'

'Again!'

'No, this time really – please.' He sank into an armchair, as if in utter exhaustion.

'You've been talking to your wife,' she said accusingly.

'Who would I talk to if not to my wife. She is my wife, you know, Nalini. We've been together for a long time and through all sorts of things. That does mean a lot. I'm a wretchedly weak person and you must forgive me.'

'You're not weak. You're sensitive. Like an artist.'

He made a helpless, hopeless gesture with his hand. Then he got up and quickly went downstairs. Mrs Crompton was waiting at the foot of the stairs. She said, 'Do have a cup of tea before you go.' Norman didn't answer but hurried away. He had his coat collar up and there was something guilty and suspicious about him which made Mrs Crompton look after him with narrowed eyes.

Mrs Crompton told Nalini about men: that they were selfish and grasping and took what they wanted and then they left. She illustrated all this with reference to Mr Crompton. But Nalini did not believe that Norman was like Mr Crompton. Norman was suffering. She could hardly bear to look at him during lectures because she saw how he suffered. These were terrible days. It was the end of winter, and whatever snow there had been, was now melting and the same slush colour as the sky that drooped spiritlessly over the town. Nalini felt the cold at last, and wore heavy sweaters and coats over her sari, and boots on her small feet. She hated being muffled up like that and sometimes she felt she was choking. She didn't know what to do with herself nowadays – she did not care to be much with the girls at college and she had lost the taste for Mrs Crompton's company. She hardly worked at all and got very low marks in all her subjects. Once the professor called her and told her that she would either have to do better or leave the course. She burst into tears and he thought it was because of what he was saying, but it wasn't that at all: she often cried nowadays, tears spurting out of her eyes at unexpected moments. She spent a lot of time in bed, crying. She tossed from side to side, thinking, wondering. She could not understand how it could all have ended like that, so abruptly and for nothing. They had been happy, and it had been radiant and wonderful, and after that how could he go back to that house with the leaking taps and the ungainly woman in it and all those children?

The weather was warmer. It was a good spring that year, and crocuses appeared even in Mrs Crompton's garden. Nalini began to feel better – not happy, but better. She went out for walks again with one or two friends, and sometimes they had tea together, or went to the music society. It was all very much like before. One fine Sunday she and Maeve took a walk outside the town. There were cows in the fields, and newly shorn sheep, and the hedges were brimming with tiny buds. Nalini remembered how she had walked with Maeve the year before, and how dissatisfied she had felt while Maeve, in her brown knitted stockings, talked of Anglo-Saxon vowel changes. Today Maeve wore patterned stockings, and she talked of her chances of a research studentship; there were several other strong candidates in the field – for instance, Dorothy Horne whose forte was the metaphysicals. Nalini listened to her with kindly interest. The air was full of balmy scents and the sky of little white clouds like lambs. Nalini felt sorry for Maeve and, after that, she felt sorry for all of them – Dorothy Horne and the other girls, and Mrs Crompton and Norman.

'Dearest Mummy, What a clever clever little thing you are! Yes you are right, I have not been happy lately . . . You know me so well, our hearts are open to each other even with such a distance between us. Here people are not like that. I don't believe that Shakespeare or Keats or Shelley or any of them can have been English! I think they were Indians, at least in their previous birth!!! Darling, please talk to Daddy and ask him to let me come home for the long vac. I miss you and long for you and want to be with you all soon. I don't think the teaching here is all that good, there is no one like Miss Subramaniam at the dear old Queen Alex with such genuine love for literature and able to inspire their pupils. A thousand million billion kisses, my angel Mummy.'

An Experience of India

Today Ramu left. He came to ask for money and I gave him as much as I could. He counted it and asked for more, but I didn't have it to give him. He said some insulting things, which I pretended not to hear. Really I couldn't blame him. I knew he was anxious and afraid, not having another job to go to. But I also couldn't help contrasting the way he spoke now with what he had been like in the past: so polite always, and eager to please, and always smiling, saying, 'Yes sir,' 'Yes madam please.' He used to look very different too, very spruce in his white uniform and his white canvas shoes. When guests came, he put on a special white coat he had made us buy him. He was always happy when there were guests – serving, mixing drinks, emptying ashtrays – and I think he was disappointed that more didn't come. The Ford Foundation people next door had a round of buffet suppers and Sunday brunches, and perhaps Ramu suffered in status before their servants because we didn't have much of that. Actually, come to think of it, perhaps he suffered in status anyhow because we weren't like the others. I mean, I wasn't. I didn't look like a proper memsahib or dress like one – I wore Indian clothes right from the start – or ever behave like one. I think perhaps Ramu didn't care for that. I think servants want their employers to be conventional and put up a good front so that other people's servants can respect them. Some of the nasty things Ramu told me this morning were about how everyone said I was just someone from a very low sweeper caste in my own country and how sorry they were for him that he had to serve such a person.

He also said it was no wonder Sahib had run away from me. Henry didn't actually run away, but it's true that things had changed between us. I suppose India made us see how fundamentally different we were from each other. Though when we first came, we both came we thought with the same ideas. We were both happy that Henry's paper had sent him out to India. We both thought it was a marvellous opportunity not only for him professionally but for both of us spiritually. Here was our escape from that Western materialism with which we were both so terribly fed up. But once he got here and the first enthusiasm had worn off, Henry seemed not to mind going back to just the sort of life we'd run away from. He even didn't seem to care about meeting Indians any more, though in the beginning he had made a great point of doing so; now it seemed to him all right to go only to parties given by other foreign correspondents and sit around there and eat and drink and talk just the way they would at home. After a while, I couldn't stand going with him any more, so we'd have a fight and then he'd go off by himself. That was a relief. I didn't want to be with any of those people and talk about inane things in their tastefully appointed air-conditioned apartments.

I had come to India to *be* in India. I wanted to be changed. Henry didn't – he wanted a change, that's all, but not to be changed. After a while because of that he was a stranger to me and I felt I was alone, the way I'm really alone now. Henry had to travel a lot around the country to write his pieces, and in the beginning I used to go with him. But I didn't like the way he travelled, always by plane and staying in expensive hotels and drinking in the bar with the other correspondents. So I would leave him and go off by myself. I travelled the way everyone travels in India, just with a bundle and a roll of bedding which I could spread out anywhere and go to sleep. I went in third-class railway carriages and in those old lumbering buses that go from one small dusty town to another and are loaded with too many people inside and with too much scruffy baggage on top. At the end of my journeys, I emerged soaked in perspiration, soot and dirt. I ate anything anywhere and always like everyone else with my fingers (I became good at that) – thick, half-raw chapattis from wayside stalls and little messes of lentils and vegetables served on a leaf, all the food the poor eat; sometimes if I didn't have anything, other people would share with me from out of their bundles. Henry, who had the usual phobia about bugs, said I would kill myself eating that way. But nothing ever happened. Once, in a desert fort in Rajasthan, I got very thirsty and asked the old caretaker to pull some water out of an ancient disused well for me. It was brown and sort of foul-smelling, and maybe there was a corpse in the well, who knows. But I was thirsty so I drank it, and still nothing happened.

People always speak to you in India, in buses and trains and on the streets, they want to know all about you and ask you a lot of personal questions. I didn't speak much Hindi, but somehow we always managed, and I didn't mind answering all those questions when I could. Women quite often used to touch me, run their hands over my skin just to feel what it was like I suppose, and they specially liked to touch my hair which is long and blonde. Sometimes I had several of them lifting up strands of it at the same time, one pulling this way and another that way and they would exchange excited comments and laugh and scream a lot; but in a nice way, so I couldn't help but laugh and scream with them. And people in India are so hospitable. They're always saying, 'Please come and stay in my house', perfect strangers that happen to be sitting near you on the train. Sometimes, if I didn't have any plans or if it sounded as if they might be living in an interesting place, I'd say 'all right thanks', and I'd go along with them. I had some interesting adventures that way.

I might as well say straight off that many of these adventures were sexual. Indian men are very, very keen to sleep with foreign girls. Of course men in other countries are also keen to sleep with girls, but there's something specially frenzied about Indian men when they approach you. Frenzied and at the same time shy. You'd think that with all those ancient traditions they have – like the Kama Sutra, and the sculptures showing couples in every kind of position – you'd think that with all that behind them they'd be very highly skilled, but they're not. Just the opposite. Middle-aged men get as excited as a fifteen-year-old boy, and then of course they can't wait, they jump and before you know where you are, in a great rush, it's all over. And when it's over, it's over, there's nothing left. Then they're only concerned with getting away as soon as possible before anyone can find them out (they're always scared of being found out). There's no tenderness, no interest at all in the other person as a person; only the same kind of curiosity that there is on the buses and the same sort of questions are asked, like are you married, any children, why no children, do you like wearing our Indian dress . . . There's one question though that's not asked on the buses but that always inevitably comes up during sex, so that you learn to wait for it: always, at the moment of mounting excitement, they ask, 'How many men have you slept with?' and it's repeated over and over, 'How many? How many?' and then they shout 'Aren't you ashamed?' and 'Bitch!' – always that one word which seems to excite them more than any other, to call you that is the height of their lovemaking, it's the last frenzy, the final outrage: 'Bitch!' Sometimes I couldn't stop myself but had to burst out laughing. I didn't like sleeping with all these people, but I felt I had to. I felt I was doing good, though I don't know why, I couldn't explain it to myself. Only one of all those men ever spoke to me: I mean the way people having sex together are supposed to speak, coming near each other not only physically but also wanting to show each other what's deep inside them. He was a middle-aged man, a fellow-passenger on a bus, and we got talking at one of the stops the bus made at a wayside tea stall. When he found I was on my way to X—— and didn't have anywhere to stay, he said, as so many have said before him, 'Please come and stay in my house.' And I said, as I had often said before, 'All right.' Only when we got there he didn't take me to his house but to a hotel. It was a very poky place in the bazaar and we had to grope our way up a steep smelly stone staircase and then there was a tiny room with just one string cot and an earthenware water jug in it. He made a joke about there being only one bed. I was too tired to care much about anything. I only wanted to get it over with quickly and go to sleep. But afterwards I found it wasn't possible to go to sleep because there was a lot of noise coming up from the street where all the shops were still open though it was nearly midnight. People seemed to be having a good time and there was even a phonograph playing some cracked old love song. My companion also couldn't get to sleep: he left the bed and sat down on the floor by the window and smoked one cigarette after the other. His face was lit up by the light coming in from the street outside and I saw he was looking sort of thoughtful and sad, sitting there smoking. He had rather a good face, strong bones but quite a feminine mouth and of course those feminine suffering eyes that most Indians have.

I went and sat next to him. The window was an arch reaching down to the floor so that I could see out into the bazaar. It was quite gay down there with all the lights; the phonograph was playing from the cold-drink shop and a lot of people were standing around there having highly coloured pop drinks out of bottles; next to it was a shop with pink and blue brassieres strung up on a pole. On top of the shops were wrought-iron balconies on which sat girls dressed up in tatty georgette and waving peacock fans to keep themselves cool. Sometimes men looked up to talk and laugh with them and they talked and laughed back. I realized we were in the brothel area; probably the hotel we were in was a brothel too.

I asked, 'Why did you bring me here?'

He answered, 'Why did you come?'

That was a good question. He was right. But I wasn't sorry I came. Why should I be? I said, 'It's all right. I like it.'

He said, 'She likes it,' and he laughed. A bit later he started talking: about how he had just been to visit his daughter who had been married a few months before. She wasn't happy in her in-laws' house, and when he said goodbye to her she clung to him and begged him to take her home. The more he reasoned with her, the more she cried, the more she clung to him. In the end he had had to use force to free himself from her so that he could get away and not miss his bus. He felt very sorry for her, but what else was there for him to do? If he took her away, her in-laws might refuse to have her back again and then her life would be ruined. And she would get used to it, they always did; for some it took longer and was harder, but they all got used to it in the end. His wife too had cried a lot during the first year of marriage.

I asked him whether he thought it was good to arrange marriages that way, and he looked at me and asked how else would you do it? I said something about love and it made him laugh and he said that was only for the films. I didn't want to defend my point of view; in fact, I felt rather childish and as if he knew a lot more about things than I did. He began to get amorous again, and this time it was much better because he wasn't so frenzied and I liked him better by now too. Afterwards he told me how when he was first married, he and his wife had shared a room with the whole family (parents and younger brothers and sisters), and whatever they wanted to do, they had to do very quickly and quietly for fear of anyone waking up. I had a strange sensation then, as if I wanted to strip off all my clothes and parade up and down the room naked. I thought of all the men's eyes that follow one in the street, and for the first time it struck me that the expression in them was like that in the eyes of prisoners looking through their bars at the world outside; and then I thought maybe I'm that world outside for them – the way I go here and there and talk and laugh with everyone and do what I like – maybe I'm the river and trees they can't have where they are. Oh, I felt so sorry, I wanted to do so much. And to make a start, I flung myself on my companion and kissed and hugged him hard, I lay on top of him, I smothered him, I spread my hair over his face because I wanted to make him forget everything that wasn't me – this room, his daughter, his wife, the women in georgette sitting on the balconies – I wanted everything to be new for him and as beautiful as I could make it. He liked it for a while but got tired quite quickly, probably because he wasn't all that young any more.

It was shortly after this encounter that I met Ahmed. He was eighteen years old and a musician. His family had been musicians as long as anyone could remember and the alley they lived in was full of other musicians, so that when you walked down it, it was like walking through a magic forest all lit up with music and sounds. Only there wasn't anything magic about the place itself which was very cramped and dirty; the houses were so old that, whenever there were heavy rains, one or two of them came tumbling down. I was never inside Ahmed's house or met his family – they'd have died of shock if they had got to know about me – but I knew they were very poor and scraped a living by playing at weddings and functions. Ahmed never had any money, just sometimes if he was lucky he had a few coins to buy his betel with. But he was cheerful and happy and enjoyed everything that came his way. He was married, but his wife was too young to stay with him and after the ceremony she had been sent back to live with her father who was a musician in another town.

When I first met Ahmed, I was staying in a hostel attached to a temple which was free of charge for pilgrims; but afterwards he and I wanted a place for us to go to, so I wired Henry to send me some more money. Henry sent me the money, together with a long complaining letter which I didn't read all the way through, and I took a room in a hotel. It was on the outskirts of town which was mostly waste land except for a few houses, and some of these had never been finished. Our hotel wasn't finished either because the proprietor had run out of money, and now it probably never would be for the place had turned out to be a poor proposition, it was too far out of town and no one ever came to stay there. But it suited us fine.

We had this one room, painted bright pink and quite bare except for two pieces of furniture – a bed and a dressing-table, both of them very shiny and new. Ahmed loved it, he had never stayed in such a grand room before; he bounced up and down on the bed which had a mattress, and stood looking at himself from all sides in the mirror of the dressing-table.

I never in all my life was so gay with anyone the way I was with Ahmed. I'm not saying I never had a good time at home; I did. I had a lot of friends before I married Henry and we had parties and danced and drank and I enjoyed it. But it wasn't like with Ahmed because no one was ever as *carefree* as he was, as light and easy and just ready to play and live. At home we always had our problems, personal ones of course, but on top of those there were universal problems – social, and economic, and moral, we really cared about what was happening in the world around us and in our own minds, we felt a responsibility towards being here alive at this point in time and wanted to do our best. Ahmed had no thoughts like that at all; there wasn't a shadow on him. He had his personal problems from time to time, and when he had them, he was very downcast and sometimes he even cried. But they weren't anything really very serious – usually some family quarrel, or his father was angry with him – and they passed away, blew away like a breeze over a lake and left him sunny and sparkling again. He enjoyed everything so much: not only our room, and the bed and the dressing-table, and making love, but so many other things like drinking Coca-Cola and spraying scent and combing my hair and my combing his; and he made up games for us to play like indoor cricket with a slipper for a bat and one of Henry's letters rolled up for a ball. He taught me how to crack his toes, which is such a great Indian delicacy, and yelled with pleasure when I got it right;

but when he did it to me, I yelled with pain so he stopped at once and was terribly sorry. He was very considerate and tender. No one I've ever known was as sensitive to my feelings as he was. It was like an instinct with him, as if he could feel right down into my heart and know what was going on there; and without ever having to ask anything or my ever having to explain anything, he could sense each change of mood and adapt himself to it and feel with it. Henry would always have to ask me, 'Now what's up? What's the matter with you?' and when we were still all right with each other, he would make a sincere effort to understand. But Ahmed never had to make an effort, and maybe if he'd had to he wouldn't have succeeded because it wasn't ever with his mind that he understood anything, it was always with his feelings. Perhaps that was so because he was a musician and in music everything is beyond words and explanations anyway; and from what he told me about Indian music, I could see it was very, very subtle, there are effects that you can hardly perceive they're so subtle and your sensibilities have to be kept tuned all the time to the finest, finest point; and perhaps because of that the whole of Ahmed was always at that point and he could play me and listen to me as if I were his sarod.

After some time we ran out of money and Henry wouldn't send any more, so we had to think what to do. I certainly couldn't bear to part with Ahmed, and in the end I suggested he'd better come back to Delhi with me and we'd try and straighten things out with Henry. Ahmed was terribly excited by the idea; he'd never been to Delhi and was wild to go. Only it meant he had to run away from home because his family would never have allowed him to go, so one night he stole out of the house with his sarod and his little bundle of clothes and met me at the railway station. We reached Delhi the next night, tired and dirty and covered with soot the way you always get in trains here. When we arrived home, Henry was giving a party; not a big party, just a small informal group sitting around chatting. I'll never forget the expression on everyone's faces when Ahmed and I came staggering in with our bundles and bedding. My blouse had got torn in the train all the way down the side, and I didn't have a safety pin so it kept flapping open and unfortunately I didn't have anything underneath. Henry's guests were all looking very nice, the men in smart bush-shirts and their wives in little silk cocktail dresses; and although after the first shock they all behaved very well and carried on as if nothing unusual had happened, still it was an awkward situation for everyone concerned.

Ahmed never really got over it. I can see now how awful it must have been for him, coming into that room full of strange white people and all of them turning round to stare at us. And the room itself must have been a shock to him, he can never have seen anything like it. Actually, it was quite a shock to me too. I'd forgotten that that was the way Henry and I lived. When we first came, we had gone to a lot of trouble doing up the apartment, buying furniture and pictures and stuff, and had succeeded in making it look just like the apartment we have at home except for some elegant Indian touches. To Ahmed it was all very strange. He stayed there with us for some time, and he couldn't get used to it. I think it bothered him to have so many *things* around, rugs and lamps and objets d'art; he couldn't see why they had to be there. Now that I had travelled and lived the way I had, I couldn't see why either; as a matter of fact I felt as if these things were a hindrance and cluttered up not only your room but your mind and your soul as well, hanging on them like weights.

We had some quite bad scenes in the apartment during

those days. I told Henry that I was in love with Ahmed, and naturally that upset him, though what upset him most was the fact that he had to keep us both in the apartment. I also realized that this was an undesirable situation, but I couldn't see any way out of it because where else could Ahmed and I go? We didn't have any money, only Henry had, so we had to stay with him. He kept saying that he would turn both of us out into the streets but I knew he wouldn't. He wasn't the type to do a violent thing like that, and besides he himself was so frightened of the streets that he'd have died to think of anyone connected with him being out there. I wouldn't have minded all that much if he *had* turned us out: it was warm enough to sleep in the open and people always give you food if you don't have any. I would have preferred it really because it was so unpleasant with Henry; but I knew Ahmed would never have been able to stand it. He was quite a pampered boy, and though his family were poor, they looked after and protected each other very carefully; he never had to miss a meal or go dressed in anything but fine muslin clothes, nicely washed and starched by female relatives.

Ahmed bitterly repented having come. He was very miserable, feeling so uncomfortable in the apartment and with Henry making rows all the time. Ramu, the servant, didn't improve anything by the way he behaved, absolutely refusing to serve Ahmed and never losing an opportunity to make him feel inferior. Everything went out of Ahmed; he crumpled up as if he were a paper flower. He didn't want to play his sarod and he didn't want to make love to me, he just sat around with his head and his hands hanging down, and there were times when I saw tears rolling down his face and he didn't even bother to wipe them off. Although he was so unhappy in the apartment, he never left it and so he never saw any of the places he had been so eager to come to Delhi for, like the Juma Masjid and Nizamuddin's tomb. Most of the time he was thinking about his family. He wrote long letters to them in Urdu, which I posted, telling them where he was and imploring their pardon for running away; and long letters came back again and he read and read them, soaking them in tears and kisses. One night he got so bad he jumped out of bed and, rushing into Henry's bedroom, fell to his knees by the side of Henry's bed and begged to be sent back home again. And Henry, sitting up in bed in his pyjamas, said all right, in rather a lordly way I thought. So next day I took Ahmed to the station and put him on the train, and through the bars of the railway carriage he kissed my hands and looked into my eyes with all his old ardour and tenderness, so at the last moment I wanted to go with him but it was too late and the train pulled away out of the station and all that was left to me of Ahmed was a memory, very beautiful and delicate like a flavour or a perfume or one of those melodies he played on his sarod.

I became very depressed. I didn't feel like going travelling any more but stayed home with Henry and went with him to his diplomatic and other parties. He was quite glad to have me go with him again; he liked having someone in the car on the way home to talk to about all the people who'd been at the party and compare their chances of future success with his own. I didn't mind going with him, there wasn't anything else I wanted to do. I felt as if I'd failed at something. It wasn't only Ahmed. I didn't really miss him all that much and was glad to think of him back with his family in that alley full of music where he was happy. For myself I didn't know what to do next though I felt that something still awaited me. Our apartment led to an open terrace and I often went up there to look at the view which was marvellous. The house we lived in and all the ones around were white and pink and very modern, with picture windows and little lawns in front, but from up here you could look beyond them to the city and the big mosque and the fort. In between there were stretches of waste land, empty and barren except for an occasional crumbly old tomb growing there. What always impressed me the most was the sky because it was so immensely big and so unchanging in colour, and it made everything underneath it – all the buildings, even the great fort, the whole city, not to speak of all the people living in it – seem terribly small and trivial and passing somehow. But at the same time as it made me feel small, it also made me feel immense and eternal. I don't know, I can't explain, perhaps because it was itself like that and this thought – that there *was* something like that – made me feel that I had a part in it, I too was part of being immense and eternal. It was all very vague really and nothing I could ever speak about to anyone; but because of it I thought well maybe there is something more for me here after all. That was a relief because it meant I wouldn't have to go home and be the way I was before and nothing different or gained. For all the time, ever since I'd come and even before, I'd had this idea that there was something in India for me to *gain,* and even though for the time being I'd failed, I could try longer and at last perhaps I would succeed.

I'd met people on and off who had come here on a spiritual quest, but it wasn't the sort of thing I wanted for myself. I thought anything I wanted to find, I could find by myself travelling around the way I had done. But now that this had failed, I became interested in the other thing. I began to go to a few prayer meetings and I liked the atmosphere very much.

The meeting was usually conducted by a swami in a saffron robe who had renounced the world, and he gave an address about love and God and everyone sang hymns also about love and God. The people who came to these meetings were mostly middle-aged and quite poor. I had already met many like them on my travels, for they were the sort of people who sat waiting on station platforms and in bus depots, absolutely patient and uncomplaining even when conductors and other officials pushed them around. They were gentle people and very clean though there was always some slight smell about them as of people who find it difficult to keep clean because they live in crowded and unsanitary places where there isn't much running water and the drainage system isn't good. I loved the expression that came into their faces when they sang hymns. I wanted to be like them, so I began to dress in plain white saris and I tied up my hair in a plain knot and the only ornament I wore was a string of beads not for decoration but to say the names of God on. I became a vegetarian and did my best to cast out all the undesirable human passions, such as anger and lust. When Henry was in an irritable or quarrelsome mood, I never answered him back but was very kind and patient with him. However, far from having a good effect, this seemed to make him worse. Altogether he didn't like the new personality I was trying to achieve but sneered a lot at the way I dressed and looked and the simple food I ate. Actually, I didn't enjoy this food very much and found it quite a trial eating nothing but boiled rice and lentils with him sitting opposite me having his cutlets and chops.

The peace and satisfaction that I saw on the faces of the other hymn singers didn't come to me. As a matter of fact, I grew rather bored. There didn't seem much to be learned from singing hymns and eating vegetables. Fortunately just about this time someone took me to see a holy woman who lived on the roof of an old overcrowded house near the river. People treated her like a holy woman but she didn't set up to be one. She didn't set up to be anything really, but only stayed in her room on the roof and talked to people who came to see her. She liked telling stories and she could hold everyone spellbound listening to her, even though she was only telling the old mythological stories they had known all their lives long, about Krishna, and the Pandavas, and Rama and Sita. But she got terribly excited while she was telling them, as if it wasn't something that had happened millions of years ago but as if it was all real and going on exactly now. Once she was telling about Krishna's mother who made him open his mouth to see whether he had stolen and was eating up her butter. What did she see then, inside his mouth?

'Worlds!' the holy woman cried. 'Not just this world, not just one world with its mountains and rivers and seas, no, but world upon world, all spinning in one great eternal cycle in this child's mouth, moon upon moon, sun upon sun!'

She clapped her hands and laughed and laughed, and then she burst out singing in her thin old voice, some hymn all about how great God was and how lucky for her that she was his beloved. She was dancing with joy in front of all the people. And she was just a little shrivelled old woman, very ugly with her teeth gone and a growth on her chin: but the way she carried on it was as if she had all the looks and glamour anyone ever had in the world and was in love a million times over. I thought well, whatever it was she had, obviously it was the one thing worth having and I had better try for it.

I went to stay with a guru in a holy city. He had a house on the river in which he lived with his disciples. They lived in a nice way: they meditated a lot and went out for boat rides on the river and in the evenings they all sat around in the guru's room and had a good time. There were quite a few foreigners among the disciples, and it was the guru's greatest wish to go abroad and spread his message there and bring back more disciples. When he heard that Henry was a journalist, he became specially interested in me. He talked to me about the importance of introducing the leaven of Indian spirituality into the lump of Western materialism. To achieve this end, his own presence in the West was urgently required, and to ensure the widest dissemination of his message he would also need the full support of the mass media. He said that since we live in the modern age, we must avail ourselves of all its resources. He was very keen for me to bring Henry into the ashram, and when I was vague in my answers – I certainly didn't want Henry here nor would he in the least want to come – he became very pressing and even quite annoyed and kept returning to the subject.

He didn't seem a very spiritual type of person to me. He was a hefty man with big shoulders and a big head. He wore his hair long but his jaw was clean-shaven and stuck out very large and prominent and gave him a powerful look like a bull. All he ever wore was a saffron robe and this left a good part of his body bare so that it could be seen at once how strong his legs and shoulders were. He had huge eyes which he used constantly and apparently to tremendous effect, fixing people with them and penetrating them with a steady beam. He used them on me when he wanted Henry to come, but they never did anything to me. But the other disciples were very strongly affected by them. There was one girl, Jean, who said they were like the sun, so strong that if she tried to look back at them something terrible would happen to her like being blinded or burned up completely.

Jean had made herself everything an Indian guru expects his disciples to be. She was absolutely humble and submissive. She touched the guru's feet when she came into or went out of his presence, she ran eagerly on any errand he sent her on. She said she gloried in being nothing in herself and living only by his will. And she looked like nothing too, sort of drained of everything she might once have been. At home her cheeks were probably pink but now she was quite white, waxen, and her hair too was completely faded and colourless. She always wore a plain white cotton sari and that made her look paler than ever, and thinner too; it seemed to bring out the fact that she had no hips and was utterly flat-chested. But she was happy – at least she said she was – she said she had never known such happiness and hadn't thought it was possible for human beings to feel like that. And when she said that, there was a sort of sparkle in her pale eyes, and at such moments I envied her because she seemed to have found what I was looking for. But at the same time I wondered whether she really had found what she thought she had, or whether it wasn't something else and she was cheating herself, and one day she'd wake up to that fact and then she'd feel terrible.

She was shocked by my attitude to the guru – not touching his feet or anything, and talking back to him as if he was just an ordinary person. Sometimes I thought perhaps there was something wrong with me because everyone else, all the other disciples and people from outside too who came to see him, they all treated him with this great reverence and their faces lit up in his presence as if there really was something special. Only I couldn't see it. But all the same I was quite happy there – not because of him, but because I liked the atmosphere of the place and the way they all lived. Everyone seemed very contented and as if they were living for something high and beautiful. I thought perhaps if I waited and was patient, I'd also come to be like that. I tried to meditate the way they all did, sitting cross-legged in one spot and concentrating on the holy word that had been given to me. I wasn't ever very successful and kept thinking of other things. But there were times when I went up to sit on the roof and looked out over the river, the way it stretched so calm and broad to the opposite bank and the boats going up and down it and the light changing and being reflected back on the water: and then, though I wasn't trying to meditate or come to any higher thoughts, I did feel very peaceful and was glad to be there.

The guru was patient with me for a long time, explaining about the importance of his mission and how Henry ought to come here and write about it for his paper. But as the days passed and Henry didn't show up, his attitude changed and he began to ask me questions. Why hadn't Henry come? Hadn't I written to him? Wasn't I going to write to him? Didn't I think what was being done in the ashram would interest him? Didn't I agree that it deserved to be brought to the notice of the world and that to this end no stone should be left unturned? While he said all this, he fixed me with his great eyes and I squirmed – not because of the way he was looking at me, but because I was embarrassed and didn't know what to answer. Then he became very gentle and said never mind, he didn't want to force me, that was not his way, he wanted people slowly to turn towards him of their own accord, to open up to him as a flower opens up and unfurls its petals and its leaves to the sun. But next day he would start again, asking the same questions, urging me, forcing me, and when this had gone on for some time and we weren't getting anywhere, he even got angry once or twice and shouted at me that I was obstinate and closed and had fenced in my heart with seven hoops of iron. When he shouted, everyone in the ashram trembled and afterwards they looked at me in a strange way. But an hour later the guru always had me called back to his room and then he was very gentle with me again and made me sit near him and insisted that it should be I who handed him his glass of milk in preference to one of the others, all of whom were a lot keener to be selected for this honour than I was.

Jean often came to talk to me. At night I spread my bedding in a tiny cubbyhole which was a disused storeroom, and just as I was falling asleep, she would come in and lie down beside me and talk to me very softly and intimately. I didn't like it much, to have her so close to me and whispering in a voice that wasn't more than a breath and which I could feel, slightly warm, on my neck; sometimes she touched me, putting her hand on mine ever so gently so that she hardly was touching me but all the same I could feel that her hand was a bit moist and it gave me an unpleasant sensation down my spine. She spoke about the beauty of surrender, of not having a will and not having thoughts of your own. She said she too had been like me once, stubborn and ego-centred, but now she had learned the joy of yielding, and if she could only give me some inkling of the infinite bliss to be tasted in this process – here her breath would give out for a moment and she couldn't speak for ecstasy. I would take the opportunity to pretend to fall asleep, even snoring a bit to make it more convincing; after calling my name a few times in the hope of waking me up again, she crept away disappointed. But next night she'd be back again, and during the day too she would attach herself to me as much as possible and continue talking in the same way.

It got so that even when she wasn't there, I could still hear her voice and feel her breath on my neck. I no longer enjoyed anything, not even going on the river or looking out over it from the top of the house. Although they hadn't bothered me before, I kept thinking of the funeral pyres burning on the bank, and it seemed to me that the smoke they gave out was spreading all over the sky and the river and covering them with a dirty yellowish haze. I realized that nothing good could come to me from this place now. But when I told the guru that I was leaving, he got into a great fury. His head and neck swelled out and his eyes became two coal-black demons rolling around in rage. In a voice like drums and cymbals, he *forbade* me to go. I didn't say anything but I made up my mind to leave next morning. I went to pack my things. The whole ashram was silent and stricken, no one dared speak. No one dared come near me either till late at night when Jean came as usual to lie next to me. She lay there completely still and crying to herself. I didn't know she was crying at first because she didn't make a sound but slowly her tears seeped into her side of the pillow and a sensation of dampness came creeping over to my side of it. I pretended not to notice anything.

Suddenly the guru stood in the doorway. The room faced an open courtyard and this was full of moonlight which illumined him and made him look enormous and eerie. Jean and I sat up. I felt scared, my heart beat fast. After looking at us in silence for a while, he ordered Jean to go away. She got up to do so at once. I said, 'No, stay,' and clung to her hand but she disengaged herself from me and, touching the guru's feet in reverence, she went away. She seemed to dissolve in the moonlight outside, leaving no trace. The guru sat beside me on my bedding spread on the floor. He said I was under a delusion, that I didn't really want to leave; my inmost nature was craving to stay by him – he knew, he could hear it calling out to him. But because I was afraid, I was attempting to smother this craving and to run away. 'Look how you're trembling,' he said. 'See how afraid you are.' It was true, I was trembling and cowering against the wall as far away from him as I could get. Only it was impossible to get very far because he was so huge and seemed to spread and fill the tiny closet. I could feel him close against me, and his pungent male smell, spiced with garlic, overpowered me.

'You're right to be afraid,' he said: because it was his intention, he said, to batter and beat me, to smash my ego till it broke and flew apart into a million pieces and was scattered into the dust. Yes, it would be a painful process and I would often cry out and plead for mercy, but in the end – ah, with what joy I would step out of the prison of my own self, remade and reborn! I would fling myself to the ground and bathe his feet in tears of gratitude. Then I would be truly his. As he spoke, I became more and more afraid because I felt, so huge and close and strong as he was, that perhaps he really had the power to do to me all that he said and that in the end he would make me like Jean.

I now lay completely flattened against the wall, and he had moved up and was squashing me against it. One great hand travelled up and down my stomach, but its activity seemed apart from the rest of him and from what he was saying. His voice became lower and lower, more and more intense. He said he would teach me to obey, to submit myself completely, that would be the first step and a very necessary one. For he knew what we were like, all of us who came from Western countries: we were self-willed, obstinate, *licentious*. On the last word his voice cracked with emotion, his hand went further and deeper. *Licentious*, he repeated, and then, rolling himself across the bed so that he now lay completely pressed against me, he asked, 'How many men have you slept with?' He took my hand and made me hold him: how huge and hot he was! He pushed hard against me. 'How many? Answer me!' he commanded, urgent and dangerous. But I was no longer afraid: now he was not an unknown quantity, nor was the situation any longer new or strange. 'Answer me, answer me!' he cried, riding on top of me, and then he cried, 'Bitch!' and I laughed in relief.

I quite liked being back in Delhi with Henry. I had lots of baths in our marble bathroom, soaking in the tub for hours and making myself smell nice with bath salts. I stopped wearing Indian clothes and took out all the dresses I'd brought with me. We entertained quite a bit, and Ramu scurried around in his white coat, emptying ashtrays. It wasn't a bad time. I stayed around all day in the apartment with the air conditioner on and the curtains drawn to keep out the glare. At night we drove over to other people's apartments for buffet suppers of boiled ham and potato salad; we sat around drinking in their living-rooms, which were done up more or less like ours, and talked about things like the price of whisky, what was the best hill station to go to in the summer, and servants. This last subject often led to other related ones like how unreliable Indians were and how it was impossible ever to get anything done. Usually this subject was treated in a humorous way, with lots of funny anecdotes to illustrate, but occasionally someone got quite passionate; this happened usually if they were a bit drunk, and then they went off into a long thing about how dirty India was and backward, riddled with vile superstitions – evil, they said – corrupt – corrupting.

Henry never spoke like that – maybe because he never got

drunk enough – but I know he didn't disagree with it. He disliked the place very much and was in fact thinking of asking for an assignment elsewhere. When I asked where, he said the cleanest place he could think of. He asked how would I like to go to Geneva. I knew I wouldn't like it one bit, but I said all right. I didn't really care where I was. I didn't care much about anything these days. The only positive feeling I had was for Henry. He was so sweet and good to me. I had a lot of bad dreams nowadays and was afraid of sleeping alone, so he let me come into his bed even though he dislikes having his sheets disarranged and I always kick and toss about a lot. I lay close beside him, clinging to him, and for the first time I was glad that he had never been all that keen on sex. On Sundays we stayed in bed all day reading the papers and Ramu brought us nice English meals on trays. Sometimes we put on a record and danced together in our pyjamas. I kissed Henry's cheeks which were always smooth – he didn't need to shave very often – and sometimes his lips which tasted of toothpaste.

Then I got jaundice. It's funny, all that time I spent travelling about and eating anything anywhere, nothing happened to me, and now that I was living such a clean life with boiled food and boiled water, I got sick. Henry was horrified. He immediately segregated all his and my things, and anything that I touched had to be sterilized a hundred times over. He was forever running into the kitchen to check up on whether Ramu was doing this properly. He said jaundice was the most catching thing there was, and though he went in for a whole course of precautionary inoculations that had to be specially flown in from the States, he still remained in a very nervous state. He tried to be sympathetic to me, but couldn't help sounding reproachful most of the time. He had sealed himself off so carefully, and now I had let this in. I knew how he felt, but I was too ill and miserable to care. I don't remember ever feeling so *ill*. I didn't have any high temperature or anything, but all the time there was this terrible nausea. First my eyes went yellow, then the rest of me as if I'd been dyed in the colour of nausea, inside and out. The whole world went yellow and sick. I couldn't bear anything: any noise, any person near me, worst of all any smell. They couldn't cook in the kitchen any more because the smell of cooking made me scream. Henry had to live on boiled eggs and bread. I begged him not to let Ramu into my bedroom for, although Ramu always wore nicely laundered clothes, he gave out a smell of perspiration which was both sweetish and foul and filled me with disgust. I was convinced that under his clean shirt he wore a cotton vest, black with sweat and dirt, which he never took off but slept in at night in the one-room servant quarter where he lived crowded together with all his family in a dense smell of cheap food and bad drains and unclean bodies.

I knew these smells so well – I thought of them as the smells of India, and had never minded them; but now I couldn't get rid of them, they were like some evil flood soaking through the walls of my air-conditioned bedroom. And other things I hadn't minded, had hardly bothered to think about, now came back to me in a terrible way so that waking and sleeping, I saw them. What I remembered most often was the disused well in the Rajasthan fort out of which I had drunk water. I was sure now that there had been a corpse at the bottom of it, and I saw this corpse with the flesh swollen and blown but the eyes intact: they were huge like the guru's eyes and they stared, glazed and jellied, into the darkness of the well. And worse than seeing this corpse, I could taste it in the water that I had drunk – that I was still drinking – yes, it was now, at this very moment, that I was raising my cupped hands to my mouth and feeling the dank water lap around my tongue. I screamed out loud at the taste of the dead man and I called to Henry and clutched his hand and begged him to get us sent to Geneva quickly, quickly. He disengaged his hand – he didn't like me to touch him at this time – but he promised. Then I grew calmer, I shut my eyes and tried to think of Geneva and of washing out my mouth with Swiss milk.

I got better, but I was very weak. When I looked at myself in the mirror, I started to cry. My face had a yellow tint, my hair was limp and faded; I didn't look old but I didn't look young any more either. There was no flesh left, and no colour. I was drained, hollowed out. I was wearing a white nightdress and that increased the impression. Actually, I reminded myself of Jean. I thought, so this is what it does to you (I didn't quite know at that time what I meant by it – jaundice in my case, a guru in hers; but it seemed to come to the same). When Henry told me that his new assignment had come through, I burst into tears again; only now it was with relief. I said let's go now, let's go quickly. I became quite hysterical so Henry said all right; he too was impatient to get away before any more of those bugs he dreaded so much caught up with us. The only thing that bothered him was that the rent had been paid for three months and the landlord refused to refund. Henry had a fight with him about it but the landlord won. Henry was furious but I said never mind, let's just get away and forget all about all of them. We packed up some of our belongings and sold the rest; the last few days we lived in an empty apartment with only a couple of kitchen chairs and a bed. Ramu was very worried about finding a new job.

Just before we were to leave for the airport and were waiting for the car to pick us up, I went on the terrace. I don't know why I did that, there was no reason. There was nothing I wanted to say goodbye to, and no last glimpses I wanted to catch. My thoughts were all concentrated on the coming journey and whether to take air sickness pills or not. The sky from up on the terrace looked as immense as ever, the city as small. It was evening and the light was just fading and the sky wasn't any definite colour now: it was sort of translucent like a pearl but not an earthly pearl. I thought of the story the little saintly old woman had told about Krishna's mother and how she saw the sun and the moon and world upon world in his mouth. I liked that phrase so much – world upon world – I imagined them spinning around each other like glass balls in eternity and everything as shining and translucent as the sky I saw above me. I went down and told Henry I wasn't going with him. When he realized – and this took some time – that I was serious, he knew I was mad. At first he was very patient and gentle with me, then he got in a frenzy. The car had already arrived to take us. Henry yelled at me, he grabbed my arm and began to pull me to the door. I resisted with all my strength and sat down on one of the kitchen chairs. Henry continued to pull and now he was pulling me along with the chair as if on a sleigh. I clung to it as hard as I could but I felt terribly weak and was afraid I would let myself be pulled away. I begged him to leave me. I cried and wept with fear – fear that he would take me, fear that he would leave me.

Ramu came to my aid. He said it's all right Sahib, I'll look after her. He told Henry that I was too weak to travel after my illness but later, when I was better, he would take me to the airport and put me on a plane. Henry hesitated. It was getting very late, and if he didn't go, he too would miss the plane. Ramu assured him that all would be well and Henry need not worry at all. At last Henry took my papers and ticket out of his inner pocket. He gave me instructions how I was to go to the air company and make a new booking. He hesitated a moment longer – how sweet he looked all dressed up in a suit and tie ready for travelling, just like the day we got married – but the car was hooting furiously downstairs and he had to go. I held on hard to the chair. I was afraid if I didn't I might get up and run after him. So I clung to the chair, trembling and crying. Ramu was quite happily dusting the remaining chair. He said we would have to get some more furniture. I think he was glad that I had stayed and he still had somewhere to work and live and didn't have to go tramping around looking for another place. He had quite a big family to support. I sold the ticket Henry left with me but I didn't buy any new furniture with it. I stayed in the empty rooms by myself and very rarely went out. When Ramu cooked anything for me, I ate it, but sometimes he forgot or didn't have time because he was busy looking for another job. I didn't like living like that but I didn't know what else to do. I was afraid to go out: everything I had once liked so much – people, places, crowds, smells – I now feared and hated. I would go running back to be by myself in the empty apartment. I felt people looked at me in a strange way in the streets; and perhaps I was strange now from the way I was living and not caring about what I looked like any more; I think I talked aloud to myself sometimes – once or twice I heard myself doing it. I spent a lot of the money I got from the air ticket on books. I went to the bookshops and came hurrying back carrying armfuls of them. Many of them I never read, and even those I did read, I didn't understand very much. I hadn't had much experience in reading these sort of books – like the Upanishads and the Vedanta Sutras – but I liked the sound of the words and I liked the feeling they gave out. It was as if I were all by myself on an immensely high plateau breathing in great lungfuls of very sharp, pure air. Sometimes the landlord came to see what I was doing. He went round all the rooms, peering suspiciously into corners, testing the fittings. He kept asking how much longer I was going to stay; I said till the three months' rent was up. He brought prospective tenants to see the apartment, but when they saw me squatting on the floor in the empty rooms, sometimes with a bowl of half-eaten food which Ramu had neglected to clear away, they got nervous and went away again rather quickly. After a time the electricity got cut off because I hadn't paid the bill. It was very hot without the fan and I filled the tub with cold water and sat in it all day. But then the water got cut off too. The landlord came up twice, three times a day now. He said if I didn't clear out the day the rent was finished he would call the police to evict me. I said it's all right, don't worry, I shall go. Like the landlord, I too was counting the days still left to me. I was afraid what would happen to me.

Today the landlord evicted Ramu out of the servant quarter. That was when Ramu came up to ask for money and said all those things. Afterwards I went up on the terrace to watch him leave. It was such a sad procession. Each member of the family carried some part of their wretched household stock, none of which looked worth taking. Ramu had a bed with tattered strings balanced on his head. In two days' time I too will have to go with my bundle and my bedding. I've done this so often before – travelled here and there without any real destination – and been so happy doing it; but now it's different. That time I had a great sense of freedom and adventure. Now I feel compelled, that I have to do this whether I want to or not. And partly I don't want to, I feel afraid. Yet it's still like an adventure, and that's why besides being afraid I'm also excited, and most of the time I don't know why my heart is beating fast, is it in fear or in excitement, wondering what will happen to me now that I'm going travelling again.

Two More under the Indian Sun

Elizabeth had gone to spend the afternoon with Margaret. They were both English, but Margaret was a much older woman and they were also very different in character. But they were both in love with India, and it was this fact that drew them together. They sat on the veranda, and Margaret wrote letters and Elizabeth addressed the envelopes. Margaret always had letters to write; she led a busy life and was involved with several organizations of a charitable or spiritual nature. Her interests were centred in such matters, and Elizabeth was glad to be allowed to help her.

There were usually guests staying in Margaret's house. Sometimes they were complete strangers to her when they first arrived, but they tended to stay weeks, even months, at a time – holy men from the Himalayas, village welfare workers, organizers of conferences on spiritual welfare. She had one constant visitor throughout the winter, an elderly government officer who, on his retirement from service, had taken to a spiritual life and gone to live in the mountains at Almora. He did not, however, very much care for the winter cold up there, so at that season he came down to Delhi to stay with Margaret, who was always pleased to have him. He had a soothing effect on her – indeed, on anyone with whom he came into contact, for he had cast anger and all other bitter passions out of his heart and was consequently always smiling and serene. Everyone affectionately called him Babaji.

He sat now with the two ladies on the veranda, gently rocking himself to and fro in a rocking chair, enjoying the winter sunshine and the flowers in the garden and everything about him. His companions, however, were less serene. Margaret, in fact, was beginning to get angry with Elizabeth. This happened quite frequently, for Margaret tended to be quickly irritated, and especially with a meek and conciliatory person like Elizabeth.

'It's very selfish of you,' Margaret said now.

Elizabeth flinched. Like many very unselfish people, she was always accusing herself of undue selfishness, so that whenever this accusation was made by someone else it touched her closely. But because it was not in her power to do what Margaret wanted, she compressed her lips and kept silent. She was pale with this effort at obstinacy.

'It's your duty to go,' Margaret said. 'I don't have much time for people who shirk their duty.'

'I'm sorry, Margaret,' Elizabeth said, utterly miserable, utterly ashamed. The worst of it, almost, was that she really wanted to go; there was nothing she would have enjoyed more. What she was required to do was take a party of little Tibetan orphans on a holiday treat to Agra and show them the Taj Mahal. Elizabeth loved children, she loved little trips and treats, and she loved the Taj Mahal. But she couldn't go, nor could she say why.

Of course Margaret very easily guessed why, and it irritated her more than ever. To challenge her friend, she said bluntly, 'Your Raju can do without you for those few days.

Good heavens, you're not a honeymoon couple, are you? You've been married long enough. Five years.'

'Four,' Elizabeth said in a humble voice.

'Four, then. I can hardly be expected to keep count of each wonderful day. Do you want me to speak to him?'

'Oh no.'

'I will, you know. It's nothing to me. I won't mince my words.' She gave a short, harsh laugh, challenging anyone to stop her from speaking out when occasion demanded. Indeed, at the thought of anyone doing so, her face grew red under her crop of grey hair, and a pulse throbbed in visible anger in her tough, tanned neck.

Elizabeth glanced imploringly towards Babaji. But he was rocking and smiling and looking with tender love at two birds pecking at something on the lawn.

'There are times when I can't help feeling you're afraid of him,' Margaret said. She ignored Elizabeth's little disclaiming cry of horror. 'There's no trust between you, no understanding. And married life is nothing if it's not based on the twin rocks of trust and understanding.'

Babaji liked this phrase so much that he repeated it to himself several times, his lips moving soundlessly and his head nodding with approval.

'In everything I did,' Margaret said, 'Arthur was with me. He had complete faith in me. And in those days – well.' She chuckled. 'A wife like me wasn't altogether a joke.'

Her late husband had been a high-up British official, and in those British days he and Margaret had been expected to conform to some very strict social rules. But the idea of Margaret conforming to any rules, let alone those! Her friends nowadays often had a good laugh at it with her, and she had many stories to tell of how she had shocked and defied her fellow-countrymen.

'It was people like you,' Babaji said, 'who first extended the hand of friendship to us.'

'It wasn't a question of friendship, Babaji. It was a question of love.'

'Ah!' he exclaimed.

'As soon as I came here – and I was only a chit of a girl, Arthur and I had been married just two months – yes, as soon as I set foot on Indian soil, I knew this was the place I belonged. It's funny, isn't it? I don't suppose there's any rational explanation for it. But then, when was India ever the place for rational explanations?'

Babaji said with gentle certainty, 'In your last birth, you were one of us. You were an Indian.'

'Yes, lots of people have told me that. Mind you, in the beginning it was quite a job to make them see it. Naturally, they were suspicious – can you blame them? It wasn't like today. I envy you girls married to Indians. You have a very easy time of it.'

Elizabeth thought of the first time she had been taken to stay with Raju's family. She had met and married Raju in England, where he had gone for a year on a Commonwealth scholarship, and then had returned with him to Delhi; so it was some time before she met his family, who lived about two hundred miles out of Delhi, on the outskirts of a small town called Ankhpur. They all lived together in an ugly brick house, which was divided into two parts – one for the men of the family, the other for the women. Elizabeth, of course, had stayed in the women's quarters. She couldn't speak any Hindi and they spoke very little English, but they had not had much trouble communicating with her. They managed to make it clear at once that they thought her too ugly and too old for Raju (who was indeed some five years her junior), but also that they did not hold this against her and were ready to accept her, with all her shortcomings, as the will of God. They got a lot of amusement out of her, and she enjoyed being with them. They dressed and undressed her in new saris, and she smiled good-naturedly while they stood round her clapping their hands in wonder and doubling up with laughter. Various fertility ceremonies had been performed over her, and before she left she had been given her share of the family jewellery.

'Elizabeth,' Margaret said, 'if you're going to be so slow, I'd rather do them myself.'

'Just these two left,' Elizabeth said, bending more eagerly over the envelopes she was addressing.

'For all your marriage,' Margaret said, 'sometimes I wonder how much you do understand about this country. You live such a closed-in life.'

'I'll just take these inside,' Elizabeth said, picking up the envelopes and letters. She wanted to get away, not because she minded being told about her own wrong way of life but because she was afraid Margaret might start talking about Raju again.

It was cold inside, away from the sun. Margaret's house was old and massive, with thick stone walls, skylights instead of windows and immensely high ceilings. It was designed to keep out the heat in summer, but it also sealed in the cold in winter and became like some cavernous underground fortress frozen through with the cold of earth and stone. A stale smell of rice, curry and mango chutney was chilled into the air.

Elizabeth put the letters on Margaret's work table, which was in the drawing-room. Besides the drawing-room, there was a dining-room, but every other room was a bedroom, each with its dressing-room and bathroom attached. Sometimes Margaret had to put as many as three or four visitors into each bedroom, and on one occasion – this was when she had helped to organize a conference on Meditation as the Modern Curative – the drawing- and dining-rooms too had been converted into dormitories, with string cots and bedrolls laid out end to end. Margaret was not only an energetic and active person involved in many causes, but she was also the soul of generosity, ever ready to throw open her house to any friend or acquaintance in need of shelter. She had thrown it open to Elizabeth and Raju three years ago, when they had had to vacate their rooms almost overnight because the landlord said he needed the accommodation for his relatives. Margaret had given them a whole suite – a bedroom and dressing-room and bathroom – to themselves and they had had all their meals with her in the big dining-room, where the table was always ready laid with white crockery plates, face down so as not to catch the dust, and a thick white tablecloth that got rather stained towards the end of the week. At first, Raju had been very grateful and had praised their hostess to the skies for her kind and generous character. But as the weeks wore on, and every day, day after day, two or three times a day, they sat with Margaret and whatever other guests she had round the table, eating alternately lentils and rice or string-beans with boiled potatoes and beetroot salad, with Margaret always in her chair at the head of the table talking inexhaustibly about her activities and ideas – about Indian spirituality and the Mutiny and village uplift and the industrial revolution – Raju, who had a lot of ideas of his own and rather liked to talk, began to get restive. 'But madam, madam,' he would frequently say, half-rising in his chair in his impatience to interrupt her, only to have to sit down again, unsatisfied, and continue with his dinner, because Margaret was too busy with her own ideas to have time to take in his.

Once he could not restrain himself. Margaret was talking about – Elizabeth had even forgotten what it was – was it the first Indian National Congress? At any rate, she said something that stirred Raju to such disagreement that this time he did not restrict himself to the hesitant appeal of 'madam' but said out loud for everyone to hear, 'Nonsense, she is only talking nonsense.' There was a moment's silence; then Margaret, sensible woman that she was, shut her eyes as a sign that she would not hear and would not see, and, repeating the sentence he had interrupted more firmly than before, continued her discourse on an even keel. It was the other two or three people sitting with them round the table – a Buddhist monk with a large shaved skull, a welfare worker and a disciple of the Gandhian way of life wearing nothing but the homespun loincloth in which the Mahatma himself had always been so simply clad – it was they who had looked at Raju, and very, very gently one of them had clicked his tongue.

Raju had felt angry and humiliated, and afterwards, when they were alone in their bedroom, he had quarrelled about it with Elizabeth. In his excitement, he raised his voice higher than he would have if he had remembered that they were in someone else's house, and the noise of this must have disturbed Margaret, who suddenly stood in the doorway, looking at them. Unfortunately, it was just at the moment when Raju, in his anger and frustration, was pulling his wife's hair, and they both stood frozen in this attitude and stared back at Margaret. The next instant, of course, they had collected themselves, and Raju let go of Elizabeth's hair, and she pretended as best she could that all that was happening was that he was helping her comb it. But such a feeble subterfuge would not do before Margaret's penetrating eye, which she kept fixed on Raju, in total silence, for two disconcerting minutes; then she said, 'We don't treat English girls that way,' and withdrew, leaving the door open behind her as a warning that they were under observation. Raju shut it with a vicious kick. If they had had anywhere else to go, he would have moved out that instant.

Raju never came to see Margaret now. He was a proud person, who would never forget anything he considered a slight to his honour. Elizabeth always came on her own, as she had done today, to visit her friend. She sighed now as she arranged the letters on Margaret's work table; she was sad that this difference had arisen between her husband and her only friend, but she knew that there was nothing she could do about it. Raju was very obstinate. She shivered and rubbed the tops of her arms, goose-pimpled with the cold in that high, bleak room, and returned quickly to the veranda, which was flooded and warm with afternoon sun.

Babaji and Margaret were having a discussion on the relative merits of the three ways towards realization. They spoke of the way of knowledge, the way of action and that of love. Margaret maintained that it was a matter of temperament, and that while she could appreciate the beauty of the other two ways, for herself there was no path nor could there ever be but that of action. It was her nature. 'Of course it is,' Babaji said. 'And God bless you for it.'

'Arthur used to tease me. He'd say, "Margaret was born to right all the wrongs of the world in one go". But I can't help it. It's not in me to sit still when I see things to be done.'

'Babaji,' said Elizabeth, laughing, 'once I saw her – it was during the monsoon, and the river had flooded and the people on the bank were being evacuated. But it wasn't being done quickly enough for Margaret! She waded into the water and came back with someone's tin trunk on her head. All the people shouted, "Memsahib, Memsahib! What are you doing!" but she didn't take a bit of notice. She waded right back in again and came out with two rolls of bedding, one under each arm.'

Elizabeth went pink with laughter, and with pleasure and pride, at recalling this incident. Margaret pretended to be angry and gave her a playful slap, but she could not help smiling, while Babaji clasped his hands in joy and opened his mouth wide in silent, ecstatic laughter.

Margaret shook her head with a last fond smile. 'Yes, but I've got into the most dreadful scrapes with this nature of mine. If I'd been born with an ounce more patience, I'd have been a pleasanter person to deal with and life could have been a lot smoother all round. Don't you think so?'

She looked at Elizabeth, who said, 'I love you just the way you are.'

But a moment later, Elizabeth wished she had not said this. 'Yes,' Margaret took her up, 'that's the trouble with you. You love everybody just the way they are.' Of course she was referring to Raju. Elizabeth twisted her hands in her lap. These hands were large and bony and usually red, although she was otherwise a pale and rather frail person.

The more anyone twisted and squirmed, the less inclined was Margaret to let them off the hook. Not because this afforded her any pleasure but because she felt that facts of character must be faced just as resolutely as any other kinds of fact. 'Don't think you're doing anyone a favour,' she said, 'by being so indulgent towards their faults. Quite on the contrary. And especially in marriage,' she went on unwaveringly.

'It's not mutual pampering that makes a marriage, but mutual trust.'

'Trust and understanding,' Babaji said.

Elizabeth knew that there was not much of these in her marriage. She wasn't even sure how much Raju earned in his job at the municipality (he was an engineer in the sanitation department), and there was one drawer in their bedroom whose contents she didn't know, for he always kept it locked and the key with him.

'I'll lend you a wonderful book,' Margaret said. 'It's called *Truth in the Mind*, and it's full of the most astounding insight. It's by this marvellous man who founded an ashram in Shropshire. Shafi!' She called suddenly for the servant, but of course he couldn't hear, because the servants' quarters were right at the back, and the old man now spent most of his time there, sitting on a bed and having his legs massaged by a granddaughter.

'I'll call him,' Elizabeth said, and got up eagerly.

She went back into the stone-cold house and out again at the other end. Here were the kitchen and the crowded servants' quarters. Margaret could never bear to dismiss anyone, and even the servants who were no longer in her employ continued to enjoy her hospitality. Each servant had a great number of dependants, so this part of the house was a little colony of its own, with a throng of people outside the rows of peeling hutments, chatting or sleeping or quarrelling or squatting on the ground to cook their meals and wash their children. Margaret enjoyed coming out there, mostly to advise and scold – but Elizabeth felt shy, and she kept her eyes lowered.

'Shafi,' she said, 'Memsahib is calling you.'

The old man mumbled furiously. He did not like to have

his rest disturbed and he did not like Elizabeth. In fact, he did not like any of the visitors. He was the oldest servant in the house – so old that he had been Arthur's bearer when Arthur was still a bachelor and serving in the districts, almost forty years ago.

Still grumbling, he followed Elizabeth back to the veranda. 'Tea, Shafi!' Margaret called out cheerfully when she saw them coming.

'Not time for tea yet,' he said.

She laughed. She loved it when her servants answered her back; she felt it showed a sense of ease and equality and family irritability, which was only another side of family devotion. 'What a cross old man you are,' she said. 'And just look at you – how dirty.'

He looked down at himself. He was indeed very dirty. He was unshaven and unwashed, and from beneath the rusty remains of what had once been a uniform coat there peeped out a ragged assortment of grey vests and torn pullovers into which he had bundled himself for the winter.

'It's hard to believe,' Margaret said, 'that this old scarecrow is a terrible, terrible snob. You know why he doesn't like you, Elizabeth? Because you're married to an Indian.'

Elizabeth smiled and blushed. She admired Margaret's forthrightness.

'He thinks you've let down the side. He's got very firm principles. As a matter of fact, he thinks I've let down the side too. All his life he's longed to work for a real memsahib, the sort that entertains other memsahibs to tea. Never forgave Arthur for bring home little Margaret.'

The old man's face began working strangely. His mouth and stubbled cheeks twitched, and then sounds started coming that rose and fell – now distinct, now only a mutter and a drone – like waves of the sea. He spoke partly in English and partly in Hindi, and it was some time before it could be made out that he was telling some story of the old days – a party at the Gymkhana Club for which he had been hired as an additional waiter. The sahib who had given the party, a Major Waterford, had paid him not only his wages but also a tip of two rupees. He elaborated on this for some time, dwelling on the virtues of Major Waterford and also of Mrs Waterford, a very fine lady who had made her servants wear white gloves when they served at table.

'Very grand,' said Margaret with an easy laugh. 'You run along now and get our tea.'

'There was a little missie sahib too. She had two ayahs, and every year they were given four saris and one shawl for the winter.'

'Tea, Shafi,' Margaret said more firmly, so that the old man, who knew every inflection in his mistress's voice, saw it was time to be off.

'Arthur and I've spoiled him outrageously,' Margaret said. 'We spoiled all our servants.'

'God will reward you,' said Babaji.

'We could never think of them as servants, really. They were more our friends. I've learned such a lot from Indian servants. They're usually rogues, but underneath all that they have beautiful characters. They're very religious, and they have a lot of philosophy – you'd be surprised. We've had some fascinating conversations. You ought to keep a servant, Elizabeth – I've told you so often.' When she saw Elizabeth was about to answer something, she said, 'And don't say you can't afford it. Your Raju earns enough, I'm sure, and they're very cheap.'

'We don't need one,' Elizabeth said apologetically. There

were just the two of them, and they lived in two small rooms. Sometimes Raju also took it into his head that they needed a servant, and once he had even gone to the extent of hiring an undernourished little boy from the hills. On the second day, however, the boy was discovered rifling the pockets of Raju's trousers while their owner was having his bath, so he was dismissed on the spot. To Elizabeth's relief, no attempt at replacing him was ever made.

'If you had one you could get around a bit more,' Margaret said. 'Instead of always having to dance attendance on your husband's mealtimes. I suppose that's why you don't want to take those poor little children to Agra?'

'It's not that I don't want to,' Elizabeth said hopelessly.

'Quite apart from anything else, you ought to be longing to get around and see the country. What do you know, what will you ever know, if you stay in one place all the time?'

'One day you will come and visit me in Almora,' Babaji said.

'Oh Babaji, I'd love to!' Elizabeth exclaimed.

'Beautiful,' he said, spreading his hands to describe it all. 'The mountains, trees, clouds . . . ' Words failed him, and he could only spread his hands farther and smile into the distance, as if he saw a beautiful vision there.

Elizabeth smiled with him. She saw it too, although she had never been there: the mighty mountains, the grandeur and the peace, the abode of Shiva where he sat with the rivers flowing from his hair. She longed to go, and to so many other places she had heard and read about. But the only place away from Delhi where she had ever been was Ankhpur, to stay with Raju's family.

Margaret began to tell her about all the places she had been to. She and Arthur had been posted from district to district, in many different parts of the country, but even that hadn't been enough for her. She had to see everything. She had no fears about travelling on her own, and had spent weeks tramping around in the mountains, with a shawl thrown over her shoulders and a stick held firmly in her hand. She had travelled many miles by any mode of transport available – train, bus, cycle, rickshaw, or even bullock cart – in order to see some little-known and almost inaccessible temple or cave or tomb: once she had sprained her ankle and lain all alone for a week in a derelict rest-house, deserted except for one decrepit old watchman, who had shared his meals with her.

'That's the way to get to know a country,' she declared. Her cheeks were flushed with the pleasure of remembering everything she had done.

Elizabeth agreed with her. Yet although she herself had done none of these things, she did not feel that she was on that account cut off from all knowledge. There was much to be learned from living with Raju's family in Ankhpur, much to be learned from Raju himself. Yes, he was her India! She felt like laughing when this thought came to her. But it was true.

'Your trouble is,' Margaret suddenly said, 'you let Raju bully you. He's got something of that in his character – don't contradict. I've studied him. If you were to stand up to him more firmly, you'd both be happier.'

Again Elizabeth wanted to laugh. She thought of the nice times she and Raju often had together. He had invented a game of cricket that they could play in their bedrooms between the steel almira and the opposite wall. They played it with a rubber ball and a hairbrush, and three steps made a run. Raju's favourite trick was to hit the ball under the bed, and while she lay flat on the floor groping for it he made run after run, exhorting her with mocking cries of 'Hurry up! Where is it? Can't you find it?' His eyes glittered with the pleasure of winning; his shirt was off, and drops of perspiration trickled down his smooth, dark chest.

'You should want to do something for those poor children!' Margaret shouted.

'I do want to. You know I do.'

'I don't know anything of the sort. All I see is you leading an utterly useless, selfish life. I'm disappointed in you, Elizabeth. When I first met you, I had such high hopes of you. I thought, ah, here at last is a serious person. But you're not serious at all. You're as frivolous as any of those girls that come here and spend their days playing mahjong.'

Elizabeth was ashamed. The worst of it was she really had once been a serious person. She had been a schoolteacher in England, and devoted to her work and her children, on whom she had spent far more time and care than was necessary in the line of duty. And, over and above that, she had put in several evenings a week visiting old people who had no one to look after them. But all that had come to an end once she met Raju.

'It's criminal to be in India and not be committed,' Margaret went on. 'There isn't much any single person can do, of course, but to do nothing at all – no, I wouldn't be able to sleep at nights.'

And Elizabeth slept not only well but happily, blissfully! Sometimes she turned on the light just for the pleasure of looking at Raju lying beside her. He slept like a child, with the pillow bundled under his cheek and his mouth slightly open, as if he were smiling.

'But what are you laughing at!' Margaret shouted.

'I'm not, Margaret.' She hastily composed her face. She

hadn't been aware of it, but probably she had been smiling at the image of Raju asleep.

Margaret abruptly pushed back her chair. Her face was red and her hair dishevelled, as if she had been in a fight. Elizabeth half-rose in her chair, aghast at whatever it was she had done and eager to undo it.

'Don't follow me,' Margaret said. 'If you do, I know I'm going to behave badly and I'll feel terrible afterwards. You can stay here or you can go home, but *don't follow me.*'

She went inside the house, and the screen door banged after her. Elizabeth sank down into her chair and looked helplessly at Babaji.

He had remained as serene as ever. Gently he rocked himself in his chair. The winter afternoon was drawing to its close, and the sun, caught between two trees, was beginning to contract into one concentrated area of gold. Though the light was failing, the garden remained bright and gay with all its marigolds, its phlox, its pansies and its sweet peas. Babaji enjoyed it all. He sat wrapped in his woollen shawl, with his feet warm in thick knitted socks and sandals.

'She is a hot-tempered lady,' he said, smiling and forgiving. 'But good, good.'

'Oh, I know,' Elizabeth said. 'She's an angel. I feel so bad that I should have upset her. Do you think I ought to go after her?'

'A heart of gold,' said Babaji.

'I know it.' Elizabeth bit her lip in vexation at herself.

Shafi came out with the tea tray. Elizabeth removed some books to clear the little table for him, and Babaji said, 'Ah,' in pleasurable anticipation. But Shafi did not put the tray down.

'Where is she?' he said.

'It's all right, Shafi. She's just coming. Put it down, please.'

The old man nodded and smiled in a cunning, superior way. He clutched his tray more tightly and turned back into the house. He had difficulty in walking, not only because he was old and infirm but also because the shoes he wore were too big for him and had no laces.

'Shafi!' Elizabeth called after him. 'Babaji wants his tea!' But he did not even turn round. He walked straight up to Margaret's bedroom and kicked the door and shouted, 'I've brought it!'

Elizabeth hurried after him. She felt nervous about going into Margaret's bedroom after having been so explicitly forbidden to follow her. But Margaret only looked up briefly from where she was sitting on her bed, reading a letter, and said, 'Oh, it's you,' and 'Shut the door.' When he had put down the tea, Shafi went out again and the two of them were left alone.

Margaret's bedroom was quite different from the rest of the house. The other rooms were all bare and cold, with a minimum of furniture standing around on the stone floors; there were a few isolated pictures hung up here and there on the whitewashed walls, but nothing more intimate than portraits of Mahatma Gandhi and Sri Ramakrishna and a photograph of the inmates of Mother Teresa's Home. But Margaret's room was crammed with a lot of comfortable, solid old furniture, dominated by the big double bed in the centre, which was covered with a white bedcover and a mosquito curtain on the top like a canopy. A log fire burned in the grate, and there were photographs everywhere – family photos of Arthur and Margaret, of Margaret as a little girl, and of her parents and her sister and her school and her friends. The stale smell of food pervading the rest of the house stopped short of this room, which was scented very pleasantly by woodsmoke and lavender water. There was an umbrella stand that held several alpenstocks, a tennis racket and a hockey stick.

'It's from my sister,' Margaret said, indicating the letter she was reading. 'She lives out in the country and they've been snowed under again. She's got a pub.'

'How lovely.'

'Yes, it's a lovely place. She's always wanted me to come and run it with her. But I couldn't live in England any more, I couldn't bear it.'

'Yes, I know what you mean.'

'What do you know? You've only been here a few years. Pour the tea, there's a dear.'

'Babaji was wanting a cup.'

'To hell with Babaji.'

She took off her sandals and lay down on the bed, leaning against some fat pillows that she had propped against the headboard. Elizabeth had noticed before that Margaret was always more relaxed in her own room than anywhere else. Not all her visitors were allowed into this room – in fact, only a chosen few. Strangely enough, Raju had been one of these when he and Elizabeth had stayed in the house. But he had never properly appreciated the privilege; either he sat on the edge of a chair and made signs to Elizabeth to go or he wandered restlessly round the room, looking at all the photographs or taking out the tennis racket and executing imaginary services with it; till Margaret told him to sit down and not make them all nervous, and then he looked sulky and made even more overt signs to Elizabeth.

'I brought my sister out here once,' Margaret said. 'But she couldn't stand it. Couldn't stand anything – the climate, the water, the food. Everything made her ill. There are people like that. Of course, I'm just the opposite. You like it here too, don't you?'

'Very, very much.'

'Yes, I can see you're happy.'

Margaret looked at her so keenly that Elizabeth tried to turn away her face slightly. She did not want anyone to see too much of her tremendous happiness. She felt somewhat ashamed of herself for having it – not only because she knew she didn't deserve it but also because she did not consider herself quite the right kind of person to have it. She had been over thirty when she met Raju, and had not expected much more out of life than had up till then been given to her.

Margaret lit a cigarette. She never smoked except in her own room. She puffed slowly, luxuriously. Suddenly she said, 'He doesn't like me, does he?'

'Who?'

'"Who"?' she repeated impatiently. 'Your Raju, of course.'

Elizabeth flushed with embarrassment. 'How you talk, Margaret,' she murmured deprecatingly, not knowing what else to say.

'I know he doesn't,' Margaret said. 'I can always tell.'

She sounded so sad that Elizabeth wished she could lie to her and say that no, Raju loved her just as everyone else did. But she could not bring herself to it. She thought of the way he usually spoke of Margaret. He called her by rude names and made coarse jokes about her, at which he laughed like a schoolboy and tried to make Elizabeth laugh with him; and the terrible thing was sometimes she did laugh, not because she wanted to or because what he said amused her but because it was he who urged her to, and she always found it difficult to refuse him anything. Now when she thought of this compliant laughter of hers she was filled with anguish, and she began unconsciously to wring her hands, the way she always did at such secretly appalling moments.

But Margaret was having thoughts of her own, and was smiling to herself. She said, 'You know what was my happiest time of all in India? About ten years ago, when I went to stay in Swami Vishwananda's ashram.'

Elizabeth was intensely relieved at the change of subject, though somewhat puzzled by its abruptness.

'We bathed in the river and we walked in the mountains. It was a time of such freedom, such joy. I've never felt like that before or since. I didn't have a care in the world and I felt so – light. I can't describe it – as if my feet didn't touch the ground.'

'Yes, yes!' Elizabeth said eagerly, for she thought she recognized the feeling.

'In the evenings we all sat with Swamiji. We talked about everything under the sun. He laughed and joked with us, and sometimes he sang. I don't know what happened to me when he sang. The tears came pouring down my face, but I was so happy I thought my heart would melt away.'

'Yes,' Elizabeth said again.

'That's him over there.' She nodded towards a small framed photograph on the dressing-table. Elizabeth picked it up. He did not look different from the rest of India's holy men – naked to the waist, with long hair and burning eyes.

'Not that you can tell much from a photo,' Margaret said. She held out her hand for it, and then she looked at it herself, with a very young expression on her face. 'He was such fun to be with, always full of jokes and games. When I was with him, I used to feel – I don't know – like a flower or a bird.' She laughed gaily, and Elizabeth with her.

'Does Raju make you feel like that?'

Elizabeth stopped laughing and looked down into her lap. She tried to make her face very serious so as not to give herself away.

'Indian men have such marvellous eyes,' Margaret said. 'When they look at you, you can't help feeling all young and nice. But of course your Raju thinks I'm just a fat, ugly old memsahib.'

'Margaret, Margaret!'

Margaret stubbed out her cigarette and, propelling herself with her heavy legs, swung down from the bed. 'And there's poor old Babaji waiting for his tea.'

She poured it for him and went out with the cup. Elizabeth went after her. Babaji was just as they had left him, except that now the sun, melting away between the trees behind him, was even more intensely gold and provided a heavenly background, as if to a saint in a picture, as he sat there at peace in his rocking chair.

Margaret fussed over him. She stirred his tea and she arranged his shawl more securely over his shoulders. Then she said, 'I've got an idea, Babaji.' She hooked her foot round a stool and drew it close to his chair and sank down on it, one hand laid on his knee. 'You and I'll take those children up to Agra. Would you like that? A little trip?' She looked up into his face and was eager and bright. 'We'll have a grand time. We'll hire a bus, and we'll have singing and games all the way. You'll love it.' She squeezed his knee in anticipatory joy, and he smiled at her and his thin old hand came down on the top of her head in a gesture of affection or blessing.

Desecration

It is more than ten years since Sofia committed suicide in the hotel room in Mohabbatpur. At the time, it was a great local scandal, but now almost no one remembers the incident or the people involved in it. The Raja Sahib died shortly afterwards – people said it was of grief and bitterness – and Bakhtawar Singh was transferred to another district. The present Superintendent of Police is a mild-mannered man who likes to spend his evenings at home playing card games with his teenage daughters.

The hotel in Mohabbatpur no longer exists. It was sold a few months after Sofia was found there, changed hands several times and was recently pulled down to make room for a new cinema. This will back on to the old cinema, which is still there, still playing ancient Bombay talkies. The Raja Sahib's house also no longer exists. It was demolished because the land on which it stood has become very valuable, and has been declared an industrial area. Many factories and workshops have come up in recent years.

When the Raja Sahib had first gone to live there with Sofia, there had been nothing except his own house, with a view over the ruined fort and the barren plain beyond it. In the distance there was a little patch of villagers' fields and, huddled out of sight, the village itself. Inside their big house, the Raja Sahib and Sofia had led very isolated lives. This was by choice – his choice. It was as if he had carried her away to this spot with the express purpose of having her to himself, of feasting on his possession of her.

Although she was much younger than he was – more than thirty years younger – she seemed perfectly happy to live there alone with him. But in any case she was the sort of person who exudes happiness. No one knew where the Raja Sahib had met and married her. No one really knew anything about her, except that she was a Muslim (he, of course, was a Hindu) and that she had had a good convent education in Calcutta – or was it Delhi? She seemed to have no one in the world except the Raja Sahib. It was generally thought that she was partly Afghan, perhaps even with a dash of Russian. She certainly did not look entirely Indian; she had light eyes and broad cheekbones and a broad brow. She was graceful and strong, and at times she laughed a great deal, as if wanting to show off her youth and high spirits, not to mention her magnificent teeth.

Even then, however, during their good years, she suffered from nervous prostrations. At such times the Raja Sahib sat by her bedside in a darkened room. If necessary, he stayed awake all night and held her hand (she clutched his). Sometimes this went on for two or three weeks at a time, but his patience was inexhaustible. It often got very hot in the room; the house stood unprotected on that barren plain, and there was not enough electricity for air-conditioning – hardly even enough for the fan that sluggishly churned the hot air. Her attacks always seemed to occur during the very hot months, especially during the dust storms, when the landscape all around was blotted out by a pall of desert dust and the sky hung down low and yellow.

But when the air cleared, so did her spirits. The heat continued, but she kept all the shutters closed, and sprinkled water and rose essence on the marble floors and on the scented grass mats hung around the verandas. When night fell, the house was opened to allow the cooler air to enter. She and the Raja Sahib would go up on the roof. They lit candles in coloured glass chimneys and read out the Raja Sahib's verse dramas. Around midnight the servants would bring up their dinner, which consisted of many elaborate dishes, and sometimes they would also have a bottle of French wine from the Raja Sahib's cellar. The dark earth below and the sky above were both silver from the reflection of the moon and the incredible number of stars shining up there. It was so silent that the two of them might as well have been alone in the world – which of course was just what the Raja Sahib wanted.

Sitting on the roof of his house, he was certainly monarch of all he surveyed, such as it was. His family had taken possession of this land during a time of great civil strife some hundred and fifty years before. It was only a few barren acres with some impoverished villages thrown in, but the family members had built themselves a little fort and had even assumed a royal title, though they weren't much more than glorified landowners. They lived like all the other landowners, draining what taxes they could out of their tenant villagers. They always needed money for their own living, which became very sophisticated, especially when they began to spend more and more time in the big cities like Bombay, Calcutta, or even London. At the beginning of the century, when the fort became too rough and dilapidated to live in, the house was built. It was in a mixture of Moghul and Gothic styles, with many galleries and high rooms closed in by arched verandas. It had been built at great cost, but until the Raja Sahib moved in with Sofia it had usually remained empty except for the ancestral servants.

On those summer nights on the roof, it was always she who read out the Raja Sahib's plays. He sat and listened and watched her. She wore coloured silks and the family jewellery as an appropriate costume in which to declaim his blank verse (all his plays were in English blank verse). Sometimes she couldn't understand what she was declaiming, and sometimes it was so high-flown that she burst out laughing. He smiled with her and said, 'Go on, go on.' He sat cross-legged smoking his hookah, like any peasant; his clothes were those of a peasant too. Anyone coming up and seeing him would not have thought he was the owner of this house, the husband of Sofia – or indeed the author of all that romantic blank verse. But he was not what he looked or pretended to be. He was a man of considerable education, who had lived for years abroad, had loved the opera and theatre, and had had many cultivated friends. Later – whether through general disgust or a particular disappointment, no one knew – he had turned his back on it all. Now he liked to think of himself as just an ordinary peasant landlord.

The third character in this story, Bakhtawar Singh, really did come from a peasant background. He was an entirely self-made man. Thanks to his efficiency and valour, he had risen rapidly in the service and was now the district Superintendent of Police (known as the SP). He had been responsible for the capture of some notorious dacoits. One of these – the uncrowned king of the countryside for almost twenty years – he had himself trapped in a ravine and shot in the head with his revolver, and he had taken the body in his jeep to be displayed outside police headquarters. This deed and others like it had made his name a terror among dacoits and other proscribed criminals. His own men feared him no less, for he was known as a ruthless disciplinarian. But he had a softer side to him. He was terribly fond of women and, wherever he was posted, would find himself a mistress very quickly – usually more than one. He had a wife and family, but they did not play much of a role in his life. All his interests lay elsewhere. His one other interest besides women was Indian classical music, for which he had a very subtle ear.

Once a year the Raja Sahib gave a dinner party for the local gentry. These were officials from the town – the District Magistrate, the Superintendent of Police, the Medical Officer and the rest – for whom it was the greatest event of the social calendar. The Raja Sahib himself would have gladly dispensed with the occasion, but it was the only company Sofia ever had, apart from himself. For weeks beforehand, she got the servants ready – cajoling rather than commanding them, for she spoke sweetly to everyone always – and had all the china and silver taken out. When the great night came, she sparkled with excitement. The guests were provincial, dreary, unrefined people, but she seemed not to notice that. She made them feel that their presence was a tremendous honour for her. She ran around to serve them and rallied her servants to carry in a succession of dishes and wines. Inspired by her example, the Raja Sahib also rose to the occasion. He was an excellent raconteur and entertained his guests with witty anecdotes and Urdu couplets, and sometimes even with quotations from the English poets. They applauded him not because they always understood what he was saying but because he was the Raja Sahib. They were delighted with the entertainment, and with themselves for having risen high enough in the world to be invited. There were not many women present, for most of the wives were too uneducated to be brought out into society. Those that came sat very still in their best georgette saris and cast furtive glances at their husbands.

After Bakhtawar Singh was posted to the district as the new SP, he was invited to the Raja Sahib's dinner. He came alone, his wife being unfit for society, and as soon as he entered the house it was obvious that he was a man of superior personality. He had a fine figure, intelligent eyes and a bristling moustache. He moved with pride, even with some pomp – certainly a man who knew his own value. He was not put out in the least by the grand surroundings, but enjoyed everything as if he were entirely accustomed to such entertainment. He also appeared to understand and enjoy his host's anecdotes and poetry. When the Raja Sahib threw in a bit of Shakespeare, he confessed frankly that he could not follow it, but when his host translated and explained, he applauded that too, in real appreciation.

After dinner, there was musical entertainment. The male guests adjourned to the main drawing-room, which was an immensely tall room extending the entire height of the house with a glass rotunda. Here they reclined on Bokhara rugs and leaned against silk bolsters. The ladies had been sent home in motor cars. It would not have been fitting for them to be present, because the musicians were not from a respectable class. Only Sofia was emancipated enough to overlook this restriction. At the first party that Bakhtawar Singh attended, the principal singer was a well-known prostitute from Mohabbatpur. She had a strong, well-trained voice, as well as a handsome presence. Bakhtawar Singh did not take his eyes off her. He sat and swayed his head and exclaimed in rapture at her particularly fine modulations. For his sake, she displayed the most delicate subtleties of her art, laying them out like bait to see if he would respond to them, and he cried out as if in passion or pain. Then she smiled. Sofia was also greatly moved. At one point, she turned to Bakhtawar Singh and said, 'How good she is.' He turned his face to her and nodded, unable to speak for emotion. She was amazed to see tears in his eyes.

Next day she was still thinking about those tears. She told her husband about it, and he said, 'Yes, he liked the music, but he liked the singer, too.'

'What do you mean?' Sofia asked. When the Raja Sahib laughed, she cried, 'Tell me!' and pummelled his chest with her fists.

'I mean,' he said, catching her hands and holding them tight, 'that they will become friends.'

'She will be his mistress?' Sofia asked, opening her eyes wide.

The Raja Sahib laughed with delight. 'Where did you learn such a word? In the convent?'

'How do you know?' she pursued. 'No, you must tell me! Is he that type of man?'

'What type?' he said, teasing her.

The subject intrigued her, and she continued to think about it to herself. As always when she brooded about any- thing, she became silent and withdrawn and sat for hours on the veranda, staring out over the dusty plain; 'Sofia, Sofia, what are you thinking?' the Raja Sahib asked her. She smiled and shook her head. He looked into her strange, light eyes. There was something mysterious about them. Even when she was at her most playful and affectionate, her eyes seemed always to be looking elsewhere, into some different and distant landscape. It was impossible to tell what she was thinking. Perhaps she was not thinking about anything at all, but the distant gaze gave her the appearance of keeping part of herself hidden. This drove the Raja Sahib crazy with love. He wanted to pursue her into the innermost recesses of her nature, and yet at the same time he respected that privacy of hers and left her to herself when she wanted. This happened often; she would sit and brood and also roam around the house and the land in a strange, restless way. In the end, though, she would always come back to him and nestle against his thin, grey-matted chest and seem to be happy there.

For several days after the party, Sofia was in one of these moods. She wandered around the garden, though it was very hot outside. There was practically no shade, because nothing could be made to grow for lack of water. She idly kicked at pieces of stone, some of which were broken garden statuary. When it got too hot, she did not return to the house but took shelter in the little ruined fort. It was very dark inside there, with narrow underground passages and winding steep stairs, some of which were broken. Sometimes a bat would flit out from some crevice. Sofia was not afraid; the place was familiar to her. But one day, as she sat in one of the narrow stone passages, she heard voices from the roof. She raised her head and listened. Something terrible seemed to be going on up there. Sofia climbed the stairs, steadying herself against the dank wall. Her heart was beating as loudly as those sounds from above. When she got to the top of the stairs and emerged on to the roof, she saw two men. One of them was Bakhtawar Singh. He was beating the other man, who was also a policeman, around the neck and head with his fists. When the man fell, he kicked him and then hauled him up and beat him more, Sofia gave a cry. Bakhtawar Singh turned his head and saw her. His eyes looked into hers for a moment, and how different they were from that other time when they had been full of tears!

'Get out!' he told the policeman. The man's sobs continued to be heard as he made his way down the stairs. Sofia did not know what to do. Although she wanted to flee, she stood and stared at Bakhtawar Singh. He was quite calm. He put on his khaki bush jacket, careful to adjust the collar and sleeves so as to look smart. He explained that the man had been derelict in his duties and, to escape discipline, had run away and hidden here in the fort. But Bakhtawar Singh had tracked him down. He apologized for trespassing on the Raja Sahib's property and also – here he became courtly and inclined his body towards Sofia – if he had in any way upset and disturbed her. It was not a scene he would have wished a lady to witness.

'There is blood on your hand,' she said.

He looked at it. He made a wry face and then wiped it off. (Was it his own or the other man's?) Again he adjusted his jacket, and he smoothed his hair. 'Do you often come here?' he asked, indicating the stairs and then politely standing aside to let her go first. She started down, and looked back to see if he was following.

'I come every day,' she said.

It was easy for her to go down the dark stairs, which were familiar to her. But he had to grope his way down very carefully, afraid of stumbling. She jumped down the last two steps and waited for him in the open sunlight.

'You come here all alone?' he asked. 'Aren't you afraid?'

'Of what?'

He didn't answer but walked round the back of the fort. Here his horse stood waiting for him, grazing among nettles.

He jumped on its back and lightly flicked its flanks, and it cantered off as if joyful to be bearing him.

That night Sofia was very restless, and in the morning her face had the clouded, suffering look that presaged one of her attacks. But when the Raja Sahib wanted to darken the room and make her lie down, she insisted that she was well. She got up, she bathed, she dressed. He was surprised – usually she succumbed very quickly to the first signs of an attack – but now she even said that she wanted to go out. He was very pleased with her and kissed her, as if to reward her for her pluck. But later that day, when she came in again, she did have an attack, and he had to sit by her side and hold her hand and chafe her temples. She wept at his goodness. She kissed the hand that was holding hers. He looked into her strange eyes and said, 'Sofia, Sofia, what are you thinking?' But she quickly covered her eyes, so that he could not look into them. Then he had to soothe her all over again.

Whenever he had tried to make her see a doctor, she had resisted him. She said all she needed was him sitting by her and she would get well by herself, and it did happen that way. But now she told him that she had heard of a very good doctor in Mohabbatpur, who specialized in nervous diseases. The drive was long and wearying, and she insisted that there was no need for the Raja Sahib to go there with her; she could go by herself, with the car and chauffeur. They had a loving quarrel about it, and it was only when she said very well, in that case she would not go at all, would not take medical treatment, that he gave way. So now once a week she was driven to Mohabbatpur by herself.

The Raja Sahib awaited her homecoming impatiently, and the evenings of those days were like celebrations. They sat on the roof, with candles and wine, and she told him about her drive to Mohabbatpur and what the doctor had said. The Raja Sahib usually had a new passage from his latest blank verse drama for her to read. She would start off well enough, but soon she would be overcome by laughter and have to hide her face behind the pages of his manuscript. And he would smile with her and say, 'Yes, I know, it's all a lot of nonsense.'

'No, no!' she cried. Even though she couldn't understand a good deal of what she was reading, she knew that it expressed his romantic nature and his love for her, which were both as deep as a well. She said, 'It is only I who am stupid and read so badly.' She pulled herself together and went on reading, till made helpless with laughter again.

There was something strange about her laughter. It came bubbling out, as always, as if from an overflow of high spirits, but now her spirits seemed almost too high, almost hysterical. Her husband listened to these new notes and was puzzled by them. He could not make up his mind whether the treatment was doing her good or not.

The Raja Sahib was very kind to his servants, but if any of them did anything to offend him, he was quick to dismiss him. One of his bearers, a man who had been in his employ for twenty years, got drunk one night. This was by no means an unusual occurrence among the servants; the house was in a lonely spot, with no amusements, but there was plenty of cheap liquor available from the village. Usually the servants slept off the effects in their quarters, but this bearer came staggering up on the roof to serve the Raja Sahib and Sofia. There was a scene. He fell and was dragged away by the other servants, but he resisted violently, shouting frightful obscenities, so that Sofia had to put her hands over her ears. The Raja Sahib's face was contorted with fury. The man was dismissed instantly, and when he came back the next day,

wretchedly sober, begging pardon and pleading for reinstate-
ment, the Raja Sahib would not hear him. Everyone felt sorry
for the man, who had a large family and was, except for these
occasional outbreaks, a sober, hard-working person. Sofia
felt sorry for him too. He threw himself at her feet, and so
did his wife and many children. They all sobbed, and Sofia
sobbed with them. She promised to try and prevail upon the
Raja Sahib.

She said everything she could – in a rushed, breathless
voice, fearing he would not let her finish – and she did not
take her eyes off her husband's face as she spoke. She was
horrified by what she saw there. The Raja Sahib had very thin
lips, and when he was angry he bit them in so tightly that they
quite disappeared. He did it now, and he looked so stern and
unforgiving that she felt she was not talking to her husband
at all but to a gaunt and bitter old man who cared nothing
for her. Suddenly she gave a cry, and just as the servant had
thrown himself at her feet, so she now prostrated herself at
the Raja Sahib's. 'Forgive!' she cried. 'Forgive!' It was as if
she were begging forgiveness for everyone who was weak and
had sinned. The Raja Sahib tried to make her rise, but she lay
flat on the ground, trying over and over again to bring out
the word 'Forgive' and not succeeding because of her sobs.
At last he managed to help her up; he led her to the bed and
waited there till she was calm again. But he was so enraged
by the cause of this attack that the servant and his family had
to leave immediately.

She always dismissed the car and chauffeur near the doctor's
clinic. She gave the chauffeur quite a lot of money – for his
food, she said – and told him to meet her in the same place
in the evening. She explained that she had to spend the day

under observation at the clinic. After the first few times, no explanation was necessary. The chauffeur held out his hand for the money and disappeared until the appointed time. Sofia drew up her sari to veil her face and got into a cycle rickshaw. The place Bakhtawar Singh had chosen for them was a rickety two-storey hotel, with an eating shop downstairs. It was in a very poor, outlying, forgotten part of town, where there was no danger of ever meeting an acquaintance. At first Sofia had been shy about entering the hotel, but as time went on she became bolder. No one ever looked at her or spoke to her. If she was the first to arrive, the key was silently handed to her. She felt secure that the hotel people knew nothing about her, and certainly had never seen her face, which she kept veiled till she was upstairs and the door closed behind her.

In the beginning, he sometimes arrived before her. Then he lay down on the bed, which was the only piece of furniture besides a bucket and a water jug, and was at once asleep. He always slept on his stomach, with one cheek pressed into the pillow. She would come in and stand and look at his dark, muscular, naked back. It had a scar on it, from a knife wound. She lightly ran her finger along this scar, and if that did not wake him, she unwound his loosely tied dhoti, which was all he was wearing. That awakened him immediately.

He was strange to her. That scar on his back was not the only one; there were others on his chest and an ugly long one on his left thigh, sustained during a prison riot. She wanted to know all about his violent encounters, and about his boyhood, his upward struggle, even his low origins. She often asked him about the woman singer at the dinner party. Was it true what the Raja Sahib had said – that he had liked her? Had he sought her out afterwards? He did not deny it, but laughed as at a pleasant memory. Sofia wanted to know more and more. What was it like to be with a woman like that? Had there been others? How many, and what was it like with all of them? He was amused by her curiosity and did not mind satisfying it, often with demonstrations.

Although he had had many women, they had mostly been prostitutes and singers. Sometimes he had had affairs with the wives of other police officers, but these too had been rather coarse, uneducated women. Sofia was his first girl of good family. Her refinement intrigued him. He loved watching her dress, brush her hair, treat her skin with lotions. He liked to watch her eat. But sometimes it seemed as if he deliberately wanted to violate her delicacy. For instance, he knew that she hated the coarse, hot lentils that he loved from his boyhood. He would order great quantities, with coarse bread, and cram the food into his mouth and then into hers, though it burned her palate. As their intimacy progressed, he also made her perform acts that he had learned from prostitutes. It seemed that he could not reach far enough into her, physically and in every other way. Like the Raja Sahib, he was intrigued by the look in her foreign eyes, but he wanted to seek out that mystery and expose it, as all the rest of her was exposed to him.

The fact that she was a Muslim had a strange fascination for him. Here too he differed from the Raja Sahib who, as an educated nobleman, had transcended barriers of caste and community. But for Bakhtawar Singh these were still strong. All sorts of dark superstitions remained embedded in his mind. He questioned her about things he had heard whispered in the narrow Hindu alleys he came from – the rites of circumcision, the eating of unclean flesh, what Muslims did with virgin girls. She laughed, never having heard of such things. But when she assured him that they could not be true, he nodded as if he knew better. He pointed to one of his scars, sustained during a Hindu–Muslim riot that he had suppressed. He had witnessed several such riots and knew the sort of atrocities committed in them. He told her what he had seen Muslim men do to Hindu women. Again she would not believe him. But she begged him not to go on; she put her hands over her ears, pleading with him. But he forced her hands down again and went on telling her, and laughed at her reaction. 'That's what they did,' he assured her. '*Your* brothers. It's all true.' And then he struck her, playfully but quite hard, with the flat of his hand.

All week, every week, she waited for her day in Mohabbatpur to come round. She was restless and she began to make trips into the nearby town. It was the usual type of district town, with two cinemas, a jail, a church, temples and mosques, with a Civil Lines, where the government officers lived. Sofia now began to come here to visit the officers' wives whom she had been content to see just once a year at her dinner party. Now she sought them out frequently. She played with their children and designed flower patterns for them to embroider. All the time her thoughts were elsewhere; she was waiting for it to be time to leave. Then, with hurried farewells, promises to come again soon, she climbed into her car and sat back. She told the chauffeur – the same man who took her to Mohabbatpur every week – to drive her through the Police Lines. First there were the policemen's barracks – a row of hutments, where men in vests and shorts could be seen oiling their beards and winding their turbans; they looked up in astonishment from these tasks as her saloon car drove past. She leaned back so as not to be seen, but when they had driven beyond the barracks and had reached the Police Headquarters, she looked eagerly out of the window again. Every time she hoped to get a glimpse of him, but it never happened; the car drove through and she did not dare to have it slow down. But there was one further treat in store, for beyond the offices were the residential houses of the police officers – the Assistant Deputy SP, the Deputy SP, the SP.

One day, she leaned forward and said to the chauffeur, 'Turn in.'

'In here?'

'Yes, yes!' she cried, mad with excitement.

It had been a sudden impulse – she had intended simply to drive past his house, as usual – but now she could not turn back, she had to see. She got out. It was an old house, built in the times of the British for their own SP, and now evidently inhabited by people who did not know how to look after such a place. A cow was tethered to a tree on what had once been a front lawn; the veranda was unswept and empty except for some broken crates. The house too was practically unfurnished. Sofia wandered through the derelict rooms, and it was only when she had penetrated to the inner courtyard that the life of the house began. Here there were children and noise and cooking smells. A woman came out of the kitchen and stared at her. She had a small child riding on her hip; she was perspiring, perhaps from the cooking fire, and a few strands of hair stuck to her forehead. She wore a plain and rather dirty cotton sari. She might have been his servant rather than his wife. She looked older than he did, tired and worn out. When Sofia asked whether this was the house of the Deputy SP, she shook her head wearily, without a smile. She told one of her children to point out the right house, and turned back into her kitchen with no further curiosity. A child began to cry.

At their next meeting, Sofia told Bakhtawar Singh what she had done. He was surprised and not angry, as she had feared, but amused. He could not understand her motives, but he did not puzzle himself about them. He was feeling terribly sleepy; he said he had been up all night (he didn't say why). It was stifling in the hotel room, and perspiration ran down his naked chest and back. It was also very noisy, for the room faced on to an inner yard, which was bounded on its opposite side by a cinema. From noon onward the entire courtyard boomed with the ancient sound track – it was a very poor cinema and could afford to play only very old films – filling their room with Bombay dialogue and music. Bakhtawar Singh seemed not to care about the heat or the noise. He slept through both. He always slept when he was tired; nothing could disturb him. It astonished Sofia, and so did his imperviousness to their surroundings – the horribly shabby room and smell of cheap oil frying from the eating shop downstairs. But now, after seeing his home, Sofia understood that he was used to comfortless surroundings; and she felt so sorry for him that she began to kiss him tenderly while he slept, as if wishing to make up to him for all his deprivations. He woke up and looked at her in surprise as she cried out, 'Oh, my poor darling!'

'Why?' he asked, not feeling poor at all.

She began for the first time to question him about his marriage. But he shrugged, bored by the subject. It was a marriage like every other, arranged by their two families when he and his wife were very young. It was all right; they had children – sons as well as daughters. His wife had plenty to do, he presumed she was content – and why shouldn't she be? She had a good house to live in, sufficient money for her household expenses, and respect as the wife of the SP. He laughed briefly. Yes, indeed, if she had anything to complain of he would like to know what it was. Sofia agreed with him. She even became indignant, thinking of his wife who had all these benefits and did not even care to keep a nice home for him. And not just his home – what about his wife herself? When she thought of that bedraggled figure, more a servant than a wife, Sofia's indignation rose – and with it her tender pity for him, so that again she embraced him and even spilled a few hot tears, which fell on to his naked chest and made him laugh with surprise.

A year passed, and it was again time for the Raja Sahib's annual party. As always, Sofia was terribly excited and began her preparations weeks beforehand. Only this time her excitement reached such a pitch that the Raja Sahib was worried. He tried to joke her out of it; he asked her whom was she expecting, what terribly important guest. Had she invited the President of India, or perhaps the King of Afghanistan? 'Yes, yes, the King of Afghanistan!' she cried, laughing but with that note of hysteria he always found so disturbing. Also she lost her temper for the first time with a servant; it was for nothing, for some trifle, and afterwards she was so contrite that she could not do enough to make it up to the man.

The party was, as usual, a great success. The Raja Sahib made everyone laugh with his anecdotes, and Bakhtawar Singh also told some stories, which everyone liked. The same singer from Mohabbatpur had been called, and she entertained with the same skill. And again – Sofia watched him – Bakhtawar Singh wept with emotion. She was deeply touched; he was manly to the point of violence (after all, he was a policeman), and yet what softness and delicacy there were in him. She revelled in the richness of his nature. The Raja Sahib must have been watching him too, because later, after the party, he told Sofia, 'Our friend enjoyed the musical entertainment again this year.'

'Of course,' Sofia said gravely. 'She is a very fine singer.'

The Raja Sahib said nothing, but there was something in his silence that told her he was having his own thoughts.

'If not,' she said, as if he had contradicted her, 'then why did you call for her again this year?'

'But of course,' he said. 'She is very fine.' And he chuckled to himself.

Then Sofia lost her temper with him – suddenly, violently, just as she had with the servant. The Raja Sahib was struck dumb with amazement, but the next moment he began to blame himself. He felt he had offended her with his insinuation, and he kissed her hands to beg her forgiveness. Her convent-bred delicacy amused him, but he adored it too.

She felt she could not wait for her day in Mohabbatpur to come round. The next morning, she called the chauffeur and gave him a note to deliver to the SP in his office. She had a special expressionless way of giving orders to the chauffeur, and he a special expressionless way of receiving them. She waited in the fort for Bakhtawar Singh to appear in answer to her summons, but the only person who came was the chauffeur, with her note back again. He explained that he had been unable to find the SP, who had not been in his office. Sofia felt a terrible rage rising inside her, and she had to struggle with herself not to vent it on the chauffeur. When the man had gone, she sank down against the stone wall and hid her face in her hands. She did not know what was happening to her. It was not only that her whole life had changed; she herself had changed and had become a different person, with emotions that were completely unfamiliar to her.

Unfortunately, when their day in Mohabbatpur at last came around, Bakhtawar Singh was late (this happened frequently now). She had to wait for him in the hot little room. The cinema show had started, and the usual dialogue and songs came from the defective sound track, echoing through courtyard and hotel. Tormented by this noise, by the heat and by her own thoughts, Sofia was now sure that he was with the singer. Probably he was enjoying himself so much that he had forgotten all about her and would not come.

But he did come, though two hours late. He was astonished by the way she clung to him, crying and laughing and trembling all over. He liked it, and kissed her in return. Just then the sound track burst into song. It was an old favourite – a song that had been on the lips of millions; everyone knew it and adored it. Bakhtawar Singh recognized it immediately and began to sing, '*O my heart, all he has left you is a splinter of himself to make you bleed!*' She drew away from him and saw him smiling with pleasure under his moustache as he sang. She cried out, 'Oh, you pig!'

It was like a blow in the face. He stopped singing immediately. The song continued on the sound track. They looked at each other. She put her hand to her mouth with fear – fear of the depths within her from which that word had arisen (never, never in her life had she uttered or thought such abuse), and fear of the consequences.

But after that moment's stunned silence, all he did was laugh. He took off his bush jacket and threw himself on the bed. 'What is the matter with you?' he asked. 'What happened?'

'Oh I don't know. I think it must be the heat.' She paused. 'And waiting for you,' she added, but in a voice so low she was not sure he had heard.

She lay down next to him. He said nothing more. The incident and her word of abuse seemed wiped out of his mind completely. She was so grateful for this that she too said nothing, asked no questions. She was content to forget her suspicions – or at least to keep them to herself and bear with them as best she could.

That night she had a dream. She dreamed everything was as it had been in the first years of her marriage, and she and the Raja Sahib as happy as they had been then. But then one night – they were together on the roof, by candle- and moon-light – he was stung by some insect that came flying out of the food they were eating. At first they took no notice, but the swelling got worse and worse, and by morning he was tossing in agony. His entire body was discoloured; he had become almost unrecognizable. There were several people around his bed, and one of them took Sofia aside and told her that the Raja Sahib would be dead within an hour. Sofia screamed out loud, but the next moment she woke up, for the Raja Sahib had turned on the light and was holding her in his arms. Yes, that very same Raja Sahib about whom she had just been dreaming, only he was not discoloured, not dying, but as he was always – her own husband, with grey-stubbled cheeks and sunken lips. She looked into his face for a moment and, fully awake now, she said, 'It's all right. I had a nightmare.' She tried to laugh it off. When he wanted to comfort her, she said again, 'It's all right,' with the same laugh and trying to keep the irritation out of her voice. 'Go to sleep,' she told him, and pretending to do so herself, she turned on her side away from him.

She continued to be haunted by the thought of the singer. Then she thought, if with one, why not with many? She her-self saw him for only those few hours a week. She did not know how he spent the rest of his time, but she was sure he did not spend much of it in his own home. It had had the look of a place whose master was mostly absent. And how could it be otherwise? Sofia thought of his wife – her neglected appearance, her air of utter weariness. Bakhtawar Singh could not be expected to waste himself there. But where did he go? In between their weekly meetings there was much time for him to go to many places, and much time for her to brood.

She got into the habit of summoning the chauffeur more frequently to take her into town. The ladies in the Civil Lines were always pleased to see her, and now she found more to talk about with them, for she had begun to take an interest in local gossip. They were experts on this, and were eager to tell her that the Doctor beat his wife, the Magistrate took bribes and the Deputy SP had venereal disease. And the SP? Sofia asked, busy threading an embroidery needle. Here they clapped their hands over their mouths and rolled their eyes around, as if at something too terrible, too scandalous to tell. Was he, Sofia asked – dropping the needle, so that she had to bend down to pick it up again – was he known to be an ... adventurous person? 'Oh, Oh! Oh!' they cried, and then they laughed because where to start, where to stop, telling of his adventures?

Sofia decided that it was her fault. It was his wife's fault first, of course, but now it was hers too. She had to arrange to be with him more often. Her first step was to tell the Raja Sahib that the doctor said she would have to attend the clinic several times a week. The Raja Sahib agreed at once. She felt so grateful that she was ready to give him more details, but he cut her short. He said that of course they must follow the doctor's advice, whatever it was. But the way he spoke – in a flat, resigned voice – disturbed her, so that she looked at him more attentively than she had for some time past. It struck her that he did not look well. Was he ill? Or was it only old age? He did look old, and emaciated too, she noticed, with his skinny, wrinkled neck. She felt very sorry for him and put out her hand to touch his cheek. She was amazed by his response. He seemed to tremble at her touch, and the expression on his face was transformed. She took him in her arms. He was trembling. 'Are you well?' she whispered to him anxiously.

'Oh yes!' he said in a joyful voice 'Very, very well.'

She continued to hold him. She said, 'Why aren't you writing any dramas for me these days?'

'I will write,' he said. 'As many as you like.' And then he clung to her, as if afraid to be let go from her embrace.

But when she told Bakhtawar Singh that they could now meet more frequently, he said it would be difficult for him. Of course he wanted to, he said – and how much! Here he turned to her and with sparkling eyes quoted a line of verse which said that if all the drops of water in the sea were hours of the day that he could spend with her, still they would not be sufficient for him. 'But . . . ' he added regretfully.

'Yes?' she asked, in a voice she tried to keep calm.

'Sh-h-h – listen,' he said, and put his hand over her mouth.

There was an old man saying the Muhammedan prayers in the next room. The hotel had only two rooms, one facing the courtyard and the other the street. This latter was usually empty during the day – though not at night – but today there was someone in it. The wall was very thin, and they could clearly hear the murmur of his prayers and even the sound of his forehead striking the ground.

'What is he saying?' Bakhtawar Singh whispered.

'I don't know,' she said. 'The usual – *la illaha il lallah* . . . I don't know.'

'You don't know your own prayers?' Bakhtawar Singh said, truly shocked.

She said, 'I could come every Monday, Wednesday and

Friday.' She tried to make her voice tempting, but instead it came out shy.

'You do it,' he said suddenly.

'Do what?'

'Like he's doing,' he said, jerking his head towards the other room, where the old man was. 'Why not?' he urged her. He seemed to want it terribly.

She laughed nervously. 'You need a prayer carpet. And you must cover your head.' (They were both stark naked.)

'Do it like that. Go on,' he wheedled. 'Do it.'

She laughed again, pretending it was a joke. She knelt naked on the floor and began to pray the way the old man was praying in the next room, knocking her forehead on the ground. Bakhtawar Singh urged her on, watching her with tremendous pleasure from the bed. Somehow the words came back to her and she said them in chorus with the old man next door. After a while, Bakhtawar Singh got off the bed and joined her on the floor and mounted her from behind. He wouldn't let her stop praying, though. 'Go on,' he said, and how he laughed as she went on. Never had he had such enjoyment out of her as on that day.

But he still wouldn't agree to meet her more than once a week. Later, when she tried ever so gently to insist, he became playful and said she didn't know that he was a very busy policeman. Busy with what, she asked, also trying to be playful. He laughed enormously at that and was very loving, as if to repay her for her good joke. But then after a while he grew more serious and said, 'Listen – it's better not to drive so often through Police Lines.'

'Why not?' Driving past his office after her visits to the ladies in the Civil Lines was still the highlight of her expeditions into town.

He shrugged. 'They are beginning to talk.'

'Who?'

'Everyone.' He shrugged again. It was only her he was warning. People talked enough about him anyway; let them have one more thing. What did he care?

'Oh nonsense,' she said. But she could not help recollecting that the last few times all the policemen outside their hutments seemed to have been waiting for her car. They had cheered her as she drove past. She had wondered at the time what it meant but had soon put it out of her mind. She did that now too; she couldn't waste her few hours with Bakhtawar Singh thinking about trivial matters.

But she remembered his warning the next time she went to visit the ladies in the Civil Lines. She wasn't sure then whether it was her imagination or whether there really was something different in the way they were with her. Sometimes she thought she saw them turn aside, as if to suppress a smile, or exchange looks with each other that she was not supposed to see. And when the gossip turned to the SP, they made very straight faces, like people who know more than they are prepared to show. Sofia decided that it was her imagination; even if it wasn't, she could not worry about it. Later, when she drove through the Police Lines, her car was cheered again by the men in underwear lounging outside their quarters, but she didn't trouble herself much about that either. There were so many other things on her mind. That day she instructed the chauffeur to take her to the SP's residence again, but at the last moment – he had already turned into the gate and now had to reverse – she changed her mind. She did not want to see his wife again; it was almost as if she were afraid. Besides, there was no need for it. The moment she saw the house, she realized that she had never ceased to think of that sad, bedraggled woman inside. Indeed, as time passed the vision had not dimmed but had become clearer. She found also that her feelings towards this unknown woman had changed completely, so that, far from thinking about her with scorn, she now had such pity for her that her heart ached as sharply as if it were for herself.

Sofia had not known that one's heart could literally, physically ache. But now that it had begun it never stopped; it was something she was learning to live with, the way a patient learns to live with his disease. And moreover, like the patient, she was aware that this was only the beginning and that her disease would get worse and pass through many stages before it was finished with her. From week to week she lived only for her day in Mohabbatpur, as if that were the only time when she could get some temporary relief from pain. She did not notice that, on the contrary, it was on that day that her condition worsened and passed into a more acute stage, especially when he came late, or was absent-minded, or – and this was beginning to happen too – failed to turn up altogether. Then, when she was driven back home, the pain in her heart was so great that she had to hold her hand there. It seemed to her that if only there were someone, one other living soul, she could tell about it, she might get some relief. Gazing at the chauffeur's stolid, impassive back, she realized that he was now the person who was closest to her. It was as if she had confided in him, without words. She only told him where she wanted to go, and he went there. He told her when he needed money, and she gave it to him. She had also arranged for several increments in his salary.

The Raja Sahib had written a new drama for her. Poor Raja Sahib! He was always there, and she was always with him, but she never thought about him. If her eyes fell on him, either she did not see or, if she did, she postponed consideration of it until some other time. She was aware that there was something wrong with him, but he did not speak of it, and she was grateful to him for not obtruding his own troubles. But when he told her about the new drama he wanted her to read aloud, she was glad to oblige him. She ordered a marvellous meal for that night and had a bottle of wine put on ice. She dressed herself in one of his grandmother's saris, of a gold so heavy that it was difficult to carry. The candles in blue glass chimneys were lit on the roof. She read out his drama with all the expression she had been taught at her convent to put into poetry readings. As usual she didn't understand a good deal of what she was reading, but she did notice that there was something different about his verses. There was one line that read, 'Oh, if thou didst but know what it is like to live in hell the way I do!' It struck her so much that she had to stop reading. She looked across at the Raja Sahib; his face was rather ghostly in the blue candlelight.

'Go on,' he said, giving her that gentle, self-deprecating smile he always had for her when she was reading his dramas.

But she could not go on. She thought, what does he know about that, about living in hell? But as she went on looking at him and he went on smiling at her, she longed to tell him what it was like. 'What is it, Sofia? What are you thinking?'

There had never been anyone in the world who looked into her eyes the way he did, with such love but at the same time with a tender respect that would not reach farther into her than was permissible between two human beings. And it was because she was afraid of changing that look that she did not speak. What if he should turn aside from her, the way he had when she had asked forgiveness for the drunken servant?

'Sofia, Sofia, what are you thinking?'

She smiled and shook her head and, with an effort, went on reading. She saw that she could not tell him but would have to go on bearing it by herself for as long as possible, though she was not sure how much longer that could be.

Expiation

I was thirteen when he was born. He was the youngest of seven of us, of whom only I, my brother Sohan Lal, and one sister (who is married, in Kanpur) are still living. Even after he had learned to walk, I used to carry him around in my arms, because he liked it. The one thing I couldn't bear was to see him cry. If he wanted something – and he often had strong desires, as for some other child's toy or a pink sweet – I did my best to get it for him. Perhaps I would have stolen for him; I never did, but if called upon I might have done it.

Our father had a small cloth shop in the town of P—— in Haryana, India. Today this town is known all over the world for its hand-spun cotton cloth, which is made here, but when my father was alive he could barely make a living from his shop. Now we take orders from all the rich Western countries, and our own warehouse is stocked so full of bolts of cloth that soon we shall need another one. I have built a house on the outskirts of the town, and when we have to go any distance we drive there in our white Ambassador car.

On that day – a cold Friday in January – I stood outside the prison gates. I wore a warm grey coat. There was a crowd there waiting, and everyone looked at me. I had got used to that. For more than two years, wherever I went people had pointed and whispered, 'Look. It is the eldest brother.' My photograph was often in the newspapers; whenever I went in and out of the court, I had to walk past all these people with cameras, from the newspapers and from the television station. So when they took my photograph outside the prison that day, I didn't mind it. I stood and waited. My brother Sohan Lal was with me, along with some cousins and one elderly uncle. We waited and shivered in the cold. Our thoughts were only on what was going on inside. I kept reading the words that are carved over the prison entrance: 'Hate the Sin but Not the Sinner'.

When they opened the gates at last, everyone rushed forward, but they would permit only me to enter. The old uncle tried to squeeze in behind me, but he was pushed back. I felt angry with him; even at that moment I had this anger against the old man, because I knew he was trying to come in not out of a feeling of love but to put himself forward and be important. They led me through the prison, which I had come to know very well, to where the body was. Everything was different that day. The courtyard and passages were empty, for whenever there is an execution they lock all the prisoners inside their cells. The officials and the doctor spoke to me in a very nice way. They stood with me while we waited for the municipal hearse, which I had ordered the night before. They had put a sheet over the face. I uncovered it to see him once more, though I knew it would not be the same face. Then I covered it again. I stood very straight and looked ahead of me. They offered me a place to sit, and I thanked them and declined. They spoke among themselves about the other body, which no one had come to claim. They would have to cremate it themselves, and they were discussing which warders should be assigned to this duty. They had neglected to place an advance order for a hearse, so they would have to wait. I didn't know where the other body was; it was not with his. They must have put it aside somewhere else.

His name was Ram Lal, but we always called him by his pet name, Bablu. Besides being much younger than I, he was also much smaller in build. All our family, including the girls, are big; only he stayed small. I could lift him even when he was grown up. I used to do it for a joke. When I put him down again I would hug him. I often hugged him and kissed him. He knew I loved him. Before my marriage we shared a bed, and when he cried out in his sleep – he often had bad dreams – I pressed him against my chest. He was six years old when I was married. A little satin coat was stitched for him, and he sat behind me on the mare on which I rode to the bride's house, with a band playing in front and cousins and friends (they had taken opium) dancing in the street. My wife's family made a good wedding for us, and he enjoyed it all. But he never liked my wife and she never liked him. From the beginning there was this between her and me. She tried to change my feelings for him and could not succeed.

It was not just weddings he was fond of but all festivals where special food is cooked and good clothes are worn. He didn't like anything that was old or ugly. He didn't like our home – two rooms in an old house in Kabir Galli, where we had to share a bathroom with eight other families. He was also unhappy sitting in the shop with me, because the bazaar is so crowded and smelly. At that time, the whole town was in a bad state, with all the old houses falling down and with dirty water from the gutters overflowing in the streets. In the old parts, it is still like that – in Kabir Galli, for instance, and in the bazaar where my father's shop used to be – but now there are also completely new areas, with bungalows and the temples that people have donated out of their black market money. When we were children, all these areas were fields and open ground where we could play. He spent many hours there alone in those days. He sat by the canal or lay under a tree – whole days sometimes.

I expected him to be a good student when he grew older, because although he was so quiet, his mind was always busy. Even at night he was alive with those bad dreams he had, while the rest of us, heavy with food and the day's work, lay asleep like stones. But it turned out he wasn't fond of studying, and whenever possible he stayed away from school. By this time, with the growing market for our cloth, I began to get free of the debts by which our family had been bound hand and foot since my grandfather's time. There was nothing to spare yet, but when he wanted some little sum he could ask me and I was in a position to give it. He was fond of going to the cinema, and if it was a good film he would see it six or seven times. Like everyone else, he knew all the film songs, though he didn't sing them out loud. He never sang and he didn't speak much, either; he was always very shy and alone, even when he was enjoying himself in the cinema or at a wedding. His face was always serious. It was unusual, almost strange, to see him smile. That may have been because his teeth were so odd – very small and pointed with spaces in between. When he did smile, his gums showed, like a girl's, and when he grew up and became very fond of chewing betel, they were always red and so were his lips and tongue.

Now I must record a small incident that I have never liked to remember. It was not just one incident, in fact, but several. The first time it happened, he was about nine years old. One day when I came home, my wife told me that she had seen

Bablu taking money out of the metal box that I used to keep under my bed. Her eyes shone as she told me this, as if she were happy that it had happened, so I frowned and told her he had taken this money at my instruction. She didn't believe me. 'Then why did he say he was looking for his slippers under the bed?' she said, challenging me. She said that he had tried to run away but that she had caught him and given him one or two slaps. When she told me that, I became angry, and said, 'How many times have I told you never to raise your hand to this boy?' For she had done it before – she is a strong woman, with a strong temper – and he had come to me crying bitterly and didn't stop until I had rebuked her. But when she slapped him because of the metal box he never mentioned the incident to me.

From then on, she was like a spy with him. She would watch his movements, and more than once she reported to me that she had awakened at night and seen him searching through our clothes. I wouldn't believe her; I told her to keep her mouth shut. She became cunning, and one night she whispered in my ear, 'Wake up and see.' I didn't open my eyes. I didn't want to see what she wanted me to, so I turned around on my other side and pretended to be angry with her for waking me. Next day, when he came to bring me my food in the shop, I said, 'Bablu, do you want money?' He said yes, so I gave him three rupees and said, 'Whenever you need money, I'm always here.' He was silent, but he looked at me as if he were saying, 'Why are you telling me this? I know all that very well.' His eyes had remained as I remembered them when he was a baby. All small children have this very serious look – as if they know things their elders have forgotten – but with him it remained till the end.

*

People say that you can learn a lot from a person's eyes. The moment I saw that one – the other one, the one whose body no one wanted to claim – I noticed his eyes. Although he was dark-complexioned, his eyes were very light – like a Kashmiri's or a European's, or even lighter, for they had no colour at all, so that at first it looked as if he had no vision but had lost it because of disease. I hated and feared him from the beginning. We all did, yet we had to tolerate his presence in our house. I even had to be grateful to him, because it was he who had brought Bablu back after he was lost to us for over two years.

When Bablu was sixteen, he wasn't like other boys – nothing like the way Sohan Lal had been at that age, when we had to find a bride and marry him off before he became too troublesome. Bablu was no trouble at all in that way – or in any other way. He never even smoked or drank anything. He was fond of nice clothes made of Terylene, and modern shoes with pointed toes. He also grew his hair long, and to keep it in place used a costly brand of oil, with a very sweet smell. But it is common for young boys to be careful of their appearance. Sohan Lal also dressed up and sat with his friends outside the Peshawar Café, and they talked among themselves the way boys do, and when girls walked past they shouted. This behaviour is to be expected before natural satisfaction is obtained in marriage.

Bablu, though he dressed so nicely, never sat with friends in the Peshawar Café. He was always by himself. Never once did I see him with a friend. He didn't care to come and help us in the shop or with the rest of the business, which was just starting to do well. Most of the time he stayed at home. We were still in our house in Kabir Galli, it was a very small place, but during the day the children were at school and

Sohan Lal's wife liked to go to neighbours' homes to talk. So usually there was only my wife at home with Bablu. She didn't like it; she kept asking me to send him to the shop or find some other work for him, but I said let him be. Although he never did anything or had anything to read except some film magazines, I could see that he was thinking all the time. I had respect for him for being such a thoughtful person and not at all like Sohan Lal and me, who were always busy and had no inclination for thinking at all.

One night when I came home, my wife called to me from the other room – the one where our beds were put out at night, and also where I kept a metal safe I had bought when the business began to progress. When I went in, she wouldn't let me put on the light, but I saw at once that the safe was open; the bundles of money I'd had in it were gone, though the jewellery was intact. My wife was sitting on the floor. 'Quickly,' she said. 'Help me.' I squatted down beside her, and she put one hand over my mouth to stifle my cry. I saw that she had tied up her arm with a bundle of cloth, but already this cloth was soaked in blood. Neither of us spoke. I threw a shawl round her and, hurrying through the other room where the family were all sitting, I took her out into the street and put her in a cycle rickshaw, and we went to the hospital. There she explained that the knife had slipped while she was cutting up a chicken that she was preparing for a feast.

We didn't see him again for two years. At first I was glad he was gone, and I told a lie to everyone about how I had sent him to Ludhiana to look after a new business I was starting there. I even told this lie to Sohan Lal, and he kept quiet, knowing there was something it was better for him not to know. If only I, too, could have remained as ignorant! But my peace was gone, even my sleep was gone. Every night my wife lay beside me, and she too was awake, and I knew she was seeing again what she had described to me – the expression on his face when he turned round to her from the safe. He had raised his hand, and though she didn't see the knife in it she quickly put her arm over her chest – and what if she had not done so! Even in the dark, I covered my eyes so as not to see such a thing. I thought also of how he had taken the key of the safe out of my pocket and had had it copied in a shop, and of how he had thought all this out while he sat with me at meals, so quiet and sweet-natured, and while he had stood before the mirror and combed his hair up into a wave, his eyes serious and pure like a child's.

So at first I was glad he was gone. Then I began to miss him. I thought of the bundles of money he had taken with him and of how unsafe it was for anyone, let alone a young boy, to travel with so much cash. Secretly, I arranged to put out a search for him. I changed my story and I told everyone, even relatives, that he had run away – probably to be in films in Bombay, like so many other boys. I inserted advertisements in many newspapers all over India, in English and in Hindi, with his photograph and, printed underneath, 'Bablu, come home. All is forgiven'. The advertisements offered a reward of two thousand rupees. There was no result.

During all this time only my wife knew the true story. She kept quiet – even with her own family, her own brothers. She told them only what I had instructed her to say: first, that he had gone to Ludhiana, then that he had probably run away to Bombay, where the film studios are. Her arm healed slowly; she was often in pain, but no one knew what had happened except me. Up to this time we had enjoyed frequent marital intercourse; now we only lay silently side by side. I thought not of her but of him – not of his turning around from the safe with his arm raised but of his travelling alone with the money and of what could have happened to him. She knew what I was thinking, and to calm me she made those sweet noises at me she makes at our children when they are sick or crying.

So two years passed, and in that time our new house was built. The house was also intended for Sohan Lal and his family, but because his wife does not get on with mine – it is the usual story with sisters-in-law – they all stayed behind in Kabir Galli. Of course, I was sad to see our joint family split in this way, but secretly I hoped that Bablu would come back one day and then I would find a wife for him and they would live with us in our precious new home. And then he did come back, and he did live with us – not with a wife but with that one, the other one, Sachu, he called himself.

Although the things Sachu had done and the way he lived only came out afterwards in court, he seemed to carry them around with him, so that wherever he was the air became foul. He was small and thin, like Bablu, and except for his colourless eyes there was nothing to notice. He wore a dirty, torn pajama, and a dirty, torn shirt over it. Bablu, too, was in rags. All the money must have gone long ago and they were destitute. They were hungry, too. When I saw my brother fall like a starving dog on the food we gave him, I said, 'If you had written one word, I would have sent whatever you needed.' Sachu said, 'Don't worry, I've brought him home now.' Neither of them ever said much, but when there was an answer to be given it was Sachu who spoke. And it was he who said, 'Don't forget the reward – two thousand rupees.' He laughed, so I thought he was joking. It was always difficult to know what he meant, because his eyes were always blank like glass.

Our new house was built in such a way that the room where visitors are received is separate from where the family lives.

This room is at the front of the house and is much larger than the rooms crowded together at the back, where we keep our cots and cooking vessels and other very simple furniture. For the front room we have bought a sofa and matching chairs and a table with a glass top, and there is a glass cabinet in which my wife keeps pretty dolls and other ornaments. Here we also have a television set and a radio. This room was now given over to Bablu and his friend, and they made themselves comfortable there. It was hard to see Sachu putting his dirty feet on the blue velvet sofa, but it was better than to have him in the back of the house with the family. So I kept quiet, and my wife also kept quiet. She had to – the same way she had to about the wound in her arm. We didn't even speak out our fear to each other.

When Sachu asked me again for the two-thousand-rupee reward, I gave it to him. After all, it was his right. And when he asked me, 'Aren't you grateful I brought him home to you?' I said yes. It was true. Now at least I knew where Bablu was – in the front of my own house – and I did not have to imagine what his fate might be. He was alive and well! – and now that he ate good food and slept comfortably, he was very well! I had never seen him so happy before. I have mentioned how rarely he smiled and looked glad, but now he did it all the time, showing his little pointed teeth and his gums stained red with betel. For the first time, he had a friend whom he loved. They were together all the time. They sat side by side on the low wall around our house, swinging their feet and holding hands, the way friends do. They both liked playing the radio and watching television. Once I saw them dancing together, holding each other the way English people dance. I had to smile then, because it was a strange sight and also nice for me to see Bablu enjoying himself. I began to think that my fears were foolish and that it was good for him to have Sachu as a friend. I can't say they were any trouble to us. My wife also had no complaints on that score. They were never disrespectful, and they behaved decently. They didn't mix very much with us but kept themselves apart in the front room. They even ate their meals there, brought to them by the servant boy we kept in the house.

Although he has nothing to do with what happened later, I must say something about this servant boy. Before he came to us he was working in a tea stall, serving customers and washing cups and plates in a bucket in the back. He also slept there at night. He had no other home and no family; no one knew where he came from. He was about twelve or thirteen years old. He couldn't read or write, but he was a willing worker. When Sachu and Bablu came, this boy changed completely. Now all he wanted was to be near them. He would sit in the doorway of the front room, waiting for them to send him out for betel or cool drinks, or to take their clothes to the washerman. They had good clothes now and were very careful to have them always nicely washed and pressed. I have seen this boy arranging their clothes and touching the fine cloth as if he were touching a woman. When my wife called him he pretended not to hear; perhaps he really didn't hear her, because all his attention was focused on those two. He tried to comb his hair up in a wave like theirs, and he begged my wife to buy him bell-bottom pants instead of the khaki shorts she had given him. Later, after the two were no longer with us, this boy became worse and worse. He mixed with bad characters and hung around the bazaar and cinema with them. He stayed out all night and could never be found for work, until at last my wife dismissed him. He got a job as a servant in another house but soon disappeared from there with money and valuables. A report was lodged with the police, but he was never found. Probably he got on a train and went to some other town. There are millions like him, and no one can tell one from the other. They eat where they can, sleep where they can, and if they get into trouble in one place they move on to another. They may end up in jail on some case that never comes up for trial, they may die of some disease, or they may live a few years longer. No one cares where they are or what happens to them. There are too many of them.

That was Sachu's defence for his crime: no one cared for him, so he cared for no one. The time of the trial and afterward, after the sentence, was Sachu's great hour. He became a big man and gave interviews to journalists and made them listen to his philosophy. He boasted of all the crimes he'd committed before he came to our town. He had been in jail many times, he said, but he had never been convicted of any of the other murders to which he now admitted. He said he would kill anyone if he wanted something they had, even if it was only a ring that he liked. He said that human beings were not born to be poor, otherwise why should the earth be so full of riches, with mines full of gold and precious gems, and with pearls scattered in the ocean? His father had pulled a handcart for a living and had had nine children. Probably those who had survived were all pulling handcarts now – all except him, Sachu. He had wanted something else, and if it had brought him death on the gallows, all right, he was ready. He had always been different from his family; he had run away from them at the age of ten, when he had overheard his father and elder brothers planning to break his leg in order to make him change his bad ways. Since that day he had been on his own.

*

My prayer to be relieved of their crime has been answered, so that it is no longer before my eyes day and night. Now it is as if it were locked away in a heavy steel trunk; this weight may be taken from me at my last hour, but until then I carry it inside myself, where only God and I know of its constant presence. After a while there is nothing more you can do or suffer. I have also prayed on behalf of the father of the victim – that the man's suffering may be made bearable for him, if such a thing were possible. Day after day I was with this man in the courtroom, but I can say nothing of his appearance, because not once in all that time did I dare to raise my eyes and look at him.

The famous Parsi lawyer I engaged for Bablu's defence believed that they never intended to kill the boy but meant to release him, after collecting the ransom money. Very likely this is true. It is certainly true that while they were living in my house they made their plan to kidnap him. At that time there was a popular film playing about a dacoit who kidnapped a high-born girl for money, but then he fell in love with her and she reformed his ways. It was one of those stupid Bombay films that people like, including my wife, who made me take her to see it because her favourite actor was in it. A mother with three children, but still she has a favourite actor! Sachu and Bablu went four or five times, and they knew all the songs and dialogue by heart. So the idea of kidnap must have got into their heads. There were enough rich people in our town – many of them like myself, who a few years ago were only humble shopkeepers and were caught up in the big boom in cotton cloth. Such people spent a lot of money on themselves and their children and lived like millionaires; some of them already were millionaires. However, it was not one of their children who was chosen.

P——— is a cantonment town, and we have always had a regiment stationed here. The cantonment area is quite separate. It has wide roads and brick barracks, and the officers live in bungalows with gardens. Everything is very clean and very well kept up. The soldiers are healthy and sturdy and look quite different from the townspeople. The officers and their families are like higher beings; they are well built, with light complexions, and they are educated gentry, speaking English with each other. Some of them even speak Hindi with an English accent, like foreigners – like sahibs. They also live like sahibs in their big bungalows, and drink whisky and soda, and their cooks prepare English-style food for them, with roast meat. The boy's father was the commanding officer – he had the rank of colonel – and his memsahib, the boy's mother, was from one of the princely families who have lost their title but still have houses and land. (She has since passed away.) The boy was their only child, and they had sent him to a boarding school in the hills to get a good education. The reason he was in the cantonment at that time was that there had been a measles epidemic in the school; all the unaffected children had been sent home as a precaution, to safeguard their health.

Everyone knows what the boy looked like. His photograph has been in the newspapers as often as Bablu's and Sachu's. Sometimes all three photos were on the same page, and even though they were not clear in the newsprint it was evident that the boy was of a different type from the other two – as if he came from some different stock or species of human being. In Sachu's interviews with the newspaper reporters, he sounded as if he hated the boy, because the boy was plump, with big eyes and a light complexion, and wore a very good blue coat, with the badge of his school on the pocket. And because he had roller skates. No one had heard of roller skates in our town till the boy was seen with them. His parents had brought them as a present for him from abroad, and the boy loved them so much that he went on them everywhere, as with wings under his feet.

It was because of these roller skates that Bablu and Sachu were discovered very quickly. It was also all they got from their crime, for although the father had put the ransom money in the place they had indicated, they did not dare collect it after killing the boy. They had so little cash that they had to sneak on to a train as ticketless travellers. When an inspector came, they had to jump off. This was in a town less than two hundred miles from ours. They took a room in a hotel in a bad part of town, and they never came out except at night, when one of them went to buy gram, which was all the food they could afford. Their room was very small, with only one bed and an old fan, but here Sachu tried to learn to roller-skate. This made the whole house shake, as if it were in an earthquake, and everyone in the hotel wondered what was happening. They also heard the noise of someone falling, and then the two young men laughing in enjoyment, so they tapped on the door of their room to inquire. Sachu let them come in and look, because he was so proud of learning to roller-skate. Everyone smiled and enjoyed his feat, but when there was news everywhere of a boy killed and of his missing roller skates the police were informed at once.

Up to that time, the two of them had been lucky, even though their crime had not been well planned. They had stolen a car from outside the interstate bus depot, and had waited near the cantonment for the boy to pass on his roller skates. They had no difficulty getting into conversation with him; he was frank and open in his manner – everyone said so later – and was always glad to talk to people and to make friends. They got him into the car and drove him to the place they had chosen for their hideout. Here they tied him up with chains, and Sachu – Bablu couldn't drive – took the car to the other side of town and abandoned it there. It was found by the police the same day, though they found the boy only when he was dead.

There are many places where a person can hide around our town. Important battles have been fought here, and it has been destroyed and built up again many times. Ruins are all around – the foundations of beautiful cities, with the remains of tombs, mosques and bathing tanks. Since it is a very dry area, very little vegetation has grown, and there are only mounds of rubble and dust, where jackals live and can be heard howling at night. The two took the boy down into a bathing tank, which had been dug so deep into the earth that there were forty steps descending into it. All round the tank were arched niches like rooms. In olden days, it must have been a beautiful, cool place for royal people to bathe and rest and take enjoyment. Now the tank is empty and dry. They kept the boy in one of the niches and stayed with him there for four days, all of them living on milk sweets.

After they were arrested, Sachu talked freely. It was as if he had waited all his life for people to listen to what he had to say. He was a person of no education, and could not express himself, yet words and thoughts always seemed to boil up in him and come gushing out freely. One thing he could never bear was to be contradicted or interrupted; he wanted to be the only one to talk, and others were there to listen. After his arrest, if any journalist challenged him or talked back to him, he went into a rage. Sometimes he seemed to fly into the same rage when talking about the boy; he spoke as if the boy were still alive and challenging what he was saying. Then anger filled his empty eyes.

The Parsi lawyer wanted to present the case in such a way as to show that Sachu had stabbed the boy with his knife during an argument between them. It was soon established that the boy didn't sit quietly and whine for mercy while he was being kept prisoner. He was a fearless boy and also a first-class debater who had competed for an inter-school trophy. He liked talking and arguing as much as Sachu did, and although he was seven years younger (he was thirteen), he was much better educated. When Sachu spoke to the boy about society and astrology and what is man's fate – the same way he later talked to the reporters – the boy could answer him and argue with him, and he could even quote from books he had read at school. The Parsi lawyer said that when Sachu was defeated by the boy over and over again in argument he became so enraged that he killed him. Sachu alone did it, and Bablu was innocent. And Sachu said yes, that was the way it happened, and then he boasted of the other murders he had committed, which no one had ever discovered.

But Bablu said no to the Parsi lawyer, that was not the way it happened. Bablu said, 'I did it – not Sachu.' Then the lawyer appointed to defend Sachu wanted to make a case that Bablu had killed the boy out of jealousy, because he saw that his friend was paying a lot of attention to the boy and spent many hours talking and arguing with him. The lawyer said that the boy was not only educated and cultured but also very handsome – soft-skinned and wheat-complexioned. (The medical report had established the fact that sodomy had taken place.) Bablu was ready to confirm what the lawyer said and to admit that he had killed the boy because he could not bear to watch what Sachu did with him. He confessed this in a very quiet voice and without raising his eyes – not out of shame, it seemed, but because he felt shy about talking of this matter.

All this time, Bablu never changed. Unlike Sachu, he hardly spoke to anyone but appeared so sunk in his own thoughts that one didn't like to disturb him. As before, his face was very serious, and his expression altered only when he read the newspaper reports of the interviews that Sachu had given. Bablu eagerly waited for me to bring him these newspapers, and when he read them he smiled – that smile, with his little pointed teeth and betel-red gums, which always gave me a shock to see. It didn't seem to belong on his face – any more than that other expression my wife had once described to me, when he had turned from the safe and raised his hand with the knife.

Since each of them was ready to plead guilty to save the other, their lawyers got together and tried to prove that they had never met the boy – that someone else had killed him and they had only stolen the roller skates. It was a very weak case, and no one believed it. In the end, both were found guilty, and both were hanged. The burden of what was done has remained with us who are living. My brother Sohan Lal and his family have emigrated to Canada, and at first I, too, intended to leave this place where our name is known. But in the end I stayed. We are still living in the same house, though at first I had intended to sell it. For a long time we kept the front room locked and lived only in the back – no one even went in there to clean – but slowly we have got used to going in there again. At first, only the children went, to look at TV if there was a good programme on, but now my wife and I also sit there sometimes, and it is becoming like an ordinary room where nothing has happened.

After the final appeal was dismissed and there was only one week left, they allowed me to visit the prison every day. I always brought his food with me. All this time, I had been providing his meals at the jail. At first, I brought his food from a cooking stall and sent it to him in the little mud pots covered with a leaf that they give you in the bazaar. But after a time, and without anything being said, my wife cooked his food herself, and it was carried to him in dishes from our house. I was glad to be able to provide this home-cooked food, which he liked and was used to. But soon I discovered that he ate only a part of it, and had the rest taken away to Sachu, for whom no one sent anything, of course. When I mentioned this to my wife, she began to send more food, and after a time there were always two dishes of everything.

On the last day, when he asked me to see Sachu and say goodbye to him, I said I would but I didn't do it. So it was that my last word to him was a lie. He asked, 'Did you see him?' and I said, 'Yes.' But next day I did something I hadn't expected. When the hearse arrived to take Bablu, I told the prison officials that I would take the other one, too. They agreed and were glad to be relieved of this charge. So I took both of them to the electric crematorium, and there I performed for both the ceremonies and prayers due to a brother. Sohan Lal and the rest of my family blamed me for this and said I had polluted the last rites. They were all angry and refused to participate in the final ceremony, when the ashes are committed to the river. I didn't care and prepared to do it on my own.

I bought two silver urns and returned to the crematorium to collect the ashes. I had determined to go to Allahabad, to the most holy and purifying place of all, where the three great rivers meet and mingle, but a lot of business came up during the next few days and I could not leave at once. I placed the two urns in the front room, and when I was ready to leave I packed them in a cardboard box I had brought from the warehouse for this purpose. The night before, I told my wife to wake me early so that I could be in time for the plane. She said, 'I will come with you,' and in the morning she was ready in new white clothes. We drove to Delhi to go to the airport there. They allowed us to take the box on board with us. My wife had never been on a plane before and was very excited, though she pretended not to be. She kept looking out of the window to see the clouds and whatever else you see. Once, she turned to me and said, 'Bablu has never been on a plane before.' I didn't answer her but I thought, yes, it is true; it is the first time for all three of them. The two others would have enjoyed it too and would have been as excited as she was. In Allahabad we took a boat, and a priest went with us, and there was a beautiful ceremony as the ashes were committed at the confluence of those very holy rivers – the Ganges, the Jumna, and the Saraswati.

Great Expectations

Pauline was a New York real estate agent – middle-aged and comfortably settled. It had taken her many years to reach her present plateau of contentment, also to build up her own business, after having worked for other people. Now she had a tiny office which was almost a storefront – it had been an unsuccessful dry-cleaner's before she had rented it and was in a row of other commercial establishments, including a deli, a nail spa, a newsagent and a jewellery boutique about to go out of business. But Pauline had converted her interior into what was almost a cosy little parlour, with flowers, prints and little armchairs done up in striped silk. The windows had curtains from inside, but from outside they were plastered with notices offering apartments in terms so attractive that passers-by often stopped to read them, even those who didn't need new accommodation.

However, there were enough people who did to give Pauline a comfortable income and a devoted clientele of her own. She took a very personal interest in her cases – as she humorously called them – and several of them remained her friends after she had accommodated them. These were mostly single women – though, unlike herself, not by choice but as a result of divorce or abortive affairs, so that they

223

were often in need not only of apartments but of solace and friendship.

And of all the needy cases who came to her, Sylvie was the most desperate. It wasn't that she was poor – some of the others were in really tight straits because of unfavourable divorce settlements forced on them by their husbands' lawyers. But Sylvie's husband had remained supportive. Of course, there wasn't only Sylvie to consider but also their daughter Amy. Sylvie and Amy came as a pair, a team: this was how they had first presented themselves in Pauline's office, two waifs in tatty but chic little frocks, so desperately in need of help that they sat in dumb despair, winding locks of their long blonde hair around their fingers.

It was Pauline's speciality to know just how to cater to the needs and means of a client. But although Sylvie always said, 'It's lovely, Pauline', to whatever she showed her, and Amy echoed, 'It's lovely, Pauline', they never took the place. Something was always somehow wrong; neither of them could say what this was. So they said, 'Lovely', or 'Fabulous', or 'Fantastic', and then looked vague or blank, or miserable at not being able to oblige Pauline by signing a contract.

Yet their situation was hazardous – they really had to have a place, for they were under duress to vacate their present quarters, belonging to a friend who was no longer a friend. 'Mona is so hostile,' Sylvie said and then clamped her lips tight, indicating that she did not want to say anything derogatory about anyone. And even when they were forced out – legal threats were involved – Sylvie still did not utter a word of complaint, but she and Amy came to Pauline's office with their bundles and suitcases, and they sat there, silent and forlorn.

Pauline had no alternative but to take them home to her

own apartment. She did not want to at all. Pauline liked – she loved – her privacy, a preference it had taken her many years to achieve. In her youth she had been like everyone else and had craved romance, or at least companionship. When these were not forthcoming, or their promise was blighted, she had slowly come to accept her solitude and self-reliance. These became an absolute necessity after her mother died. Although they had not lived in the same city for years – the mother had remained in Kansas City – Pauline had visited her home town at least three or four times a year, and they had spoken almost daily on the phone. Pauline had a married brother in Washington, and in the first years after their mother died, she was expected to spend Christmas and Thanksgiving with him and his family. But soon it was only Christmas, and then one year Pauline decided that it was easier to stay home; and after that she spent all her Christmases at home, and usually alone – which she grew actually to like: that was how independent she was.

Sylvie and Amy stayed in her second bedroom. They were very considerate and tried to make themselves useful, which was not easy with someone of Pauline's settled temperament. Pauline didn't like the way they made beds, or washed and put away her dishes, so when she came home in the evenings, she undid everything they had done – rather grimly, for she was tired after her day's work. And she didn't like the way they cooked, either – well, it wasn't really cooking, they usually prepared some sort of salad and beans (both of them were vegetarians), so that Pauline had to run down and buy herself a steak. By the time she had cooked and eaten it, she was completely exhausted and in no way inclined to be sociable or even agreeable. She went to bed long before they did – Amy was only ten, but she kept the same hours as her mother; and Pauline could hear them showering together, or laughing at the TV, and though they shushed each other and tried to walk on tiptoe, they kept her awake long after she needed to be asleep.

Still, she endured the situation. As all her friends and acquaintances could testify, she was a good sort who was always glad to help people out in their troubles. Besides, she knew the arrangement was only temporary, and that as soon as she found them a good apartment, she could have hers back again to enjoy in undisturbed comfort. This business of finding them an apartment had become a professional challenge: for whatever she came up with – and she came up with many, many – they continued to find unsuitable for their particular needs. She began to wonder somewhat bitterly how those complicated needs could possibly be satisfied in her spare bedroom: but of course they did have the place to themselves the whole day and could make full use of its many advantages, such as her washer and dryer, which were always full of their panties and tee-shirts.

Unfortunately, besides laughing and showering together, they also had fights. Out of deference to her, they tried to keep their voices down, but getting excited, they began to shout and bang doors. They fought like children – well, Amy was a child, and Sylvie reacted as if she was, too. They called each other names like stinkbag and went over old grievances, such as when Amy ruined two pairs of Sylvie's jeans with bleach. These fights often ended with Amy stuffing some tutus and her fluffy giraffe into a backpack, saying she was leaving, she was going to her daddy. However, this did not appear to be feasible, for she soon allowed Sylvie to unpack again and then they both went to sleep, earlier than usual because of being exhausted from their fight.

Pauline had met Amy's daddy once or twice, when she had come home earlier than expected, and she suspected that he spent more time in her apartment than they wanted her to know. It must have been a convenient place for them, better than strolling around the streets and shops and cafés, which were their other alternatives. This was because Sylvie was not welcome in the place where her ex-husband lived – in his mother's very grand Park Avenue duplex, where Amy went to visit, by herself, every third Sunday.

Sylvie's ex-husband, whose name was Theo, was so much like Sylvie herself, and like their daughter, that Pauline wondered they had not stayed together. They certainly seemed to enjoy one another's company, and when Theo was there, the three of them did the same sort of things Sylvie and Amy did on their own. Theo even looked like them – he was slender and pale and fair-haired; and when he accompanied them to view the apartments that Pauline was hopefully showing them, he reacted with the same 'It's lovely,' and the same unspoken opinion that it was not for them. He was also a vegetarian – in fact, he and Sylvie had met in India, in a guru's ashram where, let alone eggs, not even root vegetables, such as onions and potatoes, were allowed.

On the Sundays when Amy visited her Park Avenue grand-mother, Sylvie was so depressed that Pauline felt obliged to cancel her usual Sunday arrangements and devote herself to Sylvie. But she never succeeded in making her feel better. There was the time when she had taken her for a walk in the park, hoping to console her among the holiday crowds in spring clothes come out to enjoy the blossoms flying through the air like pink raindrops. Sylvie was in one of her long flowing pastel dresses – a bit faded because of being washed so often – and people looked at her with pleasure: only to look away again at once, shocked to see this embodiment of youthful enchantment in tears. Pauline was embarrassed, as if people were blaming her for her companion's misery. And in a way she felt guilty that it was she who walked beside this girl and not a youth as fine and fair as Sylvie herself: not, that is, someone like Theo – or indeed, Theo himself.

This was the essence of their tragedy: that they could not be together. Every third Sunday Sylvie said it, or hinted at it, in a different way; but she always ascribed the fault to fate, or destiny, or plain bad luck, never blaming their separation on any person. Yet she could, it seemed to Pauline after several of these Sundays, very easily have named Theo's mother as the agent of their malevolent fate – Pauline herself was inclined to do so, after piecing together Sylvie's various hints on the subject. But as soon as Pauline said anything subversive about his mother, Mrs Baum, Sylvie begged her to be silent; she put her hand on Pauline's and said in a gentle voice, 'No, she's Theo's mother; she's a good person.'

'She hasn't been good to you,' Pauline said in her outspoken way.

Sylvie shook her head and smiled: 'She's good to Theo and to Amy.'

She did not mention the fact – very clear to Pauline by now – that she herself was never invited to accompany Amy, or ever visit the Park Avenue place at all. Gradually Pauline came to realize that Sylvie had not even met Mrs Baum. Yet she always spoke of her with admiration: what a grand lady she was, who gave the most fabulous parties, never for pleasure but always for a good cause or for some cultural purpose, for she sat on many boards – for the opera, and the ballet, and for the educational advancement of disadvantaged youths in the inner city. She was also the chairman of her late husband's company, which was a huge undertaking for a woman alone, so that she needed all the support she could get. And the way things were in the business world, Sylvie said, looking grave as though repeating a thought that was too big for her to handle, you were surrounded by sharks wanting to swallow you and all your assets, and the only people you could trust were your own immediate family.

'That's Theo?' Pauline said.

'She has no one else. No one in the world.'

'What about you?'

But again Sylvie shook her head, smiling: 'Oh, you know how I'm just this airhead.'

Pauline said, 'I don't know anything of the sort.' This was on another Sunday, when they had gone to a museum and were looking at pictures. Pauline's favourites were sunny landscapes with graceful young people walking in them in eighteenth-century clothes. Sylvie didn't seem to have any particular favourites – but she would suddenly be transfixed by a picture and would stand in front of it as in a trance; and when she finally managed to break away, it was evident that she had had a deep experience.

Obviously, under such circumstances, it was not possible for her to look at many pictures, and they often sat out, either in one of the galleries or under the glass roof of the loggia where fountains played and sometimes splashed them with cool drops.

'No, I'm not very bright,' Sylvie said. 'Of course I never had the chance to go to college, though I'd have loved to study something. Painting, or psychology.'

Pauline put out her hand to tuck a loose strand of hair behind Sylvie's ear. 'Oh, you're wet,' she said, feeling her cheek. 'Should we sit somewhere else? I'm getting splashed too.'

'No, I like it, don't you? ... Maybe Sanskrit. Or religion. I've always been very interested in religion. But I never even finished school. It wasn't my fault,' she said, looking sad, as she usually did when talking of the past, or that part of it.

Pauline had picked up some details of this past on a succession of previous Sundays: Sylvie's difficult childhood with a divorced mother, who had nervous breakdowns and finally died in a psychiatric institution – a private one that had absorbed most of her funds, leaving Sylvie only just enough to take a trip to India in pursuit of an interest in Hindu religion.

'I bet if you had finished school you'd have done something,' Pauline assured her. 'I think you have a lot of talent.'

'Oh really?' Sylvie's interest was stirred enough for her to turn her face and focus her eyes, vague but luminous, on Pauline. 'For what? Or are you just saying it?'

'I mean it. I think you could do anything you put your mind to.'

'You think I could paint?'

'I'm sure ... And you'd be very good at business too.'

For a moment Sylvie looked at Pauline as if she were crazy. Then she lost interest in her and the subject completely; she turned away her face again and let her eyes wander, filling them with the light filtered through the glass roof and through the springing silver cascades of the fountains.

Pauline, in her anxiety to recapture her attention, became light-headed: 'If you were to come with me in the office, you'd learn the business in no time.'

'Real estate?' Sylvie laughed but was quick to explain: 'I'm laughing at me, not you. I mean, it's so fantastic, me learning real estate.'

'What's fantastic about it? Only you'd have to come in the office with me every day. To see how things are done,' Pauline explained.

There was a moment's silence between them; then Sylvie did turn her face towards Pauline again: 'Are you offering me a job?'

'Yes.' Pauline spoke resolutely, although the thought had never till that moment occurred to her. And she went further – she heard herself offer Sylvie a full-time job in her office, and when Sylvie asked, 'With a salary and all?' she said, 'Oh yes, and commissions. That can work out to a lot of money.'

'How much?' Sylvie said, not so much out of interest as out of courtesy, to keep the conversation going.

'It depends on the sale. For instance, if you were to sell a two-bedroom, two-bathroom in a good location at 450K – but I don't want to confuse you with figures—'

'No, don't. I was never any good at sums. Arithmetic and stuff. Hopeless.'

'You wouldn't have to be. Nowadays, with computers and calculators, you hardly need a brain – I'm not saying you don't have one, Sylvie, on the contrary, I think you're a very intelligent person and that's why I'd like you to come work for me. With me,' Pauline said, like a suitor ready to promise the earth.

'Let's not talk any more now. It's so wonderful just sitting here.' Sylvie raised her face to the glass roof, letting the light stream down on herself. 'It's like being under water. Like we were two mermaids.' Although it was only she who looked like one.

They did not mention the subject of Sylvie working in Pauline's office for several days. But Pauline found herself thinking about it more and more – especially in the afternoons, when she suspected, or rather knew, that Theo was with Sylvie in her apartment. What did they do there? She supposed they made love – and yet, it was difficult to think of them doing so, at least not in the way other people did it. There was something otherworldly about them; they seemed to talk to each other on an ethereal level – when they talked at all. Mostly there was a charged silence between them, which neither of them seemed to want to break with anything more substantial than 'Divine, isn't it,' while the other breathed back, 'Out of this world.'

Yet their problems were substantial. They were divorced, for one thing, or separated – Theo's mother had insisted on this, and she had also arranged the settlement, which gave Sylvie nothing more than child support. Sylvie and Theo had had to agree to everything because Theo himself had no money and was completely dependent on his mother. In any case, his mother had suggested that they weren't really married at all – which was ridiculous, as far as Theo and Sylvie were concerned, for no one could have had a more beautiful marriage ceremony. This had been in India, where they had met, in a holy place in the Himalayan foothills, with a holy river running through it. This river was turgid and had all sorts of suspicious things floating in it – the funeral pyres were built on its banks – but nevertheless everyone bathed in it, including Sylvie and Theo. They had first seen each other in this river, at dawn, pouring water over themselves out of brass vessels and praying to the rising sun. As this rose, it suffused part of the river in a pool of light; Theo saw Sylvie standing in such a pool, as if she had just risen out of it and was pouring not water but light over herself.

Sylvie was alone – she had taken a room in the town, in a hotel given over mostly to pilgrims. She ate food in the bazaar, even raw fruits, and never got sick. Theo lived with a guru in an ashram; he had quite a high position there, as one of the guru's right-hand men. But after he met Sylvie, he was no longer so interested in the teaching, although it was what he had come to India for. He put his case to the guru: how it was through their love that he and Sylvie could achieve the ascent to the Good and the Beautiful, which the guru himself taught was the purpose of all human life. The guru was not quite convinced by this interpretation of his own message, but he was sympathetic, and in fact performed the marriage ceremony. This was very beautiful, with all the members of the ashram singing while the guru chanted the benediction and Sylvie and Theo walked around the sacred fire. They were completely covered in flowers, strings of marigold and jasmine hung down over their faces, but nevertheless at the end everyone threw more flowers at them, showering them with fragrant blossoms. After all that, it was ridiculous to say they were not really married.

Pauline became restless, and it got worse every afternoon when she thought of Sylvie alone with Theo in the apartment. One day she decided she had a headache and needed to go home. Unfortunately she had an appointment with a client, which she had to cancel, but that couldn't be helped. She did have her health to consider; and it was just one more proof that her business was simply getting too big for her to handle alone, and she really needed an assistant. She decided to reopen the subject with Sylvie as soon as she got home – but when she did, there was only Amy there, back from school and lying on Pauline's bed, eating corn chips and watching an adult programme on TV. Pauline's entrance did not disturb her – she gave her a friendly little wave, then settled herself more comfortably on the white chenille bedcover.

'Where's Sylvie?'

Amy pointed at the screen, indicating that what was going on there precluded conversation. It was only when Pauline insisted that she answered, 'She's out ... Do you mind?' she said, pointing at the screen again.

'Yes, I do mind.' Pauline was grim: she minded Amy lying on her bed, she minded the greasy corn chips she was scattering over it, and most of all she minded Sylvie not being home. 'Is Theo with her? ... Where've they gone?' When Amy didn't answer, Pauline turned off the TV.

Amy was silent for a while. Then she said, 'Well. That wasn't very polite.' She spoke with quiet reproach so that Pauline felt a bit ashamed and began to make excuses: 'I don't think it's the sort of programme you should be watching. And I have a headache,' she remembered.

'Oh, I'm sorry.'

'Yes. That's why I came home. Why aren't you at school?'

'They sent us home early. Someone died ... I could give you a head massage. I do it for Sylvie all the time.'

'No thanks. I don't think you should be eating on my bed. Making crumbs.'

'Oh, sorry.' Amy got up at once and made token gestures of brushing off crumbs. 'We have some herbal stuff if you like that, but don't take aspirin whatever you do.'

'Why shouldn't I? ... Is she with Theo? Where did they go?'

Amy answered only the first question: 'It does horrible things inside your stomach. Toxic things.'

'Oh rubbish, Amy.' Pauline went out impatiently, and Amy followed her, saying, 'I swear to God. It's been proved.'

Pauline sat down heavily on her living-room sofa. She felt disconsolate: to have left her office, cancelled and maybe lost her client, and now to be trapped here with Amy. It wasn't that she had anything specifically against Amy: it was really, though she never admitted this, that she didn't like children in general. That had been the trouble with spending Christmas in her brother's home. She had done all she could to make herself liked by his children, bought them expensive presents and so on, but she had heard them making fun of her – she had rather heavy ankles and they told each other that she had elephantiasis and amused themselves with imitating the walk of such a person. It seemed to her that children were cruel, and if you did not measure up to their standard, they despised you. She had several times caught Amy looking at her in a way that told Pauline she was contrasting her with Sylvie.

Pauline looked up now and saw Amy's eyes fixed on her; but it turned out to be with compassion: 'You look awfully sick,' Amy said.

'Yes, that's why I'm home.' And Pauline did feel sick, with disappointment. She said, 'Do you think they're coming back soon?'

'I wouldn't know. There was no one here when I got back. It's not very pleasant for me, to come from school and there's no one here.'

'No. You're right. It's not.' Pauline spoke as a fellow sufferer – though in the past she had enjoyed nothing more than to come home to an empty apartment and be alone there and still.

'Do you want to know how I was born?' Amy said.

Pauline wanted to say no, but instead said, 'If you want,' without encouragement.

'I was born in India,' Amy said.

'What – in that ashram place?'

'Oh no. Theo and Sylvie didn't live there any more – they'd gone up in the mountains to be by themselves in a hut. They didn't have any water or electricity or anything. They washed in a mountain spring.'

Amy was sitting next to Pauline by this time, quite close, as if craving company. 'I'll just do it for a minute, shall I? I'm really good at it, but you can tell me to stop if you don't like it. Okay?'

She began to massage Pauline's head. It *was* soothing, although Amy's fingers were a bit greasy, probably from the corn chips. She was so close to Pauline that she was almost sitting in her lap, enveloping her in her smell. Some of this was like Sylvie's – they used the same shampoo and soap – but some of it was peculiar to Amy: natural, in the sense of non-artificial, also somewhat dewy and damp like the wool of a lamb that had been out in the rain.

'So were you born in this hut?'

'Sylvie wanted to stay, but with there being no doctor or anyone near, Theo took her down to the town – it was a holy town called Hardwar so that was all right. And they say I was so good I just waited till they had gotten her in this hospital and then guess what? I came out so fast they said it was like kittens coming out of a mother cat so we needn't have been in the hospital at all and I could have been born in the hut.'

Amy had now climbed right into Pauline's lap – this was in order to press her fingertips against Pauline's brow. It was simultaneously soothing and disturbing: Pauline was really not used to having anyone sit in her lap and touch her face so intimately.

'But then we did go back to the hut, Sylvie and Theo and I, and they were so crazy about me they couldn't stop looking at me and they'd get up at night and wake me up, just so they could play with me some more and count my fingers and toes.'

'Do you remember all this?'

'They told me but I think I remember it too. I *think*. I was only seven months old when we left. It was snowing all the time and they couldn't find any more firewood. Anyway, by that time Granny had found out and we had to leave. Leave India, that is, and go to New York. Because of Granny. Are you feeling better now?'

'Yes, I think so. Thank you very much, Amy.'

'I do it well, don't I? Sylvie likes me doing it even when she doesn't have a headache. She's very sensuous, Theo says.'

Late that night Amy and Sylvie had one of their fights. Pauline, who was already in bed, propped herself on her elbow to listen, but they were showering together so most of what they said was drowned by the sound of the water. Next morning was as usual a big rush, with Sylvie having to take Amy to school. When she returned from this mission – for which she had merely thrown a raincoat over her nightdress, which anyway wasn't much different from her usual kind of frock – she went straight back to bed. This too was her custom, so that she was always asleep by the time Pauline left for her office. But today Pauline wouldn't let her; she followed her into the bedroom and said, 'We have to talk.'

Although warm and nestled between her sheets, Sylvie roused herself to face a serious and perhaps not unfamiliar situation: 'I know, I know – and I swear we'll go the moment we find a place, I promise.'

'It's not that,' Pauline said. 'It's not that at all.' She was silent – not that there were no questions to ask but that there were too many. For instance: where had Sylvie gone yesterday with Theo? What had they fought about, she and Amy? Instead, when Pauline spoke, it was to say: 'What I asked you the other day? In the museum?' When Sylvie looked puzzled – 'Because I really do need someone, and if you can't do it or would rather not . . . ' And still receiving no answer, Pauline worked herself up a bit: 'When someone offers you a job, the least you can do is say yes or no. I mean, it would just be common courtesy.'

'Oh Pauline. I never thought for a minute you were serious.'

'Why wouldn't I be?'

'It's such a terrific compliment – to think anyone would think *me* capable of a *job*. When I told Theo, he laughed and laughed.'

'Who's he to laugh? What's he ever done for you except come around here to my place in the afternoons or whatever – where did you go yesterday? Where were you when poor Amy was sent home from school and no one here to meet her? I think that's shocking. Absolutely shocking.'

Sylvie hung her head and plucked at the satin hem of the bedsheet. It was not possible to tell whether she was ashamed or offended.

For fear it might be the latter, Pauline went on: 'I know it's none of my business but I'm so fond of you both, you and Amy.'

'You've been an angel to us, dearest Pauline. You *are* an angel.'

'Well, you see, I love you.'

'Of course you do,' Sylvie said. 'And we love you. Very, very much,' she added, but this, for Pauline, only made her reply less satisfactory.

Although Pauline felt herself so overwhelmed with work that she was ready to hire an assistant, a few days later she again shut her office early and went home. This time she found what she expected – Sylvie was there, and Theo was with her. Pauline could hear them splashing in the bathroom, but when she opened the door, she quickly shut it again. Theo was washing Sylvie's hair; she had her head bent over the basin while he massaged soapsuds into it; both were naked. But when they came out, Theo had wrapped a towel around his waist and Sylvie was in a white bathrobe. They looked like twins.

'What a surprise,' Theo said, referring to Pauline's unexpected arrival; he made it sound like a joyous surprise.

'Yes, well, you see, I have to talk to Sylvie on a very important matter.'

Theo was rueful: 'I'm afraid I can guess what it is, and I promise you that the minute we've found a halfway nice place we're going to move out, and meanwhile I cannot tell you how terrifically grateful we all are to you, aren't we, Sylvie? Do stop that and listen to Pauline,' for Sylvie was vigorously rubbing her hair with a towel.

'But it's all *wet*,' Sylvie protested. 'I'll drip on her rug and ruin it.'

Theo said, 'Oh you mustn't. It's such a pretty rug.' He looked down at it and Pauline could tell from the politely sweet expression on his face that he didn't think so at all. She had had the same impression before when she had encountered Theo in her apartment. Although she had taken a lot of trouble with her furniture and fittings – matching colours and so on – in his presence everything appeared drab, lower-class.

Ignoring him, she addressed herself only to Sylvie: 'You still haven't given me an answer – I don't think you realize how important it is, important for the business, that is, for me to have a proper assistant.'

'You're talking about the job you offered her, and that again I must say shows your incredible kindness.'

Pauline said, 'I hear it made you laugh no end.'

'Made *me* laugh–?' Unable to believe that he might be the person referred to, he put both his hands on his chest. His chest was naked, giving him an almost mythological appearance. He looked as if he might be living in a forest and carrying a bow and arrow, not to shoot down birds or other living creatures but apples from a tree for Sylvie to eat.

Theo had turned to Sylvie: 'Did you tell Pauline that I laughed?' Sylvie began to defend herself, they argued with each other, softly, sweetly, while Pauline stood by. She realized that it was hopeless to try to intervene – they would only have listened to her politely and then turned back to each other. She could not come between them, no one could; perhaps not even Amy.

Amy turned out to be receptive to the idea of Sylvie taking a job. She at once asked Pauline, 'What'll you pay her?'

Sylvie said, 'Amy, that's vulgar.'

'No it's not,' Pauline said. 'It's realistic.'

She was relieved to have been able to return to the topic in Amy's presence and away from what she could not help feeling was Theo's negative influence. But Sylvie still seemed to be under the latter: 'We don't need money,' she told Amy.

'Yes we do. We need heaps.'

'What for?'

You know very well what for,' Amy said.

She and Sylvie exchanged a conspiratorial look that excluded Pauline. Yet Pauline too wanted to ask, what could they possibly need money for? It was not in her present interest to point out that they lived rent-free, or that she paid their grocery bills – though it was true that these had hardly increased since they had moved in with her. Their vegetarian diet of cereals and pulses was as frugal as if they had been living on bird seed.

Sylvie said, 'Theo gives us whatever we need.'

'Theo doesn't have anything to give,' Amy said.

'He will, though,' Sylvie said with quiet confidence.

'Not till Grandma dies. Which she won't.' Amy raised her voice to defend her facts: 'She's terribly healthy and she has all these doctors giving her vitamin injections and all these people coming in doing massage and things on her and you know she goes swimming every afternoon because that's the only time Theo ever gets to come visit you.'

'That's not true,' Sylvie said.

'It is so! *And* she plays tennis but Theo can't get away then in case she needs him for a partner.'

'You'll have to forgive Amy,' Sylvie turned to Pauline. 'Sometimes she just doesn't know what she's talking about. No you don't! You're a silly brat, that's all.'

'*I'm* a silly brat, look who's talking. *I'm* the only one who earns any money. And I give you all my pocket money from Grandma to put in our savings and you haven't put in one single dime.'

'I haven't got one single dime.'

'Then why don't you take Pauline's job! She'll pay you—'

Pauline gladly said, 'Of course I will.' But when Amy at once came back with 'How much?' she became more cautious. She said to Sylvie, You'd be on a starting salary at first, but later of course when you really know the business—'

'How long would that take?' Amy asked. 'Because we haven't got very long. *You* think we have,' she turned again on Sylvie, 'but I'm not going to that shitty school forever or stick around here when you *promised* – you *promised*—'

'Amy, shush, darling, it's our secret.'

'Don't *pinch* me.' But Amy bit in her lips so that no further words should escape her, not even in answer to Sylvie's 'I did not'.

Next day Pauline lost another client. Unfortunately it was one whom she had been nurturing for several months, for a bigger sale than usually came her way – a converted brownstone in the East Fifties, and Pauline had made an appointment to meet her client there for what she hoped was a final and decisive viewing. But just as she was about to leave on this mission, Theo came into the office. 'Can we talk?' he said to Pauline after a pleasant greeting. When she hesitated, 'You're busy. A pity, but never mind. That's just our bad luck. Sylvie's and mine.'

Pauline hesitated again, but not for long. She dialled her client's number and left a message on the machine to postpone the meeting by an hour. Then she allowed Theo to lead her away. Although this was her neighbourhood and not his, he knew exactly where to take her. It was not a place she would have chosen herself – a stone garden created between mammoth buildings with an artificial waterfall trained to run down a brick wall.

'Isn't this fun,' said Theo, bringing two styrofoam cups of coffee from the refreshment window, and also, in case one of them felt hungry, a Danish in plastic wrap. There were only a few elderly people sitting around, some reading the newspaper, some dozing, one or two staring straight into the waterfall but probably seeing other things. The chairs were white metal, small and uncomfortable with criss-cross seats like egg slicers.

Theo said, 'I shall have to take them away.' For a moment Pauline didn't know what he was talking about, and when she realized, she cried out much too loudly, 'You're crazy!'

He smiled sadly: 'It is a shame.' Then he assured her: 'You're not to blame. You meant well, but things don't always turn out the way we intend.'

'And may I ask,' she said, 'what is it that hasn't worked out?'

He gestured into the air, indicating that the matter was too delicate to be put into words. But she wanted words and didn't care if she appeared crude and indelicate. She felt that way, anyhow, in his presence. She was dressed in a very good business suit, with a blouse that had cost her a good deal of money, but beside him – though all he wore was jeans and a shirt – she felt badly dressed. It couldn't be helped; she was what she was; so she repeated her question.

He was courteous and tried to give her a fair answer. He said, 'You see, we have to be careful. Amy's very high-strung.'

'Amy? What have I done to Amy?'

'Please. I said it wasn't your fault. But once Amy gets something in her head, it's one hell of a thing to get it out again. It was a mistake, you know,' he said. 'Asking Sylvie to work for you. You know Sylvie better than that. She can't. She wouldn't be able to.'

Pauline swallowed – controlling her rising anger for the sake of a higher good. 'I thought she might like to; to give her something to do; pass the time while Amy's at school and you're with your mother.' When he made no response, she went on – quickly, before the subject could be considered closed: 'But of course it was only an idea. She doesn't have to at all, and we'll just go on as before.'

'Yes, but now there's Amy.'

'What does Amy *want*?'

'Amy wants money. Ridiculous child.' He smiled.

Drops of water fell on them from the artificial waterfall. It reminded her of sitting with Sylvie by the museum fountain. Why should they have this association with water, with cool crystal drops, as though their place were by the side of a mountain spring? In spite of his clear eyes, his graceful figure as of a young hunter, he did not at this moment give her the impression of purity; on the contrary.

'That's why I have to take them away,' he said. 'But don't you have to meet someone? Your client?'

She gave a start. She had truly forgotten. But now she said, 'It doesn't matter.'

'Oh but it does. You mustn't neglect your business – certainly not on our account. You want all the money you can get. Everyone does.'

'Including Amy?'

'Amy wants it so badly that she's willing to send poor Sylvie to do a job she's absolutely not fit for. Not physically, not temperamentally, not in any way. I know you acted from the noblest motives – out of love and affection for us – but I wish you hadn't started this whole thing. Now Amy can think of nothing but money, a salary, all that.'

Pauline pleaded: 'It wouldn't be very hard work.'

'I'm sure not, but unfortunately Sylvie's not capable of any work.'

'She could stay home. It wouldn't be any different from what it is now.'

'You mean you'd pay her a salary for staying home? Only for staying with you? . . . You really are a saint. An angel.' In gratitude, he undid the Danish for her from its plastic wrap, but then advised her not to eat it as it was stale.

*

For the past few years Pauline had considered herself comfortably off. She had built up her business and was able to pay herself a good salary out of it. But now, after losing several clients – she told herself the market was bad – her income was declining. This was especially unfortunate now that she had begun to pay Sylvie a salary, which, after negotiation with Theo, turned out to be almost as high as her own. Often there was nothing at all going on in her office, so that on several afternoons she had just locked up and gone home. She always went hopefully, but when she arrived, Sylvie was either not there, or she and Theo were together in the second bedroom where Pauline could not disturb them. She didn't even let them know she was there but tiptoed out again and went to a movie she had no particular desire to see. At such times, she remembered other homecomings, evenings in the past before they had moved in with her, when, after a long, busy day in the office, she had lain on the sofa in her old wrap with a gin martini she had mixed for herself, savouring her silence, her solitude, her peace. Now she had no peace – whether they were home or not home. She didn't even have it when she was away from them, in the office or alone at the cinema, because of thinking about them all the time, wondering where they were, what they were doing; wanting to be with them.

But even when she was with them, she still found herself alone. Sylvie and Amy always seemed to have so much to do – their laundry, Amy's homework, cooking their gruel which needed hours of stirring – and also so much to discuss, arguing and, more and more nowadays, fighting with each other. They continued to be careful to keep their voices down, so that she could never make out what they were saying, however hard she strained to do so. And that was all she was capable of doing now – straining to hear what they were saying, to discover what they might be up to. It had become impossible for her to concentrate on anything else, like her accounts or a book. If some old friend telephoned, she hardly had time to talk, she was so afraid of missing something going on between Sylvie and Amy.

More than anything, Pauline looked forward to the Sundays when Amy was away at her grandmother's and she could have Sylvie to herself. But on each of these Sundays Sylvie became progressively more miserable. She sat hunched in a corner of the sofa, twisting a strand of hair between her fingers and staring ahead with large scared eyes. If Pauline suggested one of their usual outings, she declined – terribly politely, the more remote she was the more polite. She said Theo or Amy might telephone and she didn't want to miss their call. They never did; and when, perhaps desperate with waiting, she herself dialled their number, she put the receiver down before anyone could answer. 'They don't want to be disturbed,' she explained; once she said, 'His mother doesn't like me to phone.'

The resigned way she said this angered Pauline: 'How long are you going to stand for this?'

'What can I do?' Sylvie said. 'We have no money. Only she has.'

'And what I give you? Your salary?'

'You're so kind, Pauline,' Sylvie said, courteously acknowledging what could only be considered a mere trifle.

Pauline bit her lip – to her it was not a trifle at all; in fact, the way things were, she had difficulty paying it. But she longed to be able to say that she would increase the amount, that she would give Sylvie as much as she wanted – suddenly she said, 'You know everything that's mine is yours,' but she

246

blushed scarlet and was breathless, as if this statement had been literally wrung out of her.

'I do know it,' Sylvie said with sincere gratitude. 'We're such a burden on you, Pauline – yes we are – but I promise you it's only for now. Like Theo says, we only have to wait.'

'Wait for what? For his mother to die – that's what you're waiting for, don't tell me.' Sylvie hung her head in shame, so that Pauline's heart was filled with pity and she said, 'We don't *need* Theo's mother.'

Sylvie raised her head and stared at Pauline: 'Who's we?'

'You and I – and Amy of course.'

Pauline waited for her, expected her to say, 'And Theo?' But she did not. His name may have hung in the air, but it was not spoken. Pauline welcomed this silence, which she interpreted to her own advantage.

By the first of the next month, Pauline found herself in trouble. Her rent was due for the office, her maintenance for the apartment, she had to have her own salary and the amount she had agreed to pay Sylvie. She did not know where anything was to come from; she had made no deals for the past four months and the business account had run very low. She considered all the payments essential except her own; and for this latter, to cover her domestic expenses, she was forced for the first time to break into her savings. She did so with a heavy heart. Her savings were sacrosanct to her, they were her future, her freedom from friends, family, from all the world except herself; they were the ground on which she stood. However, for one month it wouldn't matter; she would try not to spend more than was necessary to keep their household going. It was easy to do without a new summer outfit, and also she wouldn't be taking her usual vacation in the Berkshires this year. She always stayed in a good hotel, which she could afford on her own but would be excessive for three of them – that is, if Sylvie and Amy would consent to accompany her, which they probably wouldn't. And she knew that, without them, she would not be able to derive her usual joy and consolation from her holiday, her solitary walks in the cool woods, her morning coffee under a maple tree on the summery green grounds of the hotel.

Two months later, there were still no deals, and the office account had reached an all-time low. By taking an overdraft, she might just be able to squeeze out the rent and the maintenance, but the salaries, hers and Sylvie's, would again have to come out of her savings. She had already taken a substantial cut in her own salary; and she was now trying to broach the subject of a possible reduction in Sylvie's too. 'Only for this month,' she was planning to plead. 'Only till the next deal comes through.'

To say this, she had waited for the Sunday of Amy's visit to her grandmother. But Sylvie was so edgy – waiting for the phone to ring, dialling and then putting down the receiver – that Pauline could not find an opportunity all day. In the evening Amy returned in a very bad mood. Although she handed over her pocket money as usual, she did not spread out her presents for Sylvie to see but locked herself into the second bedroom, so that Sylvie had to stand outside, calling softly for admittance.

Pauline said, 'What's the matter?' And when Sylvie parted her lips so that her teeth showed in a smile indicating everything was fine, she went on, 'Then why has she locked herself in?'

'Oh you know,' Sylvie said with the same smile.

'I wish I did,' Pauline said.

Sylvie moved away from the door. She arranged a flower in a vase, then patted a cushion or two, to show how happy and comfortable she was here with Pauline in the apartment. But soon she was back by the bedroom door, calling through it, 'Let me *in*,' in a way that made Amy open the door, though only just enough for Sylvie to slip in.

Pauline stooped to put her ear against the keyhole; she felt she had to do it, low and mean though she considered it to be, for the sake of their future. But soon she didn't have to listen at the keyhole, their voices rose enough for her to hear. And then they screeched in such a way that Pauline felt compelled to thump on the door, and when they failed to answer, she tried the handle – it was unlocked, the door flew open, and the two stood revealed, each tugging at a hank of the other's long blonde hair.

Pauline rushed between them, and though herself receiving some pinches and slaps, managed to separate them. They stood on either side of her, looking away from one another, both of them flushed and pouting with angry self-righteousness. And to Pauline's repeated inquiry of what had happened, each tilted her chin in the other's direction: 'Ask *her*.'

'Yes, ask her,' Sylvie said at last. 'Ask her why she's so mean and horrible.'

'I'm not giving it,' Amy said. She glared at Sylvie and Sylvie looked back at her with the same face. Amy said, 'All you ever do is give it to him! And he just keeps it for himself.'

'Oh wicked, wicked,' Sylvie said, bating her breath at so much wickedness.

'Then what's he do with it? Why doesn't he do what he promised for ages and ages? With my money and with what Pauline gives you?' And in response to Sylvie's shushing sound, she stamped her foot and cried, 'I don't want to have a secret any more!' Tears of rage were in her eyes.

'I'm sorry, darling,' Sylvie said. 'I've upset you. It's my fault.' To Pauline she said, 'I keep forgetting she's only a child.'

'You always say that when I want something you don't want!' Amy brushed at her cheeks, ashamed of the tears that had begun to roll and were of sorrow now more than rage.

Sylvie started forward to embrace and comfort her. But Pauline remained between them; she even stuck her elbow out to prevent Sylvie from approaching Amy. And it was Pauline herself who embraced Amy and encouraged her to bury her face in Pauline's bosom. She pressed Amy's head against herself so that she could not raise it to meet Sylvie's imploring gaze.

Most afternoons, since Sylvie was busy with Theo at that time, Amy was brought home in a car pool; but on that following day Pauline again shut her office early and waited for Amy outside the school. Amy's mood was still sullen; she hardly greeted Pauline and walked beside her, kicking at the sidewalk. But Pauline had a treat in mind for her. She took her to a palatial new hotel with a lobby that was all gold and glass and flowers in purple vases as tall as Amy. The tea room was upstairs, reached by a curving carpeted staircase, and it made Amy gasp at its beauty. Golden angels floated in a sea of glass and crystal; they played lyres and wore garlands of plaster-of-paris fruits and flowers wound around their ankles. Although the lyres were inaudible, celestial sounds came from a lady harpsichordist in a chiffon gown. The waiters were handsome and dressed as for a wedding; one of them held Amy's chair for her, but before daring to sit on it, she whispered to Pauline: 'Do you think I'm okay?' She was in her uniform and was rather grimy from a day of working and playing at school.

'You're fine,' Pauline assured her. She had never seen Amy's eyes shining so brightly.

'Wouldn't Sylvie love it here,' Amy said, looking around with those eyes.

'Yes, I wish she were with us. But I guess she's with Theo.' Pauline watched the brightness fall from Amy's face. But Pauline pressed on: 'They're together every afternoon, aren't they, when you're at school and I'm in the office. Do you think they have a lot of secrets they don't want us to know about?'

'They've got one secret and I know about it.'

'I don't,' Pauline said.

A waiter smilingly held out a silver tray of little sandwiches to Amy who took one in a very refined way and said, 'Thank you,' in the same way. Pauline encouraged her, 'Take more than that, they're so tiny.' Amy did so – it was a ham sandwich, but Pauline did not tell her.

'I don't think it's nice when people have secrets from their friends,' Pauline said. 'I think friends should tell each other everything.'

'Yes, but if they've promised their other friends that they wouldn't—' Amy frowned as one trying to grasp and state a metaphysical problem.

Pauline said, 'Oh of course, no one must ever break a promise.'

Amy frowned more: 'But what if they break *their* promise . . . '

'I'm sure they wouldn't. What are you doing?' For Amy was taking the tops off her remaining sandwiches to examine the contents.

'I want one like the pink one I ate. What was it?'

'I think it was tomato. Take mine.' Pauline put her own ham sandwich on Amy's plate. She said, 'They love you too much ever to break a promise they've made you.'

'That's what you think.' Amy chewed; she brooded; she appeared tempted to say more. Pauline sipped her tea, seemingly indifferent, enjoying the harpsichord music, and Amy gave in to temptation: 'They've promised and promised and they still haven't done it.'

'Haven't done what? But if you tell me, you'll be giving away the secret and you mustn't. You know what? I'll tell *you* a secret, but will you promise not to tell *them*? All right: the sandwich you ate? The two sandwiches? They were ham.'

'What's ham?'

'It's meat. It's meat from a pig.'

The harpsichord, sweet and mellifluous, played into the silence between them. At last Amy said, 'So what. I don't care, I liked it. I can eat meat if I want.'

'Yes, but they don't want you to.'

'Only because of going there. They say when we're there we can only eat fruit and nuts and everything pure like that ... In India, in the hut where we lived when I was born. They said we're going there as soon as we've gotten enough money, and I've given them my pocket money for years and years and you're giving them money and we're still here. Ask him if he has another sandwich like that. I'll eat all the ham I want and I'll tell them and they can do what they like.'

'You said you wouldn't tell. You promised,' Pauline reminded her.

But it seemed Amy no longer believed in promises. She told Sylvie that same evening, and went on, 'And I'm going to eat steak too like Pauline and hot dogs and hamburgers and stuff like everyone else eats every day.'

252

'You know what that means,' Sylvie said in a warning voice.

'Oh sure, yeah. It means I can't go to India with you.' And when Sylvie shot a look in Pauline's direction – 'She knows. I told her. And I told her how you're not going anyway like you said, and all you do is take my money and her money and give it to Theo.'

Sylvie, a hunted doe, glanced around wildly, wondering where help was to be found. Amy's arms were crossed defiantly; she remained adamant. But Pauline, touched by Sylvie's pale distress, said: 'He's probably keeping it in a savings account for you to earn interest so you'll have more money.'

'Yes, more money for him,' Amy replied.

Sylvie pleaded, 'And for you and for me. So we can go.'

'He doesn't want to go,' Amy said. 'He likes being here with Granny. You don't know, you haven't ever seen them! He's always messing around with her silver and stuff and those pictures she has like that stupid Picasso that's supposed to be such a big deal.'

'It is a big deal, Amy,' Sylvie said. 'And one day it'll all belong to Theo and to you and to me.'

'But I keep telling you! You can wait till you're a hundred thousand years old and she still won't be dead, she'll be swimming in her swimsuit from Bendel's and it's you who'll be old and die. You'll die and leave me,' Amy ended very differently from how she had begun.

And in response Sylvie too changed: 'I'll never leave you,' she said, utterly confident, scornful of any such idea.

Next day, while Pauline was sitting idle in her idle office, she was surprised by a visit from Sylvie. Sylvie was in a long buttercup-yellow dress and a straw hat with a buttercup-yellow ribbon. Involuntarily, Pauline rose in her chair, and then found herself blushing: she didn't know if it was in embarrassment or from the tide of warmth that surged out of her heart and suffused her.

But Sylvie at once said, 'Why did you give her ham to eat? And telling her it was tomato.'

Although this was an accusation, Sylvie spoke as usual in a mild voice; and Pauline lowered her own rather harsh one to ask, also mildly, 'Does it matter so very much?'

'It's a principle, Pauline.' Sylvie looked around her: 'It's different in here.'

It was different. The pretty striped armchairs appeared to be dusty; a bulb had gone out on one of the Chinese vase table lamps, leaving it to the other one to light up the rather dim interior.

'Is it?' Pauline looked around abstractedly. 'No, it's just the same ... Whose principle is this? Is it Amy's?'

'In a way ... When she was born, she was – I can't tell you – so shiny white, it was like you could look through her, like she was an angel. We said, we must give her nothing but angel food – it was a joke really, but we were eating very simple food ourselves, so my milk I was giving her came out as pure and white as she was ... I don't know what she eats at school; what the other girls give her. Children always want to do the same as everyone else. If only we could get her away.'

'She wants to go, more than anything.' Pauline leaned across her desk: 'But do you want to?'

'Of course. That's what we're saving for, putting everything away ... That reminds me.' She was embarrassed; so was Pauline: it was past the beginning of the month and she had not yet paid Sylvie. 'I'm sorry to ask you,' Sylvie said, acutely apologetic, 'but it's important for us.'

'No, I'm glad you did because I was going to mention it

myself ... I was going to ask you if you would mind very much waiting maybe till the middle of the month, or when I get paid for something I'm putting through now.'

Sylvie tried the switch of the table lamp; but the bulb really was dead, and moreover when she withdrew her hand, it was dusty. 'Don't you think, Pauline, you should – maybe – you know – a little bit, so it would look nice for clients who come in.'

'What clients?' This escaped Pauline, with bitterness, before she could stop herself.

'Why, Pauline, you've got hundreds of clients! And you just said there's a big deal coming through in the middle of the month – not that I care about getting paid, if you can't you can't, I mean, I would be happy to wait—'

'But Theo wouldn't?'

Sylvie leaned back in her chair with a sigh. It was so difficult to explain, but she tried. 'There's two things. One is that Theo is really quite businesslike, he doesn't look it but it's the sort of family he comes from and that's how they've made a lot of money. It's sort of in his genes.'

'And the other thing?'

'The other thing is Amy and I. He's doing it for us, saving and so on. So he can take us away. Well! Aren't you sick and tired of us, even though you are a saint, you must be counting the days till we move out.'

'And will he take you where Amy wants to go?'

Sylvie smiled her sad smile, as at something too desirable to be possible.

'Because if he doesn't, I will.'

Pauline hadn't thought she was going to say this – she hadn't thought of it at all – but now suddenly it was there: a possibility, something she could do, something not fantastic but within her reach. Too excited to stay still, she got up: 'Let's go home,' she said. It was Sylvie who protested it was only the middle of the afternoon, that a client might come: Pauline turned off the one remaining lamp and then shut the office door behind them and padlocked it.

And next day she did not reopen it. She had too much to do. She had spent the previous evening elaborating her idea, explaining it to Amy, talking it over with her and Sylvie. Amy was wild with enthusiasm, and between them they swept Sylvie along. Pauline conclusively proved to them that it was something that could be achieved within a short time. All Pauline had to do was dissolve her savings and her pension fund; and she could sell her apartment, or rent it out furnished, and maybe she could sell her business too, to some big company, and if she couldn't, she would just lock up and go away; at least she would be saving the overdue rent on it, and the landlords could do what they liked. She became light-headed, she was so busy proving to them that Theo was not the only one who was practical.

First thing in the morning, she started phoning around the airlines, to get a price on fares; from there on they could work out the rest of their budget. Amy wanted to stay home from school to help her – anyway, she argued, what was the use of continuing with school now? Pauline helped Sylvie persuade her to leave; though afterwards she wished she were back again because, without Amy there to prop her up, Sylvie began to falter. She kept biting her underlip and saying, 'Are you sure it's all right, Pauline, that you want to do this?' until Pauline, in between her telephone calls, replied, 'I've never been so sure of anything in my life.' And truly it seemed to her that she had shaken off the burden of her past and her personality – and was ready to step out unencumbered into a new world of freedom and light.

However, this mood vanished when Theo appeared in the afternoon. It was left to Pauline to tell him of their plan while Sylvie sat by, biting her lip. When Pauline had finished, Theo laughed; and then Sylvie laughed too, though glancing nervously at Pauline.

'Yes, isn't it a hoot,' Pauline said to him. 'You've kept them hanging with your promises for years together, and when I come in, it's all done within hours. Here are the figures: an economy couple ticket for Sylvie and me, and half-fare for Amy because she's under twelve.' She held out the yellow pad on which she had been scribbling all morning.

Theo peered at it, as if he were near-sighted, which he was not. He said, 'Yes, you've got it all worked out.' He looked up and at Sylvie: 'Pauline's got it all worked out, for you and Amy and herself . . . I'd like to come, I really would,' he said to Pauline. 'But I do have obligations here – unfortunately one can't just pack up and leave and turn his back on everything. Sylvie understands that.' He put his arm around Sylvie's shoulders and looked apologetically at Pauline.

Again it struck Pauline how alike they looked, like twins, a boy and a girl – though from another planet, a different one from Pauline's. But she spoke up courageously, as if there were hope of communication: 'Does Amy understand? You've been promising her since the day she was born, almost.'

Theo said, 'If you promise a child Santa Claus, you're not exactly obliged to deliver him on Christmas Day.'

'So that's all it is: Santa Claus.' Pauline looked towards Sylvie, not hopefully, not really expecting help.

Sylvie spoke gently to her, as if she felt sorry for her and wanted to explain things: 'Without Theo, it's only a hut on a hillside, and anyway it's probably fallen down by now.'

'We can always find another hut,' Pauline said.

'But why should you? When you've got this nice apartment—' Theo looked around, the way he always did, with that set smile that told Pauline what he really thought of her modest little interior. 'Two bedrooms, and everything so cosy and tasteful, not to speak of your office—'

'Pauline doesn't want to keep her office,' Sylvie told him. 'She says she owes the rent and is not making any money.'

'Oh?' Theo said.

'She says she can't pay me anything this month,' Sylvie said.

'Of course I can!' Pauline had jumped up. 'And next month I'll be able to give you more, there's some big deals coming up.' She waved Sylvie away impatiently before she could even speak. 'You don't think I would ever give up my office, turn my back on it, just pack up and leave? That's not the way I was brought up.' She was going to say more, but Theo put up his hand in warning. They all three listened to the key turn in the lock of the front door – it was Amy, delivered by her car pool, letting herself in.

'Don't tell her,' Sylvie whispered. She held out her hand for the yellow pad Pauline was holding and looked around for somewhere to hide it. Theo took it from her and slid it inside the back of Pauline's sofa. Then all three turned to face the door with that false smile of adults who have promised children something that they have no intention of delivering. Only Pauline had difficulty keeping up her smile: for Amy entered with a radiance of expectation that Pauline, settling for a lesser good, had only just managed to extinguish within herself.

Two Muses

Now that my grandfather, Max Nord, is so famous – many years after his death, a whole new generation has taken him up – I suppose every bit of information about him is of interest to his readers. But my view of him is so familiar, so familial that it might be taken as unwelcome domestic gossip. Certainly, I grew up hearing him gossiped about – by my parents, and everyone else who knew about him and his household set-up. At that time no one believed that his fame would last; and it is true that it did not revive to its present pitch till much later – in fact, till everyone had gone: he himself and his two widows, Lilo and Netta, and my parents too, so that I'm the only family member left to reap the fruits of what now turns out to be, after all, his genius.

Max, Lilo and Netta had come to England as refugees in the thirties. I was born after the war, so I knew nothing of those earlier years in London when they were struggling with a new language and a new anonymity; for it was not only his work that was in eclipse, they themselves were too – their personalities, which could not be placed or recognized in this alien society. At home, in the Germany of the twenties and early thirties, they had each one of them had a brilliant role: Max of course was the young genius, whose early novels had caused a sensation, and Lilo was his prize – the lovely young daughter of a banking family much grander than his own. Netta was dashing, dramatic, chic in short skirts and huge hats. She loved only artists – painters, opera singers – only geniuses, the more famous the better. She never found one more famous than Max, which was maybe why she loved and stayed with him for the rest of their lives. It always seemed to me that it was Netta, much more than his wife Lilo, who fussed over him, adored him, made excuses for him. Lilo sometimes got impatient with him, and I have heard her say to Netta, 'Why don't you take him home with you and make everyone happy, most of all me?' But the moment she had said this, she covered her face and laughed, and Netta also laughed, as at a big joke.

They always spoke in English to each other; it was a matter of principle with them, although they must have felt much more at home in their native German, its idiom packed with idiosyncratic meaning for them. But they had banished that language, too proud to use it now that they themselves had been banished from its precincts. Lilo had had an English governess as a child so that her accent was more authentic than that of the other two – though not quite: I myself, an English child growing up in England, never thought of my grandmother as anything but foreign. Max's accent was so impenetrable that it was sometimes impossible to understand what he was saying (always impossible for me, but then I didn't understand him anyway). Yet, although he did not speak it well, Max's grasp of the English language must have been profound; he continued to write in German but spent weeks and months with his English translator, wrestling over nuances of meaning.

Since Max's work is so well known today, I need not say

much about it. This is just as well, for his books are not the
slender psychological novels I prefer but huge tomes with the
characters embodying and expressing abstract thought. Today
they are generally accepted as masterpieces, but during his
last years – which are those that I remember – this estimate
was confined to a small group of admirers. In his own household it was of course accepted without question – even by my
grandmother Lilo, although I now suspect that she was not
as devoted a reader of his works as she should have been. In
fact, I wonder sometimes if she read them at all, especially the
later, most difficult ones. But Lilo was not really a reader. She
liked to go for long walks, to make odd purchases at antique
stalls and to play tennis. Yet as a girl she had read the classics –
mostly German, and Russian in translation – and, with all her
desirable suitors, she had chosen to marry a young writer of
modest means and background. An only child, she lived – an
enchanted princess – in her father's villa in the salubrious outskirts of the city. Max would bicycle from the less salubrious
city centre where he was a lodger in the flat of an army widow.
He brought his latest manuscript and they sat under the trees
in her father's garden – in their memories, as transmitted to
me, it seems to have been always summer – and he read from
his work to her till it got too dark to see. He was so engrossed
in his own words that he noticed nothing – it was she who
cried, 'Maxi! A bee!' She saved him from it with vigorous flaps
of the napkin that had come out with the coffee tray. This tray
also bore, besides the voluminous, rosebudded coffee pot, an
apple or other fruit tart, so that Lilo was constantly on the
alert with the same napkin; and in other ways too she was
distracted – for instance, by a bird pecking away in the plum
tree, or by Max himself and the way his hair curled on the
nape of his strong round young neck where it was bent over

his manuscript. Sometimes she could not refrain from tickling him there a little bit, and then he looked up and found her smiling at him – and how could he not smile back? Perhaps it didn't even occur to him that she wasn't listening; or if it did, it wouldn't have mattered, because wasn't she herself the embodiment of everything he was trying to get into words?

After they were married, they lived in a house – it was her father's wedding present to them – not far from the one where she had grown up; it too had a garden, with fruit trees, bees and flowers, where Lilo spent a lot of time while he was in his study, writing (it was taken for granted) masterpieces. As the years went by, Lilo became more and more of a home bird – not that she was particularly domestic, she never was, not at all, but that she loved being there, in her own home where she was happy with her husband and child (my mother). During the summer months, and sometimes at Easter, the three of them went to the same big comfortable old hotel in the mountains where she had vacationed with her parents. During the rest of the year Max travelled by himself, to European conferences or to see his foreign publishers; he also had business in the city at least once a week and would go there no longer by bicycle but in his new Mercedes sports car. And it was here, in their home city, which was also hers, that he encountered Netta – or she encountered him, for there is no doubt that, however their affair developed, it was she who first hunted him down: her last, her biggest lion.

She saw him in a restaurant – one of those big plush bright crowded expensive places she went to frequently with her artistic circle of friends, and he only very occasionally, and usually only with his publisher. He was with his publisher that time too, the two of them dining together. They were both dressed elegantly but also very correctly, so that it would have been difficult to distinguish between publisher and author, if it had not been for Max's looks, which were noble, handsome. 'Oh my God! Isn't that Max Nord? Catch me, quick, I'm fainting—' and Netta collapsed into the lap of the nearest friend (an art critic). Soon she and Max were introduced and soon they were lovers – that never took long with her, at that time; but for him it may have been his first adulterous affair and he suffered terribly and made her suffer terribly. He would only meet her when he travelled to other cities, preferably foreign ones, so that they were always in hotel rooms – he checked in first, and when his business was concluded, he allowed her to join him. She wrote him frenzied, burning letters, which have since been published, by herself— '... Don't you know that I sit here and wait and die again and again, longing for a sign from you, my most beloved, my most wonderful terrible lover, oh you of the arched eyebrows and the— I kiss you a thousand times there and there and there ...' Years passed and the situation did not change for them: he would still only see her in other cities, stolen luxurious nights in luxurious hotel rooms; and she, who had always lived by love, now felt she was perishing by it. She had divorced her husband (her second), and though she still had many men friends, she no longer took them as her lovers; later there were rumours that she had sometimes turned to women friends, her tears and confession to them melting into acts of love. Her looks, always brilliant, became more so – her hats more enormous, her eyebrows plucked to the finest line; she wore fur stoles and cascades of jewels, she glistened in silk designer gowns slit up one side to show a length of splendid leg.

It has never been clear when Lilo first found out about the affair. There was always something vague about Lilo – also something secret, so that she may have known about it long before they realized she did. But whatever upheaval there may have been in their inner lives became vastly overwhelmed by what was happening in the streets, the cities, the countries around them. They, and everyone they knew, were preparing to leave; life had become a matter of visas and wherever possible secret foreign bank accounts. Even when he went abroad, to conferences where he was honoured, Max had only to lean out of his hotel window – Netta was there beside him – to witness marching, slogans, street fights, trucks packed with soldiers. Everyone emigrated where and when they could; farewells were mostly dispensed with – no one really expected to meet again, or if they did, it would be in countries so strange and foreign that they themselves would be as strangers to each other. Max, accepting asylum in England for himself and his family, left at what was almost the last moment. Only a week later his books were among those that were burned, an event that must have seared him even more than his parting from Netta. He was by nature a fatalist – he never thought he could actually do anything in the face of opposition, and indeed he couldn't – so he did not let himself hold out any hope of meeting Netta again. But she was the opposite: she knew she had her hand on the tiller of fate. She told him, 'I'll be there soon.' And so she was – she and even some of her furniture; all were installed in a flat in St John's Wood, within walking distance of where Max lived with his family in another flat, up a hill, in Hampstead.

I always assumed that the three of them – Max, Lilo and Netta – all lived in the Hampstead flat, and on the few occasions when Netta took me to St John's Wood, I would ask why we were coming to this place and who lived there. It was very different from my grandparents' home, which was in an ornate Edwardian apartment house buried among old trees, whereas Netta's block had been built ultra-smart on a Berlin model in the thirties and had porters and central heating. Her flat was light and sparse, with her tubular furniture and her white bear rug and the large expressionist painting she had brought of a café scene featuring herself among friends – chic women and nervously intellectual men, whom I thought of as the inhabitants of this place. For Netta herself really belonged in the other household where she appeared to be in complete charge of all domestic arrangements. Had Lilo ceded this place to her over the years, or had Netta usurped it? Probably it had fallen to her lot by virtue of temperament – especially during the early years of their exile when they were aliens, refugees, with thick accents and no social circle. Only Netta knew how to cope; and when war broke out, it was she who sewed the blackout curtains for their flat as well as her own and stuck tape over the windows so that they would not splinter during an air attack. She always managed to get something extra on their ration cards, and in the winter she unfroze the pipes with hot-water bottles and managed to get a fire going with damp lumps of rationed coal. She found domestic help for them – another refugee, Mrs Lipchik from Aachen, who was still with them by the time I began to visit the household. Even so, Netta's greatest contribution was not practical but what she did for their morale, or for Max's morale: he was the pivot of everything that had meaning for them.

These must have been difficult years for Max – exiled not only from his country but also from his language, his readers, his reputation. Netta created the conditions that allowed him to write new books. She had furnished his study at the end of the passage; it was his own furniture that they had brought with them, his desk and glass-fronted bookcases and the little round smoking table with leather armchair. Even I, when I was no more than three years old, knew that I could only tiptoe down the passage, preferably with my finger laid on my lips (Netta showed me how). No one was allowed to enter the study except herself twice a day, once with his morning coffee and digestive biscuits, and again in the afternoon with coffee and doughnut. When the telephone rang, it had to be answered swiftly and in hushed tones; if he himself stuck his head out to ask who was calling, she quickly assured him that it was nothing that need bother him. Lunch, starting with a good soup, was served exactly at one – only then was Mrs Lipchik permitted to ply her noisy vacuum cleaner – and if, hungry or frustrated, he appeared before that time, Netta sent him back again. All this would come to fruition in the evenings when they would gather in the sitting-room. This too was full of their German furniture, of light-coloured wood and, though modern, more solid and conventional than Netta's, with woodcuts (I particularly remember a medieval *danse macabre*) and Daumier cartoons on the walls. While Max read his day's work to them, Netta was totally rapt, though engaged in sewing, or darning his socks; sometimes she would make him repeat a phrase and then repeat it herself and become more rapt. Lilo didn't sew; she said her eyes weren't good enough. Sometimes, sated with Netta's comments, he might look for some response from Lilo, but she either gave none or said something irrelevant like, 'Maxi, I think your hair's going.' At once his hand flew to his brow – it was true, it was getting more and more noble, nobly arched – and Netta said quickly, 'What nonsense, nothing of the sort.' 'All right, don't believe me,' said Lilo, shrugging, knowing better.

Slowly, over the years, he became if not famous at least

known again. This is the period during which I remember him best, when new admirers and literary historians came to call on him. Besides his study and the passage leading up to it, the drawing-room (known as the *salon*) also became a silent zone at certain hours of the evening. Appointments for his visitors were regulated by Netta, and she was also the only person who entered, to bring a tray of refreshments and to listen in and make sure he wasn't being tired out by his visitors. He never was – he was too appreciative of this new respect and so was Netta, to witness him again taking up his rightful place as a European man of letters. Lilo did not participate in these sessions; she sat in the kitchen enjoying a cup of coffee with Mrs Lipchik. The two of them spoke together in German – the only time I heard that language in the flat – and it must have been a funny, racy sort of German, for it made them both laugh. I think sometimes they were also laughing at the visitors – I've seen Lilo do a comic imitation of some scholar she had seen arrive with his umbrella and wet shoes – and also maybe even at Max himself. Lilo always enjoyed laughing at Max, which didn't undermine her pride, or her other feelings for him.

Also, at this time, with foreign royalty payments beginning to come in again, their financial position became more stable. During their first years in England, and especially during the war, they had been almost poor, which affected the three of them in different ways. For Max, having no money was something he had been born to fear: he had grown up with a widowed mother who lived on a shrinking pension and had had to pretend they didn't need the things they couldn't afford, like a summer holiday. These long-buried memories came back to him and often drove him to a despair that he could only share with Netta. For Lilo, who knew nothing about not having money, blithely accepted that now, for the first time in her life, she was without it. Unable to afford new clothes, she was perfectly content to wear her old ones, even if they were sometimes torn. This characteristic remained with her, so that my memories of my grandmother included a Kashmir shawl that was falling apart and holes in the heels of her stockings. When they could no longer afford to pay Mrs Lipchik, Lilo told her so without embarrassment; and she gladly accepted Mrs Lipchik's offer to wait for her money and was grateful when Mrs Lipchik, to keep herself going, took a part-time job, enabling her sometimes to help them out with her earnings.

Netta too found a job around this time – probably in response to one of the scenes she had with Max, when he buried his head in her lap: 'What are we going to do, Netta? Without money, how can we live?' Although Netta too came from a family of modest means – her father had held a lifelong position as accountant to a shoe manufacturer – she didn't share Max's fear of poverty: from her youngest days, she had managed brilliantly with her looks and personality, finding jobs in boutiques and as a model, and later, living with or marrying, twice, wealthy men. Now, a refugee in London, she took what she could get and became a receptionist to a dentist, another refugee, Dr Erdmund from Dortmund. It was a full day's work, but she continued all her previous chores in the Hampstead flat. Sometimes, when there was a difficult case and she was kept longer in the surgery, she would arrive from the rush hour in the Underground with her coat flying open to get Max ready for an appointment she had scheduled for him. She didn't even have time to unpin her hat while she brushed him down, lapels and front and back, for, whatever else, he had to be perfect, and he always was. Nevertheless, he would be complaining about the difficult day he had had, the telephone ringing and no one to answer it, both Lilo and

Mrs Lipchik off somewhere or pretending to be deaf. Netta clicked her tongue in sympathy, and having finished with his coat, she got to work on his hair with a soft baby brush for, as Lilo had predicted, he had gone almost bald. She even had time to flick quickly through his mail – he had extracted the fan letters himself, leaving the rest to her. If she found anything disturbing, like an electricity bill or a tax notice, she slipped it into her handbag to take home to her own flat, for Lilo too did not care to deal with such matters.

Lilo spent her days in her own way, devoting herself to her daughter (my mother), and afterwards to me, her granddaughter. I was often sent to stay with her and would sit in the kitchen eating plum cake while she and Mrs Lipchik talked German; or Lilo would make drawings for me, of fruits and flowers, or a whole menagerie of animals out of Plasticine. When Netta was not there, I played at trains up and down the corridor – till the study door opened and Max stood there, in despair: 'God in heaven, is there no one to keep the child quiet!' The sight of him – looming and hostile – made me burst into tears, and Lilo would have to lead me away, while throwing reproachful looks over her shoulder at Max. To comfort me, she would take me out on one of her shopping expeditions; these were never for anything dull like groceries – that was Netta's province – but to antique stalls, where she would pick out the sweetest objects for me, like a painted Victorian picture frame or a miniature bouquet in enamel in a miniature vase. She liked to play tennis, and when they were both younger, she and Netta had played together; but Netta was too competitive, so that Lilo preferred to potter around with me on a court we booked for half an hour at a time in the public park.

When Max's reputation, and with it his royalties, had grown more substantial, Netta broached the subject of leaving her job. He said, 'Are you sure? Can we afford it?' She proved to him that they could, but he remained dubious: his inborn caution, as well as the experience of the previous years, made him reluctant to give up the assurance of a steady salary. 'What's wrong?' he said. 'What's got into you? You *like* your job.' Her eyes, still darkly magnificent in spite of lines around them, flashed: 'Who told you that?' But he couldn't go into it – he never could go into practical problems, especially those of a petty nature, it took too much out of him; and usually she was the first person to spare him, removing annoyances by shouldering them herself.

And now too, she did not burden him with facts of which she had never allowed him to be conscious – that it was tiring for her to do a full day's work and then look after his affairs as well as her own. She never mentioned anything of that, but what she did now decide to mention was something else that she had spared him. It had been all right, nothing to make a fuss about, during the days of Dr Erdmund of Dortmund – well, yes, he had had a crush on her, but he was after all a gentleman and never let it go beyond a squeeze of the hand or a stolen kiss behind her ear, which it hadn't cost her anything to permit. But Dr Erdmund had become old and had had to sell his practice – 'You never told me,' Max said, and she shrugged, 'Why should I?' The new boss was a younger man, though not very young – another refugee, from Czechoslovakia, with none of the cultured manners of an earlier generation of refugees. She didn't mind that – she had always been able to get on with all sorts – but unfortunately he had wandering hands and he could not keep them off Netta, which was really a bit thick. Max genuinely didn't understand, he had never heard of such a thing, and she had to explain to him how unpleasant it was to spend all day with someone and be on your guard constantly – 'You know, Max—' 'Know what, Netta, what?' 'Coming up behind me – he says he's a thigh man – oh, it's disgusting—' But Max was not disgusted; he laughed, he protested: 'You're imagining it.' 'Imagining it!' 'But Nettalein, how could it be? God in heaven, at your age.'

For a long time, no one – not even Lilo, who wasn't told the details – knew what had happened: why Netta suddenly withdrew from the household and told my parents and everyone else that she had had enough. She started a life of her own in her St John's Wood flat and entertained old friends with whom she had re-established contact. She also had what she called her cavaliers – elderly gentlemen from Vienna or Berlin, who were very gallant and visited her with flowers and chocolates and always had a good joke for her they remembered from the old days. She kept herself trim with sports – her competitive games of tennis, and three times a week she went to an indoor swimming pool where she swam several lengths up and down, her arms pushing the water with the vigour of a much younger woman. In the afternoons she had her coffee in a restaurant in a hotel – the only equivalent of the sort of coffee houses she had known in Germany, with deep armchairs and carpets and cigarette smoke and foreign waiters and foreign newspapers stuck on wooden poles. If there was no friend to join her, she went alone; she had adventures, for she was still very attractive with her flashing eyes, and her strong teeth intact, and always chic, the large hats of her youth replaced by little saucy ones over one eyebrow. Of course men of a certain age – incorrigible wolves, she called them – were always trying to pick her up and sometimes she let them, though insisting on respect. She knew how to deal with every situation – for years afterwards, for the rest of her life, she told the story of the man who had taken, without permission, the empty chair at her table for two and had been bolder than she would permit: and she, without a word, had picked up her coffee cup and flung the contents in his face. 'You should have seen him! Dripping! And it was hot, too! With hot coffee in your face, you forget all about being fresh with a woman.'

Around this time my parents, who were documentary film-makers specializing in aboriginal tribes, went away for almost a year, leaving me in the Hampstead flat with my grandparents. So I was witness to what might be called their second honeymoon – the time alone together that they had not had since Netta had become attached to them. Max, remote and selfish as he was, began to woo my grandmother all over again. With Netta gone, it was once more only to Lilo that he read his day's work in the evenings – even sitting on the floor the way he had done in the past, though now it was no longer so easy for him, with his increased weight and his custom-tailored suit he had to be careful not to crease. As before, Lilo did not listen too attentively; some of her attention was now bestowed on me, but Max didn't seem to mind when he looked up and saw her busy helping me pick out the right colour crayon for an elephant's ear. They exchanged smiles then – maybe about me, more likely for each other – before Max went on reading; though he looked up again when, staring at his lowered head, she exclaimed, 'Oh Maxi, what a pity – it's really all gone now!' But when he ruefully passed his hand over his scalp – 'Really? All?' – she looked closer: 'There's still a little bit; so sweet.'

My grandmother's own hair was as long as it had been – she never cut it – but it had turned very grey. She continued to wear it the way she had done as a girl – loose and open down her back and around her shoulders. When people in the street turned to stare at her, I assumed that it was for her beauty. I thought she was beautiful, and I was never ashamed of her, though she dressed shabbily – there was her frayed shawl and the holes in her stockings, one of which sometimes came loose and wrinkled around her ankle. Walking tall and erect, she was completely unselfconscious; if something interested her, maybe in a shop window or a flower growing in a hedge, she would stop and look at it for a long time. She was very fond of street markets and liked to talk to people selling pottery and costume jewellery and discuss their craft with them. She always bought something from them, but if on her way home, someone admired her purchase, she might simply give it to them and walk on. She remained my grandfather's muse for the rest of their lives: there were always reflections of her in his work, but not as she was in these later years, nothing of her gypsy quality, but the girl he had wooed in their youth. This girl – several theses have already been written about her influence – was wound into his work like filigree. She was the moonlit statue of a nymph in a deserted *allée* of poplars; she was the girl shining in white at her first communion and also the cold lilies adorning the altar. She was everything – every image – that was lyrical, nostalgic, breathlessly beautiful in his work, keeping it as fresh as on the day it was written.

Although at first they enjoyed their time together without Netta, they encountered difficulties. There was now no one to arrange appointments except Max himself – Lilo had tried, but she had several times given rival scholars identical hours and tended to get not only the days but the weeks mixed up. She also didn't like the telephone and Mrs Lipchik would answer, but she never understood what anyone was saying and that made her laugh so much that she had to put down the receiver (Lilo laughed with her). So then Max had to attend to phone calls himself, which disturbed him terribly in his work;

several times he simply let it ring, but that disturbed him even more and he sat with his head between his hands. Also it was he now who had to deal with practical matters, which was very difficult for him, for though he was meticulous, he was very timid and would panic at anything with an official stamp on it like an income tax notice. In fact, these sorts of communications had such a shattering effect on him that, like Netta had done, Lilo hid them from him, if she happened to see them; but unlike Netta, she did not deal with them and only stuffed them into a drawer and forgot about them till threatening notices arrived. Then they would search for them, and if they found them – occasionally they didn't – Max would blame Lilo for hiding them, and they would be angry with each other and miserable.

Once Lilo was so hurt and annoyed by Max – this was when my parents were home again – that she left the flat and came to us. She had often told us, as a joke, how she had several times run away from Max during their first years of marriage, packing up a suitcase and going straight back to her father's house. When she came to us, it was also with a suitcase; she didn't say anything and my parents didn't ask her any questions. It must have been the same when she had gone home to *her* parents – it would probably have been as useless then as it was now to expect any explanations or accusations from her. Unlike Netta, who had gone around complaining about Max to everyone who knew him and even to those who didn't, Lilo's pride expressed itself in silence. Stubborn and upright, completely oblivious of us tiptoeing tactfully around her, she sat on a chair in our house; but as the afternoon wore on, she moved her chair nearer to the window and looked out into the street, her elbow propped on the sill, her cheek on her hand. That was the way she must have waited in her parents' house – waited for the garden gate to open and Max to come up the path to take her home; without giving him time to ring the bell, she had jumped up and opened the door for him herself and said, 'Let's go,' not bothering about her suitcase, which her father's chauffeur had to bring after her. In the same way, my mother had to take her suitcase back to the Hampstead flat – because the moment Lilo saw Max from the window, she jumped up and went straight out to meet him: leaving us to gaze after the two of them walking down the street together, two elderly people with their arms around each other. They appeared to be an odd couple for romantic attachment – he like a banker in his fur-collared overcoat and Homburg hat, and she with her long loose grey hair, a gypsy or a poetess.

After that, my mother hired a part-time secretary to take care of his business affairs and professional obligations, ignoring his protests that he couldn't afford to pay a salary. The secretary was efficient and soon everything was as it had been with Netta: but when I say everything, I mean only the practical side because in other ways there was something – even I felt it – amiss, or missing. Of course this was Netta, her absence from their lives she had shared for so long. At that time, it never occurred to me that Max was anything but this disagreeable old man who disturbed my pleasant time with my grandmother; and even if I had been old enough to know him better, how could I have understood his need for Netta any more than did my parents, who thought it would be solved by someone else taking care of his practical problems. Emotionally he seemed – he was – completely fulfilled by Lilo, as was evident not only to his family but also to people who knew him simply through his work. Nevertheless – and this is being written about today – there was another element in that work, a hidden current coursing beneath the cool stream of his lyrical love. However, no one mentioned a second muse until Netta published his letters to her, after his death and Lilo's, which was less than a year later. In her introduction, Netta spilled every bean there was, giving time and place for all their secret meetings, all the hotel rooms in all the cities where they had met and the scenes they had had there – the tears they spilled, but also how she had always managed to make him laugh. In her account, their time together was fundamentally joyous and beautiful; and in his work too it was beautiful but also full of interior struggle and guilt, painful, often renounced yet inescapable, cut down only to grow again, a cancer of dark passion.

Lilo too must have missed Netta during the years of her absence. I accompanied her several times on visits she made to Netta in the St John's Wood flat – I went under protest, for it was much more interesting for me in the Hampstead flat, and familiar, with the comfortable furniture and all the amusing objects Lilo picked up at street fairs. At Netta's, there was always the danger of hurting myself on some sharp edge of her metal furniture; and I did not care for Netta's only picture – the café scene of herself and friends, who did not look like people at all but like geometrical masks. Worst of all was Netta herself – at home I was fond of her, she was always bringing me presents, and when I said anything that amused her, she shouted: 'Did you hear that? What a child, my God!' But here all she did was talk to Lilo, in a torrent of words, all of them complaints. When I plucked at Lilo's sleeve to ask to go home, Netta pleaded, 'One moment, darling, only one more little minute, my angel,' and not wanting to interrupt herself by kissing me, she kissed the air instead, with several absent-minded smacks of her pursed lips, and went right on talking. Although everything she said was directed against

Max – how he had availed himself of her youth and strength only to throw her away like an orange he had sucked dry – Lilo did not protest or try to interrupt; the most she said was, 'No no,' which made Netta shout louder, 'Yes, an orange!' When at last I persuaded Lilo to go home, she got up reluctantly, lingering as if she wanted to say something more than only 'No no'. But she never managed to say much, and then only as we were leaving and Netta was kissing not the air but really me, kneeling down to do so and making me wet with her lips and with tears too, hot tears – Lilo, looking down at us, would say sadly, 'It was so nice when you were there.'

These words seemed to enrage Netta – not there and then but later, when she came to see my parents, as she did after each of Lilo's visits. 'Oh yes, so nice, so nice,' she cried, 'when I was there to do all their dirty work for them!' My parents tried to soothe her, they spoke eloquently, and after a while Netta sat quiet to listen to them: how much she meant to all of us, and whatever had been difficult in the past was now an indispensable part of the present so that she was missed terribly – 'Who misses me terribly?' she asked, eyes dangerously narrowed as though she were ready to leap on the answer and tear it to pieces. They said we all of us missed her, even I, though only a child, and of course most of all – her eyes narrowed more – Lilo and (yes?) Max. At that name, her eyes sprang wide open in all their dark beauty: 'Well, if he misses me so much, let him come crawling to me on his hands and knees and beg me to come back.'

With all the accusations she made, there was one thing she never mentioned: the money from her salary that she had freely shared with Lilo and Max when they were in difficulties. Nor did she tell anyone that she was now herself running short of money and needed another job to keep going. We none of us knew that she was looking for work – she may even have been searching for some time and finally had to take what she could get: this was as manageress of a continental bakery and café. It wasn't called a café but a coffee lounge; there were only half a dozen tables, usually occupied by elderly refugees who couldn't do without their afternoon coffee and cake. Nominally, Netta had an assistant, but none of them was reliable – 'Bone lazy', she called them – so that often she had to be both saleslady and waitress. She seemed to like it, moving around the place with verve, and always with a personal word for her clientele. It was only a short walk from the Hampstead flat, so Lilo and I often dropped in and stayed for quite a while, with me eating more chocolate eclairs than I was normally allowed. There was usually at least one – and sometimes more – elderly gentleman who seemed to be there as much to enjoy Netta's presence as the refreshments she served them. Their eyes followed her as she flew around the coffee lounge, and the moment she approached their table they were ready with some gallant quip. If one of them tried to hold on to her hand longer than necessary while she was handing him his change, she good-naturedly let him, while giving us a wink. Lilo watched her in true admiration – the way she handled the business and the customers – and when we went home, she described the scene to Mrs Lipchik, saying, 'Netta is so wonderful.' She also praised her to Max, but he didn't like to hear about it at all: 'What's wonderful about being a waitress? And just around the corner to us. What an embarrassment.' Lilo reared up as if it were she who had been insulted. 'Oh, I didn't know you were so *grand*,' she said, and swept out of the room, very grand herself.

One day Max surprised me by inviting me for a walk.

'Would you like to, little one?' he said with a smile that was as unnatural as the tone in which he spoke. I looked around at Lilo, but she had to nod several times and even frown at me a bit before I went reluctantly to put on my coat. Max continued to smile in a glassy way, but once out in the street, he forgot about me. He strode along, sunk in thought, with steps too large for me; when he realized I was lagging behind, he stopped to wait for me, but impatiently as though in a hurry to get to where we were going. Netta was at the counter, and when she saw us, she went right on chatting with her customer, her hands busy inserting a dozen pastries into their cardboard box. There was no table vacant, and we had to wait; Max's face had gone very red, but his head was raised loftily and he held me by the hand in an iron grip. Although I was his excuse for being there, when we were seated and Netta came for our order, he turned to me as if he didn't see me, asking: 'What do you want?' 'I know what *she* wants,' Netta said, 'but what do *you* want?' 'Netta, Netta,' he implored, his eyes downcast, in shame and pain.

And that was all he said, the entire time we were there: 'Netta, Netta'. He didn't address a word to me, and of course I didn't expect him to, he never did, and anyway I was there to eat my chocolate eclairs. He was like the other elderly gentlemen who came there and followed Netta with their eyes. Only with this difference, that she approached our table quite often – as often as she could – and lingered there to do something unnecessary, like exchanging the position of sugar bowl and milk jug. And we sat on, though there were others waiting for our table and glaring at us, so that Max felt constrained to order more pastry for me. He also tried to order another coffee for himself, but Netta said, 'Yes, and the indigestion?' for no one knew better than she what too much coffee did to him. Although totally engrossed in licking up the cream from my pastry, I was aware of the tension emanating from my grandfather. This became unbearable when Netta approached our table; and when she touched or maybe just accidentally brushed against him, he moaned: 'Netta, Netta.' Once she flicked at something on his shoulder – 'For heaven's sake, doesn't anybody ever take a clothes brush to you?' In stricken silence, he pointed at my plate, which was empty again; I looked up hopefully, but Netta said, 'I'm not having this child spoil her stomach, just to please you.' However, she brought each of us a glass of water, and ignoring the waiting customers pointing restively at our table, she still didn't give us our bill.

Over the following period of time – was it weeks, months, or even years? – I often accompanied Max on visits to the coffee lounge. But although we were now steady companions, he never became anything other for me than the remote, gloomy figure he had always been. Holding me by the hand so that I wouldn't lag behind, he communed only with himself – shaking his head, uttering a half-stifled exclamation; and when we got to Netta's place of work, he concentrated entirely on her, vibrating to each movement as she passed, now close to, now far from, our table. And there was another burden on his spirit, of which I heard him complain to Lilo: 'But don't you understand! They're sitting there looking at her as if she were – oh my God in heaven – a—' 'The child,' warned Lilo. Who was there sitting looking at her? Next time in the coffee lounge, I followed his burning eyes and saw what he saw: it was only another elderly gentleman like himself, dressed as he was, very correctly, with spats for the cold weather. One of them I knew – it was Dr Erdmund from Dortmund, retired and in the habit of taking his afternoon coffee there. Sometimes he stopped at our table, to pinch my cheek and address a word to Max, very respectfully as was befitting with a famous author. Max never answered or even looked at him, and it was not only his hands but his whole body that seemed to clench up into a fist. And afterwards he would mutter to Netta, darkly, awesomely – except that she was not awed, she tossed her head and moved around on her duties with even greater verve.

My days in the Hampstead flat were no longer as light-hearted as they had been. This was because of the change in my grandmother – *she* was no longer light-hearted: as with Max, there was a burden on her spirit, and in her case, *he* was the burden. When he was in his study, oppressive waves seemed to seep from under the door, so that, wanting to get as far away from him as possible, I gave up playing anywhere except in Lilo's sitting-room at the other end of the flat. I also refused to accompany him to the coffee lounge: since Netta regularly denied me my third round of pastries and we just sat on and on with nothing but glasses of water in front of us, I preferred to stay home with my grandmother. The first time I refused him he looked in such anguish at Lilo that she persuaded me to change my mind; but after that even she could no longer coax me – he of course never tried: it was not in his nature to coax anyone, he only knew to stand stricken till the other person's heart would melt of its own accord. But mine never melted towards him, not even when I watched him from the window – Lilo stood behind me, her hand on my shoulder – as he made his way with heavy steps towards the coffee lounge, his proud head sunk low.

Ever since I had known them, my grandparents had slept in separate bedrooms. Max's was next to his study and Lilo's, which I shared when I stayed with them, adjoined her sitting-room. But he had always come to say goodnight and stayed so long that I was usually asleep before he left. I had no interest in their conversation, which in any case was interspersed with long silences. These had once been soothing enough for me to fall asleep, with clear streams winding through the meadows of my dreams. But now all that changed, and though he still came to our room in his nightshirt and sat on the edge of the bed, there was a different silence between them; and when she took his hand, she did not tickle it as she used to but grasped it tight, either to comfort or hold on to him. Now I could not fall asleep, though I pretended to, while listening for anything they might say. This was often about Netta and her job – 'She says she can't afford to give it up,' Max told Lilo. 'She says she has no money.' 'But that's ridiculous,' Lilo said, to which he replied, 'Money is never ridiculous to those who don't have it.' 'But we have it,' Lilo said. 'Don't we? Enough for three?' 'I don't know,' he moaned, in despair. 'You know I know nothing about money.'

'Listen,' Netta said to Lilo. 'If you offered me a million pounds, I wouldn't do it.'

Lilo and I had come to visit Netta in the St John's Wood flat. It was not until I saw her sitting side by side with Netta that I noticed how much my grandmother had changed. She had lately had to have many of her own teeth extracted and the new ones hurt her, so that she was mostly without them; and she continued to wear her beloved Kashmir shawl, though the fabric had split with age in several places. I'm sorry to say that she now looked not so much like a gypsy but like some old beggar woman – especially in comparison with Netta, who was in a silk blouse and tight velvet pants, her nails and hair both red. And it wasn't only Lilo's appearance: she seemed really to be begging for something that she wanted very much from Netta; and though Netta kept refusing her, it wasn't Lilo but Netta herself who burst into tears – loud sobs interspersed with broken sentences that made Lilo say, 'Careful: the child.'

But I was busy exploring the flat, which had changed. It seemed somehow to have filled out, or rounded its contours, an impression that may have been due to additional items of furniture. Besides the tubular chairs Netta had brought from Germany, there were now low round upholstered little armchairs that people could actually sit in. And apparently people *had* been sitting in them; and they had stubbed out their cigarettes in the ashtrays that were scattered around on new little tables, and these also held glasses out of which guests had drunk wine. When I went into the kitchen and opened the refrigerator – which had always been depressingly empty – I found it stuffed with food like potato salad and roast chickens. There was also a tray of delicious little canapés, which I took back into the living room. 'Can I have one?' I asked, but just then Netta was shouting, 'A life! A whole lifetime I've given him!' so I had to say it again. 'Of course you can, my darling,' Netta said, 'you can have anything from me you want—' 'Oh thank you, Netta,' I said, and retreated politely back into the kitchen, so that they could say whatever they wanted without having to warn each other of my presence. Anyway, Netta was shouting loudly enough to be heard throughout the flat – 'That's what I'm here for, to give, always to give, but now I tell you it's my turn to take!'

Lilo's voice was low, conciliatory, which only made Netta's rise more: 'Yes, I have my friends, that's not a crime I hope, to try and get a little bit of a life going of my own?' And again Lilo murmured, mild, protesting, and again Netta cried out, 'So who asked him to come and sit there and disturb me in my work? He's welcome to come here to my home, I'd be glad to entertain him in my own place for a change, because I've had enough, up to here enough, of the dog's life he's made me lead in his.'

Whereas Netta's flat was now comfortable and lively, the Hampstead flat had changed in the opposite direction. It was as if not Lilo and Max were living there but the original Edwardian families for whom this ponderous structure had been built. It had become gloomy and oppressive – although the one person who had had this effect on me was usually absent. I no longer had to fear that Max's forbidding figure would appear in the door of his study, for he was now mostly with Netta, and not only in the coffee lounge. Now I feared – not Lilo (I never feared *her*) but *for* Lilo: that, however cute I tried to be for her sake, I could hardly make her smile. We still went on our usual outings, no longer because she enjoyed them but because she thought I would: but how could I, when she didn't? Mrs Lipchik heaved heavy sighs as she cleaned, and while she and Lilo still had their long coffee sessions in the kitchen, these were no longer full of German jokes but of secrets, problems. It was even worse when Max was there with us: Mrs Lipchik's sighs were nothing compared with his, especially those he uttered like groans when he came to Lilo's bedroom at night. Sitting as before on the side of her bed, with me curled up beside her, he spoke to her in whispers: only to get up and pace around and then return and seize her hands and implore: 'What shall I do? What *shall* I do?' And she withdrew her hands and didn't answer him.

My dreams ceased to feature pellucid streams in meadows; instead – if they were dreams – they resounded with the echo of his voice, through which the word fate struck repeatedly like hammer blows. Fate! It was the great theme of his later books. Here Fate is the main character and human beings are depicted as struggling helplessly in the grip of its iron claw. But although he witnessed the upheaval of his whole continent and the destruction of his generation, he goes beyond the epoch in which he happened to be living to embrace the entire epoch of Man: Man in the abstract, from birth to death. And this is what astonished him and made him suffer – the suffering of Man, and all he has to endure in the course of a lifetime of inevitable decline; and also the swiftness of that decline, the inexorable swiftness with which a young man becomes an old one. It is no doubt a great theme, but how could I take it seriously when I identified its author with my grandfather, whom I saw suffer because I made a noise playing outside his study door, or because his girlfriend flirted with her dentist? In his last book there is a sort of dance of death in a landscape of night and barren rock where men and women join hands and revolve in a circle, their faces raised to the moon so that its craters appear to be reflected in the hollow sockets of their eyes. This might for others be a powerful metaphor for the macabre dance of our lives; but for me it is only a reminder of a birthday party we attended.

It was Max's birthday – his last, as it turned out – and, like all our celebrations during this year, the party was held in Netta's flat. For by then Max was spending all his days in St John's Wood – even his desk had been moved there – though he still showed up in the Hampstead flat for the sort of nocturnal visits I have described. Netta also came quite often, not with him but alone. I witnessed several scenes between her and my grandmother, only now it was always Netta who was pleading while Lilo remained stubborn and silent. This made Netta desperate and she stopped pleading and was angry, or pretended to be: 'My God, think of me all these years, in *your* house, and putting up with it – yes, gladly! Laughing and pretending to be happy, so that everyone could be happy! And you can't come even once, for one afternoon, for his sake?' For a long time my grandmother remained impervious, so that Netta might as well have been addressing someone blind and deaf. But gradually, over the years – for no particular reason, or perhaps because it didn't matter any longer, or that other things mattered more – anyway, we did go to Netta's flat, to her more important parties like when it was her birthday, or Max's, or even Lilo's: everything was celebrated there.

It was always the same guests who had been invited, and they were all Netta's friends, from the social circle she had formed around herself. They included people we vaguely knew, like Dr Erdmund from Dortmund and some of the other elderly gentlemen whom I remembered from the coffee lounge. They were mostly German refugees who, like Max and Lilo and Netta, had had their youthful heyday during the time of the Weimar Republic. In fact, they might have been the embodiment of the big painting in Netta's flat of the German café scene, with geometrically shaped faces crowding each other around a café table. Now those triangles and cones had been realigned into the masks of old age, and the expression of nervous restlessness had frozen into the smile of the tenacious survivor. Their clothes were elegant – Netta insisted on glamorous attire for her parties – and they still held a wine glass in one hand and a cigarette in the other, some with a long silver or ivory holder; and they were still animated by a kind of frenetic energy, a consumptive eagerness. There was dancing too – Netta rolled up her bear rug and put on some of her old dance records, and when the music started, she stretched herself up by her clenched arms and said, 'Oh my God,' and laughed at whatever it was that she remembered.

They were all pretty good dancers – mostly foxtrots, with some very intricate footwork. Netta's favourite was the tango, and it suited her – inside her tight silk metallic dress she made movements as sinuous as those of a young siren; and the expression on her face no doubt reflected the sensations in her heart, which were those of her siren years. Her partners did their best to keep up with her, pretending they were not out of breath; but she discarded them one by one when they began to fail, and imperiously snatched up a fresh old gentleman.

The only person who refused her was Max: he would not dance, he could not, never had done, which was why Lilo had given it up too, long ago. So the two of them were always onlookers – except on that last birthday party when everyone had drunk a lot of champagne and excitement burned through the air like holes made by a forgotten cigarette. In fact, Netta was scattering dangerous sparks from the cigarette held between her fingers; and her eyes too sent out glints of fire and so did her red hair and her metallic dress. Discarding her last breathless partner, she turned to Max: he shook his head, he smiled, no, he would not. But for once she insisted and she grasped his hand and pulled him up; and at last, to please her, he let himself be dragged on to the dance floor and tried to imitate her steps. But he could not, and to help him, she pressed herself as close to him as possible to lead him and make his hips rotate along with hers. But still he stumbled and could not; at first he laughed at his own ineptitude, but when others too began to laugh, he tried to extricate himself from Netta's close embrace. She would not let him go, and perhaps to drown his angry words, she called to someone to turn up the record; and then, when it was really loud, she called out, 'Come on, everybody, what are you waiting for – New Year?' and soon they were all jigging up and down, with Max and

Netta in their centre. The more he struggled the tighter she held on to him, so that he appeared to be entangled in the embrace of an octopus or some other creature with long tentacles. His situation made them all laugh – even I did, till I saw how Lilo had hidden her face in her hands, and not because she was laughing. Suddenly she snatched at me in the same way as Netta had done to Max and made me get up with her. Although neither of us knew how, we tried to join the dance – and that made all of them turn from Max and look and laugh at us, at grandmother and granddaughter hopping and slipping on the polished floor. Although Lilo was getting out of breath, we stuck it out till the music stopped, and then she and I thanked Netta for the party and went home.

If it were not for the famous *danse macabre* in Max's last book, I might have forgotten all about that birthday party. I prefer to remember our walk home from it, Lilo's and mine, through empty streets on a cool autumn night. There was the smell of fallen leaves, and layers of clouds shifted and floated across the sky; the moon was dim, so that even when it came sliding out from between these veils, it didn't light up anything. Nevertheless, it seemed to me that it did illumine my grandmother's face when she raised it to try and identify some of the stars for me. She pointed at what she said was the Great Bear – or was it the Plough – I think she wasn't sure, and anyway her eyesight was not good enough to see that far. I don't know why I expected her to look unhappy – after all, we had just left a party with music and champagne and special birthday cake ordered from Netta's bakery; but anyway she didn't, not at all, on the contrary her face appeared as radiant as was possible by the light of that dim moon.

Ménage

Leonora was my mother, Kitty my aunt. Kitty had no children, she never married because Yakuv didn't believe in marriage, and once she met him, she never looked at anyone else. 'He treats her like dirt,' my mother used to say, the corners of her mouth turned down – an expression I knew well, for it was often how she regarded me while telling me, 'You'll end up like Kitty: a neurasthenic.' Physically, it would have been impossible for me to become either like my mother or my aunt. They were both tall, statuesque, whereas I have taken after my father who was a lot shorter than my mother. It's odd that both these sisters chose men who were short – though this was all that Yakuv and my father Rudy had in common.

Leonora dominated Rudy and he liked it. She was a wonderful manager of all practical details, but at that time I resented and perhaps rather despised her orderly bourgeois ways. I often took refuge with Kitty, who lived in three tiny rooms in a subdivided old brownstone. My parents had a large apartment in an expensive building on Central Park West, filled with some very fine furniture and pictures that had belonged to Rudy's family of prosperous Berlin publishers. Unlike Rudy and Leonora, who had funnelled out his family money through Switzerland, Kitty had arrived here in

1937 with nothing – except of course my parents, who were a constant support to her.

Kitty's apartment was always in a mess, which for me was part of its charm. I associated disorder with artistic creation, and there was usually some piece of work lying around. She had begun with etchings and woodcuts, but later became a photographer; there were prints tacked up of her charming portraits of little girls picking flowers in a meadow. Kitty herself sat on the floor, her arms wrapping her knees and her long reddish hair trailing around her. If my mother was there – and Leonora often came to check up on her sister – she would be tidying panties off the floor, washing the dishes piled in the sink, while clicking her tongue in distress and disapproval. But that didn't bother Kitty at all, she continued sitting there talking to me about some artistic matter, even when Leonora found a broom and began to sweep around her.

My parents adored New York, were completely at home here, and continued to live the way they might have done if they had been allowed to stay in Berlin. They spoke only in English, though their heavy accents made it sound not unlike their native German. They had many social and cultural activities, mostly with other prosperous émigrés from various Central European countries. It was at one of these cultural events that Kitty first met Yakuv, who had been engaged to give a piano recital after a buffet supper at some rich person's house. The house was pointed out to me later, a rococo mansion at 90th and 5th, since pulled down. At this concert Kitty had behaved in a crazy way that was not uncharacteristic of her: the moment Yakuv had finished playing, she dashed up to the piano and, kneeling down, she kissed his hand. Leonora said she nearly died of shame, but Rudy was more tolerant of his sister-in-law's behaviour, which he said was a tribute not to a person but to his art. As for Yakuv himself – I don't know how he took her gesture, but probably it was in his usual sardonic way.

On account of his art, my mother was prepared to forgive Yakuv for many things: among them, his background. He came from Eastern Europe, from what she assumed to be a tribe of pedlars and hawkers; the language they spoke was to her a debasement of the High German with which she had grown up. But this had nothing to do with Yakuv's art: 'Even if his father peddled toilet brushes,' she explained, 'an artist is born with his talent. It's a gift from the gods and comes from above.' His real background might have disturbed her more. His forefathers had been rabbinic scholars, but more recent generations had abandoned these studies in favour of Marx and Engels, Bakunin and Kropotkin. Some of them had rotted for years in jail as political prisoners, and at the beginning of the last century an aunt had been executed for her part in an unsuccessful assassination attempt. The glowering intensity that pervaded Yakuv's music, and our lives, must have been inherited from these revolutionaries. His looks were as fiery as his playing. He was very short but with broad shoulders and an exceptionally large head, which looked even larger because of his shock of black curly hair.

A year or two after his first meeting with her, Yakuv moved into the brownstone where Kitty lived. His rooms on the top floor were even smaller than hers on the second, and just as untidy. But I have seen Yakuv get much angrier than my mother at the mess in Kitty's rooms, kicking things around the floor in a fury and sweeping crockery off her table. Then she would fly at him, and a dreadful quarrel break out. These were the first passionate fights I ever witnessed, for between my parents there was only a slight tightening of the lips to indicate one of their rare differences of opinion. Kitty's fights with Yakuv frightened and thrilled me by their violence. They always ended the same way, with Yakuv going upstairs to his own den as though nothing had happened – he might even have been smiling – while she was left quivering, prostrate on the floor. But soon she would get up and rush to the door to scream up the stairs – uselessly, for by that time he was back at the piano and she could not be heard above his playing.

At the time we first knew him, in the early 1940s, there was a surfeit of talented refugee pianists, so Yakuv had to struggle to make ends meet. He played for a ballet class and gave piano lessons to untalented students, of whom I became one. At six, my eager parents had sent me for piano lessons to a little old Russian lady, who spent most of her time with me writing appeals for visas to consular officials. But when I was twelve, my parents decided that I should take lessons from Yakuv. I was very reluctant, for I had often seen his pupils coming down from their lessons in tears. I knew this would be my fate too – and deservedly, for he was a great musician and I had very little talent. He made no attempt to disguise his despair, putting his hands over his ears and imploring to be struck deaf. He begged me never to come back again, never to think of the piano again, and of course I would have liked nothing better; but however much we swore an eternal farewell when I left, I always returned on time for my next lesson. I knew – we all knew, including himself – that he needed the money, and since he had driven most other pupils away, it seemed up to me to stick it out, however painful this might be for both of us.

And actually, apart from my playing, I liked being with him. He had three little rooms, and the one in which he gave lessons was only just big enough to hold his piano. The window faced the back yard which was wild and overgrown since the first-floor tenant had no money to keep it up. At that time the mammoth apartment buildings had not yet been built, so the house was surrounded by other brownstones with similarly untended gardens and trees growing tall enough to fill his window. Yakuv, in a shabby jacket and rimless glasses, filled the room with smoke from his little black cigars. A cup of coffee stood on the piano, and since I never saw him make a new one, it must have been stone cold; but he kept sipping at it, and dipping a doughnut into it. Although coffee, dough-nuts and cigars appeared to be all he lived on, he was full of energy. He roared, stamped, heaped me with his sarcasms. Sometimes I got so mad, I banged down the piano lid, and that always seemed to amuse him: 'I see you have inherited your aunt's sweet temper.' But then he pinched my cheek, almost with affection, and walked me out the door with his arm around my shoulders.

I was not the only one in the family to take lessons from him. I don't know whether my father did this because he really wanted to learn or to contribute to Yakuv's income. He came not to play the piano but to sing Lieder; he loved music but was unfortunately as unmusical as I am. I have heard Yakuv tell Kitty that the entire neighbourhood was trilling *Die Schöne Müllerin* while my father was still struggling with the first bars. Poor Rudy – he must have endured the same sarcasms as I did, but all he would say was that Yakuv had the typical artistic temperament. Then Kitty said: 'So artistic temperament gives one the right to be a swine?' She spoke bitterly because he fought with her, wouldn't marry her, wouldn't let her have a child with him. This last always came up in their quarrels: 'All right, so don't marry, leave it, forget it – but a child, why not a child!' He wouldn't hear of it; and it really was impossible to think of him as a father, a gentle comforting presence like Rudy.

Yet he and Kitty had their tender moments together. Sometimes on my visits to her I found them in bed together. They were not at all shy but invited me to sit on the side of the bed. We played games of scissors, paper, stone, with the two of them quickly changing to scissors if they saw the other being paper; or he would teach us card games and didn't contradict when she told me that he could have made a living as a card sharp. 'Better than the piano,' he said cheerfully. Without his glasses, he looked almost gentle, probably because he was so nearsighted; and it was always a surprise to see that his eyes were not dark but light grey.

Then there were the times when he was a guest at one of my parents' dinner parties. On those evenings Leonora sparkled in a low-cut evening gown and the sapphire and ruby necklace she had inherited from her mother-in-law. Her successful dinners were her personal triumph, so that she was entitled to the little glow that made two red patches of excitement appear on her cheeks. But at that time, when I was about fifteen or sixteen, I was embarrassed by what I thought of as her smug materialism. It seemed to me that she cared only for appearances, for her silver, her crystal and china, and for nice behaviour (she even tried to make me curtsy when I greeted her guests). She was in her middle thirties, in wonderful shape, radiant with health and the exercise and massage she regularly took: but I thought of her as sunk in hopeless middle age with no ideals left, if ever she had any, which I doubted.

Except for me, everyone appreciated her dinner parties, including Yakuv whenever he was invited. In his crumpled, rumpled evening suit, he ate and drank like a person who is really hungry: which he probably was, and certainly Leonora's exquisite dishes must have been a wonderful change from his stale coffee and doughnuts. After dinner he was persuaded to sit down at the piano, and this my parents made out to be a special favour to them, though before he left Rudy's cheque had been tactfully slipped into his pocket. He played the way he ate – voraciously, flinging himself all over the keys, swaying, even singing under his breath and sometimes cursing in Polish. All this made him perspire profusely, so that afterwards he could hardly respond to the applause because he was so busy wiping his face and the back of his neck. The enthusiasm was genuine – even unmusical people realized that they were in the presence of a true artist; and I could well imagine how Kitty had been so carried away the first time she heard him that she knelt at his feet.

Kitty resented the fact that Yakuv performed for my parents' guests, that he had to do so in order to earn money; and also that he himself didn't resent it enough. He never complained, as she did constantly, about his lack of reputation and success. He probably didn't think it worth complaining about. A bitter sardonic person by nature, he expected nothing better from fate, which he accepted as being terrible for everyone. When Kitty tried to make him say that he only went to Leonora's parties because of Rudy's cheque, he said, 'Oh no, I go for the food – where else would I get veal in a cream sauce like Leonora's?' And never losing an opportunity to provoke her, he added, 'If only you learned to cook – just a few little dishes, one isn't even expecting miracles—'

'Oh yes, now you want me to be your cook-housekeeper! How you would hate it, hate it!'

He laughed and said that on the contrary, a cook-housekeeper was just what he needed; but we both knew that he didn't mean it because the three of us were on the same side – what I thought of as the artistic, the anti-bourgeois side.

*

This was the way things stood with us when I went away to college and then, two years later, on my own quest – which I won't go into now except to say that I may have been influenced by Yakuv's view of life. I mean by his pessimism, his assumption that no hopes were ever fulfilled in this life; and while he left it at that, it may have been the reason why I, and others like myself, Jewish and secular, turned to Buddhism. For a while I wanted to be a Buddhist nun – it seemed a practical way out of the impasse of human life. But then I dropped the idea and got married instead.

With all this happening, I became detached from my family in New York. I skimmed through their letters only to satisfy myself that everything was as it always had been with them. It was difficult to tell my parents' letters apart: they had the same handwriting with traces of the spiky Germanic script in which they had first learned to write. The facts they presented were also the same – the concerts and plays they had liked or disliked, an additional maid to help Lina who had got old and suffered with her knees. Kitty in her scrawl did not report facts: only excitement at a painting or a flowering tree, anguished longing for a child, Yakuv's impossible behaviour. He of course did not write to me. I don't suppose he wrote any letters; to whom would he write? Apart from our family, he seemed to have no personal connection with anyone.

The only change they reported was that the brownstone in which Kitty and Yakuv had been renting was torn down. That whole midtown area was being built up with apartment blocks where only people with substantial incomes could afford to live. Kitty gave me a new address, downtown and in a part of the city that had once been commercial but had been moribund for years. When I went to see her on my return to New York, I found the warehouses and workshops still boarded up; the streets were deserted except for a few bundled-up figures hurrying along close to the walls. This made them look like conspirators, though they may only have been sheltering against the wind, which was blowing shreds of paper and other rubbish out of neglected trash cans. But some of the disused warehouses were in the process of being revived, one floor at a time. In Kitty's building there were two such conversions, and to get to hers I had to operate the pulleys of an elevator designed for crates and other large objects. Kitty's loft, as she called it, seemed too large for domestic living, though it had a makeshift kitchen with a sink and an old gas stove. Kitty's own few pieces of furniture looked forlorn in all this space; even Yakuv's piano – for his furniture too had come adrift here – seemed to be bobbing around as on an empty sea. He himself wasn't there; he was on tour, things were better for him now and he was getting engagements around the country. And Kitty's career also seemed to have taken off: she had rigged up a dark room in one corner of her space, and in the middle of the floor was a platform with two tree stumps on it, surrounded by arc lights and a camera on a tripod.

Instead of going to my parents, I had come straight to her from the airport. I felt it would be easier to tell her about what I saw as the dead end of my youthful life – I had abandoned both my Buddhist studies and my marriage – and it was a relief to unburden myself to her. She listened to me in silence, which was really quite uncharacteristic of her. There were other changes: the floor had been swept, there were no dishes in the sink. After I had finished telling her whatever I had to tell, she murmured to me and stroked my hair. How right I had been to come to her first, I felt; I knew I could not expect the same understanding from my parents, whose lives had been so calm, stable and fulfilled.

My parents' building and all its neighbours stood the way they had through all the past decades, as stately as the mansions that they had themselves displaced. The doormen were the same I had known throughout my childhood; so was the elevator man who took me up to where Leonora was waiting for me in the doorway. She held me to her bosom where I remembered to avoid the sharp edges of her diamond brooch. 'But now it's my turn!' Rudy clamoured, caring nothing about having his good suit crumpled as I pressed myself against him, inhaling his aftershave and breath-freshener.

But, 'No not here, darling,' Leonora said when I started to go into my room. My father cleared his throat – always a sign of embarrassment with him. But Leonora exuded a triumphant confidence: 'Because of the piano,' she said, ushering me into the guest bedroom, which was considerably smaller than mine. I didn't understand her: the piano had always been in the drawing-room and was still there. 'The other piano,' she said. '*His.*' She spoke as if we had already had a long conversation on the subject. But we had not, and it took me some time to realize that this other piano was Yakuv's new one that Rudy had bought for him.

Again skipping intermediate explanations – 'It's so noisy at Kitty's,' Leonora said. 'Could someone tell me why she has to live in a warehouse? He needs peace and quiet; naturally – an artist.'

So there *had* been changes, and principally, I noticed, in Leonora. Her coiled hair was newly touched with blonde; her cheeks had those two spots of excitement I knew from her dinner parties. She kept taking deep breaths as if to contain some elation inside her.

Rudy took me for a walk in Central Park. As usual on his walks, my father wore a three-piece herringbone suit, a Homburg hat and carried a rolled umbrella like an Englishman. From time to time he pointed this umbrella in the direction of a tree, an ornamental bridge, ducks on a pond: 'Beautiful,' he breathed, loving Nature in its formal aspect. Around us towered the hotels and apartment blocks of Central Park South and West, which he also loved – for the same decorative solidity that had formed the background of his Berlin youth and his courtship of my mother.

'It's a privilege for us to give him what he has never had. A quiet orderly home, meals on time – yes yes, this sounds very – what do you call it? Stuffy? *Square*? But even artists,' he smiled, 'have to eat and sleep.'

'What about Kitty?' I said.

'Kitty. Exactly. They're too much alike, you see; artistic temperaments. Sometimes he needs – they both need – a rest from the storm and stress. Nothing has changed. Leonora and I are what we have always been.'

'Mother looks wonderful.'

'You know how she has always adored music above everything.' Then he exclaimed: 'Dear heaven, who says we're not sensible grown-up people! We've learned how to behave. You're still a child, lambkin.' He squeezed my arm, in token of my misery and failure. 'One day you too will learn that everything turns out the way it has to, for good; for our good.' He pointed his umbrella – at the sky this time, inviting me to look upward with him towards the immense perfection that was always with us, encompassing our small mismanaged lives.

A week or two after my arrival, Yakuv returned from his tour. *He* had not changed. He at once went into what used to be my bedroom – without apology, probably he didn't real-ize that it had been mine, or simply took it for granted that it was now his. He greeted me with a comradely clap on the shoulder, not as if I had been away for several years but as if I had showed up as usual for my weekly lesson. Leonora followed him into the room; she had to unpack his bag, she said, because if she didn't it would stand there for weeks. But this was said with a smile, not in the reproachful way she used for Kitty's and my untidiness. After a while, during which Rudy went for another of his walks, she emerged with an armful of Yakuv's laundry. Soon came the sound of his piano, and every day after that it seemed to fill, to appropriate the apartment. If I moved around or shut a door a little too loudly, she or Rudy, or both, laid a finger on their lips.

Leonora did everything possible to create the best conditions for his work. She arranged his schedule with his agent, whom he often fired so that she had to find a new one; and since it infuriated him to have anyone disarrange his music sheets, she cleaned his room herself. Otherwise he was calm, immersed in his work. He rarely asked for anything and good-naturedly accepted even what he didn't want – Leonora once gave him a dark blue velvet smoking jacket, and though he mildly protested ('So now I must look like a monkey'), he let her coax him into it. He also smoked the better brand of cigars she bought him to replace the little black ones he was used to. He had personal habits but was not entrenched in them, and if it made no difference to him, he gladly obliged her in everything.

That was during the day. But during the evening meal, he would push his plate back and without waiting for the rest of us to finish – he still ate in the same rapid, ravenous way – he went out, banging the front door behind him. He never said that he was going, or where; he was not expected to, and anyway, we knew. But there were times when he did not return for several days, and while I had no idea what transpired between him and Kitty during those days, I was very much aware of the effect his absence had on Leonora. She behaved like a sick person. She stayed in her bedroom with the curtains drawn, and 'Leave me alone,' was all she ever said to Rudy's and my efforts to rally her. It was not until Yakuv returned that she got up, bathed and dressed and tried to return to her normal self. But this was not possible for her; she appeared to have suffered a collapse – even physically she had lost weight and her splendid breasts sagged within her large bra. I don't think Yakuv noticed any of this; anyway, it did not affect him since in his presence she made a brave attempt to pull herself together and go about her household duties as usual, especially her duties to him. She would not have known how to stage the sort of confrontations that he was used to with Kitty; and since these were lacking, he probably assumed that everything was fine with Leonora – that is, insofar as he thought of her at all.

Rudy wanted to take her on a Mediterranean cruise. A few years earlier they had enjoyed sailing around the Greek Islands, but now Leonora was reluctant to leave. She said she couldn't; Lina was too old and cranky to look after the house properly, everything would be topsy-turvy. I could hear my parents arguing in their bedroom at night, Rudy as usual calm and reasonable, but she not at all her usual self. In the mornings Rudy would emerge alone from their bedroom, and he and I would discuss ways of persuading her. We laid stress on her health – 'Look at you,' I said, making her stand before her bedroom mirror.

She drew her hand down her cheek: 'You think I look terrible?'

'You'll see how well you'll look after a change – young all over again. Young and beautiful.'

'Really?' She continued dubiously to regard herself in the mirror.

It was only when I promised to take over all her responsibilities that she began to accept the idea of Rudy's cruise. But first she had to train me in the arts that she herself had learned from her mother and grandmother; and it was only when she was satisfied that I knew how to take care of all Yakuv's needs that she finally agreed to leave. Rudy was overjoyed; he whispered promises of another honeymoon. He packed their suitcases in his expert way but humbly unpacked them again when she, who also prided herself on her packing, pointed out how much better it could be done.

It was only when he saw these suitcases standing in the hall on the day before departure that Yakuv realized what was going on. His reaction was unexpected: he took the cigar out of his mouth and said, 'Why didn't anyone tell me?' When Leonora began to speak, he waved his hands and stalked off into his room. We waited for the piano to start up but nothing happened; only silence, disapproval seeped from that room and filled the apartment and Leonora's heart so that she whispered, 'We can't go.'

I had never seen my father so angry. 'But this is too much! Now we have reached the limit!' Leonora and I gazed in astonishment, but he went on, 'Who is this man, what does he think?' Then – 'Tomorrow he leaves! No today! Now! Hop!' He made straight for Yakuv's door, and had already seized the handle when Leonora grasped his arm. They tussled – yes, my parents physically tussled with each other, a sight I never thought to see. She pleaded, he insisted, she used little endearments (in German) until he turned from the door.

His thinning grey hair was ruffled, another unprecedented sight in my serene and serenely elegant father. In response to Leonora's imploring looks, I joined in her pleas to postpone this expulsion, at least until they returned from their trip. 'Our second honeymoon,' Leonora pleaded, until at last, still red and ruffled, he agreed.

But later that night he came to my room. He told me that by the time they returned from their cruise, Yakuv would have to be out, pronto, bag and baggage, and it was up to me to see that this was done. His mouth thin and determined – 'Bag and baggage,' he repeated, and then, in another splutter of anger: 'Ridiculous. Unheard of.'

They were to be away for six weeks, and during that time I had to get Yakuv to pack up and leave. But he gave me no opportunity to talk to him. He stayed in his room, and all day the apartment resounded with music of storm and stress. Only sometimes he rushed out to walk in the park; once I followed him, but there too it was impossible to talk to him. Hunched in an old black coat that was too long for him, he appeared sunk in his thoughts. His hands were in his pockets and he only took them out to gesticulate in furious argument with whatever was going on under his broad-brimmed hat.

I had to turn to Kitty for help. The change in Kitty was as marked as it was in Leonora, but in the opposite direction. It was Kitty who looked calm, and though no longer young, she now appeared younger than before. Instead of her long skirts and dangling loops of jewellery, she wore a flowered artist's smock that made her look as wholesome as a kindergarten teacher. Her eyes had lost their inward brooding look and were clear and intent on the proof sheets she was holding up to the light. She made me admire them with her – they were all of pretty little girls posed on her tree stumps – and she only put them down when I told her of the task my father had imposed on me.

She laughed in surprise: 'I thought Rudy was so proud of keeping his own little Paderewski.'

'He thinks Leonora is getting too nervous.'

Now she really laughed out loud: Leonora, nervous! It was the word – together with neurasthenic, or later, neurotic – that had always been applied to Kitty herself.

'And Yakuv too,' I ventured.

She put down her proof sheets: 'Oh yes. He's in one of his moods. The other night I was busy in my dark room, and that made him so mad he stamped and roared and tore down the pictures I'd pinned up. He said he couldn't stand the way I live. Well, nothing new – I've heard it a thousand times before ... But Leonora? Are you telling me he misses Leonora?'

It was then that she offered to tell Yakuv to get out of our apartment. I was glad to be relieved of this task and to have time to go about my own business. After all, I still had a divorce to take care of, as well as deciding whether to go back to college or to find a job. And what about all those existential questions that had so troubled me? I needed to become involved again with my own concerns rather than those of my parents and my aunt. I decided that, as soon as Rudy and Leonora returned, I would look for a place of my own. Picking up some old connections and making new ones, I was out and about a lot and continued to see nothing of Yakuv. I'm afraid I neglected most of what Leonora had left me to do for him, but he didn't complain and perhaps didn't notice. Whenever I was home I heard him playing a lot of loud music. I assumed he was preparing for his next tour and hoped that he would have left on it before my parents returned. He showed no intention of moving out, but presumably he would as soon as Kitty had talked to him. Meanwhile he continued to thump away behind his closed door; he seemed to be there all the time now, even at night.

Then late one evening Kitty herself showed up. It was pouring with rain, but it turned out she had walked all the way from downtown. When I tried to make her take off her wet clothes, she waved me away – her attention was only on the sounds from Yakuv's room. 'So he's still here,' she said, partly in anger, partly in relief.

It may have been because she was so drenched, with her hair wild and dangling as it used to be (though dyed a more violent shade of red), that she had reverted to the Kitty I used to know. And her mood too was charged in the old way. She told me how she had tried to call Yakuv all day and every day, though she knew he hardly used the telephone and certainly never answered it. The last time she had seen him was when she had told him of Rudy's ultimatum. Without a word and waving his hands in the air, he had rushed out of her loft and had not returned. She had begun to fear that he had packed up and left our apartment in offended pride, abandoning not only my parents but Kitty too. Tormented by this thought – that he had taken himself out of our lives for ever – she had come running through the dark and the rain: only to hear his piano as usual in the room he had been told to vacate.

Suddenly she rushed in there. I was surprised and apprehensive: even when they had still been living together in the brownstone, Kitty had rarely dared to enter his room while he was playing. If she did, there would be a fearful explosion, with objects flying down the stairs until Kitty herself came running down them, declaring, 'He's a madman, just a crazy, crazy person,' and Yakuv would appear at the top of the stairs, shouting the same thing about her. But now there was no explosion. The playing stopped abruptly. All I heard was her voice and nothing from him at all. I went to bed, expecting them to do the same. And why not? Two people who had been living together, on and off, for over twenty years.

Later that night they woke me up. They sat on either side of my bed; they appeared exhausted, not as after a fight but after long futile talk. It was almost dawn and it may have been the frail light that made them look drained.

'He claims he can't live without her ... He used to laugh at her!' She turned on him: 'Now what's happened? Because it's you she cooks for now, all her potato dishes, is that what you can't do without?'

He shook his head, helplessly. He didn't have his glasses on and looked as I remembered seeing him in bed with Kitty: mild, melancholy, his grey eyes dim as the dawn light.

'My aunts always told me, "The way to a man's heart is through his stomach". I thought they only meant people like my fat uncles. I didn't know artists were included. If that's what you are!' she cried. 'You thump your piano loud enough: what's all that about? Passion for food, or for the housewife who cooks it?'

He remained silent – he who was always so flip, so quick with his sarcastic replies. He stretched across me to touch her: 'Kitty,' he said, his voice as sad as his eyes.

'Let me be!' she cried, but obviously this was the last thing she wanted.

My parents returned two weeks earlier than expected. Their second honeymoon had not been a success. They had sailed through the classical world, and for him it had been an enchanted return to civilization: his civilization, of order, calm and balance. But she, who had upheld this rule of life with him, had seen it crumble away. She wept, she suffered. He held her in his arms, which he couldn't get entirely around her, she was so much larger than he. While promising nothing, he began to consider means of adjusting to their new situation.

It was amazing how well he managed to restore the harmony of our household. His relief at finding Yakuv still installed in the apartment was almost as great as hers. Her husband's forbearance evoked Leonora's gratitude – and maybe Yakuv's too, though he probably took his own rights for granted. Soon Leonora was herself again. She sang as she moved around her furniture with the feather duster that was her sceptre. Practical, punctual, perfect, her figure restored to full bloom, she dispensed food and comfort in return for the love of men.

Yakuv continued to practise behind his closed door, emerging only for meals. His music no longer stormed in rage but was as calm as could be expected of him. My father too was calm – that was *his* nature – but now with some hidden sorrow that made me postpone my plan of finding my own place. Sometimes I joined him on his walks, or we played chess, a game he loved though he always lost. That didn't matter to him; he was a bad player but an excellent loser.

Kitty changed – or rather, changed back again. Instead of the simple flowered smock, she reverted to her flamboyant dresses, looped with large, noisy pieces of costume jewellery. Several times she came storming into the apartment, probably after walking all the way from downtown, as she had done on that rainy night, and as on that night, ready to burst into the room from where the piano rang out. But each time she was prevented by Leonora who stood in front of the door, her arms spread across it. Then Rudy intervened; he took his sister-in-law's hand and spoke to her soothingly. Kitty let herself be led away meekly, saying only, 'Do you know how long he hasn't come to me?' Then I realized that Yakuv had been spending not only all his days but many of his nights in our apartment.

It might be thought that their rivalry would turn the sisters into enemies, but this was not at all what happened. Instead they drew closer together in an intimacy that excluded even Rudy and me. They met several times a week, not in our apartment where they could not be alone, nor in Kitty's loft – Leonora refusing to venture into that part of town, which seemed wild, dark and suspect to her. Their favourite rendezvous was the Palm Court of a large hotel, probably similar to the sort of place they had frequented in their youth, with gilt-framed mirrors, a string orchestra and ladies and gentlemen (some of them lovers) seated on plush sofas enjoying their afternoon coffee and cake. Here Leonora and Kitty exchanged their intimate secrets, just as they had done when they were young. At that time Leonora had confided the tender ins and outs of Rudy's courtship, Kitty had analysed the characters of her lovers whom it had amused her to keep dangling on a string. Now the confidences they shared were about the same man. They would also have spoken – this was their style – of Life in general, of Love. Sometimes they may have glanced at their reflections in the hotel mirror, pleased at what they saw: though older now, they were still the same handsome sisters, Leonora in her elegant two-piece with the diamond brooch in the lapel, Kitty still bohemian under a pile of bright red hair.

A decade passed in this way within my family. Meanwhile, I came and went; I saw that the situation was not going to change in a hurry, nor was there anything I could do about it. Rudy encouraged me to leave, even though I was the only one to whom he occasionally showed something of his own feelings instead of pretending he didn't have any. I went back to college to finish my degree, I read a lot, I began to write. I had one or two stories published in little magazines, and these made my father so proud that he bought up copies to give to everyone he knew.

Yakuv also came and went. He was often on tour, for his reputation was now established and he had engagements all over the country. It did not improve his temper – on the contrary, he became more difficult. He was still firing his agents so that Leonora had to find new ones and also secretaries to attend him on his tours. Usually these secretaries returned without him; either he had fired them or they couldn't stand him another day. He would cable urgently for a replacement, but by then everyone had heard about him and no one was willing to go. He blamed us for this failure – what could he do, he said, if we sent him nothing but blockheads and idiots, and meanwhile how was he to manage, again he had missed a plane and left the suitcase with his tails in a hotel? Twice Leonora went herself to take care of him, but when they came back, they were not on speaking terms and Rudy had to make peace between them. Leonora refused to undertake another tour with him; and after a barrage of urgent messages from Kansas City, Kitty was dispatched to him – with misgivings that turned out to be justified, for he sent her back within a week.

Sometimes I suspected that his tantrums were not entirely genuine. I have seen him turn away, suppressing a smile – exactly as he had done in earlier years after some wild fight with Kitty. The music we heard him play after one of these upheavals was invariably tranquil, romantic, filling everyone with good feelings. With me, too, his manner had never changed from the time I was a child and he my teacher. He gave me books he thought I ought to read, and when he wanted to relax, he called me to play some game with him – dominoes usually, to my relief, never chess at which I suspected him to be a master. When he wanted to be affectionate, he still pinched my cheek; and when he was angry with me, it was not as with the others but as with a child, wagging his finger in my face. This made me laugh, and then he laughed too. Eventually it happened that when he was in one of his moods, Leonora and Kitty would send me to calm him down. It was as though I were free of the web that entangled them – by this I suppose I mean their intense sexual involvement with him. I felt nothing like that; how could I? For me he was just an elderly little man, almost a dwarf with a huge head and a mass of grey hair. His teeth were reduced to little stumps stained brown with tobacco.

When another crisis arose with another secretary fired in mid-tour, it was natural for someone – was it Leonora, was it Kitty? – to suggest that I should take my turn with the job at which they had already failed. It was my father who objected; he said he had higher expectations for me, and hoped I had for myself too, than to be handmaid and servant to Yakuv on his travels. Leonora and Kitty reared up as one person – it was strange how united they were nowadays; they said it would be a rich experience for me as well as a privilege to be in close contact with an artist like Yakuv. Rudy made a face as though saying – perhaps he actually did say – hadn't we had enough of this privilege over the past ten years? But he gave me money for the trip and told me to wire for more when I needed it, especially if I needed it for my ticket home.

Almost the first thing Yakuv said to me was, 'You'll need some money.' This was in a cab on our way from the airport – unexpectedly, he had been standing there waiting for me. He put his hand in his pocket and drew out a fistful of notes: 'Is this enough?' He put his hand in his other pocket and drew out some more. From then on it was the way we carried out all our financial transactions: he didn't pay me a salary but just offered me everything in his pockets to pick out as much as I needed. This was not very much, since my hotel room and plane tickets and cab rides were all included in his, paid for by the sponsors. I lasted longer than anyone else had done, traveling with him from one city to another. We always checked into the same kind of hotel, I in a small single room and he in a suite that had often to be changed, due to his complaints about noise and other inconveniences. During the day, if I didn't go to his rehearsals, I stayed in the hotel by myself; I wasn't interested in the cities we were in – they were all the same, with the same sort of museums built in the early 1900s by local millionaires to house their art collections. At night I attended his performances in a concert hall donated by a later set of millionaires; I was very proud of him, his playing and the effect it had on his audience. He was not only a superb pianist, he looked the part too as he lunged up and down the keyboard, his coat-tails hanging over the piano stool, a wild-haired artist, profoundly foreign, an East European import from an earlier era. Afterwards there was always a reception and dinner for him; surrounded by rich and wrinkled women, his eyes would rove around the room, and when he found me, he shrugged and grimaced from behind their jewelled backs.

Leonora had given me careful instructions about his routine, what to do with his clothes, when he would need the first cup of black coffee that he drank throughout the day. Of course, like everyone else, I got things wrong and he flew into a rage, but always one that was tempered to me – that is, to the child I was for him. And with me he got over it more quickly than with the others, and also pitched in to help, so that somehow we muddled through together. Whenever there were a couple of hours to spare in the afternoons, we would go to a local cinema; he liked only gangster or cowboy movies, and since the same programme was always playing in the different cities we visited, we saw each one several times. At night I sat up with him in his suite, waiting for the pills without which he couldn't sleep to take effect. He read aloud to me – Pushkin in Russian, Miłosz in Polish; I didn't understand but liked to listen to him in these languages that seemed more natural to him than the English he spoke in his sharp Slavic accent. During the time I spent alone in the hotel, I continued with my own writing; it was the first time that I attempted poetry, maybe because he liked it better than prose. He encouraged me to read it to him, listening carefully, asking questions, sometimes making a suggestion that often turned out to be right.

He asked about the years I had spent on my own travels. He was particularly interested in my Buddhist period. He himself was of course a complete agnostic; that was the way he had grown up among those whose mission it had been to overthrow everything. I said that had been my mission too, to overthrow the nihilism they had left us with. 'But a nun,' he said, smiling. Although I had long ago given up that ambition, I defended myself. I said that having started on a path, I wanted to follow it as far as it would take me – I had more to say but stopped when I saw the way he was looking at me. His lips were twitching. I didn't really expect him to take me seriously; it wasn't only that I was so many years younger than he; I suspected that he took none of us seriously. He even seemed to have the right to be amused by us, as though he were a much wiser person. I don't know whether this impression derived from the fact that he was a great artist, or from the mixture of the Talmud and Marxist idealism that I thought of as his background.

Since it seemed to take longer and longer for his sleeping pills to have effect, our conversations became more protracted. He wanted to know about my marriage, a subject that I disliked talking about except to say that it had been a mistake. He drew me out about the nineteen-year-old boy who had been the mistake. I admitted that what had attracted me to him was his frailty, which I had interpreted as vulnerability (later he turned out to be hard as nails). It had started when we had bathed together in the Ganges and I saw his frail shoulder blades – it was the first time I had seen him without his robe. 'His robe?' Yakuv asked; so then I had to admit that he too had been in the religious life and had been planning to become a monk. I glanced at Yakuv, and yes, his lips were now twitching so much that he could not prevent himself from laughing out loud. I laughed too, maybe ruefully, and he pinched my cheek in his usual way. Only it wasn't as usual, and that was the first time I stayed with him all night. Although for the rest of the tour we still took separate rooms, we usually stayed in his, except when he was very tired after a concert and then he said I had better sleep in my own little nun's bed. But mostly he wasn't tired at all but with plenty of energy left in his short and muscular body. His chest and back and shoulders were covered in grey fur; only his pubic hair had remained pitch black.

He gave me no indication of what to tell or not to tell at home, but it turned out to be easier than expected. Leonora and

Kitty were astonished at the way I had stuck it out with him. All their questions were to do with the practical side of my duties – how I had managed to make him catch planes on time and tidy him up for his performances. I gladly supplied them with answers, adding an amusing anecdote or two which made them clap their hands in joyful recognition. They had been there before me. Soon everything settled down. Yakuv and I continued to play dominoes, Leonora fulfilled his daily needs, and he had another home in Kitty's loft where he kept his furniture and his other piano. Kitty visited us often and she and Leonora met to exchange confidences in their favourite Palm Court rendezvous. They still did not invite me to join them, considering me too young and immature to understand.

However, I understood more than I had done. For instance, I realized that when Yakuv was shut away in his room and there was only the sound of his piano, he was not as oblivious of us as I had always thought. Somehow he was as tied to us as we were to him. My mother and aunt never realized that I too was now part of the web that bound them. They took it for granted – and it was a relief to them – that I would accompany him on all his tours. In New York, there was no sign of what went on between us on these tours. Only occasionally, during meals, he slipped off one of the velvet slippers my mother had bought for him and placed his feet on mine under the table. While he was doing this, he kept on eating as usual with his head lowered over the plate, shovelling food into his mouth with tremendous speed.

I was never sure – I'm still not sure – about my father. It was impossible to tell if he suspected anything: he was so disciplined, so used to accommodating himself to difficult situations and handling them not for his own satisfaction but for those he loved. Every time I packed my suitcase to go on tour with Yakuv, Rudy came into my room. I said, 'It's all right: I *like* it.' He continued to watch me in silence while I happily flung clothes into my suitcase. At last he said, 'And your writing?' He sounded so disappointed that I tried to think of something to make him feel better. I said I was continuing my attempts at writing, and in fact, inspired by Yakuv's performances, I had begun to write poetry. I knew that for my father poetry and music were the pinnacle of human achievement, so perhaps he really was consoled and not only pretending to be so.

Yakuv outlived Rudy by many years; he also outlived Leonora and Kitty. He became a wizened little old man, more temperamental than ever, his hair, now completely white, standing up as he ran his hands through it in fury. He continued his tours till the end and became more and more famous, people lining up not only to hear but also to see him leaping around like a little devil on his piano stool. He made many recordings and was particularly admired for his blend of intellectual rigour and sensual passion. When he died, he left his royalties to me, as well as quite a lot of other business to take care of. Of course I have all his recordings and often listen to them, so he is always with me. I no longer write poetry but have returned to prose and have published several novels and collections of stories. These are mostly about the relations between men and women, which appears to have been the subject that has impressed itself most deeply on my heart and mind. I keep coming back to it, trying again and again to render my mother's and my aunt's experience, as I observed it, and my own. This account is one more such attempt.

A Choice of Heritage

During the latter half of the last century – maybe since the end of the 1939 war – nothing became more common than what are called mixed marriages. I suppose they are caused by everyone moving more freely around the world, as refugees or emigrants or just out of restless curiosity. Anyway, the result has been at least two generations of people in whom several kinds of heritage are combined: prompting the questions 'Who am I? Where do I belong?' that have been the basis of so much self-analysis, almost self-laceration. But I must admit that, although my ancestry is not only mixed but also uncertain, I have never been troubled by such doubts.

Many members of my father's totally English family have served in what used to be called the colonies – Africa or India – where they had to be very careful to keep within their national and racial boundaries. This was not the case with my father: at the time of his marriage, he had been neither to India nor to Africa. He met my mother in England, where she was a student at the London School of Economics and he was at the beginning of his career in the civil service. She was an Indian Muslim, lively, eager, intelligent and very attractive. She died when I was two, so what I know of her was largely through what my aunts, my father's sisters, told me. My father rarely spoke of her.

It is through my Indian grandmother, with whom I spent my school holidays, that I have the most vivid impression of my mother. This may be because my grandmother still lived in the house where my mother had grown up, so that I'm familiar with the ambience of her early years. It was situated in the Civil Lines of Old Delhi, where in pre-Independence days British bureaucrats and rich Hindu and Muslim families had built their large villas set in large gardens. This house – with its Persian carpets spread on marble floors, pierced screens, scrolled Victorian sofas alternating with comfortable modern divans upholstered in raw silk – seemed to me a more suitable background to my mother's personality, or what I knew of it, than the comfortable middle-class English household where I lived with my father.

My grandmother, no doubt because of her royal style, was known to everyone as the Begum. Every evening she held court in her drawing-room, surrounded by male admirers who competed with one another to amuse her and light the cigarettes she endlessly smoked. Her friends had all been at Oxford or Cambridge and spoke English more fluently than their own language. Some of them had wives whom they kept mostly at home; one or two had remained bachelors – for her sake, it was rumoured. She was long divorced and lived alone except for her many servants, who were crammed with their families into a row of quarters at the rear of the property. They too vied with each other to be the closest and most important to her, but none of them ever captured this position from her old nurse, known as Amma. It was Amma who had learned to mix the Begum's vodka and tonic and to serve their favourite drinks to the visitors. During the hot summer months the household moved up into the mountains where there was a similar large sprawling villa and another set of admirers – though they may have been the same ones, except that here they wore flannel trousers and hand-knitted cardigans and came whistling down the mountainside carrying walking sticks over their shoulders like rifles.

There was one visitor who was different from the rest. His name was Muktesh, and when he was expected, she always gave notice to the others to stay away. He had not been to Oxford or Cambridge, and though his English was fluent, it sounded as if he had read rather than heard it. But his Hindi was colloquial, racy, like a language used for one's most intimate concerns. He was known to be a first-class orator and addressed mammoth rallies all over the country. He was already an important politician when I was a child, and he could never visit the Begum without a guard or two in attendance (later there was a whole posse of them). He was considerate of his escort, and Amma had to serve them tea, which was a nuisance for her. Tea was all he himself ever drank, pouring it in the saucer to cool it. He had simple habits and was also dressed simply in a cotton dhoti that showed his stout calves. His features were broad and articulated like those of a Hindu sculpture; his lips were full, sensual, and his complexion was considerably darker than my grandmother's or any of her visitors'.

He was definitely not the Begum's type, yet she appeared to need him. She was very much alone and had been so for years. At the time of Partition she was the only one of her family to stay behind in India while the rest of them migrated to Pakistan; including her husband, who became an important army general there and also the butt of many of the jokes she shared with her friends. They had been separated since the birth of my mother, one year after their marriage. He took another wife in Pakistan, but the Begum never remarried. She preferred the company of her servants and friends to that of a husband.

And Muktesh continued to visit her. He made no attempt to be entertaining but just sat sucking up his tea out of the saucer; solid, stolid, with his thighs apart inside the folds of his dhoti. There were times when he warned her to make arrangements to go to London; and shortly after she left, it usually happened that some situation arose that would have been uncomfortable for her. It is said that Hindu–Muslim riots arise spontaneously, due to some spark that no one can foresee; but Muktesh always appeared to have foreseen it – I don't know whether this was because he was so highly placed, or that he was exceptionally percipient.

I always enjoyed my grandmother's visits to London. She stayed at the Ritz and I had tea with her there after school. Sometimes she had tickets for a theatre matinee, but she was usually bored by the interval and we left. Amma accompanied her on her London visits and splashed around in the rain in rubber sandals, the end of her sari trailing in puddles. She grumbled all the time so that the Begum became irritated with her. But actually she herself tired of London very quickly, though she had many admirers here too, including most of the Indian embassy staff. After a time she refused to leave Delhi, in spite of Muktesh's warnings. 'Let them come and cut my throat, if that's what they want,' she told him with her characteristic laugh, raucous from her constant smoking. And instead of coming to London, she insisted on having me sent to her in India for the whole of my school holidays.

If it had not been that I missed my father so much, I would have been happy to stay in India for ever. I felt it to be a tremendous privilege to be so close to my grandmother, especially as I knew that, except for me, she really didn't like children. I learned to light her cigarettes and to spray eau de toilette behind her ears. In the evenings when the friends came I helped Amma serve their drinks, and then I would sit with them, on the floor at the Begum's feet, and listen to the conversation. When she thought something unfit for me to hear, she would cover my ears with her long hands full of rings.

I felt totally at home in Delhi. I had learned to speak the Begum's refined Urdu as well as the mixture of Hindustani and Punjabi that most people used. All this came in very useful in my later career as a student and translator of Indian literature. I ought to explain that my appearance is entirely Indian, with no trace of my English connections at all. None of them ever commented on this but accepted it completely – accepted *me* completely, just as I was. And so did the Begum, though I bore no resemblance to her either, or to anyone in her family of Muslim aristocrats. Both she and my mother were slender, with narrow fine limbs, whereas I have a rather chunky build and broad hands and feet. My features are Hindu rather than Muslim – I have the same broad nose and full lips as Muktesh. My complexion too is as dark as his.

I always took it for granted that it was me whom Muktesh came to visit. It was to me that he mostly spoke, not to the Begum. When I was small, he always brought me some toy he had picked up from a street vendor, or made the figure of a man with a turban out of a handkerchief wound around his thumb to waggle at me. At least once during my stay, he would ask for me to be brought to him, and the Begum sent me accompanied by Amma, who became very haughty as if she were slumming. At that time Muktesh had the down-stairs part of a two-storey whitewashed structure with bars on the windows. He had three rooms, two of them turned into offices where his personal assistant and a clerk sat with cabinets full of files and a large, very noisy typewriter. The remaining room, where he ate and slept, had the same kind of government-issue furniture standing around on the bare cement floor. The walls were whitewashed, and only the office had some pictures of gods hung up and garlanded by the personal assistant. Muktesh himself didn't believe in anything like that.

However, he did have a photograph of Mahatma Gandhi in his own room, as well as that of another Indian leader – I believe it was an early Communist who looked rather like Karl Marx. Muktesh explained to me that, though he had never met them, these two had been his political inspiration. At the age of sixteen he had joined the Quit India movement and had gone to jail. That was how he had missed out on his higher education and had had to catch up by himself; first in jail, where other political prisoners had guided him, and afterwards by himself with all these books – these books, he said, indicating them crammed on the shelves and spilling over on to the floor from his table and his narrow cot: tomes of history, economics and political science.

It was through his interest in these subjects that he first developed a friendship with my mother. Since I only knew her through the memories of other people, it has been difficult for me to grasp the dichotomy between my mother's appearance – her prettiness, her love of dress and good taste in it – and the fact that she was a serious student of economics and political science. Even after her marriage to an Englishman, the development and progress of India remained her most passionate concern. Outwardly, she became *more* Indian while living in England; she wore only saris or salwar-kameez and her Indian jewellery. She often attended functions at the Indian embassy in London, and it was there that she first met Muktesh. He was a member of a parliamentary delegation – I don't know the exact purpose of their mission, something to do with tariffs and economic reform, anyway it was a subject on which she had many ideas. Perhaps her ideas interested him, perhaps she did, and he invited her to discuss them with him when she next came to Delhi. Since she was there at least once and usually several times a year to be with the Begum, she was soon able to take him up on his invitation.

They must have had long, intense discussions – about public versus private ownership, economic reform and the expansion of social opportunities. From what I have heard of her, I imagine her doing most of the talking, eager to impart all her theories. She walks up and down with her gold bangles jingling. Getting excited, she strikes her fist into her palm, then laughs and turns around and accuses him of laughing at her. And perhaps Muktesh really does smile – his rare, sweet smile with slightly protruding teeth – but mostly he remains massively still, like a stone sculpture, and only his eyes move under his bushy brows to watch her. This is the way I imagine them together.

I must have been seventeen or eighteen when the Begum first spoke to me about my mother and Muktesh. She came out with it suddenly, one day when he had just left us – as usual with all his security personnel and the convoy of jeeps that accompanied him everywhere (there had been too many assassinations). 'In those days,' the Begum said, 'he didn't need to have all those idiots hanging around drinking tea at our expense. He and she could just meet somewhere – in the Lodhi tombs, by the fort in Tughlakabad: God only knows where it was they went to be together.' This was my first intimation of the affair – I had had no suspicion of it, but now the Begum spoke as if I had known or should have known all along.

'One day I cornered him – after all he's a sensible person, not like your poor mother . . . I told him, "You know how we live here: how everywhere there are a thousand eyes to see, especially when it's someone like you . . . " He waved his hand the way he does when he doesn't want to hear something, like you're a fly he's waving away . . . "Yes," I said, "it's fine for you, but what about her? And her husband, the poor chump? And this one—" meaning you, for you had been born by that time (a very ugly baby, by the way) . . . '

After this warning, Muktesh seemed to have made some attempt to stay away from my mother. It was hopeless, for when he didn't show up on the morning of our arrival from England, she commandeered the Begum's car and drove to his flat and made a scene there in front of his staff. So even if he had been serious about ending the relationship, he never had a chance, and they went on even more recklessly. When he gave a speech in Parliament, she was up in the public gallery, leaning forward to listen to him. She gatecrashed several important diplomatic parties, and if she had difficulty getting in somewhere, she had herself taken there by the Begum, for whom all doors always opened. Consequently, the Begum told me with amusement, a new set of rumours began to float around that it was she, the Begum, who was having an affair with Muktesh. There were all sorts of allegations, which were taken up and embellished by the gossip magazines; and not only those published in Delhi but also in Bombay and Calcutta, for he had already begun to be a national figure. His appearance in these pages was an anomaly – especially in the role of lover, at least to anyone who didn't know him.

One year, when my mother had come to India with me, my father took leave for a week or two to join us. He gave no notice of his impending arrival beyond a sudden cable announcing it. My mother took it straight away to her mother: 'Do you think he's heard something?' The Begum shrugged: 'How could he not? The way you've been carrying on.'

But if he had, it seemed he gave no sign of it. I have tried to give an impression of Muktesh, and now I must try to do the same for my father. If you think of the traditional Englishman – not of this but of a previous era – then you would have some idea of my father. He was tall, upright and athletic (he had been a rowing blue), with an impassive expression but an alert and piercing look in his light blue eyes. During weekdays in London he wore a dark suit and his old school tie and always carried a rolled umbrella against the weather; in the country, where we spent most weekends, he had a baggy old tweed jacket with leather elbow patches. He smoked a pipe, which he did not take out of his mouth when he cracked one of his puns or jokes, at which he never smiled. He wanted people to think he had no sense of humour. Otherwise he did not care what anyone thought of him. He cared for his duty, for his work, for his country – for these he had, as did Muktesh, a silent deep-seated passion; as he had, of course, again like Muktesh, for my mother.

His time in Delhi was largely spent playing cards with the Begum or doing crosswords with her, finishing them even more quickly than she did. Unfortunately it was the middle of the hot season and, perspiring heavily, he suffered horribly from prickly heat. Like myself in later years, my mother loved the Delhi heat – the mangoes, the scent of fresh jasmine wound around one's hair and wrists, and sleeping on string cots up on the Begum's terrace under a velvet sky of blazing stars. My father was very interested in early Hindu architecture, like the amphitheatre at Suraj Khund, but on this visit it was much too hot for him to go out there. Since this was a private visit, he did not think it proper to call on any of the senior government officials – his opposite numbers here, whom he knew quite well from their visits to London. I think he himself was relieved when the two weeks were up and he could return home. The Begum said she certainly was; as for my mother and Muktesh, they never told anyone anything, but no doubt they were glad to have these last few weeks of her stay to themselves. She and I followed my father to England in September, after the monsoon, but we were back again the following January. She could never stay away for long.

During the months in between her visits to India, my mother led a very conventional life at home. I have this information from my father's two sisters ('your boring aunts', the Begum called them). My mother seemed to have charmed them, and they gave the impression that she too had been charmed – by England, by their way of life: the family Christmases, fireworks on Guy Fawkes night, the village pageant of medieval English history. In her country garden she gathered plums and apples from her trees and bottled jams and chutneys; although in India she had, like her mother, hardly been inside a kitchen, she learned to roast, to baste, to bake, with a rattle of the gold bangles that she never took off. Both my aunts had very happy marriages and took their devotion to their husbands too much for granted to feel the need to demonstrate it. But my mother couldn't do enough to show her love for my father. When he came home from his long day at Whitehall, she would make him sit by the fire, she would light his pipe and bring his slippers and whatever else she had heard or read that English wives did for their husbands. 'No, let me,' she would say, 'let me,' when he protested, embarrassed at having such a fuss made over him.

Yet her visits to India became more frequent, and longer. He made no objection, perfectly understood that she wanted to see her mother, was homesick for India. How could she not be? And he was grateful that, while she was with him in England, she gave no indication of her longing for that other, different place. During her absence, he wrote her long letters – which she did not open. The Begum kept them, also without opening them, so I have been the first person ever to read them.

And having read them, I can understand my mother's reluctance to do so. They express him completely, his personality shining through the small neat civil service script and his longing for her through his deadpan account of domestic trifles: how Mrs Parrot the housekeeper and the milkman had got into a fight over some cream that had prematurely gone off; how he had tried to have a quiet dinner at his club but had been caught by a very tiresome chap who knew all about India; how he had rescued a sparrow from the jaws of next door's cat and had given it water and a worm till it was calm enough to fly away ... Each letter said not once but several times that everything was fine, he was muddling through, and yes of course not to think of coming home till the Begum had perfectly recovered from her bout of flu.

My mother died of cholera – not in India but in England, where this disease had been wiped out so long ago that English doctors failed to identify it in time. One of my aunts took me away to her house and kept me for several months until my father was able to have me back. Although my aunts loved to talk about my father's happy marriage to my mother, they never spoke of her death and how it affected him. It was as if they didn't want to remember their brother – so calm, so anchored – as he was during that year. They were reluctant to return me to him but he insisted. He never remarried. My mother's portrait, painted by an Indian woman artist, hung in our living-room in the country, an enlarged photograph in the flat in town. In the former she is pensive, with sad eyes, in the latter she is smiling. Perhaps the painter wasn't very good but, to me, the portrait conveys less of her than does the photograph. Or it may be that to smile – to be lively and alive – was more characteristic of her, of the way that people told me that she was.

Muktesh never married, which is very unusual for an Indian. He spent his days and nights – he rarely slept more than a few hours – in the service of his party, of Parliament, of politics. When he said he had no time to get married, it was true. He rarely managed to get to see his old mother in Bikaner. He used to tell me how she despaired at his lack of a wife: 'And when you're sick, who will look after you?' He would smile and point upward in a direction he didn't believe in but she did. He didn't get sick but he didn't get married either. Year after year, more and more desperately, she found brides for him – girls of their own caste, modest, domesticated. But he was used to my mother, who argued with him about subjects of vital concern to them both. When they took long car rides together, he whiled away the time composing poetry; she worked on her PhD thesis that she didn't live to present.

Their last long car ride together was to Bikaner. He had to go to a meeting of his election committee in the district from which he was returned year after year. They travelled for a day and a night, across long stretches of desert. They got very thirsty and drank whatever was available – the glasses of oversweet and milky tea that Muktesh was so fond of, or buttermilk churned out of fly-spotted curds. Once, when there was nothing else, they made do with stagnant water out of an old well. Neither of them ever had a thought for disease, she out of recklessness (the Begum called it stupidity), he out of his optimistic fatalism.

I have only his account of that day in Bikaner, and he was busy till it was time to set off again the same night. All day he had left her in his mother's house, with no comment other than that she should be looked after. His mother was used to his arrival with all sorts of people and had learned to ask no questions. She was an orthodox Hindu, and for all she knew he might have brought her untouchables, beef-eaters; but from him she accepted everything and everyone. By the time he had finished his meetings and returned to the house, he found his mother, and mine, sitting comfortably together on a cot in the courtyard, eating bread and pickle. The neighbours were peering in at them, and his mother seemed proud to be entertaining this exotic visitor – her fair-complexioned face uncovered and her vivacious eyes darting around the unfamiliar surroundings, taking everything in with pleasure the way she did everywhere.

Even well into her sixties, the Begum continued to be surrounded by admirers. They came in the evenings and had their usual drinks, no longer served by Amma but by Amma's granddaughter. Otherwise everything was unchanged – including the Begum herself who still chain-smoked. At home she was always in slacks and a silk shirt and her hair was cut short and shingled; but there was something languid and feminine about her. She relaxed in a long chair with her narrow feet up and crossed at the ankles while she joked and gossiped with friends. They had two favourite targets: the crude contemporary politicians who amassed fortunes to cover their fat wives and daughters with fat jewels, and the wooden-headed army generals, one of whom had long ago had the misfortune to be her husband. 'What did I know?' she still lamented. 'My family said his family was okay – meaning they had as much money and land as we had – and at seventeen I liked his uniform though by eighteen I couldn't stand the fool inside it.'

It was only in Muktesh's presence that she was not exactly tense – that would have been impossible for her – but less relaxed. By this time he was very important indeed and his visits involved elaborate security arrangements. He himself, in hand-spun dhoti and rough wool waistcoat, remained unchanged. Whenever I was there, he came as often as he could, mostly very late at night, after a cabinet meeting or a state banquet. The Begum, saying she was very tired, went to bed. I knew she didn't sleep but kept reading for many hours, propped up by pillows, smoking and turning the pages of her books. She read only male authors and went through whole sets of them – ten volumes of Proust, all the later novels of Henry James, existentialist writers like Sartre and Camus whom everyone had been reading when she was young and travelling in Europe, usually with a lover.

Muktesh talked to me about the reforms he was trying to push through; he spoke of dams, monetary loans, protest groups, obstructive opposition parties and rebels within his own party. He spoke to me of his concerns in the way he must have done with my mother; but his mood was different. When he was young, he said, he could afford to have theories, high principles. Now he didn't have time for anything except politics; and he drew his hand down his face as if to wipe away his weariness. But I felt that, though his mind and days were swallowed up by business and compromise, the ideals formed in his youth were still there, the ground on which he stood. And I might as well say here that, in a country where every public figure was suspected of giving and receiving favours, his integrity was unquestioned, unspoken even. It wasn't an attribute with him, it was an essence: *his* essence.

Whenever Muktesh came on one of his official visits to London, he took off an hour or two to be with me and my father. We usually met in an Indian restaurant, a sophisticated place with potted palms and Bombay-Victorian furniture and a mixed clientele of rich Indians and British Indophiles who liked their curry hot. In later years, there were always several security people seated at a discreet distance from our table. My father was the host – he insisted, and Muktesh, though always ready to pick up bills and pay for everyone, gracefully yielded. He and my father were both generous in an unobtrusive way, and it was not the only quality they shared. My father was as English as it was possible to be and Muktesh as Indian, but when I was with them, I felt each to be the counterpart of the other. Although they had many subjects of interest to them both, there were long silences while each prepared carefully to present a point to the other. They both spoke slowly – my father habitually and Muktesh because he was expressing himself in English, which he had first learned as a teenager in jail. Muktesh ate rapidly the way Indians do, neatly scooping up food with his fingers, and he was already dabbling them in a bowl with a rose petal floating in it, while my father was still following his Gladstonian ideal of chewing each mouthful thirty-two times. Occasionally they turned to me, in affectionate courtesy, to ask my opinion – as if I had any! I wasn't even listening to their conversation. I knew nothing of the checks and counterbalances between an elected government and a highly trained bureaucracy – one of their favourite subjects – but I loved to look from one to the other. The evening always ended early because Muktesh had to return to the embassy to prepare papers for his next day's meetings. When we got up, so did the security personnel. Several diners recognized Muktesh and greeted him, and he joined his hands to them and addressed them by name if he remembered them, which as a good politician was surprisingly often. A splendid doorman bowed as he opened the doors to the street for him. 'Aren't you cold?' I asked Muktesh, for even in the London winter he wore the same cotton clothes as in India, with only a rough shawl thrown over him. He laughed at my question and drew me close to say goodbye. I could feel the warmth of his chest streaming through the thin shirt and his strong heart beating inside it.

In what was to be the last year of his life, he wanted to take me to meet his mother. But when I told the Begum of this plan, she shouted 'No!' in a way I had never heard her shout before. She lit a new cigarette and I saw that her hands were shaking. She always hated to show emotion – it was what made her appear so proud and contemptuous; and it was also one of the reasons, a physical as well as emotional distancing, that she didn't like to be touched. I knew that her present emotion, the mixture of anger and fear, was a revival of the past, when my mother had returned from her visit to Bikaner – travel-stained, exhausted and with the beginning of the sickness that would flare up on her journey back to England. I tried to reassure the Begum: 'You know Muktesh doesn't travel that way any more—' for nowadays there was always a special plane and a retinue of attendants.

But it wasn't only fear of the journey that upset the Begum: 'God only knows where and how she lives.'

'Who lives?'

'And she must be ninety years old now, probably can't see or hear and won't care a damn who you are or why he brought you.' Although this was her first reference to the possible alternative of my begetting, she cut it short, dismissed it immediately— 'Well, go then, if that's what he wants – but if you dare to eat or drink a thing in that place, I'll kill you.' She had a way of gnashing her teeth, not with anger but with a pain that was as alive now as it had been these last twenty years. Or if there was anger, it was at herself for not being able to hide it, or at me for witnessing even the smallest crack in her stoical surface. 'All right,' I said, 'I promise,' and I kissed her face quickly before she had time to turn it away.

But my other grandmother – if that was what she was – liked to touch and to be touched. She sat very close to me and kept running her fingers over my hair, my hands, my face. Muktesh had gone off to his meetings and left me with her the way he had left my mother, without explanation. Or had he told her something about me – and if so, what had she understood that made her so happy in my presence? We were in the same house and courtyard that my mother had visited, maybe even sitting on the same string cot, now several decades older and more tattered. Many years ago, to save his mother from the usual lot of a Hindu widow, Muktesh had taken a loan to buy this little house for her. The town had grown around it, new and much taller buildings pressing in on it so that it seemed to have sunk into the ground the way she herself had done. As the Begum had guessed, she was almost blind. The iris of one eye had completely disappeared and with the other she kept peering into my face while running her fingers over it. At the same time she tried to explain something to me in her Rajasthani dialect that I couldn't understand. When at last

Muktesh reappeared, with all his convoy of police and jeeps, she chattered to him in great excitement. Muktesh agreed with what she said, maybe to humour her, or maybe because it really was true. When I asked him to interpret, he hesitated but then said – 'She's comparing you with all her female relatives – your nose, your chin – and your hands—' she had taken one of them into her own bird claw and was turning it over and over – 'your hands,' Muktesh said, 'are mine.' 'Bless you, son, bless you, my son!' she shouted. He bent down to touch her feet, and the people watching us – neighbours had crowded every window and some were up on the walls – all let out a gasp of approval to see this son of their soil, this great national leader, bow down to his ancient mother in the traditional gesture of respect.

A university press had commissioned me to bring out a volume of modern Hindi poetry. When I asked Muktesh if he had any poems for me to translate, he smiled and shook his head: what time did he have for poetry? Yes, sometimes on his way to a rally, he might compose a little couplet to liven up a speech. That wasn't poetry, he said, it was propaganda, not worth remembering. And there was nothing else, nothing of his own? He shrugged, he smiled – perhaps he might at some time, in the heat of the moment, have scribbled something of that kind, maybe in a letter long since destroyed.

I knew that the Begum had some of his poems addressed to my mother. On my return from Bikaner, when it was time for me to return to my teaching job in London, I asked her to let me take those poems with me. At first she hesitated – I knew that it wasn't because she was reluctant to part with them, but that she didn't want me to take them away to England, where they did not belong. I had heard some of what he called his 'propaganda' verses – I had seen him write them, in a car while being driven from one election meeting to another. They were all poems with a social theme, humorous, sarcastic, homely, with a sudden twist at the end that drew amused appreciation from his audience. His poems to my mother were completely different, yet if you knew him – really knew him – it was recognizably he who breathed in them. And not only he but poets dead a thousand years, for he belonged to their tradition of Sanskrit love poetry steeped in sensuality. As they did, he loved women – or rather, a woman: my mother, and with her the whole of life as he knew it, the whole of nature as he knew it, with its sights and smells of fruits and flowers. He wrote of the rumpled bedsheets from which she rose as the Sanskrit poet did of the bed of straw on which his mistress had made love; of the scent of her hair, the mango shape of her breasts. He longed to bed and to be embedded in her. His love was completely physical – to such an extent that it included the metaphysical without ever mentioning it, the way the sky is known to be above the earth even if you don't look up at it.

After his retirement, my father lived mostly in the country, and I joined him whenever I was free from my teaching assignments. It was there that I did most of my translations, and I was working on one of Muktesh's poems when the news of his assassination reached us. My father heard it on the little radio he kept in the kitchen. He came upstairs to my bedroom, which was also my study. He sat on my bed, holding his pipe though he had knocked out the ashes before coming upstairs. I turned around to look at him. At last he said, 'Muktesh.' He was not looking back at me but out of my bedroom window. My father's eyes were of a very light blue that seemed to reflect the mild and pleasant place where he lived. Instinctively, I put my hand on Muktesh's poem. It was too alive and present with a passion I wanted to hide from my father, who had all my life hidden his knowledge of it from me.

My next visit to India coincided with the beginning of the trial of Muktesh's assassins, and every day the newspapers carried front-page stories of it, together with their photographs. Muktesh had been shot at the moment of leaving a function to commemorate the birth date of Mahatma Gandhi. Although one man had carried out the murder, it had been planned by a group of conspirators, including two accomplices ready to do the deed if the first one failed. They were all very young men – the youngest seventeen, the eldest twenty-four – all of them religious fanatics with tousled pitch-black hair and staring pitch-black eyes. If they had been older, their views might have been less intransigent, might even have approached Muktesh's tolerance (for which they had killed him). And as I read about their lives – their impoverished youth, their impassioned studies, their wild ideas – I felt I could have been reading about the young Muktesh himself. And when I went to court to look at his assassins on trial for their lives, it could have been the young Muktesh standing there – as defiant as they, fierce and fervent in dedication to a cause.

But I knew there were other sides to him. I knew it from translating his poems, and also from his manner with me. He was as reticent about my singular appearance as the rest of my family. Yet sometimes he gazed into my face the same way my father did – I knew what for: for some trace, some echo of something lost and precious. He never found it, any more than did my father, but like him Muktesh showed no disappointment. Instead he smiled at me to show his pleasure in me, his approval, his acceptance and his love, which was as deep in his way as my father's was in his, and the Begum's in hers.

She of course had her own manner of showing it. Ever since I was small, she insisted on going through my hair with a louse-comb. 'Your mother used to come home every day from school with something,' she told me to explain this practice, which she extended right into my adult years. I think she just liked to do it, it made up for the other intimate gestures that she so disdained. My hair is coarse and deeply black, quite different from my mother's, so she said, which had been silky like the Begum's own and with auburn lights in it (by this time the Begum's had turned almost red with constant dyeing). Sometimes, while wielding her louse-comb, she commented, 'Who knows where you got this hair – it's certainly not ours.' After a while she said, 'But who knows where anything comes from, and who the hell cares?' Tossing the comb to Amma's granddaughter with instructions to wash it in disinfectant, she began on a story about her ex-husband's family. His mother, my great-grandmother, had for thirty years had a wonderful cook:

'A very lusty fellow from Bihar who made the most delicate rotis I've ever eaten. Which may have been the reason why my mother-in-law couldn't bear to be parted from him for a day. May have been – and anyway, who knows what goes on in those long hot afternoons when everyone is fast asleep?'

'Did this cook have hair like mine?'

'I couldn't tell you,' she said, 'he always wore a cap.' She made a face and then she said, 'Ridiculous,' dismissing the whole subject as unworthy of further discussion.

A Lovesong for India

Although his family had been westernized for two generations, Trilok Chand – always known as TC – was the first
to bring home an English wife. She had been his fellow student at Oxford, the university both his father and hers had
attended before them. Altogether there were similarities in
their background. Like so many British families in the years
before Independence, hers had served in India as judges,
district commissioners, medical officers; and as soon as
these posts were opened to Indians, members of TC's family,
including his father, had been appointed to fill them. Shortly
after his marriage, TC himself had joined the civil service and
had begun the ascent from rank to rank that their fathers had
taken before him.

In his first years, he was posted in the districts, far from
New Delhi and from what he considered civilization. At this
time his wife – her name was Diana – was especially dear
to him. She was as mild and pastel as the English landscape
he had learned to love. She was also fair-minded in the
English way, careful to make no judgements and entertain
no prejudices. When he returned home to her, often angry
and defeated from his day's work, she tried to speak up for
the corrupt police chief or the moneylender who so disgusted

him. She told him he was applying foreign values to a society that had worked out its own arrangements, with which no one had the right to interfere. When he answered that it was his job to interfere, she had her arguments ready – after all, she had from her schooldays been taught to evaluate and debate all sides of a question. He didn't want to debate anything; he only wanted to be with her and kiss her rosy lips and run his fingers through her silky light brown hair.

The advantage of being posted to an outlying district was the allotment of spacious living quarters. Their house dated from the 1920s, when it had been occupied by the British holder of TC's present position. Although it was called a bungalow, it was very large with many rooms, each with a bathroom that had its own back door for the use of the sweeper. The kitchen was at a distance from the main house, but that didn't matter since Diana rarely had to enter it. The cook came to her sitting-room for orders; and the bearer who served their meals knew how to keep the dishes hot while transporting them across the passage to the dining-room. In winter they had a fire lit by which they sat with their books – he read mostly history, she poetry and novels; in the hot weather they enjoyed evenings on the veranda, though when storms blew in from the desert, they retreated inside with all the doors and windows shut against the dust. This neverthe-less entered through every crevice and seeped deep into their books and their carpets and their curtains, insinuating itself forever into the texture of their lives.

For the rest of her days, Diana yearned for the districts of their early years. To her, it had been a recognisable India. The English bungalow was like those her ancestors had occupied as members of the Indian civil service; it was they who had planted the grounds with seeds brought from Kent and Surrey, and they who lay in the neglected cemeteries of the small Christian churches surviving among temples, mosques and brand-new shrines. Diana never felt foreign here: although she lived in the bungalow with the English garden as in an oasis, the surrounding fields of sugar cane or yellow mustard were known and familiar to her, as were the women with loads on their heads and silver jewellery round their ankles, the wells and the bullocks circling them, and the holy man under a tree with offerings of sweets and marigolds at his feet.

TC had joined the service a few years after Independence, when all the higher ranks had been vacated by the British. Consequently, he and his colleagues were promoted much faster than earlier or later generations, and it was not too many years before he reached the higher ranks of the bureaucracy. TC was by no means a typical bureaucrat. He was ready to bend rules when necessary; he was also decisive and quick to act in accordance with his own independent thinking. There was nothing ponderous about him – even physically he remained flexible, supple, and always looked younger than his age. This was in part due to his heritage: before serving the British, his ancestors had served the Moghul court. There may have been some admixture of blood, for they mostly had the fine limbs and features of Muslim aristocrats instead of the heavy build of their own Hindu caste. He and Diana made a not dissimilar impression, both of them slender and fair, she like an Anglo-Saxon and he with what was known as the wheat complexion of an upper-class North Indian.

Their son Romesh was born in 1959, ten years into their marriage. He was completely different from either of them. Much darker and heavier than his father, he appeared to be a throwback to the original strains of Hindu ancestry. He was their only child, but he grew away from them very quickly. He was uncontrollable as a schoolboy, and for a while showed some criminal tendencies – he stole cars and freely took money from his mother's purse when he needed it. But this turned out to be only an assertion of his independence, which later showed itself in other ways. He refused to go to England to study but enrolled in business school in the US. He stayed abroad for several years, and when he returned, he had already established himself as a businessman operating on an international scale, travelling widely in the Middle East as well as in Thailand and Singapore. When he was at home in New Delhi, he fitted in completely, an integral member of young society, enjoying the clubs, the parties and the girls.

At the peak of his career, TC became the Principal Secretary of his ministry and was transferred to the central government in New Delhi. Diana never felt comfortable in New Delhi. They had been allotted a large official Lutyens residence from the 1930s, but they didn't do much entertaining in it. There was something puritanical in Diana, which made her uncomfortable at the lavish dinner parties given with such relish by the other wives of their circle. All of these were Indian and had kept their looks, and from beautiful girls had flourished into magnificent women. Their skin glowed, their eyes shone, their hair had become an even deeper black than in their youth. They loved shawls and jewellery and complimented one another on each new acquisition. But when they said something nice about whatever Diana was wearing, it was in the sweet voice in which people tell polite lies. Diana never wore saris; she didn't have the hips or bosom to carry them. Her frocks were very simple, sewn by a tailor in the bazaar; she avoided bright colours, knowing they didn't suit her complexion, which by now had the sallow tint of someone who for many years had had to shield herself from the Indian sun.

She also felt uncomfortable with her New Delhi servants. These were very different from the cooks and bearers and ayahs with whom she had had such friendly relations in the districts. Her new staff were far more sophisticated and she was rather afraid of them. Although they called her Memsahib, she felt that they didn't regard her as a real memsahib, not like the other wives who knew how to give orders with authority. Reluctant to give any trouble, Diana sometimes surreptitiously dusted a sideboard or polished a piece of silver herself. If they caught her at it, her servants would take it away from her – 'No, Memsahib, this is our work.' She suspected that they commiserated with one another for being employed by such an inadequate person.

For TC, New Delhi came up entirely to his expectations. He loved being near the seat of power, to influence and even to formulate the decisions of his Minister. In the course of his tenure, the government changed several times, and while the Minister lost his position, TC kept his and was able to put his experience at the disposal of his new chief. Of course there were difficulties – the intrigues and manoeuvres he had already encountered in the districts, now on a magnified scale – but these were compensated for by the satisfaction he derived from his New Delhi social life. He had known many of his colleagues from their earliest days in the service, and now at the height of their careers, they had remained in a bond of friendship which included their wives and families.

One of the most energetic hostesses in their set was Pushpa, whom TC had known from their college days. He had even dated her for a while, and it amused her to refer to that early aborted romance. By now she was married to Bobby, who was TC's colleague and the Principal Secretary in another ministry; husband and wife were both fat and jolly and could always be relied on to give what they called a rousing good party. Pushpa's buffet table was loaded with succulent dishes, which were mostly too spicy for Diana. Pushpa scolded her for being so thin – Diana was almost gaunt now – and Pushpa accused TC, 'You're starving the poor girl.' Then she added, 'I know what it is – you don't want her to become fat like me.' She loved to call herself the girl he dumped: 'You think I'm only good enough for someone like Bobby who is as fat and ugly as I am!' Everyone, including Bobby, laughed heartily.

But there was also serious talk – relations with Pakistan, proposals for a new dam – and here too the wives joined in. Diana mostly remained silent. She didn't feel she had the right to enter into their discussions, and especially not into their perennial jokes about politics and corruption. Whereas they could say anything they wanted, she as a foreigner would have caused offence.

The one person Diana liked to visit in New Delhi was her friend Margaret, an Englishwoman in charge of a lay mission devoted to charitable work in India. It was far away from their official residence, and Diana drove herself there in TC's car (neither of them would ever have taken his official driver or any other member of their staff for their personal use). When he was small, Diana would take Romesh with her on these visits, but he soon revolted. He disliked the sombre old mission house with its high ceilings and stone floors impregnated by the smell of disinfectant and stale curries. It was made worse for him by Margaret herself, a large-boned woman with a loud voice who ruled over a bevy of silent, humble helpers, most of them girls whom she had rescued from orphanages or bad homes. When he grew up, his antipathy became even stronger. It puzzled Diana; she asked him, 'But why, darling? Give me one reason.' He was never good at explaining his feelings, but at last he came up with, 'If you must know, I can't stand all that holiness and prayer, it gives me the creeps. Thank God you don't go in for all that stuff.' It was true, Diana had laid aside her Christian prayers, as well as the gold cross inset with rubies, a gift from her godmother on her twelfth birthday.

Margaret never spoke to Diana about religion. Instead they liked to remind each other of favourite poems or long-ago Latin lessons, gaily correcting each other's syntax. Although both of them had spent most of their adult lives in India, their original accents had not only remained but had become even more precise and English. Margaret always wore Punjabi dress, including the modesty veil, though she only used it to wipe away the perspiration caused by her long hours of trudging the streets and slums of the inner city. She was mostly cheerful and undaunted, whether it was a day of triumph when she had procured an artificial leg for a client, or a setback with a convert relapsing into alcoholism and wife-beating. Diana never could understand why Romesh said, 'Let her go and do good somewhere else.' But quite often he wrote a cheque for her, always for a substantial amount, which Margaret received with the measured gratitude of one used to accepting whatever was given, fully aware that it would never be enough.

Neither of his parents understood much about Romesh's business activities. 'Something to do with export,' Diana explained to herself and anyone who asked. 'Import-export.' She couldn't really appreciate her son's lavish lifestyle – the big car he drove around in, his constant trips abroad – but she felt proud of his enterprise. He had never for a moment considered following his father into the civil service. 'Thanks but no thanks,' he said. 'You don't catch me spending my life trapped in a job with a measly salary and ending up with a piddly provident fund.'

Although TC's only answer was a wry 'Good luck to you', Diana knew he was hurt. 'It's just that he's a different personality,' she assured him about their son. 'He really respects you enormously.' She knew this to be true, for she had heard Romesh boast on the telephone: 'Do you have any idea who my dad is?'

TC had a new Minister – his name was RK Googal, known to everyone as Googa. They had met before, many years earlier, when TC was a district commissioner and Googa sold eggs and butter in the bazaar while making a more serious living as a local politician with power to dispense municipal contracts. At that time TC had thwarted one of Googa's business operations, and in revenge Googa had tried to get him transferred. He failed, but he never forgot this transaction between them. In the meantime TC had had dealings with many more men like Googa and had learned to steer his way around them. But Googa had the character of a potentate and, unable to get rid of his Principal Secretary, he did everything he could to obstruct him, so that TC felt more frustrated than in the many crises he had suffered in the course of his career.

Romesh admired his father's new boss. He said he was a firecracker: 'Googa they call him – or Gunda.' He laughed. 'I guess he is a gunda – a rascal – but he sure gets things done. The country needs chaps like that,' he informed his father.

TC never brought his office worries home, and the only person with whom he shared them was his friend Bobby.

Bobby was well aware of the troubles a Principal Secretary could have with his Minister. His wife Pushpa also knew about such situations, and listened with sympathy while her husband gave his friend the only advice he could – which was to be patient and subtle in his dealings with such dangerous animals. TC felt soothed in their company and by the domestic ambience of Pushpa's household – the glasses of home-made sherbet that appeared on a silver tray, the smell of spices being fried in onions. After a while they passed from the unfortunate office affairs to more personal matters – gossip about their colleagues, plans for summer travel in the hills.

Once Pushpa said, 'What about your Romesh-Baba?' and to TC's inquiring look: 'Isn't it about time he settled down? These young people have no sense. They think they can run around any way they please for the rest of their lives.'

Bobby humorously shut one eye. 'And hasn't your Romesh been running around with our Sheila-Baby?'

'Why shouldn't they!' Pushpa cried. 'We're not that antediluvian. Even in our day – if you remember,' she told TC in a favourite allusion to their past college romance. 'But all the same, someone has to give them a bit of a push now and again.'

'We leave all that to you girls,' Bobby said.

TC was used to discussing everything except office affairs with Diana, and when he mentioned Pushpa's proposal to her, her blue eyes stretched wide and she said, 'That's entirely between the boy and the girl. We have no right to interfere.'

TC was amused by her reaction, which he had expected – Diana questioned everything she considered a denial of the individual's right to free choice. He teased her: 'Sheila's a very pretty girl.'

'That has nothing to do with it. Nothing at all. We shouldn't even be talking about it.' She looked righteous and pale, the way she always did in defence of her principles.

But the next time she was alone with Romesh, she asked him, trying to sound casual, 'Do you meet Sheila quite often?'

He looked up at her from his breakfast. It was usually the only meal he ate at home, and she herself cooked the bacon for him since their Muslim cook wouldn't touch it. 'Has Pushpa-Auntie been gabbing to you?' Romesh asked. She blushed, but he went on to assure her: 'Don't worry, I'm not there yet.'

'No no, I'm not worrying, of course not. I'm not suggesting anything at all, darling, it's entirely up to you.' She watched him eat for a while, which he did as he did everything, with enormous appetite and appreciation. At last she shyly asked, 'Do you like her a lot?'

He had to suppress his laughter at this innocent question. What could his mother know about someone like Sheila — a wild, wild girl, far surpassing any he had been with in America. And not only she but other Indian girls he knew; it was as though in throwing off all restraints, they were compensating for those suffered by past generations of their mothers and grandmothers.

It was Bobby who first alerted TC to the probe that was being initiated against certain government departments, including their own. So far it was being kept secret, but TC soon found that files began to go missing. His visits to Bobby became more frequent; they exchanged news and views about the situation and kept each other informed about its development. As usual, Pushpa passed in and out, though now only to bring them refreshments.

At the end of one meeting, she told TC: 'I hear your Romesh-Baba is going off again on some of his murky business.'

'Who tells you it's murky?' TC answered her in the light tone they had established between them.

'All business is murky,' she said in the same tone. Then she said, 'I wish he and Sheila-Baby would make up their minds. It'd be a big load off *my* mind, I tell you. I'm sure they like each other; whenever I ask her where she's been, she says with Romesh of course, as if that makes it all right. And it would be all right, if they'd only . . . ' She appealed to TC, her plump face full of a mother's anxiety.

When Romesh came home that night, TC was as usual awake and working. He looked at his son: the thin muslin kurta Romesh wore for his social evenings was crumpled and somewhat soiled. His eyes were reddened, maybe from fatigue and certainly from an excess of alcohol. Pretending to notice none of this, TC said, 'I hear you're pushing off again.'

Romesh swiftly glanced at him. Next moment he relaxed. 'I guess I have to. To fill this,' and he patted his stomach, which looked very full already. 'This sinful belly.'

'We'll miss you,' his father said. 'Will you be gone long? . . . Sorry to pry into what doesn't concern me, but there's something – well, I might as well mention it,' TC decided, remembering Pushpa's anxious face.

And again Romesh looked at him suspiciously, while he answered with caution: 'I don't know yet how long I'll be gone. It depends. These things always take time. It's something to do with shares, stocks and shares – I won't bother you with details.'

'No, don't. There's no chance I'd understand them. This is about Sheila.'

'Yes. Sheila. A grand girl.'

'Her mother is hoping that perhaps, before you go? But it's entirely up to you; and to her of course. We'd all like it.'

'I'd like it too, but it's not the right time. I'm not ready to get married. Not with all this on my head.' And then he got angry: 'What do they all think! Everything is left to me, I have to run from here to Timbuktu – I told you there's no point in going into detail!' he shouted, though TC hadn't asked anything.

His raised voice brought Diana into the room. She had been awake, as she was every night, waiting for her two men to be home and in bed. Now she stood there in her white floor-length nightgown, looking from one to the other.

'Romesh is tired from his night's activities,' TC explained drily.

Romesh tried to speak more quietly: 'No, I'm not tired from a little partying but from –' he paused, then rushed on – 'the harassment. The harassment from every side – everyone is sick of it, I tell you that! Foreign investors take one look at your famous rules and regulations and run for their lives. Can you blame them? No one wants to be treated like a thief and a crim-inal for trying to get a decent business going.' He swallowed, maybe to stop himself from saying anything imprudent. 'Now do you mind if I go to bed? I'm just about done for.'

Diana watched him go to his room. He was shuffling a bit, and she appealed to TC: 'Do you think he's working too hard?' But later, alone with TC in their bedroom, she said, 'I believe people tend to drink more when they're under strain.' And when TC was silent: 'Do you think he is? Upset about anything?'

TC tried to laugh. 'When you're young, every little thing is enough to set you off. You remember how it was.'

'Yes, I remember – but that's not how it was.'

This time he laughed genuinely, with pleasure at the memories they shared of a youth that, whatever their present age and appearance, was not lost for them at all.

It was only a day or two later that Bobby called TC to come to his house in the evening. They sat as usual in Bobby's study, but this time Pushpa did not walk in and out. To explain her absence, Bobby said, 'Gone shopping somewhere, spending all my money.' But soon he was more grave.

He told TC that the inquiry had now reached further into TC's department, and higher – as high as the Minister himself. 'Of course he's taking steps to make sure he's home and dry.'

'We'll see about that,' TC promised his friend, and himself too.

In the following pause Bobby looked like someone who had something difficult to say. TC waited. 'But there are others,' Bobby said at last. 'He wouldn't be so eager to protect those others.'

'You mean those who've been taking bribes with him?'

'Not only those who have taken. Also those who have given.'

'I see.' TC did his best to speak even more calmly than usual. 'Are there names?'

'There are two very big names – big Bombay tycoons – and there are smaller names. The size of the – of the "contribution" doesn't signify. All will be considered equally guilty.'

'Of course.' TC made his long thin fingers into a steeple; this was his habit when considering official matters. But now he had to clear his throat twice before speaking: 'I believe the boy's name appears only in connection with one of the issues?'

A fat and excitable man, Bobby waved his hands in the air.

'One issue, two issues, or a hundred – this time no one's going to get away. We're not letting one scrap of proof out of our hands. No file is going to disappear, I promise you.' He looked at TC across from him. Their two pairs of glasses gleamed so that it wasn't possible to see each other's eyes behind them. But Bobby could say with confidence, 'I know you want it as much as I do, whatever the consequences.'

And TC answered with the same confidence, 'Yes. Yes, of course.' And after a pause, 'Absolutely.'

That evening Diana told him, 'Pushpa was here today. Imagine! They're sending Sheila-Baby to Australia to study political science – Sheila's a wonderful girl but I never thought of her as being very academic, did you? . . . And why Australia?' Into her husband's silence, she said, 'Do you think Pushpa came to tell me something else?'

TC said, 'I think she was trying to tell you that the marriage is off.'

'You mean that's why they're sending her away? But Romesh would have said something. He'd have told us.'

'Does he ever tell us anything?' This required no answer, so TC went on to ask: 'When is he leaving?'

'I think soon. He's already packed – or what he calls packed. But of course, as usual, I'll have to pull it all out and start again.' She smiled, and TC tried to smile too.

Next morning, while serving his breakfast, she asked Romesh about his plans for departure. He was vague in his answer – something about waiting for some papers to be cleared, which she didn't understand. She changed the subject: 'And now Sheila's going to Australia.' He said nothing, so she continued, 'Pushpa seemed pleased, though I thought she had other plans for Sheila . . . And for you,' she added with a shy smile.

He shrugged. 'Sheila's a lot of fun, but marriage is not on the cards – not to me anyway. Wait,' he said. The phone in his bedroom was ringing, and he got up to answer it. Through the closed door, she heard his voice raised in excitement; he had only half-finished his breakfast, but when he returned, he was in no mood to eat. He asked, 'Where's Dad now?'

'He's in his office, probably in a meeting ... Is there anything I can do?' she pleaded. But he said no, it was just something he had to ask TC. Like his father, Romesh avoided letting her into his difficulties, though with him it was not so much to shield her as himself, against her intrusion.

A message reached TC from his minister, which he had been half-expecting. It came in a roundabout way – this too was expected – from a clerk who said he happened to be Googa's nephew by marriage and that he had a message for TC from his uncle. Although the message was clouded, it was clear enough to TC: that there were certain papers in which Googa's name figured along with some other persons; and that it would be convenient if these papers were to be privately dealt with. Fortunately it would not be difficult to obtain them since the relevant file was located in the ministry where the Principal Secretary was not only TC's opposite number but his friend. TC received this message and thanked the messenger in a calm, non-committal manner, which gave no indication of the shame that filled him like a rush of blood to the heart.

A few days later, Googa sent festive boxes of sweetmeats to all his staff. TC's was the biggest, and it was again delivered personally by a relative of Googa's, this time a brother-in-law who explained that these sweets were to celebrate the shaving of the first hair to grow on a grandson's head. 'His *grand*son!

Googaji said to remind you that it is now twenty-five years since he sent you sweets for his *son*'s first hair-shaving. So many years you have been his father and his mother.'

'Yes,' TC agreed drily. 'We've known each other many years – certainly long enough for him to know that I don't eat sweets.' And he pushed the box aside.

The brother-in-law pushed it back again. He joined his hands in supplication. 'If not you, then for your children who are also our children. Googaji says you have a son who likes sweets very much. Let him eat and enjoy.'

That evening there was a banquet in honour of a visiting foreign dignitary, attended by cabinet ministers, ambassadors and top bureaucrats. It was held in the formal hall of a royal palace taken over by the government; under the chandeliers, the long table was laid as it had been in the Maharaja's time and barefoot bearers in turbans and cummerbunds moved silently around it to serve the guests. Googa, his enormous bulk swathed in yards of white muslin, sat in his rightful place near the head of the table. He was in a fine mood and joshed the other ministers with bad puns in Hindi – he looked only up the table to where the important guests sat. There was no need for him to look down towards TC at the lower end, or to give any sign of being aware of his existence, let alone of any business between them.

Bobby sat as always near TC at the end of the table. To relieve their boredom, they were in the habit of exchanging cryptic remarks or glances to express their feelings about the guests at the superior end. But today Bobby did not notice TC any more than Googa did, engaging himself in conversation with his neighbours at the table. Once TC called across to him with their own kind of banter and, while not completely ignoring him, Bobby gave the puzzled half-smile of one who failed to understand the reference. Then TC looked down at his golden plate and again a wave of shame welled up in him.

One evening Diana surprised her husband and her son in the middle of a talk that appeared to be difficult for both of them. But they were united in their determination that she should know nothing, and it was not until she was alone with TC in their bedroom that she could ask anything. Brushing her hair, she could see him in the mirror, and the expression on his face made her turn around quickly before he could change it. Then she did challenge him, though only with: 'Romesh still hasn't packed properly – I think he's just waiting for me to do it for him.'

A flippant white lie on his lips, TC looked into her eyes. It made him say quietly, 'He's not leaving.'

They sat side by side on the edge of their bed. Even when she put her arms around him, his back remained stiff and straight. He said, 'They've impounded his passport. He can't leave because he's wanted here for questioning.'

She tried to speak lightly: 'What's he supposed to have done? They can't just hold him for nothing. If he's done nothing.'

'He says he hasn't. Or only what everyone else does.' He almost lost his patience. 'That's what they all say: "Everyone does it – what's wrong with it when everyone does it?" That's supposed to be the excuse; not the shameful admission but the excuse.'

She had never seen him like this, so bitter and hurt. 'Let's lie down,' she whispered. It did seem a relief to him to lie with her in their bed, the same they had had in all the years of their marriage. The way they lay entwined was the same too, so that for a few hours they could sleep as if there were only the two of them – two lovers alone with each other and safe from all the world.

Next morning, when she went into Romesh's room, she found him asleep with his face pressed deep in the pillow, not wanting to see or hear. His suitcases stood open, the clothes tumbling out of them. She unpacked and put everything back in the closet. When he opened his eyes, there was the momentary look of relief of one waking from a nightmare and realising it was not real. Then he realized it *was* real; also, from the way his mother was looking at him, that she knew what it was.

At once he rushed to his own defence. 'Dad doesn't understand that it's the way business is done. If you want your motor to run, you have to oil it. Grease it. Grease their goddamn palms. Dad has his job, his little salary, no hassle – you two have no idea what's going on, what I have to do. My God, if only you knew!'

'I don't know anything because you never tell me anything. If you did, I'd try and understand.'

'I wouldn't even want you to. You're so English, you've stayed English though you've been here donkey's years. You even think that the English don't do it – that they're all like you and Dad. That's just baloney! They do exactly what we do. Exactly . . . Let me get up now. I can't stay in bed all day.' But she kept on sitting there, waiting for him to say more, take advantage of her presence.

He said, 'I guess that's why they've sent Sheila away. Isn't it? . . . So she wouldn't be in a dirty country like this with a dirty person like me. God, they're all so innocent, such babies. Bobby – what a dumb name, but it suits him. Sheila-Baby. Pushpa-Baby. Baba Bobby.' Suddenly he collapsed; his face was puffed, tears ran down it. 'Dad could help me. Ask him. He's not listening to me. If you tell him, he'll listen.'

She put her arms around him; he laid his head in her lap, his face hidden against her. She stroked his hair – already it was thinning – she didn't know what she could promise, though he was begging her, the same sentence several times: 'He'll listen to you.'

Whenever she couldn't talk freely to anyone, Diana felt a need to confide in Margaret; but when it came to the point, she never could. It happened again that day. At the mission, she found Margaret out on the veranda, surrounded by her usual crowd of petitioners and upbraiding a milkman for watering the milk he sold her. She overrode his protests until he had to admit his fault, while bystanders murmured approval of the scolding he received.

Margaret's anger was assumed. She told Diana that she had already dismissed this milkman once before, but what to do? He had a family to support, four children of his own and two of his dead brother's. Anyway, she still had to find a milkman who did not water his milk; when finally caught, their excuse was always the same – '"Everyone does it, so why not I?"' Her big shoulders shook with laughter. 'I've heard it a thousand times: "Everyone does it" – it's not an excuse but a perfectly valid explanation.'

Diana smiled with her. Today she refused the mug of tea she usually drank with Margaret; she said she had to drive back, that TC was waiting for the car.

Margaret dealt all day with people in need, and it was easy for her to sense anyone's trouble. Walking with Diana to her car, Margaret asked her, 'Can I do anything for you?' Diana shook her head; she thanked her friend and drove away.

The only person Diana had ever asked for help or ever

would was TC, and she did so that night. She knew he was awake beside her and in distress; his back was turned to her and at last she clung to it, whispering, 'Won't you try – for him?' He turned and held her against his chest. She said it again, but when he was silent, she said nothing more, and neither did he, though he could feel her tears seeping through his nightshirt.

The arraignment for Romesh came at the same time as the one for Googa. While TC resigned his post immediately, Googa showed no inclination to relinquish his. He had many supporters who accompanied him to court, loudly shouting slogans in his favour. He made the most of the presence of journalists and TV cameras to declare his innocence, his forgiveness of his enemies and his determination to continue serving his country, to the last drop of his blood if this should be required of him. His well-wishers followed him inside, so that the small courtroom was soon overcrowded and fetid with their sweat and eructations. Romesh, accompanied only by his father and his lawyers, took care to appear in court newly shaved and in a suit and tie; he listened intently to the proceedings and passed notes of instruction to his lawyers. His fortunes appeared linked to Googa's, and both of them were usually granted bail. Once they were remanded in jail, and even there Romesh extracted special privileges from the wardens and the convicts he knew had the power to grant them. When he was released, he showed no signs of depression but was very busy consulting with his lawyers, whom he changed twice. His energy and pluck reminded Diana of the time when he was a schoolboy, always in trouble, up to all sorts of mischief and defiant when caught at it.

For the first time in their married life, TC and Diana

discussed money. It had never been an important subject for either of them. They had not invested anything, nor built a house. Now, with his resignation, they had six months to give up their official residence. They assured each other that they would manage. Since TC no longer had to attend an office, they could sell their car. They had also stopped going out socially. Diana continued to visit the mission and Margaret had arranged for her to be transported by one of her protégés on his bicycle rickshaw. Diana felt ashamed to be sitting behind his emaciated back while he pushed the pedals down with all his feeble strength; but Margaret, aware of her feelings, said, 'You can hardly ask this boy to stop making a living because you feel bad about it.' She was also impatient with TC and Diana when she found that they hadn't yet tried to find another house. To discuss their problems, she often came to see them. She sat in their largest chair with her legs apart and her voice cheerfully booming; her only comment on the situation was once to TC when he saw her out. Seating herself voluminously on her protégé's frail rickshaw, 'It's a mess,' she said, 'but anyway, you did the right thing.'

Romesh did not think that his father had done the right thing. In resigning his office, TC was giving up the chance of exerting pressure on behalf of his son. It might also be taken as an admission of guilt, which Romesh himself was far from making. Instead he worked energetically to extricate himself. With the help of his lawyers, he discovered the weak links obstructing his case – a chain stretching from the lower ranks up to the occupants of some top positions. He knew whom to avoid – Bobby, for instance, whom he shrugged off as useless; so were most of his father's former colleagues, though with some surprising exceptions. Romesh found himself frequently on the same track as Googa, whom he learned to respect for his ruthless energy and ability to make things work for him. 'Not a bad chap,' he said. And it was Googa who finally resolved matters for both of them. This was during a parliamentary crisis when Googa, with his command over a substantial block of votes, could make himself very helpful; and after that it was not long before it was decided that the charges against him and his co-defendants were completely baseless.

Romesh's passport was returned to him, and he was left free to continue his business. He now shifted his base of operations to Bombay, which he said was a much livelier city, geared to modern business practices, and also with even wilder girls in it. He wanted to move his parents with him, but they were now well settled in the little flat Margaret had found for them. It was far from official New Delhi, in a bazaar area that Diana soon came to know well. Over the years she witnessed many changes in their new neighbourhood. An alley that had once been occupied by vegetable stalls and cooked meat shops was now given over to motor parts. The site of a rotted old textile mill had become a propane gas plant; and there was a brand-new charitable eye hospital under the patronage of a cabinet minister whose face – it happened to be Googa's – loomed on a poster encircled by little coloured bulbs. Margaret's mission was nearby, and here everything remained unchanged. Her helpers were still orphan girls in cotton saris, and shoes and socks to save their feet from ringworm. Out on the veranda the petitioners still stood waiting for Margaret to help solve their problems, which never seemed to grow different or less.

Diana tremendously admired Margaret's selfless devotion to India, which she couldn't help contrasting with her own selfish devotion to only two Indians, her husband and her son.

But her sense of guilt left her as soon as she got home to where TC was writing his memoirs and waiting to read his day's work to her. His style had been honed for official reports: 'In November we moved to Sitapur where we encountered a variety of incidents, some of them of a humorous nature, others rather more serious.' She knew all the incidents and was able to flood his spare prose with her memories. Often, while he read, it was not the city noises outside that she heard but the jackals and peacocks surrounding the bungalow of their early districts. She didn't need to look out of the window of their cramped little flat to know that the sun setting over the city streets was the same that she had watched over the unbroken plains of their first postings. The moon too would be the same, spreading a net of silver over the people asleep outside the shuttered shops.

Romesh came to Delhi to visit his parents. Stout, middle-aged, shining in a silk jacket and some gold jewellery, he burst in on them: 'So what's new!' Of course he knew there never could be anything new for them, washed up in all their innocence, their total ignorance of life in the world. What he couldn't account for was their happiness, though he was aware that it included him, all the years of his existence as their son.

Pagans

Brigitte: calm, large-limbed and golden as a pagan goddess, she loved to lie spreadeagled on the beach or by her swimming pool, in communication with the sun. Los Angeles had been good to her. When she was young, at the time of her marriage, she had been a successful model. Her husband, Louis Morgenstern, was a small, wizened, shrewd little man, thirty years older than herself but a studio head, a powerful producer, a very rich man. It had been a relief for her to give up her career. She preferred to swim, to sunbathe, to give dinner parties for Louis (studded with stars but as dull, in their different way, as those her sister Frances gave in New York for her banker husband); also to travel in Europe and occasionally take lovers – wry intellectuals who taught her what to read and confirmed her contempt for the sorts of films made by the studios, including her husband's.

Her sister Frances had been very sceptical about the marriage to Louis. She was wrong. In spite of the lovers – kept secret, discreet – it lasted almost thirty years, and so did Brigitte's respect and liking for her husband. While Frances had married conventionally within their own circle, settled in the US for several generations, Louis was the first in his family to be born here and still had a grandmother who spoke no English. Frances and her husband Marshall were ashamed of what they considered their sister's misalliance. They felt themselves to tower over Louis and his family – socially of course, culturally, and physically too, as was clear at the wedding when tiny Morgensterns scurried among the lofty trees of bankers and real estate developers. Afterwards Marshall joked about the ill-matched couple and how Brigitte would be crushing Louis on their wedding night between her mighty thighs.

Brigitte was in her fifties when Louis died, and Frances, for whom Los Angeles was a wasteland, said, 'Now perhaps you'll come back to civilization.' Brigitte sold her house – the Hollywood mansion of indoor and outdoor pools, patios and screening rooms – while Frances searched for a suitable apartment in New York for her. Meanwhile Brigitte moved into a suite in a hotel, and although Frances found one Upper East Side apartment and then another, all close to herself and Marshall, Brigitte kept making excuses not to move into them. She liked Los Angeles; unlike New York, it was lightweight and undemanding. From one hotel window, she could see pretty houses frail as plywood scattered over the wooded hillside. From another, she had a view over the city of Los Angeles spread flat as far as the horizon; at night it was transformed into a field of shimmering flickering glow-worms fenced by the cut-out silhouettes of high-rise buildings. And the trees – the tall, straight palm trees with their sparse foliage brushing a sky that was sometimes Renaissance blue and sometimes silver with pollution but all day held the sun to pour down on the ocean, the golden beach and Brigitte herself, past menopause but still golden and firm in her designer swimsuit, and pads on her large smooth lids luxuriantly shut.

Frances was getting impatient. I suppose she has a new lover out there, she thought to herself; and she said it to Brigitte over the phone: 'Who is it now, another of those foreigners filling your head with clever rubbish?'

Brigitte laughed; she had always laughed at Frances' disapproval, whether it was of Louis, of her lovers or of her indolence. Brigitte still had male friends – she needed them to tell her what to read – but she had long since reached a stage where she could admit that sex was boring for her. With Louis, she had enjoyed sitting beside him while he explained their stocks and shares and other holdings to her. By the time he died, he had been ill for some years but was only semi-retired, for his successors at the studio continued to need his experience and his financial clout. Twice a year he and Brigitte still gave their dinner parties where the agents and the money men mixed with the stars. Louis had little respect for most of the stars; he mocked their pretensions and perversions, their physical beauty which he said was the work of plastic surgeons and monkey glands. After each dinner party and the departure of the famous guests, he kissed Brigitte in gratitude for what she was: full-figured and naturally tanned, almost Nordic, God knew how and it was not only the hairdresser and the beautician. Louis had grown-up children from a previous marriage, and when it turned out that Brigitte couldn't have any, he was glad, wanting to keep her perfect, unmarred. Actually, Brigitte was not sorry either; she didn't think she had time for children. Frances said anyway she was too slothful and untidy ever to be able to bring them up. Frances had untold trouble with her own now grown-up son and daughter, who had gone the unstable way of the young and too rich.

Two years after selling her house, Brigitte was still in Los Angeles. By this time she had met Shoki, a young Indian, and an interesting relationship had developed. It may have appeared a classic case of older woman with impoverished young immigrant, but that was not the way it was at all. It was true that he was young, very young; it was also true that he was poor, insofar as he had no money, but the word impoverished was inapplicable. He had the refinement of someone born rich – not so much in money as in inherited culture. This expressed itself in him physically in fine features and limbs; culturally in his manners, his almost feminine courtesy; and spiritually – so Brigitte liked to think – in his eyes, as of a soul that yearned for higher being. These eyes were often downcast, the lashes brushing his cheeks, for he was shy – out of modesty, not lack of confidence. As far as confidence was concerned, he reposed as on a rock of ancestral privilege, so that it never mattered to him that he had to take all kinds of lowly jobs to keep himself going. Brigitte had met him while he was doing valet parking at her hotel; he had been filling in for another boy and left after a few weeks to work in a restaurant, again filling in for someone else. There were always these jobs available in a shifting population of unemployed or temporarily unemployed actors and other aspirants to film and television careers.

He himself wanted to become a writer-director, which was why he was here so far from home. He informed Brigitte that film was the medium of expression for his generation – he said it as though it were an idea completely original to himself. He carried a very bulky manuscript from agent to agent, or rather to their secretaries, and was always ready to read from it. Encouraged by Brigitte, he sat in her suite and read to her, while she watched rather than listened to him. Maybe it was all nonsense; but maybe it wasn't, or no more than the films on which Louis had grown so immensely rich; and she wanted him to be successful, so that he wouldn't go away, or wouldn't sink along with the other young people for whom he filled in on an endless round of temporary jobs.

She introduced him to Ralph, who had started off as a producer and now had his own talent agency. He had often been among her and Louis' guests, the powerful locals who had been their friends or had considered themselves so. Actually, some of them had made a pass at her – as who did not, even when she had been beyond the age when any woman could have expected it. Usually she laughed at them, and the one she had laughed at the most had been Ralph: 'Come on, you don't mean it.' Finally he had to admit that he did not. His excuse was that she was irresistible. 'At fifty-five?' she asked. He was the only person ever to explain to her in what way, and of course it was easier for him, with his lack of taste for women, to be impersonal. He said that her attraction was her indifference – the fact that she just *was*, the way a pagan goddess is, Pallas Athene or someone, ready to accept worship but unconcerned whether it is given or not.

The introduction to Ralph was a success. Shoki came back enthusiastic about Ralph's kindness to him. When Brigitte phoned Ralph to thank him, Ralph said it was one's duty to help young talent. He sounded guarded; there was a silence, then she said, 'So what did you think?'

'About the screenplay? It's interesting. Different.'

'Yes, isn't it.'

Brigitte had hoped Ralph would have a more explicit opinion. She knew for herself that the work was different, and also difficult. The characters spoke in a poetic prose that was not easy to understand, but it sounded beautiful when Shoki read it to her, and every time he looked up for her appreciation, she had no difficulty giving it. Then he continued, satisfied – though really he did not need approval; he had the same confidence in his work as he did in himself.

When there was another crisis in his living arrangement, Brigitte solved it by taking a room for him in the hotel. He was concerned about the expense, but when she reassured him that it wasn't a suite, just a single room, he moved in with his small baggage. He liked it very much. It was on the second floor and overlooked the hotel garden with its cypress trees and silver fountain. It was also decided around this time that it was really not necessary for Shoki to take any more jobs when he could do so many helpful things for Brigitte.

Frances found the perfect New York apartment for her sister and Brigitte agreed to take it, pay a deposit, sign papers – 'Oh please, Frankie, whatever.' Frances was not satisfied; she knew she was being got rid of and asked herself, What's going on? Unfortunately she had no one with whom to share her doubts. Although she and her husband Marshall were known and seen everywhere as an indivisible couple – large and rich – the communication between them was not intimate. Whenever she tried to confide some deeper concerns to him, he answered her with an indifferent grunt or by rattling his newspaper at her in irritation.

'What's the matter with you?' she reproached Brigitte over the telephone. 'What's wrong? I thought you wanted to come.' Then she said, 'Do you have someone out there? A relationship?'

'Oh absolutely. He's sitting right here.' Brigitte smiled across the room at Shoki, who looked up inquiringly and smiled back.

'It's not a joke. And if you knew how I've been running around trying to find the right apartment for you, and at last I have.'

'Bless you,' Brigitte thanked her, but Frances remained dissatisfied.

A few days later, after a particularly annoying telephone

conversation with Brigitte, Frances decided it would be best if she went herself to Los Angeles. She proposed this idea to Marshall, who said at once, 'Impossible.' They were about to go out to someone's anniversary dinner – she had laid out his evening clothes and was putting on her jewellery.

'Only for a few days,' she said.

'Oh yes? And what about the hospital ball, the library, the God-knows-for-what fundraiser?' He was looking at himself in the mirror, adjusting his suspenders over his dress shirt. He was a big, broad man carrying a load of stomach in front, but it gave him pleasure to dress up and see himself. She, on the other hand, inserted her earrings as though she were undergoing a disagreeable ritual.

'Why?' he said. As if he didn't know that her reason for going to Los Angeles could only be her sister. But she wasn't going to spell anything out for him: if Brigitte was to be mentioned, he would have to do it. 'You hate flying,' he said, holding out a sleeve for her to insert the cufflink. 'You sit there as if the pilot's one ambition is to crash the plane with you in it. You spoil every trip you take with me before it's even started ... I thought you told me she was moving to New York.'

Frances was now concentrating on tying his black tie, something he had had no cause to learn since she did it so expertly.

'Well, is she or isn't she?'

'I don't know.'

'You don't know. That's your sister all over – playing mystery, making everyone dance to her tune.'

But later, inside their chauffeured limousine, where they took up the entire back seat as they sat side by side in their party clothes: 'Call the office to book your seat; or remind me tomorrow, I'll tell them.'

*

Frances was querulous. The flight had been as horrible as she had expected, she already hated her room and it was all Brigitte's fault for making her come here. 'Yes you did – I knew something was up, and who else is there to care except me?'

'Darling,' Brigitte acknowledged. She looked around the room. 'But it's charming, what's wrong with it?'

'It's cheap and gaudy, like a film set. And the light is giving me a headache.'

'I'll draw the curtain' – but Brigitte regretted having to exclude the sun, the bright view.

'Marshall thinks you have a lover, that's why you're sticking on here.'

'Did Marshall say that?'

'I'm sure it's what he's thinking.'

'I have a friend,' Brigitte said.

'A man?'

'God, Frances. What are you thinking?'

'Who knows, nowadays?' Frances was sad, thinking of her own children, about whose lives she could only speculate. 'How old is he?'

'Young. Very young, Frankie.'

Her sister was the only person left in the world to call her Frankie, and Frances' mood softened. She said, 'I suppose it happens, especially in this place. You'd be far better off in New York.'

'There are no young men there?'

'*I'm* there. We'd be together again, after so many years ... We don't have to be lonely.'

With her cool lips, Brigitte kissed her sister's cheek. 'You must be dropping. I'll let you rest.'

Frances agreed meekly. She really was tired – certainly too tired to call Marshall and tell him she had arrived safely.

Anyway, he would only say that, if she hadn't, he would have heard about it soon enough.

But it was he who called her. He even asked about her flight; he also asked about her return booking, and would she and Brigitte be arriving together? She told him she was worried about the New York apartment for which she was negotiating – it was very desirable and others might pre-empt it – and in reply he did what she had hoped, asked for details, so she knew that he would be following them up and far more efficiently than she could. There was no reason after that not to hang up, but at the last moment he said, 'What's she tell you?'

'About what?'

'About being a crazy woman and getting herself in a mess back there.'

Brigitte was woken up by a phone call from Ralph, asking her if she knew where Shoki was. He was trying not to sound agitated. 'He's not in his room, so I thought he'd be with you.'

'No, but he'll be here for breakfast.'

'Breakfast! Do you know what the time is? . . . Anyway, he was supposed to be here; I'd set up a breakfast meeting for him. Remember? I'm his agent.'

Brigitte said, 'Of course.' But it was true – she really had forgotten about this connection between Shoki and Ralph. Maybe she had even forgotten that Shoki was here for any other purpose than to be with her. She asked, 'Do you and he often have breakfast meetings?'

'Well. Most days. I'm trying to help him, Brigitte.' She could hear Ralph trying to choke down his anxiety. He said, 'Have you any idea where he spends the night? You think he's in his room, don't you, but have you ever checked?' His voice rose. 'Don't you ever wonder?' he asked, angry with her now.

Actually, she did wonder sometimes – not as Ralph evidently did, with anguish, but with curiosity, even pleasure. She knew it was not possible for Shoki to restrict himself to people he liked but who, by virtue of their age, were barred from one whole potent side of his nature. For that he did need – she freely admitted it – those as young as himself, and as gay (possibly in both senses). But to Ralph she only said, 'What's happening with his screenplay?'

'It still needs work.' He swept aside the irrelevant subject. 'The fact is, he needs someone to take charge, be a bit strict with him.'

'You mean to make him work?'

'Yes yes, that too. Now listen, Brigitte, we need to talk—'

'Oh,' she said quickly, 'there's someone at the door. That may be he.'

But it was Frances. Brigitte went back to the phone. 'No, it's my sister. She's here from New York.'

'Do you realize he was not in his room, not at midnight, not early this morning?'

'My sister and I are going out now. This minute. We have a dental appointment.'

When Brigitte was off the phone, Frances said, 'I don't know why you have to tell people lies all the time.'

'That's not fair, Frankie.' But she reflected for a while. 'It's mostly to save their feelings.'

Frances was silent; she drew in her lips. 'Don't ever think you have to save mine.'

After a moment of surprise, 'Of course not!' Brigitte said. 'Why should I think that? Why should anyone?' But in her heart she thought, yours most of all. A rush of love and pity filled her, and she kissed her sister.

There was a very brief knock – for courtesy, not

permission – and then Shoki came in. It was exactly the time he appeared every day. Wherever he might have been all night and this morning, now he was fresh, rested, smiling and terribly pleased to meet Brigitte's sister. As for Frances, whatever prejudice she might have had was entirely swept away: it was as if she herself was swept clean of all negative thinking. If she had come to assess the situation, she would have to start all over again with entirely different premises.

How to explain anything to Marshall? He had never in all their life together been so attentive with phone calls; and never had she been so negligent in return. It was the first time she had actually enjoyed Los Angeles. Before, on her visits to Brigitte, she had disliked being here, and so had Marshall, though he had insisted on coming with her. Everyone they met – the actors, agents, producers, publicists – appeared to them to be social flotsam. The town itself was flotsam, its houses ready to be razed as quickly as they had been put up, or collapsing into the earth quaking beneath them. But now that she was having fun with Brigitte and Shoki, all that was changed for Frances.

Shoki had accepted Frances completely. He loved the idea of family, and a sister was something almost sacred to him. With the intimacy that came so naturally to him, he at once adopted Frances and became the only other person besides Brigitte to call her Frankie. 'Doesn't Frankie look marvellous?' he would say about some new outfit. Between them, he and Brigitte had decided to change Frances' style; and although Brigitte herself loved brilliant orange and purples, for Frances they chose discreet and lighter colours, with a hint of California playfulness. Accompanying them to a boutique, Shoki sat outside the dressing rooms chatting up the salesgirls; and when Frances emerged, he said, very thrilled, 'It *suits* you.' Then the years dropped away from Frances.

She confided to Brigitte that, with Shoki, it was like being with another sister – though at the same time he was so manly, in the best way. Unlike other men, he was not hard and insensitive but the opposite. 'He must have grown up with a lot of sisters,' she guessed, 'that's how he knows about women, what we have to put up with.'

Brigitte agreed, but she too was guessing. Although Shoki had a high regard for the notion of family, he hardly ever mentioned his own. When he did, it was with a wistful, almost sad air. They speculated with each other – perhaps he was too homesick, perhaps the subject was too sacred for him. But Ralph said it was because he was too damn secretive.

Ralph – for Frances he had become as disturbing an element as was Marshall with his constant phone calls. Ralph often turned up in one of the restaurants where they had booked a table for three. 'May I?' Ralph said, having already drawn out a chair for himself. He knew a lot of people there and sometimes he took Shoki away to introduce him to a useful contact. This was very irritating to Frances – 'Shoki is with *us*,' she complained. But Ralph was dissatisfied too, as if it wasn't enough for him to be professionally useful to Shoki. Shoki was always as nice to him as he was to the two sisters, and seemed anxious that all of them should be comfortable and happy with one another. But Ralph rarely was. He talked too much, telling some insider anecdote that made him laugh or sneer. He became brittle, malicious, assuming a role that perhaps belonged to his profession but was not in his nature. Sooner or later, and sometimes before he had even finished laughing at his anecdote, he became gloomy and was silent. When Shoki tried to cheer him up, Ralph brushed this good-natured attempt aside. Instead he said something that the two sisters could not and Shoki perhaps would not hear. Then all three avoided looking at Ralph, the way a squeamish person avoids looking at someone in pain.

Marshall asked questions over the telephone. 'So what's he like – the little friend? The lover?'

'There's nothing like that.'

'Come *on*.'

There was always some threat in his attitude to her that prevented Frances from holding out when he wanted something. 'He's only a boy, Marshall.'

'A substitute son? I knew she'd pick one up sooner or later ... What about you?'

'I have a son,' Frances said with dignity. Marshall hadn't spoken to their son for two years, and gritted his teeth when he had to write out cheques for him and his dependants from various relationships.

In a thoroughly bad mood now, Marshall told her: 'Just get yourself back here. I don't want you hanging around there. In that *atmosphere*.'

Atmosphere! Frances thought to herself. What about the home, the heavy, empty, costly apartment he wanted her to come back to and live in with him? And as if guessing the new desire arising in her heart, that same day Shoki suggested: 'Wouldn't it be great if you stayed with us?' He turned to Brigitte: 'Wouldn't it?'

Brigitte said, 'Frankie's husband really needs her. They've been married for – how many years is it, Frankie?'

'Thirty-two,' Frances said, and Shoki made a gallant joke: 'I don't believe it. You're not a day over thirty-two yourself.'

'My son is thirty. And Gilberte, my daughter, is twenty-eight. They're both married. And divorced.'

Brigitte said, 'He twice, and now he's in Hong Kong with another girlfriend. And Gilberte? We don't know about Gilberte. The last time we heard she was in Buenos Aires, and that was almost six months ago. So at least she doesn't need money – unlike her brother who needs lots. He even comes to me for it.'

'I wish he wouldn't,' Frances said, speaking as freely before Shoki as when she and her sister were alone.

Brigitte laughed. 'He knows I'm loaded.'

'This is the family today,' Shoki commented. But although they waited, he still did not speak about his own family. Instead he said, 'That is why everyone is making their own arrangements.'

As though aware of this subversive conversation, Marshall arrived the next day. He had taken an early flight and went straight to his wife's suite in the hotel. Brigitte and Shoki had started on their room service orders – neither of them could ever wait for meals; that day it was not Frances who joined them but Marshall. 'What a surprise,' Brigitte said, calmly continuing to eat her croissant. But Shoki leaped to his feet, in deference to an older man. He appeared flustered, not emotionally but socially, like a hostess with an extra guest. 'Should we send for more coffee?' He lifted the lid to peer in. 'Frankie needs at least three cups.'

Marshall's eyebrows went right up. 'Frankie?' Then they went down again. 'Frances has a headache.'

'Then there's enough.' Shoki was already pouring for Marshall. 'But Brigitte has finished the entire breadbasket. So *greedy*.'

'It's all right,' Brigitte said. 'Marshall has to watch his weight.'

Marshall was certainly a weighty man. This was never so obvious at home in New York, or in his office, or at his club lunches with other weighty men. But here in Brigitte's hotel suite, where the furniture was gilded and frail and the flowers seemed to float without support of vases in a cloud of petals, Marshall in his thick business suit imposed a heavy burden.

He didn't consider Shoki worth addressing, so it was Brigitte he asked: 'Is he an actor?'

Of course Brigitte knew that to identify anyone as a possible actor was, in Marshall's view and intention, to insult him. Shoki, however, answered as though he had been paid a compliment, and it was regretfully that he admitted he wasn't – although, he added, he had done some acting in college. 'What college?' Marshall said, asking an idle question to which no adequate answer was expected. Anyway, Shoki apparently didn't hear, he went straight on – 'Just smaller roles in student productions, but the experience was very helpful to me as a writer.'

'You're a writer?' Marshall spoke like one picking up an unattractive insect between pincers.

Shoki began to bubble over with enthusiasm. He spoke of his screenplay, which his agent was placing for him – at the moment it was with Fox, who were showing interest. Of course it was a difficult subject, he confided to Marshall, partly symbolic and partly historical. The history reflected contemporary events so it was very topical, though one did have to know something of India's past as well as of her not always perfect present. Marshall consulted his watch and shifted his big thighs where he sat. He tried to catch Brigitte's eye, the way he always did, had done through all their past together, to communicate the fact that he desired her and wished to be alone with her. Shoki appeared completely oblivious of this tension – he carried on expounding his story as though Marshall's sole intention in travelling to Los Angeles was to listen to it.

But sooner or later, Brigitte knew, Marshall would create the opportunity of being alone with her. He might give the impression of being unwieldy, but he was also subtle, at least in mental calculation. By next morning he had discovered the arrangement that his wife and sister-in-law had made with Shoki for their morning meal together. By the time Frances woke up, he was fully dressed and on the point of going out.

'I need fresh air,' he told her. 'A stroll by the ocean.' He didn't usually tell her his plans, so she didn't think it worth mentioning how far they actually were from the ocean. 'How's your headache?' he said. 'You had a headache. You'd better stay in bed and rest.'

'Who is he anyway? Your little friend?' was his first question to Brigitte. After opening the door to him, she had gone back to bed and he sat by the side of it, the vast hotel bed with the padded satin backrest.

'He's a prince. From one of those old Indian princely families. What do they call them? Maharajas.' She had only just thought of this but it made sense.

'Yes, and look at you: a Maharani.'

She did look royal, leaning against her pillows, one side of her silken nightie slipped down from her broad shoulder – divine even, a goddess emerging out of a flood of rumpled shiny satin sheets. He murmured to her in a voice that had gone thick, so that she knew soon he would be climbing in next to her, and she would let him. It had happened before in their many years together as in-laws, and the only thing surprising to her was that it should still be happening.

'Frankie will be here any minute,' she said afterwards to

Marshall, who showed every indication of staying right where he was next to her.

'My wife has a headache and I advised her to rest.' But he was good-natured about letting her push him out of bed and smirked a bit as he climbed back into his trousers.

Then he became practical. He said he wanted her to return with them to New York – why wait? Everything was ready for her arrival.

'Oh, you bought it, did you? The apartment Frankie was talking about?'

'You don't need an apartment. We have one. It's enormous. It's big. Much too big for just two people now that the kids are – where are they?'

'In Hong Kong.'

'Yes, and Buenos Aires. What are Frances and I supposed to do rattling around by ourselves in a place that size? It's ridiculous.' He frowned at the impracticality of it, and she laughed at his impudence.

'So you and I would be like this every day of our lives from now on?'

'It makes perfect sense. We shouldn't be wasting time, having to commute from one apartment to another, secret rendezvous and all that nonsense.' He spoke with the decision of a man of business, the chairman of the board. She smiled a bit, but she said, 'You really have to leave now.'

He took his time about it, strolled around the suite, stood at a window to frown at the city of Los Angeles and its giant billboards. 'I don't know how you can live in a place like this. No climate. No history.'

'I didn't know you cared about history.'

'Only my own. Grandmothers, and so on. Great-grandmothers. New York.'

'What about Poland and Russia?'

'That's too far back. By the way, I saw him this morning – your princely friend.'

'He has a room in the hotel.'

'He doesn't seem to have spent the night in it. I'm just guessing of course – but he looked like someone sneaking in after a night on the tiles.'

'What would you know about tiles, Marshall?'

'Nothing. And I won't have to, if we make this arrangement I mentioned to you. No sneaking out, or back in.'

On his third and last evening in Los Angeles, Marshall hired a limousine to take his two ladies to dinner. The restaurant he had chosen was one known to other East Coast bankers and to West Coast attorneys from old established family firms. It was very different from the ones Brigitte usually went to, but she didn't mind; it was Frances who said, 'Why do we have to come here? We might as well have stayed in New York.'

Brigitte was surprised; she had never heard a note of rebellion from Frances in the face of any decision made by Marshall. And what was also surprising was that Marshall did not wither her with one of his looks but concentrated on reading the menu.

'Don't you hate it?' Frances asked her sister. 'I hate it.' She was actually sulking, and still Marshall continued to read the menu.

The restaurant was a fantasy of an opulent New York eating place recreated by earlier settlers in the Californian desert. It was dark with antique lamps throwing insufficient light, and thick carpets and velvet drapes shutting out the rest of it. There was a buffet table overloaded with silver dishes and with giant fruits and flowers that appeared to be a replica of those in the varnished still lifes on the walls.

'Lobster,' Marshall said, returning the menu to the waiter. This waiter was no out-of-work actor but an elderly professional, Italian or Swiss, who had been with the restaurant for over forty years and would soon be mourning its closing. He hovered over Frances, who was unable to make a choice of dishes, but when Marshall said, 'You could have the lobster too,' she quickly ordered a green salad with a light dressing.

'You know what?' she said to Brigitte. 'He's let that apartment go. And it would have been so perfect for you! Now where are you supposed to live in New York? In another hotel? Then you might as well stay in Beverly Hills – I should think you'd want to stay here. My goodness, who wouldn't. And I don't suppose it's occurred to anyone that I'd like to be near my sister. That I'm sick of having her live at the opposite end of the world.'

'Not the world, darling,' Brigitte said. 'Just the country.'

'Frances has always been a dunce in geography,' Marshall said. He tried to sound playful but was too saturnine. He had tucked his table napkin under his chin and was expertly excavating the meat from a lobster claw. He ate and drank the way he had done throughout his life and would continue till he could do so no more. It was natural for a man like him to be companioned by a handsome woman, even by two of them.

These two were no longer discussing the pros and cons of living in New York or Los Angeles but whether Shoki was a prince. Brigitte had raised the question, and Frances had taken it up with such pleasure that Marshall felt he had at once to squash it. He said, 'They don't have princes any more. They've been abolished. They're all democratic now, whatever that might mean. And they're all poor. No more jewels and elephants.'

'Money's got nothing to do with it,' Frances said. 'Anyone can have money. Anyone. But look at the graceful way he moves.'

'And the delicate way he eats.'

Marshall wiped the butter from his chin. He said, 'It's time I took you two back to New York.'

'I found a lovely apartment for Brigitte and you let it go.'

Brigitte felt Marshall nudge her knee under the table. She was used to this gesture from him, though today it was another kind of plea. She denied it in her usual way, by moving her knee out of his reach. But she said, 'Why don't you tell her your grand plan?'

'It's simple common sense,' Marshall said, losing no ounce of authority. 'Our apartment is big enough for ten people, let alone three.'

After a moment of shock, 'You're completely insane,' Frances told him. She turned on her sister. 'And you listened to him? You sat and listened and didn't say a word to me?'

She pushed back her chair, rushed from the table. No one looked up from their plates; even when she stumbled against their chairs, the diners carried on dining. The waiters too kept their eyes lowered, so did the maitre d' while guiding her towards the ladies' room, where he opened and held the door for her.

'Ah, the pièce de résistance,' Marshall said as their waiter came towards them bearing the chocolate soufflé. The critical moment of its departure from the oven had now been reached and it rose above its dish in a splendidly browned dome.

Brigitte said, 'You are a fool, Marshall.'

'Today is not my lucky day,' Marshall said. 'She calls me crazy, you call me a fool. Why fool? How fool? She's always telling me how she misses you, and you I guess miss her.

Sisters, after all ... I wonder how they get it to this consistency; I suppose that's why it has to be ordered in advance.'

Brigitte too was enjoying every bit of the soufflé, but she said, 'I'm going to see how she's doing.'

'Explain it to her – how it's best for everyone.'

'Best for you.' Under the table she moved her knee further away. 'I'll explain that to her; after all these years maybe she ought to know.'

'Did you ever tell Louis?'

'Tell on you? He'd have laughed. He knew how I wouldn't give you the time of day.'

'Sometimes you give it to me. The time of day.' Over the table his lips curved in a smile; under it his knee went in pursuit of hers.

'I'd better go. This table is not big enough for you and me.'

'But the apartment is enormous, as I keep saying. Have a second helping, be a devil. Well, I will then,' he said and was already digging his spoon in when she left.

A tiny old oriental attendant welcomed Brigitte into her pink kingdom. Brigitte could see Frances' elegant shoes and ankles under a stall so she took an adjoining one. She said, 'It's me.'

'I know. I can see your feet, and I wish you wouldn't wear those kinds of teenage sandals.' Frances' voice was steady; she had not been crying but she had been thinking, and now she announced her decision. 'I'm not going back with him. I'm staying with you.' But when Brigitte said nothing, Frances' voice was less firm. 'I'm staying with you and Shoki.' She pulled the lever in her stall and went out.

Brigitte lingered inside; she could hear the excited birdlike voice of the attendant communicating with Frances in what sounded like Chinese but could not have been for Frances was able to respond. When Brigitte emerged, the attendant addressed her in the same birdsong, offering fragrant soap and towel. Frances was already wiping her hands on hers, and since neither of them spoke, the little attendant took over the conversation. They gathered that she was distressed about her job, which she had held for twenty years, and now they had been informed by the management that the restaurant was closing. Suddenly she was crying; tiny tears ran down her wizened cheeks, slightly rouged. Brigitte made comforting noises at her.

Frances was staring at herself in the mirror. Her eyes were dry, her face was set. She said, 'You can't send me back with him because I won't go.'

'Who's sending you back?'

'I haven't heard you say stay.'

Brigitte was using her towel to wipe away the attendant's tears. She told her, 'You'll find another job. Anyone would like to have you in their home.'

The attendant praised Brigitte for her kindness. She went on to explain that she was not weeping for herself but for the others, the old men whom no one would ever again want to employ. She herself had a son and a daughter, both of whom did not want her to work any more. She took the towel, wet with her own tears, and gave Brigitte a fresh one.

'You don't need to feel sorry for the whole world,' Frances said. 'And you heard her – she has a son and a daughter who care for her.'

'Of course I want you to stay,' Brigitte said. 'I don't know what gave you the idea I don't. Shall we go back now?'

'I don't want to see him.'

'I mean go back to the hotel. He's all right. He's having another helping of chocolate soufflé.' She found a fifty-dollar bill in her purse and put it in the tactful little saucer. 'That's too much,' Frances said outside, though she herself, usually more careful, overtipped the valet who whistled up a cab for them.

One evening a few weeks later Shoki gave Brigitte a lovely surprise. He came to her suite dressed up in a high-collared jacket of raw silk – Indian, but he had had it made in Beverly Hills. 'I showed them exactly what to do, how to cut it – you really like it?'

'Love it, love it; love you,' and she kissed his cheek in the beautiful way of friendship they had with each other.

He had been invited to a charity premiere and he asked her to come along. He assured her his host had taken a table for twelve.

'Ralph?'

'No, someone else, another friend.' There was sure to be room, someone or other always dropped out.

'What about Frankie?'

'Of course; let's take Frankie.'

Frances said she was waiting for a call but might join them later. Her call came exactly when she was expecting it. Marshall telephoned the same time every evening. It was always when he was home from the office or a board meeting and was having his martini by the fireplace in the smaller drawing-room (called the library, though they had never had many books). She imagined him wearing slippers and maybe his velvet housecoat; or if he was going out, he might have begun to dress.

'Isn't tonight the hospital benefit?' When he yawned and said he didn't feel like going, she urged, 'Marshall, you have to. You're on the board.'

'I guess I have to. But to turn up there by myself –' He always left such sentences unfinished. She waited; perhaps tonight he would say more. Instead he became more irritated. 'Marie can't find any of my dress shirts – do you think she drinks?'

'Marie! After all this time!'

'Who knows? Servants need supervision. Someone to make them toe the line.' Perhaps suspecting that she had begun to preen herself, he said, 'I'll send from the office to buy some new ones. What about you? You want any of your stuff sent out there?'

She hesitated; it was true she was running short of the underclothes that were specially made for her by a Swiss lady in New York. But the subject of her underclothes was not one she ever intruded on her husband, so she murmured, 'I'm all right for now.'

'For now? What's that supposed to mean?' She was silent, and then he almost asked, though grudgingly, what she was waiting to hear: 'Are you intending to stay out there forever, or what?'

He sounded so put out – so fed up – and it was her fault. She said, 'What can I do, Marshall? Brigitte just likes it better here.'

'She thinks she does. She's from New York. She was born here like the rest of us, why would she want to be in that joke place out there? Where is she, by the way?'

'She's gone out. It's a premiere. A big event. She wants me to join her later. Do you think I should?'

'You should do what you want, not what she wants. Though why anyone would want to go to a thing like that. "A Premiere. A Big Event." Tcha. You'd be better off at the benefit with me.'

'Marshall? You know my dresser? In the last drawer there

are some bits and pieces I might need. If it's not too much trouble. Just some bras. And girdles.'

'I didn't know you wore girdles.'

'They look like panties but actually they're tummy control.' She was glad he couldn't see her face – it was the most intimate exchange they had had in years. 'Marie can pack them.'

'If she's not too drunk.'

'Marie is practically a teetotaller.'

'You're the easiest person in the world to fool,' he said.

Shoki had been right and there were two empty places at his host's table. This host was a powerful studio head but a far more modern type than Louis had been. He was from the Midwest and had been to some good schools in the East; still in his thirties, he was well groomed, well informed, *smart*. The guests at his table were there for their fame, their money or their youth and beauty. Brigitte's celebrity was in the past, but that gave her an aura of historical tradition, and she kept having to raise her cheek for the tribute offered to her by other guests. Each table was ornamented by someone like Shoki, with no claim whatsoever to celebrity. Some were girls, others young men or almost boys; some were very lively, some totally silent – it didn't seem to matter as long as they were visibly there and known to be attached to a powerful member at the table. Shoki and his host hardly acknowledged one another, except that from time to time the older man's eyes stabbed towards the younger, maybe just in an instinctive gesture of checking on the security of possession. He could be entirely relaxed – Shoki gave all his attention to Brigitte next to him and to the matron on his other side, a former star. He was light-heartedly laughing and making them laugh.

But there *was* tension – not emanating from their table but from elsewhere. Her eyes roaming around the room, Brigitte soon discovered Ralph. He was craning in their direction and even half-rose in his chair as though intending to leave his place and make his way towards theirs. But it was impossible – the room was packed, each table crowded and the spaces between them thronged with guests still trying to find their place or changing it for a more desirable one, while the servers weaved and dodged among them with their platters and wine bottles.

Although without an invitation card, Frances looked too distinguished not to be let in. But once inside, she had no idea which way to turn to locate Brigitte among this crowd of strangers, strange beings who all knew or knew of one another. She stood there, dazed by the din and glitter. Then she heard her name called: 'Are you all right?'

It was Ralph. He settled her into an empty chair beside him and tried to revive her with wine. She preferred water. 'For my aspirin,' she said, taking her pill box out of her evening purse.

He laughed. 'Are you sure that's what it is?'

'It may be Disprin. For my headache. It's so terribly noisy. How can anyone enjoy being in such a noisy place?'

'At least one doesn't have to hear what's going on in one's own head. They're over there. No, you're looking in the wrong direction.'

The reason it took her so long to find Brigitte's table was that all the eighty-four tables crammed into that space appeared very much the same. Everyone there sat as in a burnished cast of wealth, of costly ornament. It was she, Frances, who was out of place. Although her hair too was professionally dyed, it had a discreet touch of silver; and her jewellery was not like that of others, women and some men, who displayed diamonds and rubies and pearls of a size and quantity that, if this had been any other place, would have been taken for paste. And maybe it was paste, she thought; it couldn't be safe to walk around loaded with such immeasurable riches.

'They're waiting for me,' she told Ralph.

'I've been trying to get through myself, but there's such a crush. Maybe after they've served the dessert. Why didn't you come with them?'

'I was on the phone with my husband. He wants me to come back to New York.' Again looking around the room, she thought of Marshall at his fundraiser. He too would be with the powerful and rich, but his would be not only physically less brilliant but much more glum than these surrounding her, who were laughing, chatting, shouting and outshouting one another as though placed on a stage to impersonate characters having a festive time.

'Brigitte doesn't want to leave. But he wants both of us. They've been having sex together.' She found it difficult to say – the words, that is; to herself she still thought of it as 'sleeping together'. 'It's been going on for years. I don't blame her for not wanting to come live with us. She doesn't even like Marshall.'

'No. Not the way she likes Shoki. As a friend, that is. They're friends.'

'Yes, he's my friend too. But I really think I must go home. Of course Marshall will be angry if I come without her. But he's angry at me anyway. It's just that he needs someone with him where he can be any mood he wants. That's the only way he feels comfortable.'

Dessert had been served. A master of ceremonies tapped a microphone. Speeches were about to start. Ralph suggested they should try and squeeze through the crowd to the other table. He led the way, and when Shoki looked up, he saw them cleaving a path towards them. Shoki told Brigitte that it was very hot inside and maybe they should try to catch some fresh air? She got up at once and he took her elbow to guide her. Their host rose in his chair, but they did not appear to see him, or to hear him when he called after them.

Unimaginably, outside the noisy room there was an empty terrace hovering over an expanse of ocean and moonless sky. Although a crowd of brilliant figures could be seen agitating inside, no sound reached through the double glazing of the windows. Two faces were pressed against the glass, trying to peer out into the darkness. Shoki said, 'There's Ralph.'

'Yes, and Frankie.'

They sighed as though something was difficult for them. But it wasn't. Nothing was difficult for them. Shoki knew a way down from the terrace to the beach and soon he and Brigitte were walking there, their hands lightly linked. He told her about Bombay, where he had also walked on the beach, but it was not the same. For one thing, the sun was too hot, and then, always, there was Bombay – right there on the beach with the coconut sellers, the boy acrobats and others seeking money for food; and beyond, the whole city of Bombay with its traffic, its slums, its huge heavy Victorian buildings pressing down on the earth and the human spirit. He didn't have to explain much to Brigitte, because somehow it was how she felt about New York, where everything was just as oppressive. But here, now, the ocean was very calm and very dark and all that could be seen of it were the white fringes of its waves gliding into the sand. There was absolutely nothing, no world at all between water and sky, and it was inconceivable that, with such fullness available, anyone could be troubled about anything – apartments, desires, attachments, anything.

At the End of the Century

Celia and Lily were half-sisters, but since both their fathers had long ago withdrawn, they were united by their one parent in common, their mother, Fay. Fay took them along with her – to France, South America – wherever she had a new marriage or liaison. Celia, who was ten years older than Lily, returned to New York as soon as she could. Educating herself through a series of semi-professional courses, she set up as a psychotherapist and became quite successful, while waiting for Lily to be old enough to join her.

Lily was sent to boarding school in Switzerland, where she was miserable. Celia advised patience; she knew Lily would be miserable anywhere except with herself. As soon as she had failed her last exam, Celia made arrangements for her to take art classes in New York, though she wasn't really surprised when Lily dropped out within a month. After that, Lily spent her days wandering around the streets carrying her sketching pad. This remained blank, but perhaps for the first time in her life Lily appeared to be entirely happy, living with her sister in their apartment in an Art Deco building on the East Side.

Celia was still there – immensely old, the only one left. Even Scipio was gone (killed when his racing car overturned at São Paulo), although his name remained as sole heir in

391

Celia's will. Nowadays, all Celia could do was keep herself slightly mobile. When she managed to get up, she somehow dressed herself, usually askew, and shuffled off to the soup and salad place at the corner. Here she was served the same bowl of soup every day, which was all she seemed to need for nourishment. What was there left to nourish? The present was extinct for her; the past had vanished with all the people in it, even the dearest of them.

When Lily, at nineteen, had decided to get married, it had been unexpected: a shock. She simply produced Gavin, didn't even introduce him, murmured his name so softly that Celia failed to hear it and he had to say it himself, louder. Celia couldn't find out where and how they had met. 'I picked her up on the street,' Gavin said. He warned Celia: 'I've been telling her she really ought to be more careful about strangers.' He said it tongue-in-cheek, a joke, but afterwards, when she and Lily were alone, Celia was serious about the dangers of the street. Lily said mildly, 'I don't talk to many people and hardly anyone talks to me.' Celia believed her; there was something remote about Lily that would discourage strangers from addressing her.

Gavin's family liked and accepted her immediately. Gavin was a poet, and it seemed right for him to unite himself with his muse. Lily was fair to the point of evanescence, delicate, almost diaphanous – it was easy to think of her as a muse. She loved Gavin, everything about him. 'Why?' he would ask, amused, but she couldn't answer; she had no gift for words. She was an artist by temperament more than practice. She liked to trace Gavin's features – not with a pencil or brush but with her finger, lightly feeling him. This also made him laugh, but he kept still for her.

392

He came from a large old American family, and the wedding was quite grand. It was held in the Hudson Valley mansion where Gavin's mother Elizabeth still lived with two old uncles. China Trade dinner services were taken out of cabinets where they had been shut up so long that they had to be soaked in tubs of water to wash the dust off. Faded tapestries were hung over wallpaper that was even more faded. But it was summer and the grounds were lush, the ancient trees loaded with foliage that looked too heavy for their broken limbs to carry. A fountain spouted rusty water out of the mouths of crumbling lions. There was a band and some of the guests danced, even some very old ones in very old long dresses that got wet in the grass.

The original idea had been for the newly wed couple to live in the house with the groom's mother. Gavin was the youngest of Elizabeth's five children and the only son; his sisters were all married with children, but he was over thirty and had not been expected to marry. Elizabeth prepared one of the bedrooms for him and Lily – it had been unoccupied for years, but all that was needed was to renew the curtains and the canopy over the four-poster. Elizabeth picked flowers and filled several vases so that youth and freshness permeated the ancient room, which held a harp and watercolours of mountain streams and a broken-down castle in the Catskills. It was enchanting, and at first Lily and Gavin were enchanted. It seemed so perfect for them, for him who wrote poetry and her who painted.

It turned out that both of them preferred the city. Lily saw plenty of sky from the terrace of Celia's apartment, and birds, and buildings as fantastic as trees and more ornate; this was as much landscape as she needed. Gavin had spent his childhood in the country, but after he went to boarding school, he didn't look forward to going home; school was far more exciting to him (he made deep friendships) and even during vacations he preferred to take up invitations from friends whose parents lived on Park Avenue and had season tickets to the opera.

Six months into their marriage, Gavin and Lily were mostly with Celia in the city. At least Lily was – Gavin spent much of his time elsewhere, with friends in their studios and their weekend houses on Fire Island or the Cape. It didn't occur to him to take his wife with him on these visits; she too appeared to think it natural that she should be mostly alone or with her sister. Marriage for her meant waiting for Gavin and being very happy when he was there. And because Lily was happy, Celia too complied with the situation, at least to the extent of not commenting on it.

Then their mother Fay showed up. She did this every now and again, whenever a liaison broke down or she had to see her lawyer about increasing her remittances. She was bored easily, loved to travel, loved to meet new people. She was very skinny and very lively and dressed with tasteful flamboyance, wound around with Parisian scarves and Italian costume jewellery; her hair was a metallic red, cut like a boy's.

It was the first time she had visited her daughters since Lily's marriage. She had been living in Paris just then and was unable to attend the wedding because of undergoing an unspecified procedure. All she told them about it now was: 'You don't want to know all that ... But guess what: I'm a widow.' They didn't understand which husband she had lost, till she revealed that it was Celia's father. They hadn't heard her refer to him as anything but 'that loser', but now she became sentimental, remembered early days – 'Fay and Harry! Crazy kids!' – and then felt sorry for Celia, for being fatherless, orphaned. 'You're still here,' Celia pointed out, which irritated her mother; those two never could be together for long without irritation.

Now they had to live together, for although Fay felt most at home in hotels, she couldn't for the moment afford to move into one. Celia's apartment was large – the same one in which she remained for the rest of her life – but, with Fay there, it was no longer large enough. Fay suggested that the front part, Celia's office where she saw patients, could be made into a charming bed-sitting room for herself. 'You don't see your crazies all day,' she argued, promising to make herself scarce during office hours. Failing that, she felt it to be appropriate to move into the bedroom now given over to Gavin and Lily. 'They should have a place of their own,' she said. 'It's working class for a young married couple to be living with their families.'

'They're looking,' Celia lied. But they weren't, and she even suspected that Gavin had kept his old apartment and continued to live there the way he had done before his marriage.

Lily agreed that it was a waste for the married couple to have the larger bedroom when she herself was mostly alone in it. One morning, while Celia was busy with her patients, Lily helped Fay carry her load of possessions into the room she willingly vacated. Even Gavin, arriving from one of his excursions, didn't seem to mind that his clothes were now scattered over various closets. Also, since their new room was too small for two of them, he made himself comfortable on the living room sofa. He kept the light on all night to read, while playing records very softly so as not to disturb anyone. He was always considerate, more like a house-guest than a husband.

The second Sunday after Fay's arrival was the day they drove her to meet Gavin's family in the country. A traditional Anglo-Saxon lunch of roast lamb had been cooked by Elizabeth,

Gavin's mother. Her kitchen still had its old appliances, which had become antiques, but Elizabeth coped very efficiently, even providing a special dish for Lily, who was vegetarian. The cavernous dining-room had been opened up, and as far as possible the dust wiped out of the convoluted furniture. Only its smell remained pervading the air. There was no smell of food, since the family usually ate in the kitchen.

In outward appearance and manner, this family now seated around the table was also more or less traditional. Besides Elizabeth, who sat at the head, there were two uncles, her brothers-in-law who lived in the house with her; both wore three-piece suits, their waistcoats and bow ties slightly spotted with food. The visiting guests were three of Gavin's sisters, two of them with husbands and some children, and a few relatives introduced as cousins. All spoke in the same loud voices, guttural with good breeding and unchallenged opinions. The conversation consisted mostly of amusing family anecdotes recounted by the two uncles. At the punchline, each uncle rapped the table and coughed with laughter, which made tears rise to their sorrowful, faded eyes. Elizabeth too laughed as at something she had never heard before; and she looked around at her guests to make sure they absorbed this family history, which it would one day be their turn to pass on.

At the end of the meal, when the sisters and cousins had driven off to visit other relatives embedded in the neighbourhood, Elizabeth invited Fay on a house tour. Several rooms had to be kept shut up because of the cost of heating and the lack of domestic staff, and here the furniture – New York State and valuable – was shrouded to protect it against bat droppings. The paintings and the statuary testified mostly to the taste of the ancestors, whose portraits hung all around the house they had built and rebuilt. They featured the same type of men and women through the generations, the original tall, bony merchants and farmers – they operated gravel pits and flour mills – still visible in the later portraits of New York clubmen living on trust funds.

These portraits were the only part of the house tour of any interest to Fay. While hardly listening to Elizabeth's detailed biographies, she stepped close to examine them; but none of them in the least resembled fair, slender Gavin. At last she asked Elizabeth, 'I suppose he takes after your family?' But no – Elizabeth's family, professional people from an adjoining county, were mostly, like herself, short and sturdy. Gavin was the first to look like – well, what he was: a poet.

As they crossed an upper landing, they saw him on the stairs; he was arguing with Celia, who called to them, 'Gavin says he's going back to New York!' They walked up together to join their two mothers on the landing. Celia was angry; she said, 'He has to meet some writer from Poland.'

'Fixed up weeks ago,' he regretted. 'Just the sort of stupid thing I do. It's not even a writer, it's a critic. But I'm not going to spoil your fun. I know Mother has a whole programme for you this afternoon. The Shaker Museum; the old almshouses. It's just my bad luck … Don't look at me like that, Celia, as if you're seeing right through me. You scare me.'

'I wish I did. Maybe then you'd be nicer to Lily.'

'Oh my Lord! Ask Lily who, *who* could be nicer to her than I?' He pecked her cheek as though grateful to her for her compliance, and she watched him, lithe in his linen suit, run lightly down the stairs.

Later, Fay and Celia were standing by the window in the bedroom allotted to them. It was a bright gold afternoon, but they looked only at the figure sitting on an ornamental bench under the largest maple, which was still magnificent though half-destroyed by storms.

'She's sketching,' Celia said.

'Have you ever actually seen . . . ?'

'Gavin says she has talent.'

Lily was sitting very still. Perhaps she was taking in the scene to interpret it later. She could often be observed sitting this way, gazing in front of her, her hands folded on the sketchbook in her lap: maybe watching, maybe waiting, definitely patient.

Fay turned away impatiently. 'I couldn't bear to stay the night in this creepy room. No doubt they all died in that *bed*. Let's go: I don't need to be entertained any more. And surely the Shaker Museum is a joke.'

'No. And neither are the almshouses.'

'You just love to torment me, Celia, you've always loved to do that.'

But she wasn't serious – she was relieved to have Celia with her. Although so different in every way, she and her daughter were both out of their element here. Unlike Gavin's ancestors, theirs hadn't tilled this land nor built their houses on it. Their great-grandmothers and grandmothers had long since looked to Europe for their sustenance; this was evident in both Fay and Celia, in the cast of their thoughts as well as in their chic appearance.

Only Lily was a throwback to earlier, simpler, simply American girls. She came in, as so often barefoot, her white-blonde hair wind-blown; she was holding a branch with a few leaves on it. She said at once: 'Where's Gavin?'

'Doesn't he tell you *anything*?' Fay said, and Celia, eyebrows raised: 'The Polish critic?'

'I'm really stupid,' Lily said. 'I forget everything. Look,

there's Elizabeth. She's pruning a rosebush. She's always busy; she does a million things. Can't you see her? I wish you'd wear your glasses, Mummy.'

'I don't need them. I don't need to see anything more. I did a house tour; I sat through an entire lunch. I'm starting a headache and I want to go back to New York.'

Lily didn't look at her but trailed the branch she was holding across the faded flower pattern of the carpet. She said, 'It wouldn't be fair to Elizabeth. If we left. It wouldn't even be polite. It would really be very rude. I mean, if it were me, I'd think these were really very rude people.' Still intent on her branch, she missed the look of wry resignation that passed between her mother and her sister.

Lily became pregnant. At first she said her stomach was upset, and as for her periods, they were always irregular. When Celia wanted to take her to a doctor, she didn't want to go because doctors always discovered something horrible. 'But supposing it's not horrible,' Celia said. 'Supposing it's something you'd like, you and Gavin?'

'Oh, you think it might be a baby? Well, why not. I *am* married.' She looked at her sister out of those very candid, fairy-tale eyes that made people love and trust her.

On being informed: 'Is it possible?' Fay asked Celia.

'Of course it is,' Celia said. 'You hear about it all the time. I have friends you'd never think – and then suddenly they spring a grown-up son or daughter on you, visiting them over Christmas.'

Fay also had such friends with unsuspected offspring. But still she said, 'I can't imagine.'

'Can't imagine what?' Celia said, the more irritably because she also couldn't imagine: not about Gavin and, if it came to that, not about Lily herself. But there she was, pregnant, an indubitable fact.

Gavin's mother Elizabeth had no doubts at all. She came travelling up to the city and took Lily to her own gynaecologist, who confirmed that everything was fine, and also that the scan showed a boy. Elizabeth was delighted – another grandchild, and this time the son of her only son. She advised plenty of exercise for Lily, plenty of walking, plenty of good food and fresh air.

Lily did plenty of walking but the air she was taking in was not altogether fresh. It was what she liked best in the world – street smells, petrol fumes, leaking gas pipes, newly poured tar, pretzels, mangoes from Mexico, Chinese noodles, overblown flowers – the exhalations of the city, the densely populated streets that she traversed from one end to the other, walking lightly on sandals so flimsy her feet might have been bare and treading on grass. On warm days she wore a very light summer frock – no more than a shift – that blew with any breeze wafting up from the subway or from leaky steam pipes. She avoided parks and other open spaces unless they were from a building recently demolished; and if she sat for a moment to rest, it was on the steps of a Masonic temple or a storefront, from which she was sometimes chased away. When it rained, she sheltered under an overbridge, though she liked to get wet – very wet, with the drops trickling from her hair down her face so that she flicked out her tongue to taste them and refresh herself. She stopped occasionally to sniff the flowers arranged in the front of a grocery store. On raising her eyes to the sky, she was perfectly satisfied that all she could see of it was a bright patch inserted among tall towers. If it was night – for she wandered around for many hours – there was sometimes a slice of moon and helicopters flitting and glittering around like fireflies.

Celia summoned Gavin to her office. 'I hate it,' she told him. 'The way she walks around everywhere by herself and at all hours. It's not safe. She's not safe.'

'Lily?' He was gentle and smiling, patient as no patient of hers ever was. 'But Lily is always safe. Don't you feel that about her – that nothing could happen to her?'

'Maybe it's happened already.' She was trembling a bit – at what she was saying, the danger to Lily, but also at his *calm*, the way he sat there, cross-legged and slightly swinging one foot in its narrow shoe. She said, 'You know how innocent she is, how trusting.'

'Yes.' He smiled in recognition of these qualities in his wife, and he assured Celia, 'I love and adore her as you do.'

'I'm her sister. I love and adore her in a different way. All I'm asking is that you should stop her from wandering around the streets. Or help me stop her. Please be home tonight so that we can talk to her together.'

'Yes, we should – but unfortunately, tonight, what a pity.'

'Tomorrow then?'

'Oh absolutely,' he promised. 'Definitely tomorrow.'

But it was on that same day that he met Lily to report on his talk with her sister. They met where they usually did, in a church in midtown. It was the place where they had first seen each other, amid a sea of empty pews with here and there a few bowed figures, some come to pray, others only to fall asleep for want of food or a home to go to. Everyone was alone, maybe lonely and certainly in deep need. If Gavin and Lily were in such need, it was at least partly satisfied that time when they first met each other.

On the day of Gavin's talk with Celia, they did not go in

but sat on the steps of the church. He ran down for a moment to buy them two pretzels from a cart, and a drink to share. They picnicked there on the bank of a river of traffic, rushing and foaming in the street below. They sat close together at the side, undisturbed by people walking past them. Gavin informed her of everything that Celia had said to him and the way she had said it; he concluded, 'She thinks you may have been . . . attacked? By someone. In the street?'

'No. No.'

'Then what happened? If you want to tell me, that is.'

She did – and it was relatively easy sitting so close and he listening with the sympathy and selfless love that he always showed her. 'It was raining,' she said. He nodded; he understood that she was sheltering somewhere. 'Yes, under the 59th Street bridge. The rain was coming down really hard and I only had this –' she indicated her diaphanous dress – 'I didn't want to stay there because you know what it's like under a bridge that people who don't have anywhere else use for their, you know, their toilet, and also to store whatever they have, from the trash or whatever. No one spoke to anyone, like they don't in church, because of having so much else to think about? Different things. Except there was one person, maybe he didn't have too many worries to consider, I mean he was maybe too young to have them.'

'How young?'

'Seventeen. He told me he'd come from – I've forgotten – some African country. He'd come here to start a restaurant. That was his dream. He was looking for a job to be a waiter where he could save enough money to open his own restaurant with the special food from his African country. He was very, very hopeful that it would happen. I was the first girl he met to talk to since he'd come here. He did what you always do – touched my hair and then let it sort of run through his fingers. He was very sweet, gentle also, till he got excited. He got like . . . frantic? No, I wasn't scared; I understood he got that way because he hadn't met any girl here, so it was my fault really, in a way. And afterwards he was very nice again and said he wished he had something to give me to keep for myself. I didn't have anything either, so I told him I'd come back next day and bring him something.'

'And did you?' Gavin asked, playing with her hair the way she said the boy under the bridge had done.

After a moment she admitted it. And after another moment: 'I thought: maybe he'll never have the restaurant, maybe not even a job in one, nothing that he expects will happen, ever happen, such a lot of disappointment . . . I gave him a silver chain Fay had brought me from Peru. I'd never liked wearing it, it was so heavy, like being put in irons. But he was glad to have it and to see me again. I think he thought I wouldn't come back.'

'But you did.'

She hung her head but raised it again before answering frankly: 'That time we didn't stay under the bridge. We walked to the park; it wasn't raining that day but the ground was wet. It was chilly but much nicer than under the bridge. This was the day before you and I drove to the country with Fay and Celia, and all the time we were there, I kept thinking how he didn't have a sweater or anything, and what if he caught a cold and had nowhere to sleep except under the 59th Street bridge? So when we got back to New York, I went there with a blanket and a sweater, but he'd gone. And I keep hoping he went off to a job as a waiter in a restaurant but also I think – what if he got ill being out in the open? And it turned into pneumonia and he was taken to a hospital where they take poor people?'

'Boys of seventeen don't catch pneumonia,' Gavin affirmed clearly. 'He's working as a waiter and saving money for a restaurant. You have to believe me. I don't want you to worry in any way or have disturbing thoughts, because that's bad for our baby. OK? Promise. Only nice thoughts.'

'About you.'

'About me, if that's what you want.' He took her hand and kissed it.

Next day he took her to the country to stay with his mother. Lily liked to sleep late, and in the mornings, when Elizabeth herself had already been up for many hours and completed many tasks, she sat beside her frail daughter-in-law and the precious unborn child where they lay in a deceased great-aunt's great bed. Elizabeth was nearing seventy, strong and stocky, with apple cheeks and bright blue eyes. Although her connection with the family was only through marriage, she was an expert on each degree of their convoluted relationships and of their convoluted stories. These stories, which she was passing on to her pregnant daughter-in-law, were mostly of domestic or social interest. No one had held high office or distinguished themselves in any wars. But they had involved themselves in local politics, built additions to the house, engaged in lawsuits with neighbours about boundary lines. There had been some scandals: divorces as long ago as the beginning of the century, also the stigma of gambling debts, and more than one case of temporary confinement in a mental institution. But mostly they had led long and uneventful lives, with several of them celebrating their hundredth birthday. They had done some travelling – honeymoons and study tours in Italy, safari in Africa – but they had all spent their last years at home and with each other. In the end family loyalties triumphed over everything, even property disputes between brothers and sisters.

Elizabeth encouraged Lily to walk around the grounds. It was the end of what had been a very wet summer, and the estate had become a wilderness of tall grass with trees sweeping down into it. The trees themselves had survived their centuries with hollowed trunks; some of them had split apart and had been kept from falling by iron chains that had grown rusty and appeared to be part of the trunks they were meant to hold. Besides age, storms had ransacked the land, and every winter one of the great trees – copper beech or red maple – had given way and crashed to the ground, to be cut up into firewood to feed the giant fireplaces inside the house and warm the chill bones of its inhabitants.

Although Lily traversed city streets in complete confidence, here she tramped through the grass with misgiving of what might be lurking there – poison ivy, or a snake she knew would not be harmless to herself. Passing two blighted apple trees – the remains of what had once been an orchard cultivated for profit – she picked up one of the apples that lay half-hidden in the grass; soft and rotten, it split apart in her hand and maggots crawled out of it. She miserably counted the minutes until she could say she had had enough fresh air and return to the house to be near the telephone on which Gavin called her regularly, at the same time every day.

Celia, also calling every day, asked her, 'When are you coming home?' Lily was evasive – for Celia, this was something completely new in her. Lily said she needed the home-cooked meals Gavin's mother provided instead of the gourmet takeout Celia usually sent for. 'I thought you liked it,' Celia said, and Lily replied yes she did, when she had only herself to think of.

Celia told Fay: 'She's lying to us. They're both lying to us.'

'What if they're not?'

'I'll find out. We'll go there this weekend. She'll tell me the truth. She always does. Don't *you* want to know the truth?'

'Not always,' Fay said. 'Will Gavin be there with her, do you think?'

'Is Gavin ever with her,' Celia said in exasperation.

Suddenly Fay said with more energy than she usually produced, 'Whatever's happened has happened. So let it rest, Celia.'

But, 'No,' Celia said. 'No.'

On the weekend, challenged about her husband's absence, Lily remained calm. 'He's trying to get away, but there's always something.' Her shy-violet eyes were large and solemn with truthfulness. 'Gavin knows a lot of interesting people. Everyone wants to meet him.' She sounded as proud and pleased as Gavin did when he spoke of her. 'He's so wonderful – different from everyone in the world. More wonderful,' she explained.

Celia said, 'That's what I'm saying: he *is* different; all right, more wonderful, if that's how you want it ... You don't have to go through with this,' she continued. 'It's a very easy thing to do nowadays, almost legal, certainly with someone as small as you ... ' She tried to span her hands round Lily's waist not only to demonstrate its smallness but to touch her in affection.

Lily disengaged herself. She said, 'If you don't believe me, you don't love me. People don't love people they think are liars.'

She went out and took the only action she knew – she called Gavin, and from her voice he realized he could not delay any longer. He told her he would be there on Sunday morning and, confident that he would, she got up early and accompanied her mother-in-law to church.

So when Gavin drove up to the house, he met only Fay, unsuccessfully trying to make coffee for herself in the stone-age kitchen. He did it for her, and she thanked him, and then she said she was glad he had come, to help intervene in the situation that had arisen between her two daughters. The difficulty was, she told him frankly, that Celia couldn't stand the competition, always having had Lily completely to herself.

'And now you're here,' he said.

'Not for long. I'm going away. But you're not. And the baby is not, I presume.'

'Yes, he and I are here to stay.'

'Isn't it exciting? I'm excited.' She stroked his arm, lingering over the sleeve of his summer jacket; she had always appreciated good-looking men. She said, 'It was so kind of you to have married my little Lily.'

'No no, not at all; quite the contrary. It's Lily who is kind. Mother adores her. For her sweet temperament,' he explained, 'and for being so much part of the family. I hope when they've finished praying together, Mother will show her around the churchyard. It's full of us, going back two hundred years. Of course there've been ups and downs – two hundred years is no joke! – but that's how it goes. Kingdoms like the orchard flit russetly away, and all the rest of it.'

'But the name is still there,' Fay said. 'And you're carrying it on. You and my Lily. That's so mysterious and lovely.' She pressed his shoulder, massaging it a bit in affection.

The Sunday lunch Elizabeth served on her return was the same Fay and Celia remembered from their previous visit. So were the family anecdotes told around the table, and they seemed endless to Celia, leaving her tense with frustration. But afterwards she managed to manoeuvre herself and Fay to be alone with their hostess in the parlour. Elizabeth was embroidering a little muslin shirt, and she explained that the pattern – of birds, daisies, violets – was copied from a framed sampler with a faded signature and the date 1871. Beside it hung some watercolours of local scenes – a waterfall, a horse and cart in a field – painted years ago but still there, Elizabeth said, to be rendered by anyone with artistic talent. She herself had no such talent – which made her all the more thankful to have Lily in the family. Fay confirmed that Lily had always loved sketching and had gone to art school.

'She lasted a week,' Celia said. 'Lily is really too frail – physically and otherwise – to see anything through. That's why we're worried about her present condition: if she's strong enough to carry it full term.'

'Our Dr Williams said everything was perfectly normal,' Elizabeth said with satisfaction.

'Perfectly normal,' Celia repeated. She threw a swift glance at her mother, but despairing of help from there, rushed in on her own to tell Gavin's mother: 'We hardly see him. We have no idea where he is, with whom. All we know is he's not where he should be. At home, Lily never knew if her husband was on the sofa where he had chosen to sleep, or if he'd been out all night.'

Snipping off a thread, Elizabeth smiled in reply. 'Gavin has always been a nightbird. I suppose poets usually are, that's when they get their inspiration. Luckily dear Lily is an artist herself, she understands him perfectly. A perfectly matched couple.' She smiled again.

'A poet and his muse.' Fay smiled back.

*

Two slender figures in light clothes, Gavin and Lily wandered among trees and bushes in the grounds. When he lifted a branch to let her slip through, they appeared to vanish – tenuous as shadows, insubstantial. But for each other they were substantially there. They hardly touched; only sometimes he held her hand, or guided her by her elbow. The grounds were different for Lily when he was there. Now she saw that here and there the ancient and broken trees had sprouted new branches with leaves on them. He led her to where there was a fishpond with water lilies unfolded and goldfish swimming beneath them. They sat on a pile of stones forming a bank, and he lightly laid his arm across her shoulders while she traced his features with her finger, in silence and contentment.

It did not last very long; he looked at his watch. He had to go back to the city, an appointment.

She said, 'Let me come with you.'

He smiled and kissed her hair. 'Mother so loves having you here, and she can look after you better and cook you all those dishes. I know you don't like them, neither do I, but you need them. The baby needs them.'

'And afterwards? Do we have to live with Celia? Can't I come live with you?'

From his sad smile she realized how impossible this was. She knew he had a place where he needed to do things of his own, write his poetry and meet poets and other friends.

'Celia lives near the park. You can take the baby there.'

'I don't like the park.'

'Then walk in the street with the pram – I'll meet you every day and I'll push the pram. I'll love to do that.'

'Really?' She laughed out loud with pleasure.

'Oh yes. Yes. It'll be fun. Our own baby ... I'm so much looking forward to it. We all are. Mother can hardly wait.'

They were silent. After a while he said, 'Mother will stay with you while he's being born. She did it for all my sisters. She'll be the first to see him.'

A leaf dropped from an overhanging tree; a frog croaked. Gavin said, 'Tell me about him again.'

She waved her hand before her face as though waving away something she did not want to see; but on the contrary, it was a gesture of conjuring up a vision that was imprinted on her mind. 'He was small, very small and skinny. Like those pictures you see of children starving in Africa? Only it was the way he was built, he wasn't exactly starving, though he was hungry. I could tell from the way he ate my pretzel and then asked for another and two hot dogs. It may be because teenagers can never get enough to eat. His hair was very curly and it sat on him like a cap, and his ears stuck out from his head like two handles. His eyes were the biggest thing about him, they were huge, huge, and they shone in the rest of his face – I mean his face being so dark and it was also dark under the bridge.'

'Yes,' Gavin said. 'I think I can see him. In fact, quite clearly.'

'I see him all the time and I'm scared.'

'Why should you be? I'm here. It's my son.'

'Scared that he may have gotten sick from being in the rain and having nowhere to dry his shirt. I don't think he had another one, and it was very thin cloth so you could see his shoulder blades sticking out.'

'I thought you trusted me,' Gavin said, sounding so sad that she gave a little cry of reassurance and for a brief moment laid her hand on the shoulder of his jacket.

'If you trust me, you have to believe me.'

'I do believe you, and last week I went around to all the

Ethiopian restaurants I could find in New York, but he wasn't there. But maybe he wasn't Ethiopian.'

'No, maybe he was Nigerian, but you wouldn't want to go around to all the Nigerian restaurants. He's working and saving his tips for the restaurant. You have to believe me without proof. That's what faith is – believing without proof.'

They got up from the bank of stones. It was getting late, the shadows lay cool and lengthened on the grass and the tops of the trees had the stillness around them that means the end of the day and its liquidation in the setting sun. They retraced their steps back to the house where his car was parked, and when they passed through the blighted orchard, he picked up an apple for her and she ate it. She didn't even have to look; she knew it would be whole, without worms or decay.

Nevertheless, some of the things he had promised her did not happen. The baby was born and, as Gavin had predicted, Elizabeth was the first to see him emerge with his little cap of black hair. Gavin chose the name Scipio for him (after the Roman general Scipio Africanus, he explained to Lily). But Lily did not often push Scipio in his pram. Instead she pushed Gavin in his wheelchair through the streets they both loved. Poets traditionally die young – in the past often from consumption, but Gavin was an early victim of a new disease. He had been moved to Celia's apartment and stayed in the bedroom that he now shared with Lily, he alone in the bed and she on a folding cot placed at the foot of it. She cared for him entirely by herself, refusing to engage a nurse and only sometimes grudgingly accepting Celia's help. It was easy for her to carry him; he had become as light as a child, and he looked up at her with perfect trust in her ability to hold him.

A week after he died, she climbed up to the roof of an

office building that Gavin had pointed out to her as a typical example of post-war commercial architecture. He had told her it was architecturally very boring, but it suited her purpose after she discovered that the fire escape stairway leading to the roof was kept open during office hours. So it was by day that she took the long climb to arrive at the top. From here she gazed down over the city: the churches and the bridges and the ribbons of river, and the streets with their shoals of cars and glittering towers of museums and stores and theatres and restaurants and dreams of restaurants – dreams of glory and gold pouring down from the sky that, now she was so close to it, turned out to be much larger and brighter than she had anticipated.

While he was growing up, the orphaned Scipio mostly lived in the country in the family house permeated by the family history that his paternal grandmother transmitted to him day by day. He didn't listen to her stories very carefully; at this time his principal interest was in horses and he often accompanied his two great-uncles to the races at Saratoga. His ambition was to become a jockey, for which he was small and wiry enough, and even slightly bow-legged. But after spending a vacation with his grandmother Fay in Monte Carlo, where she had settled for tax reasons, he grew enthusiastic about motor-car racing. This led to his subsequent career as a racing-car driver. He became famous and was photographed for magazines, leaning against his car with his crash helmet under his arm, his radiant smile stretching up to his ears where they stuck out like two handles.

This photograph, and many others of him, stood in Celia's living-room. She looked at him with pleasure, but as the years passed she began to be puzzled by these pictures of Scipio.

She wondered what he was doing there among all the others, especially next to the photograph of Gavin and Lily on their wedding day. But after some more time she also couldn't remember who this couple was – she wiped the dust off the glass, but failed to make them or her memory any clearer. No one heard her mutter to herself; if she muttered some names, she had no faces to put to them, even though they were smiling all around her. There was a film over her eyes, and a film over her mind. Only sometimes there was a glimmer – a shimmer of two figures in light-coloured clothes on the verge of disappearing from sight, between trees or around a street corner, or simply fading into the ether. The ether! Even that – a poetic idea but a false hypothesis – has ceased to exist.

The Judge's Will

After his second heart attack, the judge knew that he could no longer put off informing his wife about the contents of his will. He did this for the sake of the woman he had been keeping for twenty-five years, who, ever since his first attack, had been agitating about provisions for her future. These had long been in place in his will, known only to the lawyer who had drawn it up, but it was intolerable to the judge to think that their execution would be in the hands of his family; that is, his wife and son. Not because he expected them to make trouble but because they were both too impractical, too light-minded to carry out his wishes once he was not there to enforce them.

This suspicion was confirmed for him by the way Binny received his secret. Any normal wife, he thought, would have been aghast to learn of her husband's long-standing adultery. But Binny reacted as though she had just heard some spicy piece of gossip. She was pouring his tea and, quivering with excitement, spilled some in the saucer. He turned his face from her. 'Go away,' he told her, and then became more exasperated by the eagerness with which she hurried off to reveal the secret to their son.

Yasi was the only person in the world with whom she could share it. As a girl growing up in Bombay, Binny had had many friends. But her marriage to the judge had shipwrecked her in Delhi, a stiffly official place that didn't suit her at all. If it hadn't been for Yasi! He was born in Delhi and in this house – a gloomy, inward-looking family property, built in the 1920s and crowded with heavy Indo-Victorian furniture inherited from earlier generations. Binny's high spirits had managed to survive the sombre atmosphere; and, when Yasi was a child, she had shared the tastes and pleasures of her Bombay days with him, teaching him dance steps and playing him the songs of Hollywood crooners on her gramophone. They lived alone there with the judge. Shortly after Yasi was born, the judge's mother had died of some form of cancer, which had also accounted for several other members of the family. It seemed to Binny that all of the family diseases – both physical and mental – were bred in the very roots of the house, and she feared that they might one day seep into Yasi's bright temperament. The fear was confirmed by the onset of his dark moods. Before his first breakdown, Yasi had been a brilliant student at the university, and although he was over thirty now, he was expected shortly to resume his studies.

More like a brother than like a son, he had always enjoyed teasing her. When she told him the news of his father's secret, he pretended to be in no way affected by it but went on stolidly eating his breakfast.

She said, 'Who is she? Where does he keep her? I don't know what's wrong with you, Yasi. Why can't you see how important this is for us? Why are you asking me why? Because of the *will*. His will.'

'And if he's left it all to her?' Yasi asked.

'He'd never do that. Oh, no.' Better than anyone, she knew the pride the judge took in himself and his ancestral possessions. 'I'm sure she's a you-know-what. He must have taken her out of one of those houses – he owns half of them, anyway,' she said, stifling her usual wry amusement at that sector of her husband's substantial family properties.

A day or two later, the judge had to be returned to the hospital. He stayed there for a week, and when they sent him home again he began to spend all his time in his bedroom. Apart from a few irritated instructions to Binny, he accepted her ministrations in silence; now and again, he asked for Yasi – reluctantly, as if against his own inclination. It took him some time to overcome his pride and demand a visit from his son.

Binny was so excited. It was probably to do with his will, with the woman. 'You have to go! You must!' she urged Yasi. He agreed, on condition that she not listen at the door. 'As if I would!' she cried indignantly, though both of them knew that she would be crouching there – and, in fact, when he emerged from his father's bedroom he found her hastily scrambling up from that position.

'What is it? What did he say?'

On the rare occasions when the judge had tried to talk alone with his son in the past, Yasi had recounted the conversations to his mother, with some embellishments: how the judge had had to clear his throat several times and had still been unable to come out with what he wanted to say, and instead had babbled on about his student days in London and the wonderful English breakfasts he had enjoyed, bacon and eggs and some sort of fish – 'kippers, I believe they are called', Yasi had repeated, in the judge's own accent, to entertain his mother.

But now it was as if he were protecting his father: he wouldn't tell her anything. It wasn't until she challenged him, 'Whose side are you on?' that he said, 'He wants to see her.'

'He wants to bring her *here*?'

'He's sending the driver.'

'The fool, the first-class *idiot*,' Binny said. Her scorn for the judge soon turned to angry defiance: 'What do I care? Let him bring her – bring all the women he's been keeping for twenty-five years.' But, beneath it all, there was a sort of thrill – that at last something dramatic was happening in their lives.

There was nothing dramatic about the woman the driver brought the next day. She arrived in a plain white cotton sari and wearing no jewellery – 'as if she were already a widow', Binny commented. Binny herself was a far more appealingly feminine figure: short and plump, in tight-fitting harem pants and very high heels, draped with the costume jewellery she preferred to the family jewels; at the salon they had bobbed and curled her hair and made it gleam with golden streaks. By contrast, Phul – that was her name, Phul, meaning 'flower' – was as austere as a woman in constant prayer. Leaving her shoes at the threshold, she glided into the judge's bedroom; and though Binny lingered outside, no sound reached her to indicate what might be going on.

This performance, as Binny called it, was repeated the next day, and the next. After the fourth visit, she declared to Yasi, 'This can't go on. You have to do something.'

She had always depended on Yasi to get her out of difficult situations. In earlier years, when she still had a few woman friends, Yasi had helped her cover up some secret expenditures – such as losing at cards, which she and her friends had played for money. She appreciated the way Yasi had circumvented the judge's disapproval. She had always been proud of her son's intelligence, which he had inherited, she had to admit, from his father.

*

Friends had asked her why she had married the judge, who was in every way so different from her. But that was the answer. Before meeting him, she had lived in an adolescent world of flirtations carried on in the cafés and on the beaches of Bombay. The judge, some twenty years older than she, was already a highly regarded lawyer with a private practice in Delhi when she met him. He was working on a professional assignment in Bombay with Binny's father, an industrialist, who had invited him to the family table – usually the dullest place in the world for Binny. But, with the judge there, she had sat through every course, not understanding a word but understanding very well that the guest's attention sometimes strayed in her direction. Afterwards, she lingered in the vestibule to give him the opportunity to talk to her, though all he did was ask, in the weighty tones of a prosecutor in court, about her studies. A tall, heavy person, he habitually wore, even in the humid heat of Bombay, a suit, a waistcoat and a tie, which made him stand out from everyone else, especially from her friends, who floated around in the finest, flimsiest Indian garments. She loved describing him to these friends, who exclaimed, 'But he sounds *awful*!' That made her laugh. 'He *is* awful!' By which she meant that he was serious, sombre, authoritarian – everything that later oppressed her so horribly. One day, after posing his usual question about her studies, he went to her father to ask for her hand – for her hand! How she laughed with her friends. Wasn't it just like an old-fashioned novel – Mr Darcy and Elizabeth Bennet! Or, from another book on their matriculation list, Heathcliff. In fact, she began to refer to him as Heathcliff, and to think of him as the gypsy lover who had come to steal her away.

The driver was sent to Phul every day, and every day she remained with the judge in his bedroom. Although this bedroom had meant nothing to Binny for many years, now her thoughts were concentrated on it, as they had been at the beginning of the marriage. The judge had been an overwhelming lover, and those nights with him had been a flowering and a ripening that she'd thought would go on forever. Instead, after about two years, the judge's presence in their bed was changed into a weight that oppressed her physically and in every other way. It had been a relief to her when Yasi was born and she could move with him into her own bedroom. She never returned to the judge's, and, when he came to hers, she was impatient with his need. Mostly she used Yasi as an excuse – 'Sh-h-h! The child is sleeping!' – ignoring her husband's protest that a boy that age shouldn't still be in his mother's bed. The judge's visits became less and less frequent, and finally they ceased altogether.

She hardly noticed, and, until Phul came, thought nothing of it. On his good days, Yasi was always there for her, and she for him. He had a large group of friends and went out most nights. She would wait up for him, and, however late he came home, he would perch on the edge of her bed to tell her about the music festivals he had attended, the poetry recitals, the places where he had dined and danced. He was quite frank with his mother about the girls he slept with – she knew the sort of modern, fashionable girls who formed his social circle, and had even learned to recognize the subtle Parisian perfumes that clung to him.

Then there were his bad days, when he didn't get out of bed, and, when he did, he was silent and sombre – yes, just like his father. But whereas the judge's anger was always contained, controlled, Yasi's was explosive – sometimes he would hurl a glass, a vase, a full cup of coffee, not caring where it landed. A few times he had struck her, suddenly, sharply.

Afterwards she pretended that it hadn't happened, and never spoke of it to anyone, and certainly not to him. This silence between them was a mutually protective one. Living so closely together, perpetually intent on each other, each was wary of disturbing the other's balance, so precariously achieved, of anger and resignation, revolt and submission.

Alert to every sound from Yasi's room, one night she heard voices from there that made her tiptoe to his door. She found it open and the judge standing inside, ghostlike in his long white nightshirt. He was talking to Yasi, but as soon as he saw her he shut the door in her face. She had every right to open the door, to know what her husband was saying to their son, but it was not only the judge's prohibition that prevented her, it was Yasi's, too; for there were times when he was as forbidding as his father.

The next day, she impatiently waited to question him. But he had hardly begun to speak when she interrupted him. 'Probably he's left her everything. Very good! Let her have everything. Only don't think I won't get the best lawyer in the world to see that she has nothing.'

'He knows how difficult it will be for you to accept the will. To accept her. He says she has no family at all.'

'She doesn't? Then where did he find her? Wasn't there a whole tribe of them, in one of those rooms where they play music and people throw money?'

'He took her away before she was fifteen, and she's stayed all those years where he put her. So now he thinks she's like some tame thing in a cage – with a wild creature waiting to get her as soon as she's released. He made me promise to protect her.'

'Against *me*?'

She shouted so violently that he shushed her. They were speaking in English but they knew the servants would be listening and, even without understanding the language, would be perfectly aware of the drift of the conversation. Now she spoke more quietly, and more bitterly. 'That's what he's wanted from the day you were born. To turn you against me. To have you on his side – and now on hers, too.'

Tears, rare for her, streamed from her eyes, streaking her make-up, so that she did at that moment look like a wild creature. At first, Yasi felt like smiling, but then he felt sorry for her, as he had felt sorry for his father, that proud man pleading for a promise.

Binny had never allowed her circumstances to depress her. She had been very impatient with her women friends' constant complaints about unreliable servants, bad marriages, worse divorces. By the time she was in her fifties, she had dropped all of them except one. And, finally, there came the day when this friend, too, had to be abandoned. It happened over cocktails in their favourite hotel lounge. Binny was speaking about her close relationship with her son when the other woman interrupted her: 'It's all Freud, of course.'

'I see,' Binny said, after a long silence. 'Freud.'

She got up. She took out her purse and deposited her share of the check on the table. She gave a brief, cold laugh. 'Freud,' she repeated. It was the last word she ever spoke to this friend.

So nowadays she comforted herself with her own amusements: shopping for new outfits and jewellery, intense sessions at a salon run by a Swiss lady. Her last stop was always Sugar & Spice, for Yasi's favourite pastries. If the judge warned her that Yasi was getting too fat, she suppressed her own observation that Yasi *was* getting too fat. She countered that it was the judge himself who should be careful: a man with two heart attacks, she reminded him.

But that morning when she arrived home with the pastries and said to the servant, 'Call Yasi Baba,' she was told that he had gone out. 'In a taxi?' she asked casually, licking cream off her fingers. The servant said no, Judge Sahib had sent Yasi in the car – and by the way he said it, with lowered eyes, she realized that it was something she wasn't supposed to know. She stood fighting down a flush of anger, then suddenly she shouted, 'Don't we have any light in this house?' All the shutters and curtains were closed to keep the sun out. The servant turned on the chandelier, but its lustre was absorbed by the Turkish rugs, leaving only a thin shaft of silver light. Binny alone illuminated the dark room, with her embroidered silks and the golden glints in her hair.

The judge's long-time driver was always at her disposal, and she had arranged with him that some of her destinations should be kept secret from his employer. She hadn't realized that the judge had made a similar arrangement. It didn't take her long to persuade the driver, to whom she had always been generous, to reveal the address where he had taken Yasi, as well as his instructions to take him there again the following night. She called for a taxi for the same time and went there herself.

It was across the river, in one of the first new colonies to be built in the area some twenty-five years before, far from the judge's prestigious neighbourhood of shady old trees and large villas. Binny's taxi took her into a lively bazaar – the open stalls lit up with neon strip-lighting, the barrows of fruit and nuts with Petromax lanterns. Radios played film songs; chickens hung in rows from hooks. Opposite Phul's residence was a clinic, with patients waiting inside, and next to it a shoe shop, where Binny could try on a variety of ladies' footwear. This absorbed her so much that she almost missed Yasi's arrival. She glanced up at the opposite house when she heard the downstairs tenant assuring Yasi that the upstairs tenant was at home. Then she quickly returned her gaze to her feet, which were being fitted into a pair of bright blue sandals with silver heels, which she liked so much that she bought them there and then.

Yasi returned home very late, and as usual he perched on his mother's bed to tell her where he had been and what he had done. He had attended a music festival, he told her, and he sang her a phrase and swayed to it, his eyes closed. He loved music, which was something he'd got from Binny, though for him it was classical music, whereas she loved swing and jazz.

'So that's where you were all night?'

Alerted by her tone, he opened his eyes.

She said, 'That's not what I was told.'

Yasi said, 'He sent me with the driver. I couldn't say no. She played her harmonium and sang. It was horrible, and I left as soon as I could.'

'Then where were you until two in the morning?'

'I told you: I was at the music festival. You always think the worst of me. Oh, I'm sick of it! No, don't talk to me! My head's bursting!' And, indeed, his face had changed in a way she knew and had dreaded since the first breakdown.

The next day, he slept late, and she sat beside him in his bedroom, where he lay with the tousled, tortured look of his sickness. She blamed herself for having been angry at him. She looked at the array of medicine bottles on his bedside table – she didn't know which were his sleeping pills and which were those prescribed for his moods, or how many he had taken. Usually so particular in his personal habits, he hadn't even changed out of the shirt he had been wearing the night before. A faint smell rose from it, not the delicate scent of his girlfriends but the heavy bazaar perfume she smelled whenever Phul entered the house.

Her pity for him turned into rage against his father. In earlier years, whenever she had felt her life to be intolerable, she had packed her suitcase and announced her decision to return to Bombay. At first, the judge had used a defence attorney's arguments to dissuade her; later, he had said nothing but simply waved his hand dismissively over the packed suitcase. And after a while she had unpacked it again. But this time she would not do so, would not retreat from her decision; for now it was not she who had to be considered but her son.

Leaving Yasi asleep, she walked through the house, through the many unused rooms, some shrouded, others shuttered, and, before she had even closed the judge's door behind her, she announced, 'I'm taking him to Bombay.'

These days, she hardly ever entered the judge's bedroom. Everything was still in its place – his colonial armchair with the extended leg rest, his big bed and bigger chest of drawers, its brass handles too heavy for her to pull, and the mirror too high for her to look into – but there was a subtle change of atmosphere. Well, not so subtle! For there was Phul squatting on the floor by the judge's feet, massaging them as any devoted wife might do. He was gazing down at her with a look that Binny recognized as the expression – of father as much as of lover – that had so thrilled her in her youth.

When Binny entered, Phul turned and smiled – partly in apology but also with some pride at fulfilling a duty that she clearly felt was her right. She was a woman in her early forties, but her smile was peculiarly childlike: her teeth were as small as milk teeth and her gums showed up very pink against her complexion, which was much darker than Binny's. When she noticed that her sari had slipped off her shoulders, she tugged it back, though not before Binny had seen that she was very thin and with no breasts worth mentioning.

'Get up, child,' the judge told Phul, his voice as tender as his gaze on her.

Child! Binny thought. Never since the day of their marriage had he called her anything except Bina – never Binny or Baby, as everyone had called her at home in Bombay. And now, as he shifted his eyes from Phul to her, his expression changed completely: for Binny was not at his feet but standing upright and facing him in hostility. She said, 'We're taking the evening plane.'

'The boy stays here,' the judge pronounced.

'Here with you? And with *her*?'

Since the judge's last return from the hospital, a carved Kashmiri screen had been placed around the washstand installed for his minor ablutions. Although husband and wife were speaking in English, which she couldn't understand, Phul had quietly retreated behind this screen. Her absence made no difference to Binny, who continued, 'And now you're sending him to her house at night! Shame on you – your own son! To take her off your hands and do what with her, with a woman old enough to be his mother?'

'You're an educated woman,' the judge said. 'You can count. You know that she would have had to be a very precocious seven-year-old to become a mother.'

'Not a day longer in this house! We're going to Bombay. He has to see a doctor.'

'We have very good doctors here.'

'And what have they done for him, stuffing him full of drugs meant for psychos. He's nervous, high-strung, like his mother – yes, I know you think I'm strong as a horse and, yes, I've had to be, to bear almost forty years of marriage with you. But now – today, he and I . . . '

The judge was facing the door and he saw Yasi before she did. 'Your mother wants to take you to Bombay,' he told their son.

Binny spun around. 'Tonight. The seven thirty plane.'

'Why do I always have to be caught between the two of you?' Yasi said. 'Between a pair of scissor blades.' He spoke in Hindi, and his parents looked warningly towards the screen. There was no sound or movement from behind it. Binny said, 'Come out,' but it was not until the judge repeated the command that Phul emerged.

Yasi made a sound that was not like his usual laugh but was meant to express amusement. 'I think we're in the middle of an old-fashioned French farce.'

'This is what your father has become, an impotent old man in a farce with his young what's-it, except this one isn't young.' She smiled grimly, expecting Yasi to smile with her.

Instead he was looking at Phul, as was the judge. She stood humbly, wrapped from head to foot in her widow-like sari, and she pleaded in a low voice, 'Send me home.'

'Home?' Binny cried. 'You *are* home. This is your home. You can move in right now with my husband – please, I beg you, the house will be empty. I'm taking my son to Bombay.'

Before she had finished speaking, Yasi had sunk to a footstool, embroidered years ago by a great-aunt now deceased. He buried his head in his hands and sobbed.

His parents exchanged helpless looks. Binny said, 'He's not well. It's his headaches. He mustn't be upset.'

And the judge said, 'You're right. We mustn't upset him.' United in concern like any two parents, they spoke as though they were alone in the room.

Now Phul came up behind Yasi and laid her hands on his

forehead, pressing it as she had done with the judge's feet. He seemed to relax into her touch, and his weeping stopped.

Binny noticed – and hoped the judge did, too – that Phul's fingers were thick and coarse, unlike Binny's own, which were adorned with several precious rings, some of them inherited from the judge's mother.

Yasi resumed his lively social round and soon became so preoccupied with helping one of his girlfriends with a private fashion show that he was often out all night. So he was absent the morning the driver returned alone from his daily mission with the report that Phul was sick. At once, the judge asked for his three-piece suit, but when Binny found him trembling with the effort of getting his thin legs into his trousers – how frail he had become! – she put him back into his nightshirt and forced him into bed again. He pleaded with her to ask Yasi to take a doctor and some medicine to Phul. 'She's alone,' he told his wife. 'She has no one.' Binny regarded him with angry concern, then turned away. 'Yes, yes, yes,' she agreed impatiently to his request.

It was almost night when she called for the car and driver. The bazaar was even more alive than on her previous visit – music and lights and announcements on megaphones, vegetables trodden into the gutters, bits of offal thrown for the overfed bazaar dogs. She took the outside staircase that Yasi had climbed as she watched him from the shoe shop. The room she entered had a very different ambience from the one in which Phul presented herself in the judge's house. Gay and gaudy, with little pictures and little gods, and hangings tinkling with tiny bells, it seemed more innately Phul's, as though arising from memories of the places and the people among whom she had lived before meeting the judge. A garland of marigolds had been hung around an image of a naked saint with fleshy breasts. Among the few bolsters scattered on the floor, there were only two pieces of furniture, both large: a colonial armchair, the twin of the one in the judge's bedroom, and a bed, on which Phul lay. She wore a sort of house gown, as crumpled as the bed and with curry stains on it. When she saw Binny, she started up, and her hand flew to her heart – yes, Binny thought, she had every reason to fear the judge's wife, after he had kept her holed up in this secret den for twenty-five years.

But it turned out that her fear was for the judge – that there was bad news about him that would leave her forever penniless, alone, unprotected. She let out a wail, which ceased the moment she was reassured. Then her first words were of regret for her inability to serve a guest. She blamed her servant boy, who regularly disappeared when needed. She spoke in a rush and in a dialect that Binny found hard to follow.

When the servant boy reappeared, Binny sent him for the doctor from the clinic next to the shoe shop. Phul lay resigned and passive on her bed, though her moaning grew louder at the doctor's arrival. He was dismissive – some sort of stomach infection, he said. It was going around the city; he saw dozens of cases every day. He scribbled a prescription, ordered a diet of rice and curds. To Binny, it seemed that the room itself was a breeding ground for fevers and infections, with sticks of smoking incense distilling their synthetic essence into the air shimmering with summer heat. There was only one window, which was stuck. Watching her visitor wrestle with it, Phul got up and tried to help her and in her weakness almost fell, before Binny caught her. Struggling then to free herself – 'No, no!' she cried – she threw up in a spasm that spattered over Binny's almost new blue and silver shoes. Then she allowed herself to be carried to the bed and lay there with only her lips moving. What she seemed to be saying was the English word 'sorry' – Binny thought how typical it was of the judge that among the few English words he had taught her was this abject one of apology.

Binny was wiping the judge's face after his meal when he asked, quite shyly, 'Is she better?'

'For all I know, she may be, but not well enough to come here and infect us all.'

She wrung out the facecloth in the basin behind the screen. When she emerged, she saw that he was deep in thought. He made a gesture as though communicating with himself; his hand was unsteady but his voice was determined.

'Yasi must take care of her. He promised. Send him again; send him every day.'

'If you go on fretting this way, you'll have another attack and kill the rest of us with having to nurse you.'

But it was she herself who went every day, with specially prepared dishes of healthy food. She ascribed the slowness of Phul's recovery to the unfresh air in her room. With the one window now propped open, the incense and the bazaar perfume blended with the street smells – wilted produce, motor oil and a nearby urinal. And what was worse were the unhealthy thoughts in Phul's mind, the despair that kept her moaning, 'What will happen to me?' One day, Binny found her up and dressed and ready to go to the judge; she sank back only when Binny asked her, did she really want to expose that sick old man to her infection? Then, for the first time, Phul spoke of Yasi and begged to see him.

It was also the first time that Yasi was told about her sickness. 'Oh, the poor thing,' he said. 'I'd go to see her, but you know as well as I do that I catch everything.'

'No, no, of course you mustn't.'

He promised to go once the danger was past. Binny couldn't help warning, 'Only don't stay with her all night and then tell me lies about music and poetry.'

'If you'd just listen for once in your life!' His exasperation lasted only a moment and he continued patiently, 'I never stayed all night. I tried to get away as soon as I could, but she's very clinging. And she's also very stupid. And her singing, oh, my God, I wanted to pay her to stop. It's his fault. It was her profession to entertain but he took her away to keep for himself before she could learn anything. Would you believe it, she can hardly read and write. I'd try to teach her, but it would be hopeless. Poor little Phul, and now she's over forty.' He had accumulated a fund of feeling, first for his mother and then for all women whom he considered to have had a raw deal.

In the early years of their marriage, the judge had taught Binny to play chess. Now, alone with him in his convalescence, she brought out the neglected chessboard and set up a table in his bedroom. He was a keen player, but that day his mind was not totally on the game. Instead of deploring her wrong moves, he asked if Yasi was looking after Phul. She said, 'He's done enough for you. Send someone else.'

'There is no one else. I have no one.'

'No one except her? And all she's thinking is: what will happen to me? That's all I ever hear from her – Yasi ever hears,' she corrected. 'That is what she thinks about. Not about you, about herself.'

'I've told her about the will and the boy's promise, and still she's afraid.'

'Of me? Tell her she can vomit all over me and still there's no need.'

The judge clicked his tongue in distaste. He pointed at

her castle, which she had just stupidly exposed. He wouldn't allow her to take the move back, but scolded her for not keeping her mind on the game. It was true: she was distracted. If she hadn't been, she wouldn't have made her next move, which put his bishop in jeopardy. She was usually more careful – she knew how much he hated losing. Intensely irritated, he reproached her, 'It's as impossible to have a serious game of chess with you as it is to have a serious conversation.'

She reared up. 'Then let me tell you something serious. Whatever happens, God forbid, she's safe in her cage: there's no wild creature waiting for her outside. She can have everything. Tell her! Yasi and I want nothing.' Without a qualm, she took his bishop.

In a voice like thunder, the judge shouted, 'Call him! Call your son!' He had leaped up and with one sweep of his hand he scattered the chess pieces, so that some fell in her lap, some on the floor. This sudden strength frightened her. She grasped his shoulders to make him sit in the chair again and, though withered, they still felt like iron under her hands. She had to match her strength against his; it didn't take her long to win, but what she felt was not triumph.

She bent down to pick up the pieces from the floor and tried to replace them on the board. He waved her away, as though waving everything away.

'You can't do this,' she said. 'In your condition.'

'Yes, my condition,' he echoed bitterly. 'Because of my condition, I lose my bishop to someone with no notion of the game.'

He allowed her to lead him from the chair to his bed. She brought him water, and after he had drunk it he gave the glass back to her and said, 'I'm sorry.'

'Oh, my goodness!' she cried in shock. He had often done

this – scattered the pieces when he was losing – but he had never before apologized for it. She understood what this was about and tried again to reassure him. 'Everything will happen as you want it, the way you've written it. You have my promise, and Yasi's promise.'

'The boy is weak. It's not his fault – no, not yours, either. You've done your best.'

'Who knows what is best and what is not best,' she said. Freud, she thought, bitter in her mind against her friend.

'Fortunately, you're strong enough for both of you. Sometimes too strong.' He smiled, though not quite in his usual grim way.

He was looking at her, *considering* her, as she was now, as she had become; and though what she had become was not what she had been in her youth, he showed tolerance, even affection. It made her put her hands to her hair; she could guess what it looked like, what *she* looked like to him, how wild. She was overdue at the salon. She had been meaning to go for weeks – but what time did she have, between the judge and Yasi and this home and the secret one across the river, day after day, running from here to there?

The stories in this collection first appeared in the following publications:

'A Loss of Faith' – *Like Birds, Like Fishes*, John Murray, 1963
'The Widow' – *New Yorker*, 1963
'A Spiritual Call' – *Cornhill Magazine*, 1966
'Miss Sahib' – *A Stronger Climate*, John Murray, 1968
'A Course of English Studies' – *Kenyon Review*, 1968
'An Experience of India' – *An Experience of India*, John
    Murray, 1971
'Two More under the Indian Sun' – *New Yorker*, 1971
'Desecration' – *New Yorker*, 1975
'Expiation' – *New Yorker*, 1982
'Great Expectations' – *East Into Upper East*, John Murray,
    1998
'Two Muses' – *East Into Upper East*, John Murray, 1998
'Ménage' – *My Nine Lives*, John Murray, 2003
'A Choice of Heritage' – *My Nine Lives*, John Murray, 2003
'A Lovesong for India' – *A Lovesong for India*, Little, Brown,
    2011
'Pagans' – *A Lovesong for India*, Little, Brown, 2011
'At the End of the Century' – *A Lovesong for India*, Little,
    Brown, 2011
'The Judge's Will' – *New Yorker*, 2013